Under Review

An Academic Thriller

Sid Stark

Helia Press

Published by Helia Press
Winston-Salem, NC
Paperback ISBN: 978-1-952723-41-4

Want to keep in touch and hear about news and special offers first? Get your free novella and sign up for my mailing list (but only if you want to!) by scanning the QR code below.

1

JUST WHEN I THOUGHT my life couldn't get any worse, Madison came back into it.

I was returning from a physical therapy session for my busted-up left knee when I spotted someone sitting on the stairs leading up to my apartment entrance.

Jeez, she looks familiar, I thought. And then: *Nah, it* ***can't*** *be. It's gotta be someone else who looks kind of like her.*

I should have known better. On the radio, Bruce Springsteen was belting his heart out about being on a downbound train. This should have been a warning. But, like a moron, I ignored it, pulled into the closest parking spot I could find, got blithely—as blithely as a woman with a brace and crutches can get—out of the car, and started hobbling towards the two long flights of stairs currently looming like Everest between me and my apartment.

"Hey, Professor H! Whoa! What happened to you? Were you, like, in an accident or something?"

"Madison! What the f—what are you doing here?"

She unfolded herself from her seat on the stairs and came over to me in the coltish lope I remembered from when she'd been my student two years ago. Her straight brown hair was just as lank as it had been when she'd been napping her way through Intermediate Russian. As she came up to me, she wiped her nose on a raggedy sleeve. So maybe she was still doing coke like she'd been then, too.

You'd think nearly dying from an overdose while being chased by angry mobsters would be sufficient reason to stay clean, especially when your dad was paying for the best rehab money could buy. But Madison, I suspected, had gotten bored, the way people like Madison always would, and drugs were the only way she had to bring a little excitement into her carefully curated, lovingly organized, unspeakably dull and meaningless life.

"I got into a ginormous fight with my dad—major surprise, right?" She rolled her eyes. "But this time my mom turned on me too." She swiped at her nose again. Her wrists were too bony and frail where they poked out from the sleeves of her ratty hoodie. She hugged herself as if cold, despite being wildly overdressed for the heat radiating off the blacktop at 2:15 on an August afternoon. In Georgia.

"Here." I fished a tissue out of my purse and handed it to her, unable to stand the sight of her wiping her nose with her filthy sleeve any longer. "Was it about drugs?" I asked. "Are you doing coke again?"

"Jeez, Professor H!" The outrage in her voice seemed unfeigned. "I thought you'd trust me, at least, even though my dumbass parents don't. I said I'd go clean, and I did!"

"Then why is your nose running like a leaky faucet?"

She shrugged. "Allergies, I guess. It started as soon as I got on the bus, it got even worse once I got off the bus, and it's been going non-stop ever since."

"Okay." Georgia was notoriously bad for allergies, that was true. "But you look awful, Madison. You must be twenty pounds underweight. Drugs seem like the best explanation."

"Hey!" She stopped wiping her nose to give me a bright smile. "Can't a girl have an eating disorder without getting sh—without getting a bunch of hassle over it?"

"No," I said.

"Anyway," she said, giving me another bright smile. "You're one to talk, Professor H. You used to be super skinny back at TLASC, like you had an eating disorder or something too. And now you're...*and* you're on crutches. Looks like *you're* the one who needs to, like, practice some self-care or something."

I resisted the urge to argue that I hadn't been unhealthily thin back in New Jersey, and that I hadn't gained any weight since then. Well, not any appreciable weight. But I had the irritating feeling that she was dead right on both counts. I had been flirting with anorexia and overtraining until my knee nightmare had begun and I'd had to stop running. Now I was finding myself surreptitiously checking my fly before going out in public to make sure the zipper hadn't unzipped from the press of my expanding abdominal flesh.

If pride and poverty hadn't been such large stumbling blocks for me, I would have bought a new, larger wardrobe over the summer. But since pride and poverty both featured heavily in my decision-making process, I was still squeezing into the same three outfits I'd been wearing for close to half a decade now, and telling myself that getting serious about that diet would be good for my bottom line in both senses of the word.

"Probably we both need to practice some self-care," I said, striving for just the right balance of patience, diplomacy, and conspiratorial cheerfulness in my voice.

"Yeah, whatevs," said Madison. I guessed I had failed to hit that perfect balance I had been striving for. "So, your apartment's, like, up at the top of the stairs, huh? Want some help getting up there? Can I carry something for you?"

"Um," I said. "I guess. You still haven't told me why you're here."

"I..." She hugged herself again, now looking distinctly frail and scared and much younger than—I calculated quickly—twenty-one. "I told you. I got into a big fight with my parents. Like, a really big fight. And then"—she looked away and scuffed the toe of her dirty sneaker on the sidewalk—"I, like, left. Like, I, like, I guess I kinda...ran away. *Can* you run away if you're no longer a minor?" she asked, looking up again, a shadow of her usual cockiness returning.

"I don't know," I said. "I don't think so. Not exactly. But...your parents are probably looking for you, aren't they?"

"Nah." She wrinkled up her nose. "They said they were done with me. 'Course, they say that kind of sh—stuff all the time. But this time I think they really meant it."

"In my experience," I said, "parents say all kinds of sh—stuff all the time without really meaning it. We need to tell them where you are."

"No!" She actually took a step back at the idea. "No! They really...I really...and I don't know who they are anymore! They're not who I thought they are, Professor H, they really aren't! Turns out they've been keeping all kinds of sh—secrets from me all along. 'Specially my mom. Turns out I never knew who she really was. And, like, I mean that literally. Like, she kept all kinds of sh—stuff about our family secret, and now I don't know who she is, I don't know who I am...and, and, what I found out was *so* bad, I couldn't, I couldn't..."

Her skinny shoulders were starting to shake. "Hey," I said. "Hey, it's okay. We'll get it sorted out. Let's go inside and sit down and get something cold to drink, and we'll get it sorted out. But first of all, let me just send a quick text to your dad that you're safe. I'm sure he's worried sick about you."

"Hah!" said Madison.

"Well, at least it might keep me from getting sued for kidnapping or something," I said.

"Yeah." She was brightening up, recovering her composure. "He's such a d—such a jerk he'd probably do something like that."

"Mmm," I said. I didn't actually have such a low opinion of Erik Johnson, Madison's father, but I was already starting to worry about the legal implications of having a former student and known drug user show up unannounced at my apartment, apparently on the run from her parents.

I carefully organized myself and my crutches, and pulled out my phone. Erik Johnson was still in my contacts. I'd just send him a quick text, then get me and Madison out of this sweltering heat and into the blessed AC, and come up with a plan that would solve everything, or at least get Madison off my hands.

A text notification was already up on my screen. I had a flash of paranoia, sure it was Erik Johnson telling me he knew about Madison and demanding to know why I was hiding her from him. But no. The message was in Russian, not English.

Dearest Inna, it read. *Mama and I have an appointment with the American embassy for our visas))))) Normally the wait time is 6-8 months, but because of her health they say they might be able to expedite it. And she has already spoken with a specialist at that clinic in Atlanta. We may be with you very soon)))) Hugs, Dima.*

2

MADISON DID, SOMEWHAT to my surprise, shadow me solicitously up the stairs, carrying my purse and jumping ahead to open the door when we finally reached my apartment.

"Jeez," she said when we stepped in. "It's not much of a place, is it?"

"Well," I said. "It's the nicest place I've ever had."

That, alas, was all too true. It was a one-bedroom apartment with fixtures so cheap, I worried about accidentally punching through the kitchen sink while washing dishes, but it had reeked of new paint and new carpeting rather than mold and mildew when I had moved in, so I counted that as a win. The migraines that had plagued me my first week there had gradually receded, along with the chemical smell that had filled the air, so I counted that as a double win. Now if only the migraines I got whenever I went into my office or my classroom would dissipate just as easily.

"I thought professors were rich," she said. "My dad's house is really swank."

"Your dad," I pointed out, "is a provost. That's different. I'll bet he was pretty poor when you were a baby; you just don't remember it."

"Huh," she said. She looked around some more. "Does he know you live in a dump like this?"

"I don't know," I said. "I haven't been in touch with him in a while. But he came to my apartment in New Jersey, and that was even worse than this one."

"No way!"

"It had rats," I said. "And cockroaches. And mold."

"Ew!" She wrinkled up her face in disgust again. Then a speculative, and slightly horrified, look came into her eyes. "Why'd he come to your place, Professor H?"

"To thank me for saving you."

"Oh." She relaxed for a nanosecond before stiffening up again, her distaste at the idea of her dad getting it on with her former Russian professor replaced by her discomfort at the memory of our near-death experience.

I hoped there was some measure of shame mixed in with the discomfort, given that she'd been heavily culpable in our shared brush with death. Madison had never struck me as being particularly sensitive to shame, but near-death experiences could change a person, as could simple maturity. Two years ago, at nineteen, she'd still been more than half a child. Now, at twenty-one, she was not only of legal drinking age, she was, despite her lack of manners and her adolescent coltishness, more of an adult. She looked me in the eye when she spoke, and she was shepherding me into a chair and getting us both ice water without being prompted.

I snatched a glance at my phone while she commented on my mismatched glasses and the cracks in my single ice cube tray. The message from Dima was still there.

That's great! I wrote back. *How's Galina Ivanovna?*

Her kidneys are getting worse ((((The doctors say they don't know how long she has until she'll need a transplant. And she's having problems with her heart as well, and her vision. But you know what they say: if the patient really wants to live, doctors are helpless)))))

I know, I wrote back. *Has she been to see any more specialists in Moscow?*

Galina Ivanovna, Dima's mother, had type 1 diabetes and now, it seemed, kidney disease. She was a doctor herself and had always been scrupulous about managing her condition, but she was also in her sixties and had been under a lot of stress for a long time. Dima's father had been killed in the Soviet war in Afghanistan when Dima was a baby, and she had found herself a widow and a single mother during the incredibly turbulent years of the collapse of the Soviet Union.

Then Dima, her only child, had been sent to fight in Chechnya during his mandatory military service, and had re-enlisted, this time in OMON, the special forces riot police, and done another tour of Chechnya with them. Then he'd left OMON and become an investigative reporter, which in Russia was maybe more dangerous than serving in a war zone. Death threats were just another day at the office for him. But sometimes the threats didn't stop with him, and had extended to Galina Ivanovna and to me.

Dima had broken off our engagement and sent me back to America in order to get me out of harm's way—hahaha—but Galina Ivanovna was neither willing nor able to leave Russia. For the past two and a half years Dima had been hiding out in Ukraine, if reporting from an active war zone could be termed "hiding out," while Galina Ivanovna fended for herself in Moscow. I knew Dima wasn't happy about that, but he hadn't been able to convince her to leave, not even to go live with her brother in Murmansk.

The end result was that Galina Ivanovna was an older woman in fragile health who was also living a tough life, and it wasn't surprising that her condition was deteriorating. But it was still unwelcome news. For years, she had been a kind of stand-in mother for me, and an academic advisor, to boot. Cutting off contact with her had been almost as painful as cutting off contact with Dima, but, she'd told me when I'd asked, he had begged her to stay away from me for all our sakes, and that's what she had done.

She's gone to see all of them. But most of them won't so much as talk to her, even though she's a colleague. She says she hasn't been getting any death threats since I left Moscow, but this is maybe even worse. Seems like no one wants to treat her, because of who her son is.

Surely there has to be someone!

Her brother says he thinks he can find someone in Murmansk, but that's Murmansk. The provinces. And I think the trip will be really hard for her. But since it's her best chance of seeing a specialist before we leave for America, I'm going back to Moscow tomorrow so that I can take her up there.

Be careful, I texted. After a brief trip to, of all places, St. Petersburg over the spring, Dima had ended up back on the front in the Donbass. Of course. He always ended up back on some front or another.

I'm always careful, he texted back.

Khakhakhakhakha! I wrote.

))))))))) Dima wrote back. *But seriously, Inna, no fooling: I'll be careful. I don't want to fuck anything up for mama. But I wanted to say goodbye to you first before I left, just in case.*

Do you really think it's that dangerous? I asked.

I don't know. In my mind Moscow has become this terrifying place, overflowing with hired killers and the people who hire them. I know that's not true, but I haven't spent more than a couple of days there since—well, you know when. The last thing I remember from Moscow was a couple of thugs holding a gun to your head. It's turned me against my native city)))))) Even the front feels safer. At least there people aren't trying specifically to shoot me—or worse, my women)))))

All the hair on my neck and arms stood up, like I was about to be sick or lightning was about to strike. I opened my mouth as if he were there in the room with me and I could reply to him verbally. What that reply would be, I didn't know, but I knew I really, really needed to say it...

"Jeez, is my dad giving you a hard time already?" Madison came over, two sweating, mismatched glasses of ice water in her hands.

"No." I instinctively moved as if to hide the phone. Then I realized how guilty that looked. Plus, while Madison had picked up a surprising amount of Russian despite coming to class high as a kite half the time, I sincerely doubted she would be able to understand more than one word in ten from our texts.

"Someone I know from Russia," I said. "Let me just answer this real quick, and then we can talk about what you need to do."

I'm pretty sure there's some special prayer or spell I'm supposed to say to keep you safe, I wrote. *But I don't remember what it is.*

I'll settle for "I'll pray for you / So that you don't forget your earthly path / I'll pray for you / So that you return unharmed")))))

So be it, I wrote. It was from a famous poem recited in the popular movie *The Irony of Fate*. Dima, like most people from the former Soviet Union, knew all three hours of it by heart.

What are you doing now? Are you busy?

I looked up at Madison, who had seated herself across the rickety table from me, and was watching me with a mixture of curiosity, impatience, and poorly concealed desperation. I suppressed a groan. Normally I was happy to help people. One might even say I had a helping problem in the same way that Madison had a drug problem or Dima had a combat zone problem. But right now, I could sense, Dima wanted to talk. And I, for better or for worse, wanted to listen.

I'm with a student, I wrote. *A former student who's gotten into trouble.*

Got it. I'll leave you in peace, then. But I might come bother you again soon, okay?))))

Please do, I wrote. *I'm always happy to talk to you, you know that. And please tell me when you get to Moscow, and say hi to Galina Ivanovna for me.*

I obey! Good night))))

Good night. It was after ten o'clock in the evening where Dima was. Probably cooler, too. If I were there, we could be getting ready for bed together right now. So it was a war zone. It was a "frozen conflict," right? How bad could it be?

Very bad. Even when we hadn't been speaking at all, I had read all of Dima's articles, and I knew that this frozen conflict that had slipped out of the consciousness of most of the world was still very much a hot war for the people caught up in it. I was better off here. Definitely. Probably. I caught Madison giving me another look of impatience and poorly concealed desperation. Maybe I was better off here. Whatever problems she had, at least they weren't anything like what Dima and Galina Ivanovna were facing, right?

"So," I said, putting down my phone and giving her what I hoped was a sympathetic and reassuring smile. "What brings you to my door?"

"It's my mom," she said. "Well, actually, my mom's grandpa. Turns out he was, like, KGB or some shit like that. Only they didn't call it that back then. Anyway, turns out he was, like, whatever the KGB was back then, and then he, like, turned traitor or something and, like, collaborated with the Germans or something, and then, like, somehow half the family ended up over here. They kept it all, like, a big secret, but I found out about it."

"Oh," I said. "Well, it was a difficult, complicated time..."

"And that's not the worst part," she went on. She swiped at her nose again, this time, I thought, from tears as much as allergies. "Turns out we've still got family there, and they're, like, involved in some pretty bad shit too, and, and, and...my mom *lied* to me! She lied to me my whole life!"

"Well..." I said feebly. "It's a hard thing to explain to a child..."

"And now," she pressed on, speaking quickly, as if afraid to stop in case she lost her nerve before she got all the words out, "it turns out I've got cousins wanting to come to America, and I'm pretty sure they're going to do something bad while they're here. And my mom is going to help them."

3

"OKAAAAY," I SAID. "LIKE, um, what kind of bad stuff?"

"Like...you know those crazy survivalist groups? Like, the ones with tons of guns and shit?" Apparently Madison had given up on not swearing in front of me.

"Ye-es." I had a hard time imagining Madison's mother as part of a backwoods survivalist group. Admittedly, I had never met her, and everything I knew about her came from the extremely biased reporting by Madison, her father, and Alex. Alex...I quickly turned my thoughts back to the incongruous thought of Madison's supposedly tennis-coach-boffing socialite mother dressed in camo survival gear and toting a machine gun through the American hinterlands. Did they even allow people like her to join those kinds of groups? Sure, if they said the right words and wrote big enough checks, I told myself cynically.

"Are you saying your cousins are part of a group like that in Russia?" I asked. I didn't know much about survivalist groups in Russia. Probably they had them too, although my impression was that they were less of a threat there than they were here. One of the benefits of an semi-authoritarian regime was that it either shut down groups like that, or co-opted them for its own aims.

"Not in Russia," Madison said. "In the Ukraine. Ukraine. Whatevs."

"Ah," I said. Things were starting to become clearer. According to everything I'd heard from Dima and other sources, Ukraine was overrun with paramilitary organizations. Some of them had indeed been co-opted by the various regimes laying claim to sovereignty over the various regions, some of them served their local oligarchs, and some of them were probably still running wild.

"Did your mom's grandpa have anything to do with the OUN?" I asked, circling back to an earlier part of the conversation.

Madison's mouth dropped open. "How did you *know*, Professor H?"

"I put two and two together." This was true. The OUN, or Organization of Ukrainian Nationalists, had been a WWII-era fascist terrorist organization dedicated to achieving an independent, ethnically pure Ukraine. For reasons that no doubt had seemed excellent at the time, this had meant collaborating with the Nazis when they came rolling into that part of the world. It wasn't a stretch to guess that's what Madison's great-grandfather had been involved in.

"He's lucky he got out alive," I said. "I thought pretty much everyone involved in that was killed by one side or the other." The Germans had considered their Ukrainian collaborators to be, when all was said and done, untrustworthy turncoats, dangerous terrorists, and Slavic *untermenschen*, and had imprisoned or killed a lot of them. The Soviets, for obvious reasons, had persecuted the organization with extreme prejudice when they had retaken Ukraine, exterminating most of the members who had survived the war. All in all, it had not turned out well for those involved.

"I told you: He was in the, like, KGB or whatever it was called back then," she said.

"Probably the NKVD," I said.

"Yeah! Wow, how'd you know that too, Professor H?"

"Knowing the basic outlines of Soviet history is a major job requirement," I said.

"Whoa. Yeah, I guess so. Anyway, I was, like, super bored this summer, so I started going through the attic just to get away from my mom, and I found, like, all these old documents and shit. A bunch of it was in, like, Russian. I recognized it even though I could only read a little bit of it. So I asked her about it, and she said it was her grandpa's. He'd brought it with him when he'd left the Ukraine. Ukraine. Whatevs. She said he'd joined the partisans and then, when things got really bad, he'd just started walking west. He walked all the way to Germany, where he got picked up by some American GIs. And he came to the US, and met her grandma, and...here we are. I'd been hearing this story my whole life. It's one of the reasons I wanted to study Russian. My great-grandpa was from the Ukraine—Ukraine—and then my grandma, my mom's mom, who married the son of my Ukrainian great-grandpa, was from Petersburg, so my mom, like, got it from both sides, if you get what I'm saying. My grandma came over later via, like, Israel, I think. I guess they were letting a lot of Jews out then."

"Something like that," I said.

"Anyways," said Madison with a shrug. "It was just, like, a thing, you know? Like, part of my family was from over there. So I figured it'd be cool to, like, learn the language and shit. Especially when my mom didn't want me to. She, like, had a *major* cow when I told her about it. She told me our family'd been, like, horribly oppressed by the Russians and they were, like, super bad, and I was betraying everyone by studying it. So of course"—she grinned at me—"I did it."

"Of course you did," I said.

"But then..." She stopped and swallowed hard. "Then I took the documents and stuff to my grandma, the one from Petersburg, and she read them, and then she was all, like, *crazy* mad at what she found out, and she like, told me some of it, and it turns out *we're* the bad guys. Like, super bad!"

"You're not responsible for what your ancestors did," I said.

"No, but, like, my mom's been telling me my entire life about how hard her family had it, and how lucky we were to be here, and how we were the good guys suffering under totalitarian dictators and shit, blah dee fucking blah bah, and then it, like, totally turns out that we *were* the totalitarian dictators! Or at least their henchmen."

"Well," I said. "There were a lot of totalitarian henchmen back then. It was kind of a thing. You couldn't really avoid it. And once again, it's not your fault. *You* weren't a totalitarian henchwoman."

"Yeah, but I feel, like, *dirty!* Like all that dirty blood is running through my veins." She paused, a thoughtful look crossing her face. "Like a Mudblood, huh, Professor H?"

"I don't think you need to think of yourself as a Mudblood," I said. "We've all got a lot of bad blood running through our veins."

"I guess." She didn't sound convinced. "But it was all a *lie*. And it turned out my great-grandpa was, like, a big liar all the time! He, like, joined the OUN, and then he joined the NKVD, and he was kind of working for both at once, and *then* he worked with the Nazis—which I can't fucking *believe*, I can't fucking believe that, like, my own great-grandpa was a Nazi, but it's true!—and then he got some job working for the Americans, and he came over here, and he was supposedly, like, working for freedom and democracy and shit, but that was probably the biggest fucking lie of all!"

"Maybe he just wanted to live," I said. "So he did whatever he had to do in order to survive."

"Maybe." She didn't sound very convinced. "But anyway, now my grandma and I are super angry with him, even though he died before I was born so there's no point at being angry at him, is there? Except I *am*. I'm so mad! And then it turns out that, like, my mom already knew about it! He'd told her before he died. Not his son, not anyone else, but he told *her*. 'Cause he thought she'd understand or something. And the worst part is that she *did*. She, like, totally tried to defend him and everything to me."

"Well, he was her grandfather," I pointed out. "And like I said, it was a complicated time. A lot of people found themselves doing bad things." I thought about telling her that a lot of people found themselves doing bad things these days too. Her own father had poured out at least a little piece of his heart to me about the moral quandaries he'd found himself in. That probably wouldn't be helpful right now.

"That's what everyone keeps saying." Her nose was scrunched up in disgust again. "But I mean, *seriously*, Professor H! Would *you* do something like that?"

"I don't know," I said.

She looked startled.

"I don't think so," I said. "My life history so far has included a lot of not doing what was convenient or expedient because I didn't think it was right. I *think* I've demonstrated the courage of my convictions more than once. But I don't actually know what I'd do under those specific circumstances."

"Yeah." She nodded, cautiously relaxing. "But you, like, you'd never actually *believe* in that Nazi shit, right? 'Cause I think he actually believed in it. I think that was the thing he really believed in. The NKVD stuff and the freedom and democracy stuff was just a cover for what he really thought, which was Nazi all the way."

"It's very unlikely that I'd ever actually believe the Nazi stuff," I admitted. "But, like I keep saying, that was a very different, and very difficult, time. Especially for people in western Ukraine. Fascist ideology had a lot that was pretty attractive to them."

Madison favored me with some truly excellent side eye. "You're, liking, joking, right, Professor H? You're not *really* defending them, are you?"

"Well," I said. "Not really, no." In fact, one of the peculiarities of my position was that I spent a lot of time defending moral and political beliefs I didn't actually share. A major part of being a Russian professor in America was explaining to people that yes, Vladimir Putin was genuinely very popular in Russia, and yes, there were very real and legitimate reasons for that popularity, and that he was therefore the rightful leader of the Russian people, like it or not. This despite my own disagreement with many of his policies, and my belief that his administration was personally targeting Dima, possibly with the intent of killing him.

And now here I was defending Ukrainian Nazi collaborators. Although in that, it seemed, a lot of western liberal intellectuals were way ahead of me. My friends and colleagues had been making truly jaw-dropping statements ever since the Euromaidan uprising of 2013/14. If I heard one more time that the people wearing swastikas were just cosplaying, or that they didn't really represent the Euromaidan movement since they spoke Russian, or it was okay to use them to do the killing and dying since that's what they were good for, or conversely, that the Donbass miners shouldn't be allowed to have political representation since they weren't educated enough to use it properly, I thought I'd scream. I increasingly felt like most of my colleagues were blindly marching down a dangerously extremist path that was likely to tear Ukraine apart and maybe take a bunch of other countries out with it. And I was left behind, afraid even to shout a warning at them.

"Anyways," Madison continued. "Now my whole family is, like, fighting about this. Especially once we found out the worst part."

She paused and looked at me expectantly. I dutifully fulfilled her expectations.

"What's the worst part?" I asked.

"Some of my mom's cousins—*my* cousins—are part of some modern-day Nazi group over there. And my mom supports them."

4

"SUPPORTS THEM HOW?" I asked. "Supports them as in shares their ideological position? Supports them as in she's sending them money? Or supports them as in she's planning to go over and join them?"

"I don't think she's planning to go over and join them," Madison said. "Although with all the crazy shit she's been saying recently, maybe she will. But what she *said* was that, like, she was planning to help bring them over here."

"Ah," I said. Rather than making me feel better, this made me feel worse. Ukraine was becoming a global center for neo-Nazism and white supremacy. Many of these groups had sophisticated outreach programs that, like ISIS, were using social media to recruit people from all over the world. Including in the US. I'd already had to tell some of my own students, seduced by the snazzy videos for the training camps they were running over there, that you probably had to be white to be a white supremacist. Actually, I wasn't sure that was true, but I decided I needed to nip this thing in the bud as soon as possible, at least in my own classes.

In any case, I was not surprised to hear that people were coming over to the US. "Soooo," I said. "Do you happen to know what they're planning to do while they're over here?"

Madison shrugged. "I think meet with other, what do you call 'em, 'like-minded individuals.'" She shuddered. "That means, like, those crazy survivalists, right, Professor H?"

"Maybe," I said. "Or maybe it means smooth-talking intellectuals making a plausible case for Ukrainian nationalism or national security or the protection of European values and the white race, whatever plays best with their particular audience." I resisted the urge to point out that, as a Southerner, a lot of this sounded awfully familiar to me. There was a certain ring of "states' rights" and "heritage, not hate" to a lot of the statements coming out of the Euromaidan movement. I had already learned not to say things like that out loud, though.

"Yeah." Madison's gaze was turned inwards, as if she were replaying old conversations over in her head. "That would make more sense if my mom were hooking them up with, like, professors and shit. 'Cause that's who she knows. I just figured only crazy survivalists would listen to someone like that."

"It depends on how you spin it," I said.

"Yeah. So, like, anyways, she and my grandma got into it big time, and they both blamed *me* for it, 'cause I was the one who dug up those old documents and showed 'em to 'em, and then me and my mom got into it even more, and, and...and then I left. I just, like, walked out the fuckin' door and *left*. Finally!" She grinned, momentarily triumphant at her strength of spirit to do what she'd been wanting to do for years.

"But then I couldn't figure out where to go," she went on. "I thought about my dad, of course, but, like, well...he was already pretty pissed with me over this whole thing. He thought I was just, like, stirring up trouble to be a pain in the ass—his words—like I always do."

An expression of acute pain crossed her face, before she wiped it away with another cocky grin. "So then I was, like...pretty desperate, actually. Running away was even scarier than I thought. But then I thought of you, and I looked you up. It was easier to find you than I thought it'd be. Did you know you can find pretty much anyone these days?"

"Scary," I said. "But useful for you."

"Yeah. I know I should've called ahead or something. But I was scared you'd say no. I figured if I just showed up, you wouldn't kick me out, so that's what I did. Uh, sorry."

"No problem," I said. "Glad to help." It was only sort of a lie. I was, of course, already getting sucked into Madison's family drama. I wasn't thrilled at the idea of having her as a roommate, and I really wasn't thrilled at the idea of getting on her father's bad side, but I certainly wasn't going to turn her away now.

"And now I'm afraid that my whole family is, like, crazy and shit. *Evil,* even. And I'm so...I'm just so fuckin' disappointed in them! Angry, and disappointed, and, and...they're just *so* stupid! *So* bad! Am I, like, wrong to be this mad at them, Professor H? Does this mean there's something wrong with *me*?"

"No," I said. "Maybe it's a good thing. I'd say you can only be this disappointed in the stupidity and evil in humans when you believe strongly in their potential for goodness."

"Huh," said Madison. "I don't think I've ever believed in my mom's potential for goodness."

"The fact that you're so upset about it now suggests that you did," I said.

"Yeah. I guess. But this *sucks*! I hate how mad I am at her, and my dad, and my great-grandpa, and my cousins, and everyone! If this is what believing in goodness does to you, I don't think I want to!"

"Yeah," I said. "Sometimes I think I'm right there with you. But you can't appreciate the good people are capable of until you accept the evil they can do."

"That sounds very, like, what is it...it was in some class I took...Zoroastrian," said Madison. "Like, no light without darkness, evil is inevitable, blah blah fucking blah."

"I guess, but what I really mean to say was that you can't fight monsters until you acknowledge their existence and turn and face them. Until we acknowledge the monster within us, we won't be able to do anything about it. And in the meantime, yes, good will be pretty meaningless without evil. If you go through life with a fluffy-bunny view of the world—if you think fluffy bunnies are nothing but cute, instead of sentient beings capable of the full range of feelings and behaviors—you'll miss out on all the good you can do because you'll be so focused on ignoring the evil."

"No shit," said Madison. "Now how does that help me with my mom?"

"I don't know. Other than maybe you'll be able to have some kind of a reconciliation with her someday. But in the meantime, let's call your dad, okay?"

Madison opened her mouth, probably to say no. I hit "call" before she could get the word out. I didn't want her to dissuade me from something I didn't want to do myself.

Maybe he'll be out, I told myself encouragingly. *I'll just leave a quick voice message, and then I can screen his calls when he calls back. I'll never actually have to speak to him at all.*

"Hello?" He had picked up on the first ring. "Rowena, is that you?"

5

"OH!" I SAID. "UM, HI. Um...I wanted to let you know that, uh, Madison's with me. She's safe and she's with me."

"Thank God." His words, loud enough to fill the whole room even though he wasn't on speakerphone, sounded genuine. Across my rickety table, I could see Madison relax, some tension in her I hadn't even known was there release at his spontaneous outburst of relief.

Then he ruined it by saying, "I don't know what she was thinking, Rowena, inconveniencing you like this, but you shouldn't have to put up with her another minute longer. Send her back to me immediately. I'll send you the money if she doesn't have enough left on her credit card limit to cover it."

"Um," I said. Madison was curling up on herself, shrinking away from me as if she were about to slide off her chair, slither under the door, and disappear. "Thanks, but we're good for the moment. She just showed up, and we're not sure yet what she's going to do. If she wants to go back to New Jersey and she needs money to get there, we'll be sure to let you know. But in the meantime, she's welcome to stay here. I just wanted to let you know she's okay."

"I appreciate that." I could hear him taking a slow, deep breath on the other end of the call, probably trying to keep from blowing up completely. "I really do. And I appreciate your willingness to help her out. But you shouldn't have to deal with her, and she needs to be home."

"I don't mind having her here at all," I said. It was only very marginally true, but I could see Madison curl up smaller and smaller with each word he said.

"That's very kind of you, but I can't ask you to deal with her mess," he said. "I'll be down by tomorrow at the latest to come get her. And I'll pay for any trouble and expense she causes you, as well as for your time, of course. Just tell me where to find you."

Madison was practically in a fetal position on her chair. She wiped her nose again on her raggedy sleeve. This time I was sure it was from tears.

"That's okay," I said. "Madison's welcome to stay with me as long as she wants. Free of charge."

"Are you still in Charlotte? I can get a direct flight there this afternoon. I can have her off your hands by dinnertime."

"That's okay," I said again. Then, before I could think better of it, I ended the call.

Madison uncurled herself enough to look me in the face. She wiped her nose on her other sleeve. Her eyes looked very red. "That was awesome, Professor H," she said. Her voice was high and shaky, with none of its usual cockiness. "You hung up on him! I've, like, wanted to do that a million times, but I've never had the balls. Or whatever. I guess I don't have any balls anyway, do I?"

"Balls are wimpy and weak," I said automatically. "But, uh, female reproductive organs are, um, extremely tough."

She laughed. A watery laugh, but a laugh nonetheless. "*And* you turned down his money!" She was starting to perk up as she ran over our conversation in her head. "I don't think I've ever seen anyone do that! Normally he, like, buys up everyone around me so they do what he says."

She shivered a little at the thought. "I always feel like I can't trust anyone around me. Like, they're all there for the money. They're nice to me when he wants them to be nice to me, and mean to me when he wants them to me mean to me, and none of it's real, you know what I mean? Like, it's all just been bought and sold. Like, when everyone's goal around you is making money, there's no one you can trust. But *you* threw his money right back in his face!" She looked around my apartment. "And you probably need the money more than anyone else."

"Jeez, thanks," I said. "I'm not *that* poor." Actually, I was, but I wasn't going to tell her that.

"It looks like you are." She seemed much younger than her twenty-one years as she casually discussed my poverty in front of me. I replayed my conversation with her father in my head too. No wonder she was so immature. She was still being treated like a child. Worse than that, she was being treated like a burden. So she didn't know how to be anything but a burden.

"So, like, what do we do now?" she asked.

"I don't know," I said. "Do you have a plan?"

She shook her head. "All I could think about was getting away from all that."

"Fair enough. But now that you've gotten away, you need to figure out what you're going to do next. Are you supposed to be starting school this semester?"

"Yes." Her shoulders drooped. "My senior year. Pretty fucking crazy, huh? I can't believe I made it this far. Except maybe I didn't, right? Like, I'm supposed to be starting classes next week in New Jersey, and here I am down in Georgia. Maybe I'll just skip senior year, whaddya think?"

"I think if that's what you want to do, you should have a really good plan for something else to do instead," I said.

"Yeah. I guess. I probably can't live with you here all year, huh?"

I carefully kept my face from showing what I thought about that. At least, I hoped I did. "I think," I said carefully, "you'd find that pretty boring, pretty quick."

"I could get a job," she offered. "Probably. I've never actually had a real job before. But how hard could it be?"

"It depends on the job," I said. "And getting a job would be a good thing. But there might not be a lot of jobs here. It's not a very big town. You almost certainly couldn't get a very *good* job."

"So you're saying I should go back, huh?" She was starting to curl up on herself again.

"Not necessarily," I said. "But there will be some pretty inconvenient consequences of not going back and starting school next week, so if I were you, I'd want something pretty good on hand to make up for it."

"Yeah. Okay. That makes sense." Her gaze was turning inward, becoming introspective in a way I'd never seen on her before. Madison was a smart girl, but I didn't think she was by nature a philosopher, and she'd never been encouraged to think deeply about life before. Thinking deeply about life can get in the way of being the perfect child, and as far as I could tell, her parents had spent her whole life trying to mold her into their idea of perfection. So far it had worked out poorly for everyone.

"My dad likes to keep talking about how actions have consequences," she said. "But it was always, like, his way of controlling me. All the consequences were about him being unhappy and taking it out on me. He's, like, *obsessed* with rules, and making other people do what he says. Hey—do you think that's because he's a teacher? 'Cause he is, right? He was, like, a professor for a long time before he was, like, a provost and shit. When I was little he was still teaching, and he was always going on and on about how the students never read the syllabus and never followed instructions, blah blah

blah. And he's still like that. It's like school is just there to teach you how to, like, do what you're told, instead of how to think."

"Well, you know what they say," I said. "School prepares rich kids to be cogs in the machine of capitalism, and poor kids for prison."

Madison's mouth fell open. I regretted my outburst. But it *was* true.

"So I guess I'm, like, supposed to become a cog in the machine of capitalism?" she said.

"Yep. Pretty much."

"So, like, what do I do? Run away?"

"You've already done that," I pointed out. "And I don't know that it would save you."

"Yeah. 'Cause I'd still have to work, right? And my parents would still be my parents, even if I'm here and they're there."

"Uh-huh," I agreed.

"I just...I just *hate* school!" she burst out. "I've spent my whole life doing nothing but going to school, and I've hated every minute of it! It's, like, all rules and no real life."

"Yeah," I agreed. "Way too many rules, and not nearly enough real life. Probably because people use the rules as a way to shield themselves from real life, and then let other people pay the consequences. But that's the case in lots of places."

"Oh. Okay. Ugh. So, like, what *do* I do now?"

"First," I said, "you take a shower and wash your clothes. You can wear some of my old stuff while you wait for them to dry. Then we think about supper. And then, tonight or maybe tomorrow, we make a plan."

"Cool. And a shower sounds really good right now." She jumped up from her seat, then paused. "So, like, my dad doesn't know where you live, right?"

"I guess not," I said. "Since he asked if I was still in Charlotte."

"And then you hung up on him." The beginnings of a mischievous smile quivered at the corners of her mouth. "So...whaddya think? Is he going to get on a plane to Charlotte tonight? Where *is* Charlotte?"

"North Carolina," I told her. "He might. He has friends there. That's how he got me the job there, the semester after I left TLASC. But I don't know how much it will help him." I thought for a moment. "Actually, I think Brent—his friend there—knows I started a job here in Georgia. So he'll probably be able to track me down pretty quickly. And even if his friend doesn't tell him, he'll still probably be able to track me down pretty quickly. After all, *you* did, didn't you?"

"Yeah. Yeah, I did. But I didn't figure my dad'd be able to do it."

I could feel my mouth opening to ask if she'd engaged in a little illegal computer wizardry as part of hunting me down. She did have a history of doing that kind of thing. Or maybe, like a lot of adolescents, she just thought her dad was irredeemably stupid. And he probably didn't know how to dig around in other people's data as well as she did. But he had connections, and that was even better for getting what you wanted. I gave us twenty-four hours, tops, before he showed up at my front door. And that was if I didn't cave and give him my full street address first.

My phone buzzed under my hand. I glanced down at it. Speak of the Devil. He'd obviously decided texting was a better way to go than talking.

"Go take a shower," I told Madison. "You can take whatever clothes you want out of my closet. There's a spare towel in the drawer to the right of the sink. And then we'll figure out what to do next."

"Sure thing!" She set off with a remarkably bouncy step, considering how her day had gone so far, towards the bathroom. And I braced myself to read the text from Erik Johnson.

6

I'M SORRY IF I WAS short with you, or if I pushed too hard, the text read. *I just don't want you to get dragged into Madison's drama.*

I bit my lip at that. Not "I'm really worried about Madison," but "I don't want you to get dragged into Madison's drama." It could be read as concern for me. Maybe it was. But it was also a lack of concern for Madison. I believed that he cared about Madison. I also believed that care mainly expressed itself as frustration and resentment at her inability to fulfill his carefully considered plans for her and her future. For Madison as she really was and really needed him, the main thing he seemed to feel was disappointment and dislike.

I understand, I wrote back. *But I think Madison maybe needs a little time on her own. She's not causing me any trouble right now. We've already talked about her going back to New Jersey in time to start school next week.*

Thank God! Do you think she'll do it?

A shriek came from the bathroom. I leapt to my feet and then shrieked myself, almost going down as my left knee rebelled against the sudden weight.

"What is it?!" I shouted, clutching at the table to keep myself upright.

"Cool cat, Professor H!" Madison shouted back. "She came, like, jumping out from under the sink, and I, like, totally thought she was gonna attack me, but now she's letting me pet her."

"Be careful!" I warned. "It's normally best not to pet her, in case she bites."

"Nah," said Madison. "She's, like, totally sweet. She's purring and rubbing her head on my leg. I think she wants to get into the shower with me."

For a moment I considered rushing into the bathroom to make sure that Madison wasn't hallucinating, or that there wasn't some other, alien cat who had snuck in somehow and swapped places with Fevronia, my own cat. Although I was very fond of Fevronia, I would never have considered calling her "totally sweet." She was a long-haired tan cat of unknown heritage and a disposition that even I could only call "vicious." I was normally sporting at least one bandaid at any given moment from a bite or a scratch, and she categorically refused to sit in my lap or let me pet her like a decent cat should.

I listened carefully. No screams of pain emanated from the bathroom. Instead, there was some indistinct crooning, followed after a moment by the sound of running water.

My phone buzzed again, reminding me that I hadn't responded to Erik's last text.

I don't know if she'll go back to NJ, I wrote. *But she's not completely against the idea. In the meantime, though, I don't know that it would help for you to come down here and get her.*

I get that. In fact, I think you're probably right. I just hate the thought of letting her get away with this kind of thing, and dumping it all on you.

It's no trouble. I tried to think of what else to add to that text. I wanted to point out in some helpful, constructive way that the very concept of "letting her get away with this kind of thing" was probably a major source of the problem. But I couldn't think of how to phrase that, so I sent the text as it was.

Be honest, Rowena. How much trouble is she really causing you?

She's taking a shower right now, I wrote. *That's not very much trouble at all. She can spend a night or two here without it being any problem.*

I'm glad to hear it. As long as it doesn't go beyond that. And I'm serious, Rowena: I'll pay for any expenses you incur because of her. And I'll pay you for your time. I imagine your financial situation still isn't great. Brent said you got a visiting position at a small college in Georgia. That can't pay well.

On the other hand, living expenses are very low! I replied.

Fair enough. But I mean it: don't hesitate to ask for help. Don't hesitate to ask for money. Even if it's just for yourself. I feel like I still owe you for the last time you saved Madison from herself.

I wanted to text something snippy about how I hadn't done it for the money. But I'd already made that point to him. Several times. He'd probably even heard it. He just needed to feel like he was helping out, or at least offering to help out, in any way he could. And being snippy and defiant rarely solved problems. Madison was an object lesson in that.

Thank you, I wrote instead. *I appreciate it. I'll definitely let you know if I need any help.*

*Thank you, Rowena. And...I hope you don't mind me asking...what *do* you think I should do here? I feel like I've fucked up big time and I don't know what to do next. So I guess I might as well ask you what you think, since you seem to understand, or at least get along with, Madison better than most of us. What am I doing wrong? How can I do right? Be honest!*

I bit my lip again, and stifled a groan. When people say they want you to be honest with them, that's the worst, because they don't actually want the truth, the whole truth, and nothing but the truth. What you have to give them is a collection of carefully curated half-truths to make them feel like they're getting the truth without actually making them freak out. I was hungry and tired and I still had a lot to do today, and I didn't feel like coming up with a bunch of tactful half-truths right now. I wasn't sure I *could* come up with any tactful half-truths right now. My knee was starting to throb and cramp in a sinister way, making it hard to focus on anything except trying to find a comfortable position.

I don't think Madison responds well to discipline and control, I finally wrote. *The more people attempt to apply it to her, the more out of control she gets. And she's justifiably upset about what she found out about her family history. I only got some of the story, but anyone would be thrown by it. And I think she's worried she might get drawn into something unsavory.*

No response. Probably I'd been too honest and direct. In fact, I was sure I had. That was exactly the kind of full, unvarnished truth that people hate so much. In the bathroom, the shower shut off, and I could hear Madison moving around as she got dressed. I was going to have to end this conversation before she came out. I wasn't exactly going behind her back here, but I wasn't exactly not going behind her back, either.

My phone buzzed. Erik was finally responding.

I hear what you're saying about discipline and control, he wrote. *I've just never been brave enough to let go. A character flaw that people keep pointing out to me. But of course my daughter is going to be the most merciless about it, isn't she? LOL. Thanks for saying it. Maybe I'll finally do something about it.*

"Professor H?" Madison called from the bathroom. "Is it okay if I use your deodorant?"

My first instinct was to refuse. I'm not actually a very share-y person. But I'd grown up on a commune, and then moved to Russia and lived in a much more communal society than most Americans are used to. Once again, that training stood me in good stead.

"Go ahead!" I yelled back. "Use whatever you like."

My phone buzzed again. Another message from Erik Johnson.

*And as for the actual cause of Madison's sudden departure—it is, in point of fact, pretty concerning. *I'm* at least as concerned as she is. I'm still mulling over what to do. And I guess this is your area as well? I may consult you about this, too.*

Any time, I replied. The bathroom door opened. *Got to go now*, I wrote. *I'll check back in later*. I silenced my phone and turned to face Madison as she came back out.

7

"FEEL BETTER?" OR AT least, that's what I meant to say. But the words got caught up in a strangled laugh.

"It was the only thing I could find," Madison said defensively.

"I do need to do laundry, it's true," I agreed, as solemnly as possible. She was wearing my running shorts, a particularly ratty sleeveless scoop-neck t-shirt that had once been sexy and was now just sad, and my interview blazer. All of it was two sizes too big. I wondered if this was how I looked to other people most of the time. Probably a bit. Hopefully not quite this bad.

"At least it should be comfortable," I said.

"If by 'comfortable' you mean I can, like, get into it, then yeah, I guess it's pretty comfy," she said. "Most people tell me I'm tall, but you're even bigger than I am."

I repressed a twinge of appearance-related pain. Madison was at least 5'7", maybe 5'8", but I was a solid 5'10". It was kind of a good thing. I had a lot more strength and reach than most women, which was handy when, say, grappling with criminals and crazed attackers. It made finding clothes hard, though, and no matter how much I tried to fade into the background, I always loomed in whatever company I found myself.

"Let's put your clothes in the washer," I said. "Then we can figure out what to do next."

One of the surprising luxuries of my little apartment was that it had its own tiny washer-dryer combo. We tossed Madison's frankly filthy clothes in it, and then surveyed our resources.

They were pretty slim. One of the many things I had on my to-do list was to go grocery shopping. Currently, the only thing I had on hand was enough leftover lentil soup for one person, one single-serving yogurt, a few coffee beans, and about two tablespoons of cream in the bottom of the cream carton. In other words, just enough to get through tonight and tomorrow morning. The plan was for that to tide me over until I could swing by the grocery story.

But now that Madison was here, it was clearly inadequate. Also, it was embarrassing. By the look on her face, she'd never seen such a poorly stocked kitchen. I resisted the urge to make defensive excuses or say something about how she'd left the easy pickings of her parents' house, and now she had to get used to what it meant to fend for yourself. The real issue was that A) I didn't want to spend a cent more than I had to before I got my next paycheck, and B) shopping was a challenge when you were hobbling around on crutches.

My knee twinged again. Hard. Going shopping now was not an attractive proposition. I contemplated handing over my car keys to Madison and sending her to the store on her own. Maaaayyyybeeee not. I was okay—barely—with her borrowing my clothes and using my deodorant. Letting her use my car was a whole different story. Especially since it was a finicky beast with a touchy clutch. Unless Madison had a hidden passion for difficult cars, I doubted she'd be able to drive it at all.

"Maybe we can get takeout for supper," I suggested. "Order pizza or something." I couldn't really afford it, but I couldn't face anything else right now. Maybe I'd be taking her dad up on his offer of money after all.

"Okay," she agreed. Perkily. She had perked up a lot since the shower. "Meanwhile, where's your TV?"

"I don't have one," I said. This elicited an even more horrified look than the meager contents of my kitchen.

"So, like, what am I going to do all afternoon?" The words held more than a hint of a wail of desperation.

"Read?" I suggested.

She was already opening her mouth to reject the idea with scorn when there was a knock at the door.

"My dad!" Her eyes went so wide in alarm I could see white all the way around the iris.

"Surely not," I said. "He's figured out we're in Georgia, but unless he's learned how to Apparate, he couldn't possibly have made it here yet."

Madison still retreated into the bedroom. I went to answer the door. Not at all to my surprise, it was not Erik Johnson, but Mel Wilson. She was a fellow instructor at Crimson, although she taught Arabic rather than Russian. We lived in the same apartment complex, and had taken to checking up on each other and carpooling back and forth to campus. She was at least as tall as I was, but while I was the picture of Black Irishness, with blue eyes and wavy dark hair that came to my shoulders, she wore her dark blonde hair in a boyish pixie, and frequently hid her hazel eyes behind a pair of overlarge aviator sunglasses. As she was doing right now.

"Hey, Ro," she said, slipping off her sunglasses as she stepped into the comparatively cool darkness of my apartment. She was now the second person in my life who called me Ro. Well, the second person who did so with my permission. My brother John did it because he hadn't been able to pronounce "Rowena" back when I'd been born, and now it was an expression of affection. Frank McAvoy over in California did it too, but that seemed more like an expression of dominance than affection. I'd developed a grudging respect for Frank after everything we'd been through this summer, but I still wished he wouldn't call me Ro. From Mel, though, it was welcome.

"Just thought I'd check and see if you needed me to pick up anything for you at the store this afternoon," she said. "Seeing as how you're still all crippled. How'd PT go, by the way?"

"Are you supposed to be more crippled afterwards than before?" I asked.

"That's what they *tell* you, but I have my doubts," she said.

"Yeah, me too. Anyway, um, are you heading out right now? I was thinking of going shopping, but I need to put together a list first. And, oh, wait, I don't have any cash on me. You just go. I'll get stuff later."

"You can pay me back," she said easily. "I know you're good for it."

"Thanks. But I think I need to do some menu planning and put together a list, and I should probably talk to...anyway. You just go."

Mel's eyes roved around all the visible areas of the apartment. "What is it?" Her voice was a low hiss. "Is it Alex? Did he come back?"

"No," I said, my voice an equally low hiss. "It's not Alex, and he hasn't come back."

"Oh. But...you *do* have company, right? *Secret* company?" She nudged me playfully on the arm. "Another man already?"

"Alas, no. It's...oh, whatever, you might as well meet her. Madison! Hey, Madison! Why don't you come out and meet Mel."

After a moment, Madison came sliding out of the bedroom and sidled over in the general direction of where Mel and I were standing, stopping before she got halfway there.

"Madison, this is Mel—uh, Doctor Wilson. She's another professor at Crimson—at the college I currently teach at. Mel, Madison is a former student from New Jersey."

Lightning-fast calculations went on behind Mel's eyes. I'd told her a little bit about what had happened in New Jersey, and I could see her putting two and two together.

"Nice to meet you," she said, giving Madison both a curious once-over and a friendly nod. "I've heard a lot about you."

"Oh," said Madison. She didn't sound thrilled. Nor should she have. A lot of what I'd told Mel about her had not been complimentary. Of course, if you want people to say nice things about you, it helps to actually do nice things.

"So what brings you to fabulous Greenfields, Georgia?" Mel asked her. "And how long are you here for?"

"Um," said Madison. She rubbed her foot against her calf. "Not sure yet."

"Kind of an unplanned visit, I'm guessing," said Mel. "Seeing as you're wearing an eclectic ensemble composed of Rowena's clothing."

"Um," said Madison. She switched her stance and rubbed her other foot against her other calf. "Yeah. It was, uh, kind of, like, spur of the moment."

"Uh-huh," said Mel. She gave a decisive nod to herself. "Well, I'll leave you to it, but let me know if you need anything. Always happy to help out a friend, especially if it means less time answering email." She turned to look at me. "Have you seen the latest one from Karen yet? I swear to fuck..." She remembered Madison's presence, checked herself, and said, "Anyway, we can talk about it later. Meantime, let me know if you need me to pick up anything. Nice to meet you, Madison. Ciao, *habeebah*." She nudged my arm again, slid her overlarge aviator sunglasses back on, and stepped back out into the August afternoon sunlight.

8

"DO YOU THINK SHE'LL tell my dad?" Madison demanded as soon as Mel left.

"I don't think she knows your dad," I pointed out.

"Oh. Yeah." She hugged herself as if she were cold, then stopped and attempted a smile. "I guess I'm just paranoid, huh?"

"Maybe a little," I said. "But you've been through a lot recently. Anyway, I sincerely doubt Mel knows your dad, and even if she did, she's not the kind of person to go behind your back and snitch, so I think we're safe. But she *will* help out with grocery shopping, so you should make a list, at least of anything you want for breakfast tomorrow, and she can get it."

"Oh. And...I have cash. I got a bunch before I left Princeton. I still have some left." TLASC, where Madison was a student and her father was provost, was in New Brunswick, but New Brunswick didn't have a lot of desirable neighborhoods for people of their social class, so they lived in Princeton.

"Um," I said. I wanted to tell Madison I could take care of it. But I really didn't have any cash on hand. I'd given my last $20 to Mel when she'd gone shopping for me a couple of days ago, and I hadn't withdrawn any more since then. Nor did I want to. I had $235.71 in the bank right now, $362.87 left on my credit card limit, and eleven days until my next paycheck. Somehow, despite a whole year with a full-time teaching job *and* summer school, I was still flat broke, with a maxed-out credit card and a car that careened closer and closer to total breakdown with each passing day.

"You hang onto your cash," I told her. "You might need it to get back to New Jersey, or to wherever you need to go next. Don't worry about food here: I'll take care of it."

"Okay. So...um...what does *habeebah* mean?"

I was pretty sure that had not been the question she had originally been meaning to ask. I was pretty sure she had originally been meaning to ask me how soon I wanted her to be gone. I was pretty sure I had inadvertently made her feel just as unwanted as everyone else in her life. She'd chickened out from putting it to me directly, and had chosen to ask about something innocuous instead.

"It means something like 'girlfriend' or 'sweetheart,'" I told her.

Madison's forehead wrinkled up. "I thought that was, like, *dorogaya* or something like that."

"In Russian, yeah. But that was in Arabic. Mel—Professor Wilson—teaches Arabic."

Madison's forehead wrinkled up even more. "I didn't know you speak Arabic, Professor H."

"I don't. I just know a couple of words."

I tried to say it lightly. It was hard. My heart gave a little squeeze every time I found myself saying something that revealed my tiny store of knowledge of Arabic. 90% of the Arabic I had learned had come from Alex. I wanted to talk about it, and yet every time I did, it hurt. I should just shut up and move on—but doing so seemed like slamming a door on something that had meant something to me.

"Oh. Yeah. You were friends with Professor Miller, right?"

"Right." The word came out surprisingly normally. And in this light, Madison probably couldn't see the flush spreading over my face.

"I sent him a whole thank you letter and everything while I was rehab. They make you do stuff like that. But I haven't talked to him since. It's kind of embarrassing, you know? Are you still in touch with him?"

"Sometimes." It was getting harder and harder to speak lightly. "Anyway," I said quickly, "why don't you make a list of anything you want from the grocery store, and look up what to get for dinner, and...I don't know, think about what you want to do next, and I'll check my email and get some work done, and then it'll be suppertime. Maybe we could invite Mel over; you might like her."

"Does she like *you*?" Madison was looking at me with an intensity that was slightly unnerving.

"I mean, we're friends, so yeah, obviously."

"No, I mean...like...I didn't, like, know you were, like, you know...into, like, women..." Madison was staring down at the cheap carpet and rubbing her foot against her calf again.

"We're just friends." Now I was able to speak lightly again. It was true that Mel *was* into women, and there was a certain...something between us sometimes, but I was determined that it would go no further. I was all too painfully familiar with doomed love affairs, and there was no way I would ever want to do anything like that to Mel. Maybe it was arrogant of me to think she might be interested in a doomed love affair, or a love affair of any kind, between us, but I was determined to play it safe for both our sakes. I knew what it was like to be desperately in love with someone who kept failing you in some fundamental way, and I would do almost anything to avoid being that person for Mel. Especially since she had one of those people in her life already.

"Go take stock of our supplies," I told Madison. "Think about what we need for our resupply. And I'll go see what that dreadful email Mel was telling me about was."

9

KAREN, THE CHAIR OF the Department of Modern Languages at Crimson College, the small private liberal arts college where Mel and I were both Visiting Assistant Professors, aka VAPs, was not, to put it mildly, my favorite person. I don't think she was anyone's favorite person. Which was horribly tragic. Considering I'd spent the summer hanging out with torturers, I should maybe be a little more understanding towards her. But she was still a representative of a very deep-seated sort of evil. An evil that I, too, might be part of.

The fact that you hang out with the three of us means you're bad on the inside, even if you don't know it. Frank had said that to me at our last meeting. The words had played through my head as I had limped, with my busted-up knee and piece-of-shit car, all the way across America, from California to Georgia. They were still playing in my head at least ten times a day, every day, even though there was a continent between us. And it wasn't because they were a revelation, or because I was determined to deny them. I was pretty sure Frank was right. I just wasn't quite sure in what way he was right, so now I was scrutinizing my every action, trying to find those seeds of evil I was sure were there.

Interactions with Karen were certainly fertile ground for them. I could feel a headache start in the back of my neck and spread around to my temples, before extending down into my stomach, triggering low-grade nausea, as my fingers reached for my laptop. By the time they were actually striking the keys on the keyboard to log me in, I was feeling distinctly ill.

You need a better job, I told myself. *One that doesn't make you sick with dread every time you have anything to do with it.* Masha, my best friend from grad school, had often joked with me about taking up stripping, or possibly streetwalking, as a cleaner, safer, and more honest, or at least more remunerative, way to make a living. I thought it was unlikely to actually be much better. It probably meant getting even more up close and personal with insecure, egotistical assholes on a petty power trip than working in higher ed. But maybe, if you did it right, you could bank more cash, more quickly, and retire sooner.

Something to consider if/when I lost this job. I was on a year-to-year contract, with performance reviews every semester, and a three-year maximum term of service. Karen had repeatedly threatened to terminate me, but in the end had renewed my contract for this academic year. I suspected most of her threats were bluff, since finding someone qualified who would be willing to move to small-town Georgia would probably be challenging, but I still had to assume she would follow through. I already had a list of jobs to apply to this fall. Maybe this would be the year I got a permanent position. Maybe not. Either way, right now, August 20th, 2016, I had to deal with whatever my current, very precarious, position might throw at me.

Steeling myself, I opened my Crimsonmail. There were notifications about parking lot closures for new construction, the agenda for the college-wide faculty meeting on Monday, reminders to attend the barbecue event for incoming students this evening, which I deleted since I had no intention of hobbling across campus and standing around in the heat for several hours, and yes, an email from Karen titled "IMPORTANT!!!!"

Nothing else to indicate what might actually *be* so important. Maybe it was part of her cunning plan to whet our curiosity and get us to open an email I was sure most of the faculty were just as disinclined to read as I was. I clicked on it.

Dear Colleagues!

It has come to my attention that certain colleagues have been using the department copier to copy personal items. As a reminder: due to budget restrictions, ONLY department-related copying is allowed on our copier.

Well, that wasn't too bad. Departments were always trying to restrict printing and copying in order to cut costs. I often wondered how much money they actually saved. How much could ten or fifteen people actually spend on personal printing and copying? I was pretty sure I did less than $5 a year on personal printing. And I spent a lot more than that on printing off syllabi and handouts on my own dime—but the fact that I could afford to do it meant it was a minuscule amount of money. Meanwhile, the college was putting in a new football stadium. With private prison money...I wrenched my mind away from that enraging thought and turned back to the enraging email in front of me.

I also must inform you that, as part of the college-wide quality survey in preparation for our upcoming SACS re-accreditation, our department received low marks across multiple dimensions. We will therefore be undergoing a comprehensive overview of our practices and standards during this upcoming academic year. This will involve multiple observations of every faculty member's teaching, mandatory training in current pedagogical best practices, and a reassessment of our hiring methodology in order to avoid repeating the mistakes made in some of our recent hires.

"AGH!"

"Professor H! Are you okay?" Madison's voice from the kitchen was high and anxious.

"Just an icepick headache," I told her. I pressed at the spot of blinding pain next to my right eye.

"Oh, yeah, my dad, like, gets those all the time. He says they suck big-time."

"Yeah. But they pass quickly." Already the pain was easing, allowing me to read the rest of the email.

I should not have to tell you that the Department of Modern Languages is under considerable pressure in the area of student recruitment and retention. As I have repeatedly stated in my communications, both written and verbal, with the department, we are being held up as a negative example to the rest of the college for our class enrollments. There is a very real possibility that the department will be dissolved completely and our subjects phased out. The move by the administration to break up our department into multiple departments, while being sold to us as being in our benefit by allowing greater flexibility, is in fact likely to destroy the teaching of language as it has been practiced for decades at Crimson College. As we know, this is part of a nationwide trend to discredit the teaching of foreign languages and the humanities in general. If we do not ACT NOW, by this time next year we could all be flipping burgers at the fast food joints of our choice.

Therefore, I call on all of you to DO YOUR PART to stem this tide. Above all, we must rededicate ourselves to raising our teaching standards to those expected for faculty at Crimson College. And we must act quickly and do everything we can to stop the destruction of our department before it is too late.

Yours in solidarity,

Karen Dupont

Associate Professor of French

Chair of the Department of Modern Languages

Crimson College

"Aaaaaagh," I said again. This time it came out as more of a low groan. The icepick headache was mostly gone. This was largely an expression of emotional pain. I was, just as Mel had warned me I would be, beyond furious at the contents of the email. The phrase about "mistakes in some of our recent hires" *had* to refer to me and/or Mel and/or Chloe Taylor, the third person hired last year by the department. And the stuff about the dissolution of the department seemed like a pointed attack on the plan to create a separate program for the LCTLS—Less Commonly Taught Languages—which, again, we taught. So the whole thing was basically a personal attack on the three of us. I couldn't help but think that what felt like pointed attacks and deliberate bullying of me, Mel, and Chloe fell somewhere between deep incompetence and actual evil, and I couldn't tell which way the scales would tip. Maybe we'd only know once we'd fulfilled the cycle of abuse and become abusers ourselves.

On the other hand, I shared some of her concerns about the future of language teaching in general and the fate of our programs here at Crimson in particular. That might be the most awful thing. Some part of me agreed with some part of what she was saying. Stockholm Syndrome? The fact that the enemy of my enemy was a friend? Or a sign of the underlying *badness* Frank had seen in me, and that I now felt as a visceral taint of my whole being?

And maybe she was right about me being a bad professor and a big mistake for the college. After all, here I was, harboring a runaway former student with a drug problem and, apparently, family ties to white supremacist extremist groups. If the Crimson administration found out about this, they'd probably have a collective coronary at the bad press it could bring thundering down on the college like a ton of runaway bricks.

"Hey, Professor H? Can we go ahead and order some takeout? I'm *starving*," Madison called from the kitchen. "I haven't, like, had anything to eat since last night. And maybe your friend can go get some stuff at the grocery store? I made a list. And I really can give you some cash for it. I know I'm, like, a pain in your ass. I'd like to pay my way, at least a little."

"You're not a pain in anyone's ass," I said automatically. "And sure, we can go ahead and get some takeout. Pick whatever you'd like. I think the choices are pizza, subs, or Chinese."

"Chinese," she said immediately.

"Great. That's my favorite too."

"Awesome." She came over to stand by where I was set up with my laptop at my rickety table. "It's weird, isn't it, Professor H? We've got, like, a lot of stuff in common, don't we? I noticed it right away."

"Sure," I said. "I noticed it right away too."

She gave me the first genuinely happy smile she'd had since she'd shown up at my doorstep. It made up for the lie, and even a bit for the whole mess she'd dragged me into. And maybe it meant I wasn't such a bad teacher or a bad person. Maybe the fact that Madison Johnson, notorious troublemaker and fuckup whom even her parents had given up on, had come to me when she really needed help, meant that I was a good person and good at what I did.

You keep telling yourself that, I told myself, and went to order enough takeout Chinese food for at least three meals.

10

WE ORDERED AND ATE Chinese takeout with Madison's credit card, and gave some of Madison's cash to Mel so that she could do a grocery run for breakfast supplies, and watched a movie on my laptop and ate more Chinese takeout, and then I declared it was time for bed. At least for me. Madison could stay up as late as she wanted, as long as she was quiet.

"Normally my sleep hygiene's, like, terrible," she said, yawning hugely. "But I, like, didn't sleep at all last night on the bus, so I think I'm going to hit the hay too. Or the floor."

I didn't have a spare bed, or so much as a spare camping mattress, so Madison was going to sleep on a kind of bedroll we'd made for her with my one spare comforter. To her credit, she didn't complain about it at all. Well, she hadn't yet. The next morning might be a different matter.

But the next morning found her remarkably bright-eyed and bushy-tailed. I had been expecting her to be sleep-deprived and possibly in serious withdrawal, but instead she greeted both the new day and me with a broad smile.

"I came up with a plan!" she announced as she brewed us both coffee. "Just as I was dropping off to sleep last night, it came to me! It was awesome."

"That's how ideas are sometimes," I said.

"Yeah. Guess so. Anyway, my idea is—have I ever told you about my aunt?"

"I don't think so," I said.

"Yeah, my dad's sister. Not my mom's sister, obviously: she's, like, *totally* fucked up. A complete alkie. Can't go to *her*. But my dad's got a much older sister. She's more like a grandma to me than an aunt, really, but she's pretty cool even though she's old."

"Sometimes old people can be surprisingly cool," I agreed.

"Yeah. So she lives in, like, New York. She's got, like, one of those rent-controlled apartments you hear about it. It's not, like, super fancy, but it's nicer than this place." She cast a disparaging gaze around my apartment, which, admittedly, deserved all her censure.

"Uh-huh," I said encouragingly.

"I don't know why I didn't think of her before! Well, I do. She's been majorly on my case about rehab and shit."

"Uh-huh," I said, more noncommittally.

"Yeah." Madison shrugged. "But then I thought, hey, maybe it could work out. Like, except for the rehab shit, she's pretty cool. And I'm clean now. Maybe she wouldn't be on my case so much if I could convince her of that. So, like, maybe I could go stay with her for a while. It only takes, like, an hour to get from New York to New Brunswick by train, and I only have classes three days a week this semester anyway. I could stay with her and take the train back and forth and, like, I don't know, get a job or something."

"That could work," I agreed cautiously. "And a job would be good. Although it might be pretty hard. That's a long commute, and working on top of that wouldn't leave you a lot of time for actual schoolwork."

She shrugged. "It's not like I spend a lot of time on it anyway. Sorry! I guess you didn't want to hear that, huh? Although you might have already guessed it."

"I'd already guessed it," I said. "But I don't want to *encourage* it."

"Yeah, guess you gotta tell me to do my homework and shit, right?"

"Something like that."

"Anyway, I'm going to give her a call in a bit, as soon as I know she's up, and then if she says yes I'll just get on a bus or a train or something—maybe a train would be nicer, huh?"

"Probably," I said.

"Or maybe my dad would be so thrilled he'd, like, spot me for a plane ticket."

"He might very well," I agreed.

"I should talk to him about it right now!"

"That's a *great* idea," I said.

A weird look suddenly crossed Madison's face. "But then I'd, like, have to talk to him. To, like, *speak* to him."

"Well," I said, "yes."

"Can you do it, Professor H? Please?"

"Um," I said. "Sure. I'd be happy to." Had I ever said that phrase and actually meant it? Right now I couldn't think of any instances of that.

It was only seven in the morning, but Erik Johnson picked up the phone on the first ring. "Rowena? What's going on?"

"Madison has an idea," I said.

11

ERIK JOHNSON WAS, AS Madison had predicted, thrilled at the idea. It was vastly better, he told me, than any outcome he had been expecting. He even offered to call his sister and talk to her about it himself.

I relayed this to Madison, expecting her to leap at the idea. But instead, she shook her head.

"I want to do it myself," she said. "It should, like, come from me. I don't want this to be, like, just another case of Madison fucking up and being shoved off somewhere out of sight for someone else to deal with."

She said it to me, but loudly enough that Erik heard it just fine at the other end of the line. I heard him suck in a breath. Then he said, his voice as smooth as if he were leading a difficult meeting full of fractious faculty members, "Of course. That's without question the best approach, if this is something Madison is willing to do."

I didn't have the phone on speaker, but Madison heard him even so. "I want to do it," she said. "I just..."

I could see her confidence faltering, now that it came to the crux of the matter, which was asking him for money.

"Madison's been paying her way while she's been here," I said. "She bought dinner last night for both of us, and breakfast this morning. But she doesn't have a lot of cash left. I thought it would be quickest for her to get to New York by plane, but it would be easier if you got the ticket."

"Of course. *Of course.*" Erik was trying to keep his meeting-smooth voice, but overwhelming relief kept breaking through. "What airport would be best for her to fly out of?"

"Atlanta," I told him. "I can take her there myself any time today—well, it takes an hour and a half to get there—or later tomorrow afternoon or evening, after my faculty meetings in the morning."

"That's a long drive for you. Surely there's a shuttle."

"Maybe," I said. "But it would be expensive, and maybe not super...safe. I'd feel better taking Madison to the airport myself."

There was a short pause at the other end of the line. Then Erik said, "Of course. You're completely right. And Atlanta is a very large and confusing airport. It would be ideal—I'd be very grateful, Rowena—if you could walk her to security yourself."

"I'd be happy to," I said, while Madison called out, aggrieved, "I can make it through an airport! I'm not a *baby*."

"It's fine," I said. "It'll be fun for us to go together. Like a fun adventure. A lot more fun than me dumping you off at some shuttle pickup spot and driving away."

Madison gave me a narrow look, like she could tell I was trying to placate her. But she nodded in agreement.

"Great," said Erik. *"Great.* Madison, as soon as you talk to Cybil, let me know, and I'll get the ticket."

"Sure," said Madison. "I mean, we're all assuming she's going to yes, right? She's, like, going to say yes, isn't she?"

"I'm sure she is," said Erik, with the tone of someone trying to convince himself.

12

CYBIL, MADISON'S AUNT, was not as immediately into the idea as I'd hoped. It took at least half an hour of discussion before she would even consider it. And, she told Madison, she traveled a lot, so Madison might have to find other places to stay for part of the semester.

"I could stay at your place by myself," Madison said.

"I don't think so," Cybil said dryly. "If you're going to be on your own in Manhattan, you're not going to be doing it in my apartment."

I heartily sympathized with the sentiment, although I could see by the droop of Madison's shoulders how much her aunt's distrust hurt her. Had Madison ever been trusted with anything? I didn't think so. And now she was completely untrustworthy. Someone needed to trust her in order for her to learn how to be trusted. But I couldn't bring myself to want to be the one who trusted her. I didn't even want to loan her my car keys for a quick trip to the grocery store.

By midmorning, though, it had all been arranged. Madison would spend the first month of the semester, at least, with her Aunt Cybil in Manhattan, commuting to New Brunswick three times a week to attend class. Cybil predicted that she would grow heartily sick of the train ride by then and be begging to move back in with her father. I suspected she might be right, but kept my opinions to myself.

"At least you won't have time to get into trouble—and you won't be spending any more time with Brenda," Cybil said, her tone acidic.

Brenda was Madison's mother. Apparently Cybil felt no compunction about badmouthing her sister-in-law in front of her sister-in-law's child. Cybil, I sensed from what I could catch eavesdropping on the conversation while pretending to check over my syllabi prior to uploading the final versions onto the course pages on Sakai, was hell on wheels and a real piece of work. Cybil, I guessed, had a lot more in common with Madison than Erik did. Living with her would either do Madison loads of good, or drive her to rebelling and running away even more thoroughly than she had from her own parents.

Let it work out! Let her not come running back to me! I can't deal with that. Then I felt ashamed of that thought. But I *did* have a lot on my plate, and Madison really should be someone else's problem. Ideally, her own.

We ran into a minor snag over the tickets. Erik, with whom I was texting while Madison talked on the phone with her aunt, wanted to put Madison on a plane that afternoon. Cybil, though, said she was going to a show that evening, and wouldn't be able to meet Madison when she arrived. Madison said she could let herself in, if Cybil left a key with a neighbor, or she could hang out on her own and explore Manhattan until Cybil got back.

"I don't think so," Cybil said again, her tone even drier than before. "You can arrive when I'm able to meet you. Come tomorrow evening."

Erik said, via text, that he didn't want Madison to have to spend another night at my place. I couldn't tell if he felt sorry for Madison, he was trying to spare me more trouble, or he didn't trust me to keep a sharp enough eye on her. Probably all three.

It's fine, I assured him. *We'll be fine.*

Maybe I should come down and get her after all, he texted back. *I could be in Greenfields*—I had finally revealed where, exactly, we were—*by this evening, spend the night there, and fly up to NYC with Madison tomorrow.*

Something inside of me squirmed at the thought. I couldn't quite tell what it was. I didn't want to spend another day and a half being responsible for Madison, although if the situation weren't so fraught, it could have been fun. When she wasn't dragging me into potentially career- or life-ending adventures, she was enjoyable to be around. At least, I thought so. I'd always liked zany, different people who marched to the beat of their own, extraterrestrial, drummer.

The thing squirming inside of me, I thought, was about her father, not her. There had always been a certain...*something* between us. A something that wasn't quite full-blown attraction, but that threatened to bloom into it if we gave it a chance. Even though he was at least fifteen years my senior. I had never been the slightest bit interested in older men, but with Erik Johnson, there was a real danger that I might become interested. And, of course, an older, more powerful man falling for a younger woman over whom he had a certain amount of control was a tale as old as time.

Ugh! Ugh! Vomit! You might be younger than him, but you're old enough to know better!

My internal pep talk allowed me to text back to him that we would be just fine and he shouldn't bother himself, especially when I knew he must be extremely busy with the beginning of the semester.

You must be at least as busy, he texted back. *What courses are you teaching? Sorry. Got sidetracked. But we should really talk about your career and how it's going at some point when this has blown over and things have calmed down again. Although with Madison, things never do seem to calm down, do they?*

I'd be happy to, I wrote, my fingers on autopilot. Someday I was going to get myself in really big trouble—even bigger trouble than I already had—with my automatic response to requests. It was probably a trauma reflex, too.

I firmly put that out of my mind, and mediated the three-way argument between Madison, her aunt, and her father over when she would arrive in New York. Eventually it was decided that I would drive Madison up to the airport Monday afternoon to catch the 4:52pm nonstop flight to LaGuardia. Cybil, after some cajoling—I understood that Erik was texting her separately—agreed to meet Madison at the airport on her end. Erik wanted Madison walked from door to door, with as few opportunities as possible to deviate from the route or get into trouble. At one point he floated the idea of me flying up with her, but fortunately nixed it before I could. He also suggested twice more that he should come down to fly back with her, but Madison set up such a howl at the idea that I talked him out of it.

She's 21! I thought but didn't say. *She can vote, get married, join the military, own property—you've got to let her off the leash!* Then I started to fret that maybe she *did* need someone to babysit her all the way to New York, and I was making a big mistake, one that she would be the one to suffer from.

Maybe she needs to suffer from a few mistakes, I told myself. *Like you just said, she's 21. She's got to grow up someday, and her parents will never let her unless she forces the issue.*

In the end, everyone agreed that Madison could fly by herself, as long as I drove her to the airport in Atlanta and Cybil picked her up in LaGuardia. Erik was still agonizing over the advisability of it, and Cybil seemed mildly amused by the fuss. Madison herself was ecstatic.

"It'll be the first time I've ever flown by myself!" she announced to me, elated, when she finally hung up the phone.

"Good Lord," I exclaimed before I could stop myself.

Her face froze. I mentally kicked myself.

"Yeah," she said. She tried to smile her usual cocky smile. "I know, right? Like, my parents never let me do *anything*. This is the first trip I've ever taken by myself; isn't that crazy?"

"Well, it's never too late to start," I said.

13

AFTER THAT, MADISON mooched around the apartment looking bored while I finished the final check-through of all my syllabi and materials and uploaded them onto the course Sakai sites. Then we had lunch with Mel, who was glad of the break, and more than happy to see more of the infamous Madison. Then we drove over to campus, just for something to do. Madison was already getting antsy, and she'd spent barely 24 hours in Greenfields.

"How do you *stand* it here?" she demanded, as we drove down the single main street leading from the tiny downtown area to the small campus. "There's, like, *nothing* to do here."

"Mainly I'm too busy to be bored," I told her.

"With work?"

"Yeah, and with applying for more jobs."

"Yeah. Like when you were with us. We were only going to keep you for a semester and then kick you out, right?"

"Right," I confirmed.

"My dad was pretty upset about it," she confided. "He talked about it a bunch. He kept saying it wasn't right, especially with someone as promising as you. And he went on this whole big rant about how people are, like, disposable commodities these days. Adjunctification in higher ed, 'just in time' scheduling for retail and food service, hookup culture—he went on and on about how it's all part of the same thing."

She wrinkled up her nose. "He was, like, trying out online dating, I think, and he didn't like it. He and my mom got back together for a while last year, after...after, uh, you left, and we went to Russia and Ukraine together. That was *awesome*. Although"—she frowned—"I think it got my mom back together with these cousins who're such a bad deal...anyway. Things fell apart between them pretty quick after we got back, *of course*. I don't know *why* they keep trying to get back together. It's never going to work, and it just causes everyone a bunch of problems.

"Anyway, after a few months, my dad must have decided to try to, like, get out there in the cyber scene, but I don't think he liked it very much. He went *on* and *on* about hookup culture and how everyone just treats you like a means to an end, all they care about is what you can do for them, not what they can do for you, and then he went on this big rant about his Grand Unified Theory of Modern Society, or some shit like that. Then I think he quit with the cyber-dating. I *hope* so, anyway."

She shuddered. "I don't, like, wanna even *think* about him, like, getting it on over the internet with some random chick." She shuddered again, as if shaking off the disgusting thought, and looked out the car window to where a group of students were playing volleyball in the sand volleyball courts by the dorms.

"Seems *way* too hot for that," she said.

"They're probably from the Southeast," I said. "They're used to it. And they're probably antsy and bored like you, and they have to do something. Move-in was this weekend, and now they don't have anything else to do. At least," I added, "faculty didn't have to help with move-in this year."

"Wait, what?"

I told her the story of my ill-fated forced labor experience at the beginning of last fall, when I and most of the other faculty members had been press-ganged into helping students move into their dorms.

My knee disaster had started then, when a student and his father had run a moving cart over my foot, catching it in the wheels and twisting my knee.

I wasn't sure if that had anything to do with the administration's decision not to repeat the faculty-as-bellhops experiment this year, although I suspected it did. That, plus one faculty member had slipped a disk in her back, and another had collapsed from heat prostration and been stretchered away by paramedics. The legal implications had probably seemed too alarming to repeat the experience.

At first the revised plan had been for faculty to simply stand by the front gates in full regalia and wave at incoming students as they drove by. Then, following vehement faculty protest, that had been changed to having the football team and mascot stand by the front gates and wave at the incoming students. Much better. Most of the football players were on sports scholarships and couldn't fight back against that kind of thing without endangering their place on the team and maybe their college career. Plus, they were young and strong and supposedly used to that kind of punishment.

Only after the fact did it occur to a lot of faculty members that we may have won a Pyrrhic victory. Yes, we didn't have to risk life, limb, and dignity by parading around in the Georgia August heat in full doctoral regalia, or by hauling thousands of pounds of luggage up and down the stairs of the elderly, AC-less dormitories. On the other hand, we had now made the football team and Crimson sports mascot the first official encounter with the college that the students had. It was probably apt, given that at Crimson, like at many American colleges, sports mattered more than academics. But we, the faculty, were supposed to be fighting back against that. And we'd handed the football team a prime spot of prestige on a platter.

Not your problem, I reminded myself. *You'll probably be out of here, one way or another, by next year anyway.*

I was gratified that Madison was horrified by my story of bellhopping ignominy and subsequent maiming. At least some students didn't think that kind of thing was appropriate. Maybe there was hope for the younger generation, after all.

Madison wiped her nose on her sleeve—she was now back in her own clothes, still ratty but cleaner after a trip through my washer and dryer—and said she was hot and bored, and could we go back to my apartment.

"Sure," I said.

"I thought TLASC was a dump, but this place is even deader," she said as we drove away. "But this means you'll want to come back to New Jersey, right, Professor H?"

"Um," I said. "Maybe."

14

MONDAY MORNING BROUGHT the first week of the fall semester. Oh joy. Classes didn't start until Tuesday, but we had the delight of two back-to-back meetings on Monday to get things off on the right foot.

This meant leaving Madison on her own in my apartment. When we had been making plans the day before, I had blithely said it would be fine. Now, though, I was getting cold feet.

She doesn't know anyone here, and she doesn't have a car. How much trouble could she get into? As soon as I had the thought, I imagined at least a dozen ways she could get into lots of trouble. And while I was bringing my car keys with me, I was leaving my actual car parked outside the apartment in plain sight. Mel was driving both of us over to campus in her elderly Jeep Grand Cherokee, which meant Madison would have a solid three hours to figure out how to hotwire my ancient Honda Civic, should she feel so moved.

"Hey," said Mel, glancing over at me as we pulled out of the parking lot. "It's gonna be okay."

"I know. I think. I'm just all caught up in catastrophizing."

"I hear that. So...what do you think? Is Karen going to get rid of us this semester?"

"It certainly sounds like she's going to try."

"It sure as fuck does, doesn't it?" Mel glanced over at me again. "Don't know how I feel about that. I really fucking need this job. But I don't know if I can survive it."

"Yeah. Me too." We both glumly surveyed my left knee, carefully angled sideways to allow it to be as straight as possible. The original injury from the bellhopping debacle had been exacerbated by forced participation in a faculty 5k last fall, followed by an unpleasant run-in with a two-person lamb costume in the spring, and a near-death experience on California's sunny coast this summer. To be fair, I hadn't done it any favors by then driving—stick—from California back to Georgia. I mean, from a certain angle, I had only myself to blame.

"How's the doctor search going?" I asked, in order to take my mind off how I might be complicit in my own maiming. Better to focus on Mel's much more mysterious medical issues that she had been battling for the past year.

Mel blew out a sigh. "Bad. I spent all summer shuttling from office to office, getting told it was probably all fucking PTSD. I finally put in an application with that clinic your brother's friend Jase told you about, but there's a three-month wait, at least, to see anyone there, *if* they decide to accept you."

"Oh. How do you feel?"

She blew out another sigh. "I got a bit better over the summer. Only two episodes of what felt like the flu. The freaky seizure-y-things calmed down, with just a little twitching here and there. The Bell's palsy seems pretty much gone—right? Can you see it?"

I looked over at her. Last semester the right side of her face had suddenly become paralyzed, leading me to think she was having a stroke. After a scary high-speed drive to the closest ER, we had discovered it was "just" Bell's Palsy. Awkward, but unlikely to be fatal, and, the ER doctor had told her, likely to go away on its own. Now, five months later, her face was almost completely normal.

"It kinda came back whenever I got sick again," Mel said. "But then it went away pretty fast. I still don't like it. And my knees are fucking killing me. And my thumbs. And now my elbows are all weird, too."

"Oh," I said. "When do you think the clinic will be able to see you?" Mel had already seen the local doctor in Greenfields and various VA doctors, and had had every test and scan they would consent to give her. All of them had come back negative or normal. All her doctors had assured her she was in the pink of health. But people in the pink of health don't get sick every couple of weeks, or have debilitating joint pain that appears and disappears for no reason, or scream and convulse from random electric shocks, or have half their face go paralyzed out of the blue.

After several months of this, and talking to my brother John's best friend Jase, who had gone through something similar, Mel and I had both begun to suspect that she had Lyme disease, or something from that murky collection of poorly understood problems. Bringing this up with all the doctors she'd seen so far had led to a lot of laughter and belittlement. Jase had suggested the clinic he'd seen, where he'd finally gotten at least a little help, but, as Mel was discovering, it was expensive and difficult to get into.

"Maybe by October—*if* they agree to take me on as a patient," Mel said. "Meanwhile, I guess I'd better hope for the best."

"Yeah," I agreed.

We pulled into the faculty parking lot on the far side of the football stadium. The old football stadium. The college was building a new stadium, courtesy of their sponsorship deal with Security Solutions, the private security and prison company who'd decided to give them a lot of money in a deal that smelled ever so slightly of money laundering. What a college the size of Crimson was going to do with *two* football stadiums was an open question. What we were all pretty sure of was that the old stadium was not going to be converted to classroom space or anything educational.

The walk from the parking lot to the basement at the bottom of Bedford Hall, where the first of our back-to-back meetings was being held, was long and arduous. Mel had offered to drop me off closer to central campus and then go park, but we had decided it would be quicker and easier for us just to walk over together. That was proving to be a bad decision.

We had both worked up a good sweat by the time we stepped into the blinding cool darkness of Bedford. Maybe that was why we both began to shiver. By the time we had taken our seats in the auditorium, an orange-tinged gray blob was forming in front of my eyes. By the time opening remarks were made, it had turned into a spiky, shimmery, castle-y thing and spread out to fill half my vision.

"Ugh," Mel murmured, rubbing the back of her neck. "I'm getting that tasing feeling again." The twitchy, seizure-y episodes were often preceded by the sense of electricity building up under the skin of her scalp, neck, and shoulders, like she was hooked up to a taser and the power was slowly being turned up.

"Ugh," I whispered, massaging my temples.

"Oh, hi, Rowena. Did you have a good summer?" The woman sitting in the row behind me leaned forward to talk to me, but then broke off abruptly as the woman next to her suddenly stood up.

"Panic attack," she gasped, and started stumbling towards the aisle.

"Gotta go," said the woman who had leaned forward to talk to me. "Hang on, Julie!" She jumped up and followed the other woman out of the auditorium.

"It sure is hot in here," whispered the woman a couple of seats to our left. She was flushed and fanning herself. "Or am I just going into premature menopause?"

"I feel kinda hot too," said Mel. "Don't they have the AC on here?"

"I'm freezing," I said. "Like I'm coming down with something."

"I feel kind of feverish myself," said the woman fanning herself. Evelyn from Math, I thought. "Maybe something's going around."

Mel groaned to herself, and then put her hand to her mouth as if to quell a sudden bout of nausea. Evelyn was now fanning herself with both hands. I closed my eyes, but the shimmering, spiky blob still filled my vision. Theresa, the dean, was saying something up on the stage, but the ringing in my ears drowned out her words.

"I've got to get out of here," I said. My chest felt tight. I lurched to my feet and started stumbling towards the aisle, weaving slightly and blinking as the migraine scotoma blinded me.

When I stepped outside, the bright morning sunlight blinded me even more, but my chest eased. I took a deep breath. My shivering stopped.

"Fuck," said Mel, coming out the door after me. "That was awful."

"Really," said Evelyn from Math, joining us where we leaned against the wall. "I've been having little hot flashes here and there, but that was by far the worst."

"It's that place." Julie, looking pale and shaky, had just come out the door too. "I always get the worst panic attacks there. My doctor put me on a new set of anti-anxiety meds this summer, and I was doing so well, but as soon as I set foot in Bedford Hall—bam."

"Or maybe you're allergic to meetings," said the woman with Julie. Diane, I thought, from Biology. "I always think I'm going to have an asthma attack when I'm in there." Her words came out with a faint whistle.

"I do hate meetings, that's true," agreed Julie. "But they're much worse when they're there. Maybe I *am* allergic to something there."

The door swung open, and Chloe came staggering out. Chloe was the third new hire for the Department of Modern Languages last year. She taught Chinese, and had the dubious distinction of being Crimson College's only African-American faculty member.

"Oh my God," she said. Her teeth were chattering audibly. "I thought I'd be okay, but nope, I didn't even make it fifteen minutes into the meeting before a danged panic attack got me!"

"Me too," said Julie. "Solidarity, sister." They made weak clenched-fist gestures at each other.

I took another deep breath. My chest was easing more and more. "Maybe we really are allergic to something in there," I said.

"Yeah," said Diane. "Deans and other senior administrators." The whistle in her voice was fainter, but still there.

"No, I'm serious," I said. "We all started feeling sick within minutes of going in there. Maybe there's...I don't know..."

"Mold," said Mel darkly. "I bet it's moldy as fuck. I've been reading about that shit, and apparently it can be really bad. A basement-level auditorium sounds like just the thing for it. Either that, or maybe there's a carbon monoxide leak or some shit like that down here."

We all stared in horror at the door into Bedford Hall. Diane found her voice first.

"Well," she said. "That will make the administration hate us, for certain."

15

AFTER A VERY SHORT debate, we decided to skip the rest of the meeting, and trooped off to Brew's Up, the campus coffee shop. There was a spontaneous pause at the entrance as we all suddenly realized it might be full of mold or other problems too. When we went inside, though, the only thing that greeted us was pleasant coolness and the scent of coffee.

"What a relief," said Julie, once we had all ordered and were sitting around a large table at the back corner. "I was afraid for a minute there that I'd never be able to come back here. But I feel fine. Maybe it *is* all meeting-induced stress."

"How did you feel when we had that meeting over WebEx this summer?" Diane asked.

She and Julie both contemplated the question with the air of scientists. Julie, I thought, was also in Biology. No doubt they were running through their memories and trying to figure out if they'd accidentally done a series of double-blind experiments on themselves and their colleagues.

"A little anxious, but basically fine," Julie said eventually. "The same with the meetings we held in the biochem building last semester. I'd feel a little nervous, but nothing like the debilitating panic that hits me whenever I go into the all-faculty meetings in Bedford or Lee."

"Oh, shit," said Diane. "Lee too?"

Bedford was one of the main classroom buildings around the central quad, and where Mel, Chloe, and I all taught. Lee was the main administrative building.

"I kept getting this weird tightness in my chest the last few times I was in Lee," I volunteered. "But I thought it was just nerves too. And I do have a lot of problems in Bedford. Especially in my office. Which has no windows and lots of water damage. I've been having worse and worse migraines all year, and also episodes of..." I trailed off, unsure what to call them.

"Panic attacks?" put in Julie.

"Hot flashes?" suggested Evelyn.

"Seizures?" asked Mel.

There was an unpleasant pause while we thought about what all that might mean.

"No," I finally said. "More like...I feel like I'm floating above my body. I guess it's a kind of out-of-body experience."

"I'd tell you all that it's all in your heads, except that on top of the asthma attacks I get in the auditorium in Bedford, I get this scratchy sore throat whenever I go into Lee, and if I spend too much time in it, I get full-blown laryngitis," said Diane. "And my eyes itch and my nose runs. That sounds like allergies to me. But this other stuff...I don't know. What I *do* know is that if we complain about it, we're likely to bring a world of hurt down on us. Julie, Evelyn, and I have tenure, but I don't know that even that will protect us. You three don't have tenure yet, do you?"

I shook my head. "Chloe is tenure-track, but Mel and I are VAPs."

Diane turned to Chloe. "You're probably in the most vulnerable position," she said. "Because you have the hope of a permanent position. You two"—she nodded to me and Mel—"you can't stay here for more than another year anyway, right?"

"Right," we agreed.

"But Chloe here *could* get tenure. Or they could find a pretext to toss her out before or during the tenure process. Lack of research productivity, probably."

"I have a book contract," Chloe said. "Surely that means they can't complain about my research productivity, right?"

"If you have one book under contract, they'll say you should have one book out and a second under contract," said Diane. "If you have two books out, they'll say you should have published more articles, or that you've neglected your teaching and service and haven't been appropriately collegial. Trust me, they'll find a way."

We all nodded in glum agreement. I hadn't had any experience with the tenure review process firsthand, but I'd heard enough stories to be sure that Diane was telling the truth.

"So... what are we going to do?" Chloe asked in a small voice.

Diane shrugged. "If I knew, I'd tell you. I'd tell *me*. But first, the scientist in me wants to find proof." Her eyes were going distant as she spoke. "Maybe there are tests I could run. It could be a good study. I *am* a microbiologist, after all. This should be right up my alley. I'll do it on my own time, see what I find, and then..." She shrugged. "Publish or perish, I guess," she finished.

We all nodded.

"Meanwhile, we should avoid Bedford and Lee as much as possible. I guess that's not really an option for you three, is it?"

"We can only come in for classes and meetings," I said. "Not hang out there too much outside of that."

"My therapist wants to me to keep working on exposure training," Chloe said. "I'm supposed to come in on the weekends and spend more time there, to train myself to relax and not have panic attacks."

"That might not be such a good idea," said Diane. "Of course, we could be barking up completely the wrong tree, and we're all crazy and we do need exposure therapy, but just to be on the safe side, I'm going to tell you to treat it like a biohazard area."

"Oh, goodie," I said. I checked my phone. "At least our next meeting is in Saunders."

"Not sure Saunders is much better," said Mel.

16

"WHAT DO YOU THINK?" Chloe asked as the three of us left Brew's Up and set off across the quad towards Saunders Hall, where the Department of Modern Languages held their meetings. We were, appropriately, a split department, with half our offices and classrooms in Saunders, and half in Bedford. Both buildings, incidentally, were probably named after prominent KKK members. Chloe had previously thought that her panic attacks whenever she stepped inside them were triggered by the poisonous atmosphere of being in spaces named in honor of pro-slavery racists. Now, though, we were all wondering if her panic attacks were being triggered by straight-up poison.

"I think something stinks about this place," Mel declared. "Maybe it's toxic mold or some shit, or maybe it's just so emotionally toxic it tears you down from the inside, but either way, it's not good for us."

"Yeah." Chloe sighed. "You know, I've never been much of a Marxist. My friends in grad school were always going on and on about it, and I thought they were all talking through their hats. But now that I'm actually out in the 'real world,' I'm starting to see their point. I see the way they treat me—us—here, and it makes me so mad! We're all just things to them. No, it's worse than that. If we were things, we'd have value to them. They want to pour money into buildings, computers, football stadiums—all things. And then they treat those things like people, and the people like things, to be used up and thrown away like a plastic fork. We're all just cheap plastic forks in their eyes, and if they break us, they toss us out and get a new one without batting an eye."

"Preach," said Mel. "Ro, how's your knee?"

"Fine." I meant to say it jauntily. It came out as more of a ragged pant. We were not setting a brisk pace across the quad. But I was still breathless and falling behind. Crutches are not the most efficient way to get around. Maybe I needed one of those scooter things. But then I'd have to bend my knee and put weight on it. No, crutches were best. They just weren't very good.

"So," said Mel, slowing her already slow walk down to a crawl, "we got a strategy for this meeting? Anything we want to say to those mofos about that email Karen sent out this weekend?"

"Oh." Chloe groaned. "The email! I'd almost forgotten about it. Do you think...could she really be...I mean, that was so rude! Could she really have been talking about us?"

"I don't know who else she could have had in mind," said Mel. "So: we gonna do anything about it?"

"Do you have any suggestions?" I was falling farther and farther behind, despite the snail-like pace Mel and Chloe were setting.

"No. I was hoping one of you'd have a brilliant suggestion."

"Nope." Chloe shook her head. "No brilliant suggestions. Other than to keep our heads down and...I don't know."

"Yeah," said Mel. "I don't have anything better either."

Saunders was pleasantly cool when we stepped inside. For a moment. Then I started to shiver again. The pain in my head, which had calmed down after the infusion of caffeine in the coffee shop, spasmed fiercely around my eyes.

It's just the light change, I told myself. *You stepped from bright sunlight to indoor lighting. Fluorescent indoor lighting. That's probably it.* I was only somewhat comforted by that. If my migraines were being triggered by fluorescent lighting, that was a big problem. Fluorescent lights were everywhere. It still seemed better than being poisoned, though.

"I'm breaking out into a cold sweat," Chloe whispered.

"Funny; I feel hot," said Mel. "I'd tell you to take a few deep breaths, but now I don't know about the wisdom of that."

Breathing shallowly, we made our unsteady way to the department conference room. We were the first faculty members to arrive. Kim, the department admin, was setting out agendas and muffins. Everyone else must still be caught up in the college-wide faculty meeting.

"What do you think?" Mel asked. "Anywhere you can actually get in and find a seat, Ro?"

We surveyed the seating possibilities. The conference table was too big for the room, allowing only slender and agile people access to most of the seats. Given that college faculty members were not known for their athleticism, this was a problem. Normally I took one for the team and sidled into the seat in the far corner that no one else could squeeze into. But with crutches it was totally out of the question. I was going to have to take the seat closest to the door. That would block the way for everyone else, so I was going to have to stand, guarding my chosen seat like Cerberus, until everyone else had filed past me and sat down.

"Is that a water stain in the ceiling tiles over there?" Chloe asked, pointing to the far corner of the room.

"Looks like it," said Mel.

"I wish we could open a window," I said, trying to fan myself and hold onto my crutches simultaneously. My chills had switched to unpleasant flush, and my chest felt tight again. I normally felt that way in basements and windowless rooms. I'd always assumed it was from claustrophobia. But now I was wondering if my claustrophobia was something more sinister than a mere meaningless fear.

"In order to open a window, there'd have to be a window," said Mel. Like many of the rooms on campus, this one was completely windowless.

You can breathe! You can breathe! You can breathe! If I said to myself often enough, it would be true. Right?

"Oh, *there* you are. We missed you at the college faculty meeting." Karen had come into the room, and was smiling at us. Or her version of a smile. I wasn't sure she was actually capable of smiling. Her wide, slack-lipped mouth in her jowly face was weirdly toad-like. As I always did when I was around her, I reminded myself that I was above judging people by their appearance. So what if she was dumpy and awkward, with flyaway gray hair and unflattering clothes? Lots of people were not blessed in the looks lottery. That didn't mean they weren't nice people.

It's the eyes, I thought to myself. *There's something wrong with her eyes. And her mouth.* It wasn't that she looked stupid. There was a certain sharp, cunning light to her eyes. But there was no kindness. There wasn't even any competence. Something indefinable radiated incompetence and ill humor from her face, even when she was smiling and making what were meant to be friendly remarks.

Although in this case I didn't think the remarks were meant to be friendly. I thought they were meant to be mean. She thought she had caught us out in an error, and she was determined to call us out on it in front of the rest of the department faculty, who were currently filing in around us.

"We were there," said Chloe quickly, at the same time as Mel said, "We had to leave. Allergies and stuff. Didn't want to go coughing up a storm in the middle of the meeting."

"Funny how *all* of you had to leave simultaneously," said Karen.

"Yeah," said Mel. "Real funny how a bunch of us all got sick at once."

"Really, Melissa, you should plan better," said Karen. "If you think you're going to have an allergy attack at a meeting, you should take an antihistamine beforehand and bring some tissues with you. It's not that hard..." The rest of her words were broken off by a racking cough that left her breathless and speechless.

"You see," she gasped, once the cough had eased off enough to allow her to speak again. "You just have to manage it..." Another coughing fit overtook her, bringing tears to her eyes.

"Mmmm," said Mel, while Klaus, from German, murmured something sympathetic about how she was still suffering from that cough. Karen had gotten sick before spring break, and coughed uncontrollably for the rest of the semester. Apparently she still hadn't gotten over it, almost six months later. I hoped it wasn't contagious, whatever it was. Probably, I thought gloomily, it was allergies to something in the building, which meant the rest of us weren't safe either. I tried to take a deep, calming breath to ease my chest without actually inhaling any of the air around me, and broke into a coughing fit of my own.

Soon the whole room was coughing. It wasn't until Kim brought in a box of bottled water and handed it around that we were able to bring our coughing under control and take our seats.

"Well," said Karen. She was still pink-faced and breathless, with a faint wheeze as she spoke. "Welcome to Fall 2016, everyone. I was hoping for a more *auspicious* start to our semester, but I suppose..." She couldn't figure out what it was she supposed, and switched topics. "We have a *very* busy agenda for this meeting," she announced. "Especially as we are holding all our meetings late this semester. Normally we hold them the week prior to the start of classes, but with classes starting on a Tuesday, and at the request of several members who *apparently* couldn't make it back to Greenfields any earlier, I agreed to hold our meeting today."

She paused, as if waiting for her beneficence to be acknowledged. A few wan smiles shone here and there around the room.

"I already sent you an email detailing the most *important* items to cover today," she said. "Let's start with the situation with the copies and our paper and supply budget. It's getting simply *critical*."

I tried to stay awake and focused while she droned on about budget-cutting measures, and how we were now going to have to enter individual codes into the copier to make copies. This devolved into a tirade on the part of several faculty members about Big Brother and totalitarianism. I agreed, but I simply couldn't keep my eyes open. It felt like all the oxygen was being drained out of my brain, but I was too tired to care. If I didn't get up and move around soon, I was going to fall asleep right here on the conference table...

I jerked upright. Mel had elbowed me hard in the ribs.

"...The matter of our hiring practices," Karen was saying.

"Of course, of course." Jennifer, from German, was nodding emphatically. "We really *must* raise our standards. We want to make sure we get people who are actually a good fit for Crimson and the department, and are able to perform to our rigorous demands."

In my somnolent state I couldn't tell if people were actually giving me side eye, or if I was just imagining it. Everyone was nodding in agreement with Jennifer.

"And so I propose forming a committee to write up a department-wide description of basic minimum requirements for candidates," Karen said. "It should be more than simply 'PhD in hand,' although I think that should be part of it. No more ABD candidates!"

More nods. ABD stood for "All But Dissertation." Since the hiring process could take up to a year, it was common for people to apply during their last year of grad school, before they had actually defended their dissertation, in the hopes of having a job lined up for the next fall. However, given the tight job market, departments could be choosy. Some no longer accepted applications from ABD candidates. Some still welcomed them with open arms, on the (generally correct) assumption that they were cheaper and easier to exploit.

I started to relax. This couldn't be about me. I had had my PhD in hand at the time of application. I looked around the room. Chloe appeared to be trying to sink down under the table. She, I remembered, had been hired straight out of grad school. She must have been ABD during the application and interview process. This must be an attack on her.

"Teaching experience is the most important thing!" Karen was saying vehemently. "We *can't afford* to have inexperienced teachers at Crimson! Especially not in this department. We are *under pressure* from the Dean's office to raise our enrollment, retention, *and* our research productivity! We need to be focusing on getting the *best* candidates we can possibly get. Something we should keep in mind as we start the hiring process for our tenure-track Russian and Arabic positions."

Now I was fully awake. Karen had made vague promises of the possibility of a permanent position in Russian last year. I had assumed this was just part of her general control trip. But maybe there had been more to it.

"Yes." She nodded towards me and Mel. "The department has gotten permission to hire a Russianist and an Arabist. But, I should emphasize, that is only if those programs remain within the Modern Languages department. If they split off into this new LCTL department, as *some people* are suggesting"—another death glare at Chloe, who had been press-ganged into a committee to look into the feasibility of that—"all bets are off the table. Who *knows* when *that* program would actually get permission to open a new tenure line."

She appeared to be waiting for some kind of a response. I cleared my throat, which felt painfully tight. "Oh," I said feebly.

"Of course we'd want to have a general search," she said. "We have to—and we'd want to see who we can get. There are *so many* qualified candidates out there. But you two"—she nodded at me and Mel again—"would be welcome to *apply*, if you wished."

"Oh," I said again. "Um, that's, uh, great. When will the deadline for applications be?"

She flinched. Oops. I had asked a concrete question about practical matters. I should have known better by now.

"The *full announcement* will be released in the JIL next month," she said. The JIL, or Job Information List, was a kind of hiring board for language and literature jobs. "Of *course* I can't tell you anything about it before then. It's a matter of *equity*."

"Of course," I said.

17

I SHOULD HAVE BEEN happy at the news. Despite Karen's veiled hints and open threats to the contrary, I had to believe I was a strong candidate for any tenure-track position that opened up here at Crimson. I had already demonstrated the most important quality: the willingness to live in Greenfields, Georgia.

But, as I listened to her detail the extensive observations and performance reviews everyone in the department—"*especially* the newer faculty members; we want to make sure you receive the mentoring necessary for you to *succeed* here at Crimson"—my heart sank further and further, until when I finally stood up to go, I was surprised not to find it somewhere under the chair. Yes, I needed this job. Or rather, I needed *a* job. Until a couple of weeks ago, I had had very good reason to believe that I might find that job elsewhere, probably in California, as part of my whole life plan of moving in with Alex. When our relationship had fallen through, so had my life plan. Now I had to rely on Crimson College once again.

Well, maybe not. At Frank's suggestion, I had put in an application with the FBI last spring. I had undergone one round of testing and interviews in May. Now I was waiting to hear back about that. Three months, Frank had assured me, was not too long. It could take six months or more before things moved on. He would, he'd said, do everything he could to help get me that job, preferably in the same San Francisco office as himself.

I hadn't been thrilled at the idea of working with Frank. I still wasn't thrilled at the idea of working with Frank. I spent the hobble out to Mel's Jeep contemplating my choices: stay here at Crimson, with the petty bullies and low-level sociopaths, or go work for the government, possibly with Frank, a serial sexual harasser and all-around asshole?

And that was assuming I could get either of those jobs. The most likely scenario was for neither organization to want me, and for me to be unemployed and destitute before the year was out.

"Can you fucking believe this shit?" Mel, it seemed, was not sinking into melancholy like I was. Mel was descending into righteous rage. We were circumnavigating the football stadium on our way back to the Jeep, and I was falling farther and farther behind as she strode along wrathfully.

"Yes," I panted. "Wait up! Or go get the Jeep and come back and pick me up."

"Sorry." She stopped. "You're right. I'm so fucking mad I've gotta run or I'll blow a gasket somewhere serious. You wait here while I go get the Jeep."

I leaned gratefully against the wall of the stadium and pulled out my phone. Half a dozen text notifications popped up on my screen. My heart jumped from nerves. I'd been feeling anxious all morning about leaving Madison on her own in my apartment. Mainly I'd been worried about her burning the place down, or destroying my computer in some way, or possibly heading out to score drugs and getting caught in the act and plunging me into trouble.

I'd also been worried about my colleagues back at Crimson finding out about her being there. Even if she didn't do anything illegal while she was with me, I was afraid that her very presence would be considered inappropriate in some way. Even though we were both legal adults, no longer had any sort of teacher-student relationship, and were not engaged in any illicit activities, letting an ex-student spend the night seemed like the just the kind of thing that Karen & Co. would jump at the chance to use as grounds for termination.

The first text was indeed from Madison. I opened it with trepidation, but it only said, *Hey, Professor H! When are you getting back? We need to leave soon if we're going to make my flight.*

I texted back to assure her that I would be there in a few minutes and we were in no danger of missing her flight.

The next was from her father. *Just checking in, Rowena, to make sure everything is still in order for Madison to get to NYC tonight.*

I texted back to assure him that I was about to set off to the airport with Madison and that so far, all systems were go for her safe and timely arrival at the handoff zone. I resisted the urge to tell him to stop fretting. If everything went pear-shaped with Crimson and the FBI, Erik Johnson might be my best hope for employment. Back when I'd actually been teaching at his university, he'd offered me a position as, essentially, Madison's companion, in the style of an impoverished woman of genteel background during the Regency period.

There had been the ever-so-faint suggestion that there was the opportunity to rise through the ranks to be his companion too. I hadn't been sure how I felt about that at the time, and I still wasn't sure how I felt about it. No, I was sure. I was sure that I'd rather do many, many other things, including, possibly, continue teaching here at Crimson. But I was also sure I'd rather be Madison and/or Erik's "companion," whatever that might entail, than be completely destitute and homeless. I might even prefer it to throwing myself on the charity of John, my one and only older brother.

Therefore, it seemed only politic to be polite to Erik. Besides, I did in fact feel a certain amount of sympathy for him. The man was obviously suffering, and didn't, as far as I could tell, have many people with whom he could share his suffering. But for whatever reason, he felt safe unburdening himself to me.

Two more messages. I certainly was a popular girl this morning. I glanced at their senders. My heart skipped a beat and my underarms broke out into a sweat before my eyes even had a chance to consciously register what the little blocks of text were telling me. Then my brain caught up, and my heart beat even faster. The first text was from Dima. And the second was from Alex.

18

FOR AN INSTANT I WAS frozen in indecision. Which one to read first? The choice felt somehow weighty and binding on a cosmic scale.

It doesn't matter! It will only take a second either way. Just read them! Dima's text was at the top of my notifications queue, so I read it first.

Darling Inna. I arrived safe and unharmed in Moscow. Mama says hi.

I'm so glad! I texted back. *Say hi to Galina Ivanovna for me.* Then, feeling as if I were going mad in some way, I added, *Hugs and kisses to both of you.*

I looked up, cold sweat trickling down my sides, to see Mel's ancient Jeep trundling along slowly towards me. Just enough time, I estimated, to check the text from Alex. I took a deep breath and opened it.

Hi Rowena. Just wanted to check in with you. I know your semester is about to start. How are things? How is your knee? Are you getting around okay? Please let me know. Things are fine here. Erin is recovering well and it looks like she will be able to keep her job for now. She asked me to pass on her thanks. Frank says hi too :) I guess I'll never be rid of him :) :)

Seriously, please let me know how you're doing. I worry about you a lot.

Mel's Jeep stopped in front of me. I levered myself away from the stadium wall and began the laborious process of climbing into the passenger seat. All vehicles were bad. The Jeep, since it was high up, was particularly bad. I should have suggested that Mel take my car. Or I could have driven us myself. I could drive. I'd just driven all the way across the country.

That's probably why your knee is so bad now, I thought. It was true. But I still considered it a better deal than the alternative, which had been for me to fly home while Alex drove my car and Fevronia across the country himself. He'd offered. I appreciated the offer. But I couldn't bear the idea of being beholden to him. Not when some part of me felt like he'd run off and left me.

I knew that was unfair. I couldn't fault Alex for running away when things got hard. He'd seen someone he cared about in trouble, and run straight towards her. As he should have. But that meant he'd run straight away from me.

"That's not a happy face," said Mel, once I'd hauled myself into the front seat and organized the crutches in the back, almost braining her only once in the process. Amusingly, or maybe tragically, "Girl Crush" was floating out of her speakers, just on the edge of hearing.

"Not a fun morning," I said. I made sure to speak loudly enough to drown out the song lyrics. I might have listened to them way too many times already. I'd hated myself every time, and told myself that I *definitely* didn't feel an obsessive need to be like the woman my man had chosen over me. Maybe if I said it enough times, I'd believe it.

"Nope," Mel agreed. Her eyes half on the road, half on me, she reached up and turned the volume all the way down to zero. Mel was good that way.

"And..." I said. It came out as a gusty sigh. "I just got texts from Dima *and* Alex."

She let out a whistle. "Shi-it! So what're you going to do?"

"Answer them, I guess. I've already answered Dima's text. It was just letting me know that he'd made it to Moscow safely. And I guess I'd better answer Alex's text too. He just wants to know how I'm doing. We did agree to stay friends, after all."

"Yeah," said Mel. "Good luck with that."

"It could happen!"

"It could," she agreed. "But in my experience, it rarely does. Not if you really loved the person. And you really loved him, didn't you?"

"Sort of," I said.

We had pulled up to a four-way stop where the exit for the football stadium met the entrance to the dorms. Mel took the opportunity to pull off her sunglasses and give me a look, brows raised.

"Weren't you thinking of marrying the guy?" she said.

"Yeah. I was. And I *did* love him enough to do that, I'm sure of it. But I was also still all hung up on Dima. So I don't know how it would have gone. And now I'll never know, since they both pushed me away before we could find out."

"Yeah." Mel replaced her sunglasses and pulled forward through the intersection. I resisted the impulse to put my head in my hands and say some harsh words about life and fate, or life, the universe, and everything, or whatever it was that was steering my life in what I considered to be absolutely the wrong direction. I'd vaguely desired lots of things in my life, but the only things I'd ever really, truly wanted was love and family. And yet for my whole adult life, it had seemed like I was always running towards true love—but everyone else was always running away from it. There was some kind of tragic disconnect going on there.

"Hey," said Mel. "It's gonna be okay. And whatever else, you'll always have that glorious piece of paper that says 'Doctor of Philosophy,' right?"

"If I can find it," I said. "I think I might have lost it in one of my many treks around this fair land."

"There's probably a moral or something in that," said Mel. "But I'm fucked if I can say what it is."

"Yeah," I said. My phone buzzed. Simultaneous anxious texts came in, one from Madison, one from Erik, demanding to know when we were going to set off to the airport.

"At least *someone* needs me," I said.

19

MADISON WAS WAITING for me at the door when I got back.

"Are you ready to go, Professor H?" she asked anxiously.

I checked my phone. "We've got plenty of time."

"Yeah, I know, I just..."

"Really want to get out of here and over to the Big Apple?" I suggested.

She fidgeted. "Is it weird that I'm really looking forward to it?" she asked.

"No," I said. "It's exciting."

"It is, right? Like, I'm actually going off and doing something that was my own idea, on my own. I mean, not, like, *exactly* on my own, I guess. Aunt Cybil will be there. But I won't be living with my mom or my dad anymore. And it was my plan, and I did it. Well, I hope I'm gonna do it. I'm just worried something'll happen to, like, mess things up at the last minute."

"I know," I said. "And it's great that you're doing this. Come on. Grab your stuff and let's set off. Unless you want to get some lunch first."

She shook her head. "Can't we, like, have lunch at the airport?"

I checked the time again. 11:00am. If we left now we would get to the airport around 12:30, providing the traffic gods smiled upon us. That was more than four hours before Madison's flight. I had hoped to bundle her through security as quickly as possible, and then pray that the presence of TSA agents would keep her on the straight and narrow until she boarded her flight. But of course, there was nothing—other than her own good sense, which was a slender reed to lean upon—stopping her from going back out through security and catching a bus or a taxi and setting off for anywhere other than New York. I didn't think she'd do that. But now that I was thinking about it, I couldn't be 100% certain.

"Sure," I said. "No problem."

While Madison gathered her things, I sent Alex a quick text telling him I was glad to hear from him, glad to hear that Erin was doing okay, I was doing great, and I had to take someone to the airport but I'd be in touch that evening. My fingers moved with surprising fluidity over the phone keyboard, considering that they felt like they belonged to someone else's body. I got a "thumbs up" emoji in response. I told myself we were doing an excellent job at the staying friends thing. Then I put the phone away and told myself not to think about it for the rest of the afternoon.

Ten minutes later we were on the road. Since Madison didn't even have a change of clothes with her, packing hadn't taken long. I was surprised she hadn't at least brought a laptop with her, but, she explained, she had stormed out of her house so quickly she hadn't even thought to bring something as important as a computer.

"And it's a good thing I had my phone in my pocket, or I'd've probably forgotten it too," she said. "I was that mad. I don't think I've ever been that mad." She was quiet for a little while. "Do you think it's possible?" she asked. "For me and my mom to make up?"

"Sure," I said. "It might take some work, but people can make up almost anything."

"Really? What's something really big you've made up with someone over, Professor H? Or something where you've, like, overlooked something they're doing that you, like, totally disagree with?"

"Well," I said. The first example of making up with someone that came to mind was with Dima. The second was with Alex. But that wasn't quite true. I was gingerly polite with both of them. But I couldn't say that I'd wholeheartedly forgiven either of them, or that our relationships had been completely repaired. Whatever happened, my relationship with one of them never could be completely repaired, because ending up with one of them would mean keeping the other at arm's length forever. Or maybe I'd have to keep them both at arm's length forever, or—more likely—they'd keep me at arm's length.

And either way, I felt betrayed by both of them, and I hadn't entirely gotten over it. I doubted I ever would get over it until I had the husband and family that had been the lynchpin of my life plan for at least ten years now. Morosely, I thought about the various women around me who'd been left pregnant and abandoned by their exes. I'd avoided that thus far. Instead, my exes had actively avoided any possibility of pregnancy before abandoning me, leaving me childless and alone rather than a desperate single mother. Either way, it felt like betrayal. But that seemed like way too personal a conversation to have with Madison while trying to shift gears with a bad knee and a tricky clutch.

"I get along pretty well with my brother," I told her. "Or at least, we're still close, even though we disagree about lots of things, and fight all the time."

"Oh yeah? Like what do you fight about?"

"Um," I said. One of the main things we'd been fighting about the past couple of years had been my unmarried, childless state. Best to skip over that if I could. "We disagree about politics sometimes. Although the main person he fights with over that is my dad. But they still love each other. They don't let it come between them. In fact, I think it's how they bond."

"Oh." Madison contemplated that for a while. Then she said, "But does your brother, like, support political stuff that's really bad? Like what my mom does?"

"Well, no," I admitted. "He likes to joke about voting Republican, but I don't think he even does that. I think he's a pretty mainstream centrist, to be honest. He just likes messing with people by playing a persona. But he'd never have anything to do with white supremacy, I'm sure of it. I know the military can have a bad reputation, but John's made it clear that he's had his, um, butt saved more than once by his non-white fellow Marines, and he doesn't put up with any trash talk about them. At heart, I think he and I agree about all the big things, like honor and justice and fairness and doing right by other people. We both might be part of institutions with questionable morals, but I'd say we ourselves do the best we can to live up to the noble missions we're supposed to be representing. It's one of the main things we have in common."

"Oh." Madison was silent for several miles.

"That's the thing," she said finally, jumping back into the conversation as if it had never been paused. "I don't think my mom and I have that in common. She and my dad—and the rest of my family, and my teachers, and, well, basically *everybody*—are always on my case about being, you know, *bad*, but I don't think I'm bad like that. I know I've done some pretty bad shit—you've seen just about the worst of it—but I've never done anything like *that*. Like, something that's fundamentally rotten at its core, something that's fundamentally about hurting other people as its main mission. I've never done anything like that. But that's what my mom is doing, and I..." She clenched and unclenched her fists. "I don't know if I can forgive her for it! Even if nothing bad happens because of it, I don't know if I can forgive her for it, and I'm afraid something really bad will happen because of it!"

"Oh," I said. "Well, that's a reasonable fear, I guess. As ye sow, so shall ye reap, and all that."

"It's not just that!" she cried out. "It's that I think they're planning something bad. Like really, terrorist-y kind of bad. And I don't know what to do about it!"

20

"OKAY," I SAID, AFTER it became apparent that Madison wasn't going to reveal more. She was staring out the window, watching the highway stream by, deliberately not looking at me. "You've brought it up several times already, so it's obviously weighing on your mind. What kind of terrible thing, exactly, do you think they're planning? And what do you think you *should* do about it?"

"I told you they're all into that, like, survivalist crap, right?" she said.

"Uh-huh."

"So, my cousins, like, run this training camp in Ukraine. It's part of this group called 'Glorious Future.' It's supposed to, like, 'build the strong, healthy youth of tomorrow.' At least, I think that's what the slogan says. But it has these weird symbols kind of worked into the logo. So I looked them up."

"Uh-huh," I said again.

"Have you ever heard of a *sonnenrad*?" she asked. "Or a *wolfsangel*?"

I decided to switch things up a little. "Yep," I said.

"Well, I never had. I thought they were just, like, fun symbols at first, although they did look a little creepy. Like, something didn't feel right about them, you know? I guess it was, like, subconscious or something. Like they were just Nazi enough for me recognize it, even though I didn't know that's what I was doing. Anyway, I looked them up, and it turns out they're both, like, supposedly ancient runic symbols that the Nazis started using. And now wannabe Nazis use 'em too. I mean, the ADL says not everyone who uses them is a Nazi, because they have all kinds of meanings, but a lot of people who use them do seem to have Nazi leanings, and when I read more of Glorious Future's manifesto, it, like, totally creeped me out. I mean, they never 100% came out and *said* 'white supremacy, neo-Nazi, blah blah blah,' but it had that *feel,* you know what I mean?"

"Uh-huh," I said, going back to my faithful standby.

"So when my mom started talking about bringing these cousins over and having them do something at the resort she manages—that's her 'job'; Dad always makes comments about how, like, it's not a real job, and then she tells him what *he* does isn't a real job either, and it's, like, super nasty to be around—anyway, we went and visited them last summer when we were over there, and my mom started talking about bringing them over, and I started reading about them, because I thought it was, like, cool, but then I realized it wasn't, like, cool at all."

"Mmmm," I said.

"They say all this good stuff about building a glorious future by raising the youth of today, and also all this stuff about building a glorious Ukraine that's part of Europe, and it all *sounds* really great, but the more I looked into it, the more I realized it was, like, all creepy and Nazi. And I...I started looking into what else they do."

She fell silent and stared some more out the window at the highway racing past. I guessed that she had made use of her computer skills of dubious legality, and was debating whether or not to tell me.

"And I can't be 100% sure of what I found," she said. "A lot of it was in Ukrainian. Actually, weirdly, a lot of it was in Russian too, even though it was all about making Ukraine free of Russia and cleansing the land of the Russian taint. At least that's what Google Translate said."

"Sounds about right," I said. "And Eastern European neo-Nazi ideology is...full of paradoxes."

"Yeah. I mean, my cousins are, like, part Russian, and have Russian names and all. Names ending in -in and -ov are Russian, right? And names ending in -ko and -uk are Ukrainian?"

"That's right," I said. "I'm impressed you remembered that."

"I mean, my mom's last name is Melnichuk, so it stuck with me. Plus it was, like, a whole *thing* in our class. You kept making us practice declining names. And then, after you left, Danila and Vitya"—Danila and Vitya were two other TLASC students—"joined our lit class, and they kept talking about it too. So it's not, like, I could forget or anything. And it really stuck in my mind when I started thinking about how my cousins' names are things like Smirnov and Zhuraev, which are, like, really common last names in Russia, right? Like, totally Russian names, right?"

"Right," I confirmed.

"Yeah, I thought so. Far as I can tell, everyone from that side of the family other than my great-grandpa fled East during the war and ended up married to Russians. So anyway, these cousins are all, like, about as Russian as can be, except that they're, like, these giant Ukrainian nationalists and go around talking about how Ukraine is, like, totally separate and different from Russia and always has been. It's, like, super weird."

"People are weird," I agreed.

"But I guess it, like, gives them status or something? Like, this is how they prove themselves? Like, in that lit class, which was pretty lit"—she turned to me and grinned at the pun—"we read this story about a goose, and how this guy has to prove himself to, like, Cossacks, and they tell him he has to commit, like, rape or murder, but he can't, so he, like, kills a goose instead as a way to, like, show he's one of the gang. And it's like these cousins are doing the same thing. You know what I mean?"

"I know the story, and I know exactly what you mean," I said.

"And my mom, she ate that shit they're spouting right up. She said that's what her grandpa had always been saying, that's what he'd been trying to do back in the war, and she was glad they were still trying to keep up his work, and she'd do whatever she could to help. And I was, like, WTF, Mom, when she was explaining this to me. And then...and then..." Madison stopped and gulped for breath. "And then she said she'd failed with me, but with Glorious Future, she had a chance to right that wrong. She'd be able to provide someone else's child with a glorious future, even if she couldn't with me, and maybe..." Her voice broke again. She swallowed hard and continued. "And maybe I'd see the good in what she was doing, and I'd come around, and this would save me too."

21

WE BOTH SAT IN SILENCE and stared at the highway streaming past for a while. I was desperately trying to come up with something to say. Let's see...let's see...Oh shit, that eighteen-wheeler is going to cut me off...

I gripped the wheel and hit the brakes as a swaying eighteen-wheeler passed much too close for comfort and tucked itself into a slot I would have considered more appropriate for a compact car. It was, I saw, crammed full of pigs, trapped in a hideous journey on their way to an even more hideous destination. I caught a glimpse of terrified eyes staring out of filthy faces. An apt summing-up of the horrors of the past hundred years. And just like so many others, there was absolutely nothing I could do to save them. We were all in this together, but I couldn't get them out of it.

"She didn't fail with you," I said, once I'd gotten the car back under control. I dropped back so that I didn't have to see those pleading eyes, didn't have to bear witness to my own helplessness in the face of evil. "You're not a failure, Madison." There wasn't a lot I could do to rescue anyone who really needed rescuing, but maybe I could make Madison feel a little better, and that would be better than nothing.

"It sure *seems* like I am." She had bent her head so that her hair had fallen over her face, hiding her eyes. "I mean, let's, like, look at the facts. I'm barely scraping through the college I only got into because my dad pulled some strings, I've been in and out of rehab since high school, and I just ran away from home. And I'm 21, so it's pathetic that I'm still living with my parents. Oh, and I fucked up real bad and kinda got my friend killed, and almost got you and Professor Miller killed too."

"That wasn't your fault," I said.

"It felt like it was. It *was*. I did a lot of bad shit, and people got hurt because of it. I got hurt too, but not nearly enough, you know what I mean? Like, I'm still walking around free after all that. I even got an all-expenses paid trip to Europe and Russia out of the deal."

"I don't mean to say that you didn't have anything to do with what happened," I said. "But there were a lot of bad people doing bad things, and that's on them. You were just a kind of...catalyst, I guess you'd say. Although I think a lot of that would have happened anyway."

"Maybe." She twirled a strand of hair around her finger and yanked on it hard enough to hurt.

"Sometimes you might...do stuff without thinking it through," I said. "But you've also tried to do the right thing and fix things. At least whenever you've been around me. And now you're trying to figure out how to fix things again. You say you don't know what to do. Do you think your mom or your cousins are planning...I don't know... you hinted at terrorist activity. Do you really think they might do something like that?"

"I don't know." She wound another strand of hair around her finger, and pulled hard. "No. I think it's more, like...training. Like, they're planning some kind of training thing. That's what they do. And the people they train...I don't know what they might do."

"Okay," I said. "I don't know how reportable that is. But I could ask around for you. I have...um...I have a contact in the FBI. I could ask him. And in the meantime, do you think it would be helpful to talk to your Aunt Cybil?"

She released her hair. "Actually, it might. She's, like, pretty smart about stuff like that. She's not all super sweet and cuddly, but I think she might have some good advice in a sitch like this."

"Okay," I said. "Why don't you talk to her about it, see what she suggests. And in the meantime, I'll run this by my, uh, contact in the FBI, see what he says."

"Great!" She was sitting up straight in the seat, looking more alive than she had since she'd shown up at my doorstep. "Thanks, Professor H! And is that our exit?"

22

AFTER MUCH TRAFFIC, trouble, aggravation, and expense, we made it into the airport, parked, got into the terminal, found a restaurant, and sat down to eat. Madison insisted on paying for it with the last of her cash.

"You might want to hang onto your money," I counseled her.

"Nah, I'm sure Dad'll give me more."

Ah, to be so young and so full of that blithe assurance that parents could and would give you whatever money you needed or wanted. My parents had never been stingy or miserly, but we hadn't had much money when I was a child. There had been the commune years, which had been awesome in many respects, but had not involved a lot of economic prosperity. Then my parents had left the commune and started grad school (my dad) and med school (my mom), and things had been even tighter, since we'd been trying to survive in a currency-based economy without much currency.

Things had been a little better once they'd graduated and started working, but both of them had chosen fields that paid largely in gratitude and goodwill rather than cold hard cash. So, while I suspected that my own father liked me rather more as a person than Madison's father liked her, he had never given me much money. I guess you give what you can. Maybe Erik gave Madison so much money and material support because he knew he wasn't capable of giving her the things she really needed. And she responded by throwing it in his face and wearing the oldest, nastiest clothes she could find.

After a meal of airport food, I walked her over to security.

"Let me know when you get there," I told her.

"Jeez." She rolled her eyes. "Now you're keeping track of me all the time too!"

"I always say that to people when I see them off on a journey," I told her.

She started to roll her eyes again, then stopped. "I guess I should just, like, say thank you, or something, right? Like, you actually really helped me out, in, like, a really big way. Like, not many people would've done that. And they, like, *certainly* wouldn't have been so cool about it. So, like..." She scuffed the toe of her shoe on the floor. "Thanks. Like, a lot. Like, I owe you big-time."

"I was happy to help," I said. And I actually meant it. Madison could be a pain, but whenever I thought about not helping her, I decided that helping was by far the better option. And it was rewarding, in its own way. I hadn't even expected the thanks. Helping people who needed help was its own reward, at least for me. And right now it felt like I was stepping in to help Madison when Madison's own mother couldn't. That was good, right? Or was it all I was good for? Picking up the pieces of other people's children?

Madison moved like she was going to hug me, which was a welcome distraction from my thoughts. At the last moment she thought better of it and hovered, awkwardly, a little too close to me. "Well," she said. "I guess I'd better, like, go or something before I miss my flight."

I looked at the long line snaking towards security. "I guess so," I said. "But seriously, let me know when you get there. And keep in touch, okay? And I'll let you know if I get any good advice on what to do about your mom."

"Okay. And, like, I really will try to pay you back. You keep saving my ass, and I...I guess I'd like a chance to save *your* ass someday." She looked up and grinned at me. "A girl can dream, right?"

"Absolutely," I said. Privately, I shuddered at the thought of how bad things would have to get for Madison to be the one to save my ass.

Hopefully it will never come to that, I told myself. *"Schastlivovo puti,"* I said out loud.

"Whoa, I actually recognize that! It means, like, 'have a good trip,' right?"

"Right," I said. "Have a good trip. Let me know when you get there."

"Will do!" She was smiling broadly now. She gave me a thumbs-up, slung her ratty backpack over her shoulder, and headed off into the line of people shuffling through security. I watched her until she was through and had disappeared into the depths of the concourse.

23

BY THE TIME I GOT BACK to my apartment, it was almost evening. I wasn't particularly hungry, thanks to the heavy airport meal, but I was tired. And my left knee was very, very unhappy.

It's never going to get better if you keep going like this. I squelched the thought as hard as I could. But it wasn't hard enough. I was definitely subjecting it to way more abuse than it could take. And some of that abuse, I suspected, was the PT I was doing. It had felt significantly worse after Saturday's session, and it wasn't getting any better.

Don't give up yet! Maybe I needed to give it more of a chance. Maybe I just wasn't trying hard enough. That was a seductive thought, since it suggested that success was achievable through my own individual effort. Seductive thoughts were often dangerous in their power.

Another seductive thought was the idea of throwing myself facedown on the bed and not moving for at least 12 hours. But I resisted. First of all, Fevronia needed feeding and attention. Second of all, I needed to call Frank.

I checked the time. It was only early afternoon in California. He would be at work. Probably busy with much more important things...no, wait. This was *important*. Not just to me. This was exactly the kind of thing that the ATF, DHS, FBI, NSA, and all the other letters in the alphabet were there specifically to fight.

Well, in theory. In practice, while they were all over Islamist terrorist groups, neo-Nazi or white supremacist organizations seemed to get more of a pass. I spent a moment wondering if Frank would blow this off. Maybe *he* was a neo-Nazi too...

No. Frank was a lot of bad things, but I had the sense that he was a reasonably good FBI agent, and not a crazed neo-Nazi. It just wasn't his style. I couldn't see him getting into the whole purity thing they seemed to have going on. And I suspected that, like John, he was smart enough to recognize all the times he'd been helped out by non-Aryans, and to realize that he didn't want to antagonize them. I even thought he had some morals, in his own way, and they didn't involve being part of a dangerous extremist ideology. Frank was not a nice guy, and he'd done a lot of really not nice things in his past, but he wasn't a terrorist.

On the other hand, I didn't really feel like talking to him, even if he was available. I settled for texting him instead.

I half expected him not to get back to me at all. Instead, I got a reply five minutes later.

This sounds serious. Give me a call in half an hour. On my office phone. Meanwhile, try to come up with every detail you know.

He included his office number. There was not so much as a hint of an inappropriate innuendo. That was scary. Maybe this was even more serious than I thought.

Half an hour later I called him on his office phone, as requested.

"Hi, Ro," he said. "Good to hear from you. And thanks for calling me here. I didn't want to take this call out on the street, on a cell phone."

"Sure," I said. "Although I'm not sure how serious it actually is..."

"Let's assume it's serious." His voice was all business, more so than I'd ever heard it before, even when we'd been on the hunt for Erin, his then-girlfriend, this summer.

"Okay," I agreed. "Actually, I think it might be pretty serious too. And I wasn't sure who to take it to..."

"Taking it to me is good. I can make sure it gets to the right people. So tell me what you know.

I outlined, in as coherent a fashion as I could manage, everything Madison had told me about her mother, her mother's cousins, and Glorious Future.

"And you don't actually know what they're called? The cousins? Or what organization the mother works for?"

"No," I admitted. "But I could probably find out for you..."

"We'll take it from here." He cut me off before I could finish. I got the distinct impression he didn't want me messing around with this. Fair enough. *I* didn't want me messing around with this either. This seemed like a business for the professionals if there ever was one.

"Great," I said. "Thanks a lot. I really appreciate it."

"This is what we do." His tone was still brusque. Then he said, "And of course I'm always ready to do anything to help *you*, Ro."

Damn, damn, damn! Seemed like I wasn't going to escape without a little obligatory flirtation and sexual innuendo after all.

Worst of all, I could feel myself actually cheering up a little at it. Noooooo. *Nooooooooo*. I must be even more depressed and desperate than I thought. Frank had grown on me a little during our time together this summer, it was true, in the sense that I went from despising him to developing a grudging respect for him, but that didn't mean that starting any kind of a romance with him was a good idea. Aside from the fact that he was a whole continent away, even the most cursory examination of our behaviors and values would suggest that we were completely incompatible. He was brash, bossy, rude, arrogant...the list could go on and on. And he generally treated women with a total lack of respect. I was a partial exception, but that was little comfort.

He had a certain animal magnetism—I always thought of him as a vigorous clan chieftain in the Highlands of Scotland—and he seemed to think I had a certain animal magnetism too, but animal magnetism would only get you so far. Namely, into bed. It wouldn't solve your problems out of bed, and soon those problems would come creeping into the bedroom, and you'd have nothing. So all in all, I needed to steer clear of Frank.

"Um," I said. "Thanks. I, uh, like I said, I really appreciate it. Let me know if you need anything more from me."

"I'm sure there's lots I need from you, Ro, but as far as this case is concerned, we'll take it from here."

"Great," I said. "Well, I'll, uh, let you go. I'm sure you have lots to do." I hung up before he could say otherwise.

24

THE NEXT DAY DAWNED bright and hot. Only the slightly shorter day length indicated that the school year was officially starting.

I had gotten texts from Madison the day before letting me know she was boarding, and then again when she had landed at LaGuardia, and when she had made it home to her aunt's apartment. I got a lengthy and fulsome text from Erik telling me the same thing, and thanking me for all my help with Madison, and promising to help me with whatever I needed, however he could. I got the sense that he wanted to have a long heart-to-heart, probably over the phone, about it all. That seemed like a dangerous idea, so I sidestepped it as neatly as I could.

The evening had ended with a long text from Alex. He, too, I sensed, wanted to have some kind of heart-to-heart over the phone. After my moment of weakness while talking to Frank earlier, that seemed like a very bad idea. Instead, I'd very determinedly texted him questions about Erin until he'd given up on talking to me about anything else and said good night.

I felt bad about it, but I was pretty sure I'd have felt a lot worse if I'd gotten involved in a lengthy late-night confessional with him. I did think it was good and right to help others in their time of need, but I also thought that all of these men in my life had ended up taking more than they had given me, and maybe they needed to stand on their own two feet a little more, or at least get their support from someone they could support in turn.

All those good intentions still hadn't meant a good night's sleep. I had tossed and turned, my knee letting me know in no uncertain terms that it had not appreciated the three-hour drive I'd put it through that afternoon. At least that had taken my mind off my personal problems.

Now Mel was driving us towards campus in the blinding August morning sun. We were both slouched down in our seats, sunglasses shading our eyes.

"We should probably be more excited about the start of the semester," she said. "Do you remember when it was a big thrill?"

"Distantly," I said. "I think I was pretty excited that first time I led a class on my own. That was a big deal. And I was all into pedagogy and stuff for a few semesters there in grad school. By the time I graduated, I was already over it."

"Yeah, me too. I mean, don't get me wrong. I still care about teaching, and I think about how I teach. I'm pretty sure I'm actually a good teacher now, unlike when I was all into that pedagogical theory shit. And most of the motions they make us got through seem like bullshit to me."

"Yep," I said. "Do you have first and second year too this semester?"

"Sure do." Last year, when we'd started, we'd both had two sections of first-year language classes. Now that our programs were in their second years, we had one section of first year and one section of second year. What would happen next year was anyone's guess. It wasn't clear to me whether Crimson intended to offer Russian or Arabic beyond the intermediate level. It might not be clear to anyone. Someone had come up with the brilliant idea to hire some LCTL instructors and start Russian, Arabic, and Chinese programs, but no one really knew what to do with those programs, now that they'd been started. Enrollment had been too high to shut them down, but not high enough to create a full-fledged major or even a minor.

I suspected that the plan, inasmuch as there was one, had originally been to end the programs after Mel and I had served out our three years and couldn't have our contracts renewed. What they'd do with Chloe, who was tenure-track, was unclear. They could give her a negative performance review and terminate her before she went up for tenure, of course, but given that she was Crimson's only African-American faculty member, brought there on a special diversity hire, that would be some very bad optics. Of course, the people making the decisions would have to be capable of recognizing just how bad those optics would be, and I wasn't sure they could.

But now they were talking seriously about tenure-track positions for the other LCTL programs as well. So maybe someone in the provost's office had taken a shine to our programs, or gotten some federal money for them, and now they had to spend it. How long that would last was anyone's guess. In the meantime, I had a new crop of first-years to woo and amaze. I glanced down at my knee. Well, that should certainly make an impression.

This time, Mel dropped me off as close to Bedford Hall as she could get. I hobbled the few dozen yards across the quad to the front entrance, where I stood there, trying to figure out how to get in. I was weighed down by my crutches and a very awkward book bag. I had trimmed it down with the diligence of an astronaut trying to reduce flight weight, but it was still bigger and heavier than I could easily manage. Every time I tried to open the door, the bag slipped over my shoulder and slid painfully down my arm, no doubt raising a nasty friction burn, before slamming to a halt at my wrist and almost pulling me over.

There was a big square button that in theory you could push to open the doors. I went over and, after a couple of failed attempts, managed to push it with my elbow. Nothing happened. I pushed it again. No dice. I tried with the other elbow, in case it was a left-elbow-only kind of device. Still nothing.

"Professor! Hey, Professor. Jeez. Are you still on those things?"

It was Miranda, one of my students from last year. It took me a moment to recognize her. Last August she had been wearing a jagged bob with an aggressive undercut and blue and purple streaks, along with way too much eye makeup. She had let the hair grow out over the winter and spring, and now, as I had predicted, she had ditched the eyeliner and was projecting an image of wholesome do-gooderness. I was pretty sure those were vegan organic sandals she was wearing, along with linen pants and an organic cotton shirt that harkened, ever so gently, back to the Flower Power era. It was a look I was very familiar with. I also thought it suited her better than her desperate attempts to be a goth rocker. Miranda had been born to try to make the world a better place, and she seemed to finally be embracing her destiny.

"Oh here, let me get that for you," she said, inserting herself into the stream of incoming students and holding the door open. "Those buttons don't work. We're actually working on a whole piece about it for the *Champion*."

Miranda wrote for the *Crimson Champion*, the college paper. Unsurprisingly, it was a hotbed of student rabble-rousers. They must have some fairly powerful faculty and administrative rabble-rousers protecting them, since, despite all the complaints about their critiques of the college, they were still putting out two issues a week like clockwork. It was comforting to know that someone other than me was cheering them on.

"The college spent a bunch of money a few years back to make everything ADA compliant," Miranda was saying, "but most of what they did has broken, or never worked at all. The automatic door opening buttons are pretty much all broken, all over campus. And forget about trying to get anywhere without stairs..." She looked my crutches up and down critically. "I guess you're finding out about all this the hard way, huh, Professor?"

"Yep," I said, waiting for a slow moment in the stream of students before hauling myself forward in an ungainly lurch and hopping through the door before anyone could knock me over.

The cool darkness of Bedford Hall was a relief. For a few seconds. Then a stabbing pain hit me in my left temple. Urgh. I sniffed deeply, trying to catch a whiff of mold. Oh whoa. No need to wonder. That was *definitely* some nasty mildew there, along with a dense miasma of cleaning products, fabric softener, artificial fragrances, and who knows what else. My chest started to tighten.

You're fine! I told myself. *Look: everyone around you is fine!*

Unfortunately, the person I chose to look at was pulling an inhaler out of her backpack. I hustled past her as quickly as I could, telling myself it was all just anxiety and a general beginning-of-semester malaise.

"I guess we're back in our old classroom again, huh, Prof?" said Miranda. "Hey, you want me to carry your book bag for you?"

"Sure." A few months on and off of crutches had taught me to have no pride when it came to letting other people fetch and carry stuff for me.

I almost knocked us both down during the bag transfer operation, but we managed it without actually collapsing, and then set off again towards the classroom. As we drew closer, Miranda's face got tighter and tighter. It was the same classroom where, last December, we had hidden from a gunman who'd come to shoot her. We had survived, but Miranda was still obviously carrying the emotional trauma. As anyone would.

"I wish they'd put us somewhere else," she said softly as we stepped through the door.

"Yeah, me too," I said. "You'd think they'd, I don't know, close off the room entirely or something. But I guess they can't afford it."

"Yeah." She set down my bag and shook her shoulders, physically shaking off the memories. "Anyway, this year is going to be *awesome*, right, Prof? I'm actually super excited about studying Russian again. I felt like a learned a lot last year, but I couldn't really *talk*, you know? But this year we'll actually be able to talk, right?"

"A bit." I tried to be just the right amount of encouraging. The sad truth was that Russian was difficult, and it took most English speakers a minimum of three years to be able to say much at all. No need to tell her that now, though.

"It would be cool to do some study abroad or something, too," she said. "And I'm definitely majoring in journalism, so maybe I could, I don't know, combine the two? There's a lot of stuff you could write about, isn't there?"

"There certainly is," I told her. "And...maybe I should introduce you to a friend of mine, a Russian journalist..."

Miranda opened her mouth to say something. But before she could, my phone *pinged*. I pulled it out of my pocket. Madison. I resisted a groan.

Hey, Professor H! So, I guess you already talked to someone about what I told you, right? Because I just got a call from a really serious guy. Can I talk to you about it? Right away?

25

"JUST A SECOND," I SAID to Miranda. "Um..." More students were starting to file into the classroom, and the space by the door was rapidly filling up. This classroom, like many of the others here on campus, had a table that was much too large for it. The board and lectern were on the far side of it from the door. The only way to them was to sidle, sucking in your stomach and trying not to trip over chairs, backpacks, and other hazards, around the edge of the table. It was a challenging maneuver at the best of times. With a bad knee, two crutches, and an overloaded book bag, it was nearly impossible.

I glanced at my phone again. 8:57. Class started at 9:00. I needed to get to the front of the classroom. I also needed to respond to Madison. Okay, I could do both within the next three minutes. I started towards the board.

I made it past the first chair with no problem. The second chair was a little trickier, but I made it safely past that obstacle, too. The third chair, though, was pulled slightly out from the table, blocking the twelve-inch path completely. Both my hands were taken up by my crutches and bag. I tried balancing on my good leg and pushing at the chair with my bad leg. Ugh, no, definitely not. The chair remained firmly stuck in the elderly carpeting, doing nothing but torquing my knee in a direction it didn't need to be torqued. I tried balancing on my bad leg and pushing the chair with my good leg.

More torquing of my already fragile injury, with no discernible movement in the chair.

My phone buzzed in my pocket, reminding me of Madison's text. The clock on the wall read 8:58. The classroom was now full to overflowing with students. If I couldn't get to the front of the room, not only would I not have access to the board, but there wouldn't be enough chairs for the students.

"Let me, Professor." Miranda jumped forward and pushed the chair up against the table. I eased past, catching the tip of my right crutch on a chair leg, but I recovered before doing a full faceplant. Victories. You have to take your victories where you can get them.

The room was filling up with an excited pre-class buzz. Half the students were looking up at me expectantly, and half were studiously ignoring me, focusing on their conversations and showing that they wouldn't be interrupted until they had said everything they wanted to say. Thank goodness. I could text Madison really quickly without looking too negligent.

I'm about to start class, I wrote. *Let's talk this afternoon.* Then I put away the phone and looked up.

The pre-class buzzing was dying down. More and more eager student faces were looking at me. They seemed even more curious than usual.

"Yes," I said. "As you can see, I'm still on crutches. I got a bit better over the summer, but then I had a bit of a setback."

"Jeez, Professor, sorry about that," said Jackson. "But that's not what we were wondering about. We wanted to know...is it true that you know this guy?"

He held up his phone. I squinted at it from across the classroom. The only thing I could make out was the reflection of the overhead light, blinding me.

"I don't know," I said. "What guy? What is it?"

"It's a guest article in *The Guardian*," he said. "A friend of mine knows I study Russian and he sent it to me 'cause he thought I might find it interesting. It's about, uh"—he squinted—"Chechnya. You know what that is?"

"Yes," I said. "I do."

"Anyway, the guy that wrote it...there's a rumor going around...well, from something he says here it kinda sounds like...like he knows you."

26

"UM," I SAID. "WHAT'S his name?"

Jackson squinted at the screen. "Di-mi-try Kuz-net-sov," he said carefully.

My first instinct was to tell him that, for God's sake, after a year of Russian he needed to be able to pronounce one of the most common Russian names in existence. Dmitry Kuznetsov was basically the Russian equivalent of David Smith. I quelled that impulse. Berating students for incompetence was ineffectual at the best of times. Besides, that was not what this conversation was about.

"I do know him," I said, as calmly as I could. "Although I don't see how that could possibly come up in any article he wrote."

"See, it's an article about for-profit prison and security companies," he said. "Part of a whole series of them."

"Uh-huh?" I said. I wasn't liking where this was going.

"And so his article is mainly about some company called"—Jackson squinted at his screen again—"Kav-boy-ets."

"Uh-huh," I said, liking this even less. The fine folks from Kavboyets had once kidnapped me and held a gun to my head in order to pressure Dima into giving up his investigations into them. He had agreed to break off the investigation—and then he'd broken up with me. Now, it seemed, he was back with them, at least. Not so much with me. I still couldn't see what this article had to do with me, though. Surely he wasn't sharing the story of that awful night with the world. He'd said then that he was addicted to chasing a story, but not that much, surely not that much...

"And it also talks about Security Solutions," Jackson continued. "It says that maybe there's a connection between them? And he mentions that Security Solutions has given a bunch of money to an American college, which *we* know is Crimson, and he says something about how he kinda knows someone at that college, and my friend and I, we were, like, thinking it had to be you."

27

"UM," I SAID. ALL EYES were glued on me with a keen interest they had never shown for Russian grammar. "Well, it is true that we do know each other..."

"How well?" Jackson asked. He seemed much too fascinated to realize that maybe that wasn't the most appropriate question.

"Very well," I said.

Everyone was absolutely agog now.

"We, ah...we lived together for a while," I told them. *That* was probably inappropriate. It would have been better to tell them that we had been engaged, which was also true. But somehow that was much harder to say. Breaking up with a boyfriend you happened to live with for a little while was one thing. Calling off a solemn engagement was something else entirely. I didn't want to be an even more tragic figure to them than I already was, with my crutches and my involvement in the shooting, not to mention the whole thing with that frat last semester.

"Send me the article," I told Jackson. "I'd like to read it."

"Can't we talk about it, Professor? Like, it seems *way* more important than, like, case endings or whatever."

"If you knew your case endings, you could read it in the original," I told him tartly. "Which is always the best way to read anything. But tell you what: you send me the article, and I'll read it, and tomorrow we'll talk about it." Like a coward, I hoped by tomorrow they'd forget about it, and I wouldn't have to chat lightly about painful personal problems in class.

The students agreed, reluctantly, that that was acceptable, and settled down to a short and agonizingly stilted conversation about what they had done over the summer. That involved reviewing the past tense, which most of them had forgotten. We had to give up on it after a while, and switch to introductions. This felt silly, since everyone had spent all of last year in class together, but, as it turned out, they had forgotten most of their actual Russian, and so they got a good review out of it anyway.

Fifty minutes of excruciatingly halting language practice later, and I declared them done for the day, but exhorted them to review A LOT before tomorrow's class. Everyone but Miranda rushed off to their next class.

"So, is that the person you were going to introduce me to, Professor?" she asked. "The one Jackson was asking you about?"

"Yes," I said. "I guess I should check out that article."

"He already showed it to me." She held up her phone. "And I, uh, kind of read some of it during class."

"Oh," I said. "Well...was it interesting?"

She nodded her head vigorously. "That's *exactly* the kind of thing I want to be doing, Professor! Like, writing stuff that really makes a difference!"

"I don't know how much of a difference Dima's writing actually makes," I said. Then I regretted it.

"It made a difference for *me*, Professor! He said a lot of the things I've been thinking, but that no one else seems to be willing to say. It made me feel like at least one other person out there actually cares! I mean"—she looked around, then lowered her voice—"all that stuff about private prisons and 'security'—basically mercenary—companies. No one seems to think anything of it! That new football stadium that's going up? Paid for with blood money! I...well, I guess you know how I feel about that, Professor."

"I do," I said. "And I feel the same way. And yes, I do think that it's good that Dima—and you, and other people who do this kind of thing—are out there saying this kind of thing. It's just easy to get frustrated at how little a difference it seems to make sometimes."

"Yeah. But anyway. It would be *awesome* if you could introduce me to him someday. I'd *love* to pick his brain, ask him about how he works...does he speak English?"

"Not much," I said. "It could be a great workout for your Russian, though."

"I don't think my Russian's up to that quite yet, Professor. But...maybe you could translate for us?"

"Sure," I said. "I'd be happy to. I'll see what I can do."

"Thanks, Professor! I really appreciate it. I guess—is this your next class coming in? I guess I'd better let you get to it, then. But I really would like to talk to him."

"Sure," I said. "I'd be *delighted* to set that up."

28

I HAD TO TEACH MY SECOND class before I could do anything about Madison's text or Dima's article. At 10:50 exactly, I extracted myself from the dozen bright-eyed 101 students and hauled myself to my office. Mel had class at 9:00 and 11:00, so I had scheduled my office hours for 11:00.

As usual, no one was waiting for me. I dutifully held my office hours every week, but 90% of the time, no one came to them. Office hours, I'd decided, were an anachronism of the pre-email age. These days, everyone made an appointment before showing up.

The office felt even more airless and claustrophobic than I remembered. I eyed the giant water stain in one corner with distaste. I had always assumed it was more an aesthetic problem than anything. But now I was wondering how much it was contributing to my low-level headache and the general sense of distress I always felt in this office. Ugh. I tried to put it out of my mind.

I started by calling Madison. She was practically hyperventilating with anxiety over the call she'd gotten at 8:00am that morning.

"What if my mom finds out!?!" she cried into the phone.

"Why would she? Are you going to tell her?"

"No, but...what if they start investigating her, and she finds out I'm the one who snitched on her to the FBI...she's already so disappointed in me..."

"You didn't snitch on her to the FBI," I said. "I did."

"Yeah, but because I told you to!"

"Are they going to tell her that?" I asked.

"No...they said everything I told them would be in confidence..."

"That's probably the case, then," I said soothingly.

"I guess...I just...do you think I did the right thing?"

"How would you feel if you hadn't done it?" I asked.

She paused. "Worse," she said eventually. "I really, *really* don't want these guys coming over here and doing something bad. Even though they are my family. Actually, that'd make it even worse. I'd feel *horrible* if they did something bad and I'd been able to stop it."

"Then you did the right thing," I said.

"I guess."

We went round and round about that for a few more minutes, before Madison calmed down enough to hang up the phone. I glanced up at my door. Still no one. I decided to read Dima's article.

Jackson still hadn't sent me the link, but I was able to find it after a quick search. As promised, it was part of a series of exposés on private prison and security firms, co-authored by Dima, his friend Dave Wilkinson, and a couple of others I didn't know. Dima's piece was on Kavboyets, the private army made up of Chechen orphans, and their deployment in both Eastern Ukraine and Syria.

I read through it. Boys left orphaned after the recent Chechen wars were recruited and given a safe place to stay and a stable community that promised them money, honor, and a sense of belonging. Then they were trained up as fighters and sent off to places were it was convenient for Grozny and/or Moscow to have soldiers with a certain amount of plausible deniability to their pedigrees.

It is easy for us in Russia to think that this is a specifically Russian problem, Dima wrote at the end of the article. *But in fact, this is just another example of the "adaptation to our customs" of foreign imports that has been our long-time practice. Mercenary companies have existed the world over for centuries. In the past few decades, they have gained considerable power and prestige in the West, in America in particular. Everyone knows the name of Blackwater. But there are many smaller companies that are profiting by their example, and by their own, uniquely American, innovations. Private prisons, used largely to extract money and labor from ethnic minorities by incarcerating them, are one such innovation that I fear will soon be adapted to our customs here in Russia as well.*

At least one such American firm is stretching its tentacles into Russia right now. In a twist that might surprise even the most inventive novelist, this firm has gained control not just of various prisons, but—I am informed by both official sources and my personal connections—of at least one American college. The college is conveniently located in a Southern state with a long and shameful history of imprisonment—read: forced labor, also known as slavery—of its African-American populace. Not, I argue, a coincidence. This makes it all the more convenient for this company to whitewash its image and rinse its dirty money clean. And now this very company, which goes by the benign name "Security Solutions," is in negotiations with Kavboyets. The result for both Russians and Americans could be disastrous.

Well, that was clear enough. The thought of Security Solutions joining forces with Kavboyets was alarming indeed. I was glad someone was reporting on it, and proud of Dima for having the courage of his convictions—although when did he not?—and continuing to investigate Kavboyets when they had gone to such lengths to scare him off. I was also worried that others would make the same connection Jackson had, and figure out that Dima was talking about Crimson College, and that he knew me.

I opened up Signal to text him about it, and ask him how dangerous he thought it was. My hands were shaking. Cold sweat, I noted, was running down my sides.

"Hey, Ro. Whoa. You don't look so good." It was Mel, back from teaching her second class.

"I think I'm having a panic attack," I said. My mouth felt like it belonged to someone else. I was surprised I was able to get words out at all.

"Did Karen just come and harass you?"

My heart jumped in my chest. "No, why? Is she roaming the halls?"

"Yeah. She just grabbed me on my way out the classroom and started talking about the new performance review thing she's doing this semester."

"Oh, fuck!" That came out louder than I'd intended. Mel and I both instinctively looked towards the door, then laughed.

"Let's get the hell out of here," said Mel. "We can answer our forty billion emails just as well from home. Besides, I'm starting to get real paranoid about this mold thing."

We both looked towards the water stain on my ceiling.

"Yeah," I said. "Let's go home. And get some lunch. Maybe that will make me feel better."

"Always worth a shot," said Mel.

29

MEL SET OFF TO GO GET the Jeep. I started my slow and painful way down the corridor after her.

"Oh, Rowena, *there* you are."

I froze. Then, moving slowly and carefully in order not to fall over or show my horror, I turned around.

Karen was coming up behind me. Her face was set in an expression of even greater distaste than ever. "Really, Rowena, I can't believe you're *still* on those things," she said. "How long are you going to be on crutches anyway?"

"I don't know," I said. "I was off them for a while, but I got reinjured a couple of weeks ago..."

"You should really be more *careful*, Rowena. We can't afford for you to be out sick or injured!"

"Oh," I said. I wasn't sure if that was a compliment or not.

"And of course, anything that negatively affects your fitness will have a negative impact on your candidacy for the tenure-track position here as well!"

"Ah," I said. I debated over whether to say anything about anti-discrimination laws. Being on crutches was a major pain, but I was still able to teach. Denying me a job because of it was probably a lawsuit waiting to happen. But then, our department did seem to want to get sued over something. At least, that was one potential interpretation of their treatment of me, Mel, and Chloe. A more likely interpretation, and one I had already offered, was that bullying and exploitation were endemic in education. In our case they were being expressed in ways that felt tinged with racism, sexual harassment, homophobia, and, apparently, ableism, but really it was just good old-fashioned bullying. This was not comforting.

"Speaking of such things, we need to set up your first observation for your performance review. As I've said many times before, we *must* bring your teaching up to the standards expected of a Crimson faculty member!"

"Uh-huh," I said. Then, impelled by some irrepressible spirit of mischief, I added, "I looked at my student evaluations for the past year. According to their metrics, I'm in the top 10% of the department." Student evaluations were currently being done online, and we were given a handy-dandy chart showing our placement within the department. I, I was pretty sure, had come out on top.

Karen inhaled sharply, and promptly fell into a coughing fit that took more than a minute to quell. When she could speak again, she said, "You *know* that student evaluations are not a reliable metric *at all*, Rowena!"

"True." And it was true. Student evaluations were notoriously biased, with little correlation to learning outcomes but a high correlation with the race and gender of the instructor being evaluated. One might be tempted to argue that this made my high scores even more indicative of excellence in teaching, since female professors often scored lower than their male peers. I looked at Karen's mouth, as pursed up as if she'd just bitten into an unripe persimmon, or possibly a stick of antiperspirant, and decided not to attempt that line of reasoning.

"Next week!" she said. "I need to come observe you next week!"

"Sure," I said. "I teach at 9:00 and 10:00, Monday-Tuesday-Wednesday-Friday."

"I..." Now she looked befuddled. "I need to check my calendar! I'll email you!"

"Great," I said. "Looking forward to it."

Karen looked like she wanted to say something more, but then she lost her nerve, and, with a final admonishment about my poor teaching performance, beat a hasty retreat.

30

"LET ME GUESS," MEL said when I hauled myself into the Jeep. "Karen caught you."

"Jeez, how'd you *know?*"

We both laughed. "Normally you go around with this, what's the word I'm looking for, beatific expression on your face," she said. "But right now you look like you want to chew nails so's you can spit them out as bullets."

"That is about how I feel," I agreed. I outlined my conversation with Karen, dwelling at length on her warnings about the potential negative effect my injury would have on my candidacy for the tenure-track job, should it appear.

"Yeah, well, you know how these motherfuckers roll," said Mel. "They want to work you to death, and then they get really pissed if you get cancer or something and interfere with their plans."

"And what pisses *me* off the most is that I got this injury here," I said. "At Crimson. Doing my job. It's a workplace injury. At least the first time, it was. And you could argue that the second time it was too. It certainly happened while I was here at Crimson. Saving, I should mention, Crimson's ass from what could have turned into a really nasty incident. And now Karen is hinting that it could be grounds for termination! They talk about how we're all one big caring family. And I guess some of the people here do care about us as people. It's just that most of them care about us more as commodities."

"Yeah," said Mel. "And instead of trying to help us out, they try to tell us we have to help ourselves by getting their fucking corporate enlightenment and Zen you can buy at the dollar store. They keep trying to get us to 'have a good attitude' and 'think positive,' and look what the result is."

"Yeah," I said.

"Although maybe they're right to push us towards meditation. Maybe we're in the same situation as people in medieval China or whatever, forced to rely on mind control for our medical care because it's the only thing we've got."

"Also true," I said.

"And hey, it's cheap—at least if you avoid all the hucksters and shysters trying to sell you your soul back at $200 dollars a private session."

"Man the barricades," I said. "Oops. I meant...um, woman the barricades? What is it we're supposed to be doing, anyway?"

"Nothing," said Mel. "Abso-fucking-lutely nothing. We can't even sit around looking pretty without getting shit for it."

"We need to stop this conversation before we become radicalized beyond redemption," I said.

"It sure makes you realize how people can become fucking jihadists and shit, don't it?"

"Yes," I said. "It does. Not that that's helping my peace of mind right now."

"Oh? There's *more* than Karen and her bullshit eating you up right now?"

I told her about the article about Kavboyets and Security Solutions, and the (true) rumor going around that I was, or at least had been, involved with its author.

"Oooooooh shit," said Mel. "The college isn't going to be happy about that."

"No," I agreed. "One might be tempted to point out that if they didn't want to get bad press for crawling into bed with Security Solutions, they shouldn't have done it. But I doubt that argument will hold much weight with them."

"Fuck to the no," said Mel. "They'll just shoot the shit out of the messenger."

"And I'm afraid...I'm afraid...I'm afraid they'll blame me for it, even though I had nothing to do with the article at all, and I'll get in trouble for it. That would *certainly* be grounds for termination. And...I'm afraid of Kavboyets," I admitted, my voice hardly above a whisper, barely audible against the rushing of the air through the open windows. The Jeep, most inconveniently for a vehicle in Georgia, didn't have working AC.

"I'm afraid they'll take up their vendetta against Dima again, and they'll go after him, and his mom...and me," I said, looking down at the door handle because I was too frightened and ashamed by the words I was uttering to look Mel or even my own reflection in the face. "I'm afraid they'll track me all the way here, and go after me to stop him. And...I'm angry. At Dima. I'm angry at him for putting me in this position. Again. And I'm angry at myself for being such a coward."

"Mmmm." Mel was silent for a moment as she pulled through an intersection. "Was that a bone of contention between you?" she asked once we were through. "You didn't want him putting you at risk?"

"No," I said. "I was always so proud of him, and—let's be honest—so proud of myself for standing by him. I felt like we were both doing something important, something worth fighting for...worth dying for, if it came down to it. When they—the guys from Kavboyets—were holding that gun to my head, all I felt was rage. I swore to myself that this was a blood feud now, and I would show them they hadn't stopped me, I would make them pay.

"But...I don't know...I'm so *tired*. I'm tired of fighting noble rearguard actions that can't be won. I don't want any more blood feuds, or brave fights, or...anything like that. I just, for once, want things to be pleasant and easy. Or at least, I want a husband who loves me, and a couple of kids who are, you know, just normal, nice kids, and a house that's a normal, nice house, and a job that isn't always full of gut-wrenching misery and pays enough that I don't have to calculate every single purchase to the penny every time I go to the grocery store. Is that too much to ask?"

"It shouldn't be," said Mel. "But somehow it is."

"I know. And, you know, it makes me sick sometimes when I think about it. And the worst part is that Dima, and Alex, and my brother John—they all sold their souls for money in one way or another. They all signed up for things that involved doing really, really bad stuff that now they'll have to live with for the rest of their lives, because they needed the money. And still none of them can really support a family. Not on just their paycheck. I mean, Dima's all about truth and justice *now*, but when he was younger, he was in OMON. If you know what that is."

"Russian riot police, right?" said Mel.

"Right. Not nice guys at *all*. And he did it mainly for the money. Alex and John both did ROTC, which we think is so great, but a lot of Russians consider to be horrible blood money. And they all ended up with way too much blood on their hands to ever wash clean. And they're still broke, or at least, not rich."

"Yeah," said Mel. "It fucking sucks. Believe me, I know. Every day, I ask myself what it was all for, and if this fucking guilt will ever go away, and why the fuck I'm not at least bathing in one of those fucking golden bathtubs they supposedly found in Saddam's palaces when they 'liberated' them. I mean, if I had to go in and wreck the shit out of Iraq, I should at least get something out of it other than a TBI and PTSD, right?"

"I don't think you singlehandedly wrecked the shit out Iraq," I said. "I think it was a group effort."

"Yeah, and I don't think you're a coward," said Mel. "I think you're just asking some fucking important questions, like what the fuck we're all doing here, and what kind of consequences our actions have, and whether it's worth it. And if you ask me, Dima should have asked you before writing that article. It's not just his life on the line there."

"Yeah," I said. "But he always has to do what he thinks is right, regardless of what it does to the rest of us."

"You know how it is with men," said Mel. "They want 110% from you, while only giving back 10% in return. And as the words are coming out of my mouth, that sounds like extremism even to me."

"Like I said, getting radicalized is so easy," I said. "As is getting co-opted by the totalitarian state. And a lot of the time, that seems like the only two options."

"We need to make some better fucking options," said Mel.

"Yeah," I said. "We should get right on that."

31

I TOLD MYSELF THAT the first thing I should do on getting home was do my lesson plans for tomorrow. Then I told myself I was just using that as an excuse not to confront Dima, and I should do that first. So I opened up Signal and started a text message.

It immediately became apparent that I didn't know what to say. I didn't even know what I wanted to say. I needed to figure that out. Then I could figure out how to express it in a calm, non-confrontational manner in Russian. All of that seemed so difficult that I almost gave up. I could just ignore it completely. Maybe it would just blow over.

But even if it blew over on the work front, I really felt like I needed to say something on the personal front. It was just that everything I thought of saying sounded accusatory or whiny.

I eventually went ahead and did my lesson planning first, to give myself time to let it all percolate through subconsciously. When I was done, I wrote *Just saw the article in The Guardian. Congratulations! Are you talking about me when you mention having a personal connection to the college? Some students saw the article and were asking.*

I sat there and waited for a few minutes after sending the text, in case I got an immediate reply. Nothing. I told myself I couldn't spend all day staring at my phone. So I made myself pull up my spreadsheet with this year's job postings, and get to work.

The academic hiring calendar follows a strict annual structure. In August through October, institutions post their ads for tenure-track jobs, with first-round interviews taking place between November and January, and second-round interviews (also often called campus visits, since they normally involve multi-day visits to campus) taking place between January and March. Job ads for visiting positions and post-docs could be posted anywhere from August to March, with the more desirable positions normally posted earlier in the cycle. Very short-term visiting positions, emergency replacements, and adjunct positions were normally posted in the spring and summer. Those were the least desirable positions, but also becoming more and more numerous.

At this point, the majority of US faculty were contingent, meaning they were on a short-term contract of 1-3 years, and many of them were part-time adjuncts, meaning they were paid a few thousand dollars a semester, with no benefits. This kept labor costs down dramatically in the short term. It also kept the teaching staff in a constant state of demoralization, poverty, and turnover. Students who needed advising, mentoring, or even a simple recommendation letter were increasingly out of luck.

My job at Crimson was a comparatively good visiting position, with a salary of $45,000 a year and benefits, and the possibility of renewal for up to three years. But after those three years, I was out, unless I got this tenure-track position that the college had been promising ever since I'd started there. And while $45,000 was enough to squeak by on in small-town Georgia, it was not enough to pay off debt, which most of us recent grads had in abundance, or to save up for retirement. So a major part of my current job was looking for a new job. Again, this provided non-trivial short-term benefits for the institution. The long-term problems seemed obvious to me, but not, apparently, to the senior administration or the board of directors.

The upshot of all this was that I was, once again, preparing to go back "on the market." I tried to convince myself that this was not a terrible thing. The good news, I had to admit, was that I no longer had an instinctive aversion to writing cover letters and submitting application materials. At first it had felt like, as my friends and I had all agreed, prostitution. But after a few years we had grown hardened to it—as, I supposed, all good prostitutes did.

The even better news was that I had a large selection of application materials to choose from now, so each individual application shouldn't take me much more than an hour or so to do. I hoped. Sometimes they threw you major curveballs about what they wanted and how it had to be formatted, which could mean hours spent on the application for a job that I had a maybe 1% chance of getting.

The bad news was that the mere act of opening up my spreadsheet made me nauseous. When I opened up the JIL (Job Information List), my heart jolted painfully in my chest, and when I actually got to the Russian listings, cold sweat was trickling down my sides. By the time I had finished entering all the listings I'd found in the JIL, the AATSEEL job listings, HERC, and SEELANGs, a tight band of pain was wrapped around my head. And I only had half a dozen possible jobs. None of them were for Crimson. That job ad hadn't shown up yet.

It will be okay! It will work out. Maybe the Crimson ad will show up soon, and you'll apply for it, and everyone will be blown away by your awesomeness, and you'll get the job. Or maybe this thing with the FBI will work out. Or maybe some third, fabulous, opportunity will show up. Or maybe you'll go chuck this in and become a landscape gardener. In any case, you'll have some kind of a job.

I found myself idly researching salaries for landscape gardeners. They topped out at $35,000 a year. Okay. Maybe that wasn't such a great idea. I looked up "administrative assistant." That was a little better, but not much. And I would probably be a terrible administrative assistant, anyway. I couldn't tolerate being in an office for more than a couple of hours at a stretch. I looked up "daycare assistant." I was a nurturing person who was good with younger people. Maybe this could be my new future. Jesus Christ. $22,000 a year for the top earners. Maybe not. Maybe I needed to stick with the thing that I'd spent years and years getting the highest possible level of qualification for.

My phone *pinged*. Dima. My heart jolted in my chest again.

I hinted at you a bit in the article, but of course that's not where I'm getting most of my information, don't worry)) I have other sources))) But you really should consider leaving that place.

I need the work, I texted back.

Find other work, he advised.

What if I can't?

What do you mean, what if you can't? You're smart, you're hardworking, AND you have a doctorate. The world should be in the palm of your hand!

But it's not, I wrote. *And—I feel terrible even saying this—but I'm scared. I'm scared about this story. I'm scared that it's going to get us both into really big trouble.*

Being scared is the sign that it's a good story)))))

I know. I don't know what's wrong with me. I just don't have a lot of courage left in me, I think.

The next text took a long time to come through. When it did, I could almost feel the outrage vibrating across the ether. *Are you asking me to quit? To abandon this story?*

No, I wrote. *I would never do that. But I am scared. It seems like I've used up all my reserves of bravery. I've never lacked the courage of my convictions, you know that, but...it feels like it's getting awfully thin and fragile.*

There was another long pause between texts. *Mama says the same*, he finally wrote. *She also isn't asking me to stop, but she says the same. And Polya has hinted at it too.*

Are you still seeing Polya, then? Polya was a young woman—practically a *baby*, at *least* ten years younger than us, I sometimes found myself thinking snidely—whose family had emigrated to Canada from the former USSR when she had been a child. She had gone to Ukraine after college to "find herself," or some such thing. The main thing she'd found, as far as I could tell, was Dima. And Dima had let himself be found. He'd mentioned several times that he was considering marrying her in order to get Canadian visas for himself and Galina Ivanovna. But I hadn't heard her name for the past month at least, and I'd somehow assumed that he and she were no longer an item. He'd certainly given me reason to make that assumption.

I don't know, he texted. *But she still seems interested, and I might need that Canadian visa.*

Is this how you show the courage of your convictions? By marrying an impressionable young woman for her citizenship? I wrote that text. Then I erased it. Then I re-wrote it. Then I erased it again. I thought about how Dima could see the three dots showing that I was writing and erasing things, so I'd better send him something.

You have to act as you see fit, I wrote.

Inna. I know you wanted to say more. You were writing and writing))))

You're right. I did want to say more. I wanted to say that I don't think it's right to use her like this. Marry her without love.

Maybe I do love her, in a way.

In that case, I wrote, *you should marry her as soon as possible.* I almost added *if you can—you never could bring yourself to get married before*. But I stopped myself just in time. Some things were better left unsaid.

32

I SPENT THE REST OF the afternoon in a funk. It was not improved by my attempts at my at-home PT regimen, which caused ominous sharp pains in my injured knee that didn't go away after I stopped the exercises. I had brought this up with my therapist, and she had told me to push through the pain. But I was doubting more and more in the wisdom of that advice.

I was still in a funk when I headed off to campus the next morning. The students made me feel slightly better, especially since they seemed to have forgotten all about Dima's article. The fact that I escaped without running into Karen made me feel much better. She still hadn't emailed me about setting up an observation. I suspected she was feeling overwhelmed by the enormity of the task she had set herself, and was shirking her own self-imposed busywork.

Chloe, who was not shirking her own work, self-imposed or otherwise, came up to me after my second class and suggested that she, Mel, and I get together on Thursday to hammer out a research plan for the rest of the semester.

"Best to get a jump on it now," she said. "Otherwise we'll keep putting it off and putting it off, and before we know it, it'll be December and we'll have lost another semester."

"True," I agreed. I was a lot less enthused about research than Chloe. Of course, Chloe had a tenure-track job, so research was more important for her to avoid termination. She also, she had admitted to me once, preferred research to teaching in any case. I strongly preferred teaching to research. Teaching brought a lot of stress and headaches, but it also brought a lot of rewards, many of which were immediate.

Research, on the other hand, mainly just brought tedium, criticism, and abuse. Creating teaching materials or writing a lesson plan felt like you were doing good in the world, and oftentimes the students expressed appreciation for what you'd done. With research, you spent hour upon painful hour writing something that would only ever be read by a handful of people, most of whom who would respond by telling you how wrongheaded, uneducated, and possibly terminally stupid you were. There was little wonder, I often thought, that scholars had such a hard time getting any writing done. We had carefully set up a system designed to disincentivize it as much as possible.

Left to my own devices, I tended to slack dreadfully in the research department. I preferred to engage in "productive procrastination," where I created lots of worthy-looking handouts, spreadsheets, and other seemingly useful items. Their utility was mainly in preventing me from doing my most important work.

When I said as much to Chloe, she said, "Oh, everyone's that way! That's why it's so important to have an accountability group. So what do you say? Shall we get together tomorrow? Maybe first thing in the morning so we don't put it off? At my house?"

Accordingly, Mel and I found ourselves driving to Chloe's house at 8:55 the next morning. Chloe lived in a modest suburban neighborhood on the other side of town from us. She had actually bought her own house. It was a single-story Cape Cod of less than 1,000 square feet with a postage-stamp sized yard and minimal landscaping, but it was still more than either Mel or I could currently dream of, so it seemed like an astounding feat to us.

Inside, I noted, there were still cardboard boxes lined up against the wall, awaiting unpacking. Chloe clearly took the same approach to unpacking that I did, which was that it was mainly a waste of time. Better to leave everything boxed up, in order to make the next move easier. As a bonus, once you realized you didn't actually need those things you'd been hauling so laboriously from place to place, you could toss the entire box without having to do any extra sorting.

Chloe had tea and coffee sitting out waiting for us, along with a plate of cookies.

"I thought we might need the energy," she said. "And if it's already prepared, we won't have an excuse to stop working."

"Good thinking," said Mel.

"And I really...I don't know...I'm having such a hard time focusing today...I need all the help I can get."

"The first week of the semester can be tough," said Mel. "Good on you for holding a research meeting even so."

"Yeah...it's not just that...it's...it's so stupid...I'm embarrassed even to bring it up, but it's just *eating* at me...do either of you ever follow your exes on social media?"

Mel and I both instinctively sucked in our breath. "Sort of," I said. "Fuck yeah," said Mel. "Much as I hate to admit it."

"I know...me too...and I guess it's all my fault...but there was this guy I was absolutely head over heels for in grad school for a while...and he seemed pretty interested in me, too, and I guess we kind of went out for a little while, but then he called it off, said we were going through a complicated phase in our lives and he wanted to be 'just friends.'"

"Uh-huuuuuuh," said Mel.

"So we've kind of kept in touch ever since then, mainly on social media. And lately...I hate myself for even talking about it...he's been posting lots of pictures of him with some girl."

"Uh-huh," Mel and I said together.

"And I always knew it would hurt like heck when he started seeing someone publicly and I had to witness their relationship. I kept imagining her as being incredibly glamorous and successful, and how much that would hurt. But...the reality is very different."

"Mmmmm-hmmmm," Mel and I said together.

"Because she's *not* glamorous or successful. She's...it's so awful...I've kind of stalked her a little, I guess you could say, on her own social media pages, and she...she reminds me a lot of myself. Only...and this is the part that's killing me...she's *less* glamorous and successful than me. Isn't it awful that I'm even thinking that? But the first time I saw her, I thought, 'Wait, what? *Her?* How? She's just a, a, I guess I want to say *less accomplished* version of me.' Isn't that terrible? I'm a terrible person even for thinking it."

"Not if it's true," said Mel. "You got any pictures of her you can show us?"

"Yes...I guess we're not doing any research-related work, are we?"

"Whatever," said Mel. "No way are we going to be able to focus on anything until you show us a picture of her and tell us all about her."

"I guess...anyway, here they are together."

Chloe pulled up Instagram on her phone and showed us a post. It had a picture of an extremely handsome man with warm brown skin, large bright eyes, high sharp cheekbones, a head that had probably been shaved by the best barber in town, and a suit that looked like it cost more than my whole wardrobe. He was sitting at a table at an outdoor cafe and looking at a woman sitting across from him. She gazed back at him with the look of a woman gazing upon her god made flesh.

"Yeah, I see what you mean," said Mel. "She does look kinda like you, only...plumper."

Chloe had been on the "pleasantly plump" side of things, although she had mysteriously started losing weight here at Crimson, and was now flirting with slightly alarming thinness. The girl in the picture could only be called curvaceous in the extreme. Less kind people would straight up call her fat. She had skin that was the same light brown as Chloe's but less clear and luminous, straightened hair that was slightly less competently cut and styled than Chloe's, and eyes that held all of Chloe's low self-esteem and very little of her intelligence. Her full lips were slightly parted in what appeared to be breathless adoration.

"It's the caption that really gets to me," Chloe said.

Mel and I leaned in close to read the caption. It said *Three months today with this amazing woman! The bravest, smartest, most knowledgeable person I know! Congratulations on starting your MEd program, babe! I couldn't be more proud of you.*

Mel made faint retching noises.

"I know, right?" said Chloe. "And, I mean, I know it makes me a horrible snob and probably an all-around horrible person to even think it, but, I mean...he keeps going on and on about how smart and educated she is, and, well..."

"She's about to *start* a Master's in Education," Mel finished for her.

"It's terrible that I'm even thinking that, right?" said Chloe. "But..."

"But," I agreed.

"He was working on his Master's when we were...whatever we were," Chloe said. "He kept saying it didn't bother him that I was getting a PhD and he was only getting an MBA, but...I guess it did. So now he's found someone who's behind him, academically."

"Uh-huh," I said.

"*And* she's shorter than me!"

Mel emitted an involuntary snort. "Sorry," she said when we both looked at her. "It's just that I kinda did the same thing as you, and it looks like my ex has hooked up with someone who's almost the spitting image of me in every way, right down to being ex-military, but she's six inches shorter and is finishing up her Associate's degree at a community college. I thought only men pulled that kind of shit, but I guess lesbians can too."

"Yeah," I said. "Alex chose someone who's enough like to me to be my sister, except she's six inches and two degrees shorter. On the plus side, she's got a drug habit and another man, though. And Dima..." I swallowed, and then forced myself to continue, "Dima has apparently been seeing some girl who's ten years our junior and, of course, also has a lot less college. From what I've heard about her, she kind of reminds me of myself when he and I first met."

"She's just so *basic,*" said Chloe, still staring at the picture on her phone. "I mean, I know I shouldn't be judging her like that, and she could have this amazing inner life that I know nothing about, but..."

"In my experience, people's inner lives often shine through unstoppably, even in Instagram photos," I said. "A lot of times, when people look boring or basic, it's because they are."

"Yeah...that's just so mean..."

"Oh, whatever," said Mel. "Sometimes you gotta be mean. And the mean thing I'm gonna say right now is that this guy, for all that's he's damn fine, chose the Lite version of you instead of the real deal for a reason. If that's the kind of woman he wants, you're better off without him."

"I guess...I just...I was totally head-over-heels for him, like I said, I thought he was my soul mate, and...I don't know if I can face spending years and years being single, and seeing this, hearing what you two just said...it makes me feel like it's my fault, you know what I mean? Like, it just shows that most men don't want women like me."

"Sometimes I think women want men they can admire, but men want women they can despise," I said.

"Fuck yeah," said Mel. "Although I don't know where that leaves me. But if you want my take, you straight women need to spend less time blaming yourselves for being single, and more time blaming misogyny, male entitlement, and late-stage capitalism. For us lesbians, you can take out the male entitlement, but other than that it's basically the same. Either way, you gotta stop sitting around feeling sorry for yourself, and get back out there."

Chloe groaned. "But I'm such a...I don't know what when it comes to that kind of thing. I thought I knew lots about human nature because of all the reading I'd done, but a lot of that reading had prepared me for how to deal with some rich but arrogant man from the North of England declaring his undying passion for me. There was nothing about what to do about men who can't be bothered with you because they'd rather watch hentai porn. Ick! I hate that I know what that is now. I feel dirty just thinking about it.

"I did try online dating for a while, and talking to men on dating apps and social media is either like a hostile job interview, or they demand an in-depth qualitative and quantitative analysis of your pubic hair. And lots of talk about hentai and trans porn, like I said." She shuddered. "Either way, all they care about is what you can do for them. I just don't think I can face that right now. I feel like I get that too much at work already."

"Yeah," I said. "I just heard a theory that adjunctification is like hook-up culture—everyone is there to be used, everyone is disposable. It rang too depressingly true. But I need a job, and I really want a family, so I guess I have to put up with it. I just feel like either way, my best impulses are being used."

"I know what you mean," said Mel. "Sometimes...you're gonna laugh, but it's true...I doubt my own sexuality. I mean, I like women, don't get me wrong. But how much of my rejection of men is because I sensed from an early age that everyone around me was constantly trying to use my sexuality and reproductive abilities and shit to control me and use me. The only thing worse than not being married and having kids would be being married and having kids and knowing that the people you loved most in the world were using that love to use you."

"This is probably the most depressing conversation I've ever had," Chloe said.

"Yeah, but you're smiling a little now, aren't you?" said Mel. "So it can't have been all bad."

Chloe sighed. "It *did* make me laugh. And I'm glad I'm not the only person who had those horrible thoughts about that girl. *And* now research is sounding a lot more palatable."

It was true. All of a sudden, scholarly research had gained a freshness and attractiveness it had never held for me hitherto. I sat down at my laptop and began working on an article with astonishing zeal.

33

FOR THE NEXT WEEK, things went surprisingly smoothly, given that it was the beginning of the semester. I held my classes, which went well, and did my PT exercises for my knee, which hurt more and more. When I brought this up at my next appointment, I was told that this was normal and I needed to keep pushing through the pain. My doubts were growing by the day, but I decided to give it another week or two.

Madison texted me a couple of times to tell me that she was having a great time in New York and that she had successfully taken the train down to New Jersey to attend class. It was, she said, a real adventure and made her feel a new sense of courage and purpose. Until she'd gotten on that bus to Georgia, she'd never traveled by herself. But now she was spending hours every week traveling around by subway, bus, and train, completely on her own. Not only that, but Cybil had sent her on several grocery runs. This, too, was a new and heady experience for her. She didn't use the word "empowering," but it seemed like it might be appropriate.

After that first, frightening phone call from the FBI, she had been left in peace. She had spent several days in terror of being called up by her mom and accused of treachery and betrayal, but so far nothing like that had happened. In fact, her mom hadn't spoken to her at all, which she said was an improvement. Maybe, she said, it would all blow over into nothing, or whatever bad thing her family had been planning would be stopped at the source, and no one would ever have to know about our involvement in thwarting it.

Could be! I texted encouragingly. After that, I stopped hearing from her.

I had also stopped hearing from Dima. That could be normal. He often went for long periods in complete radio silence, until it suddenly became convenient for him to talk to me. I was aware of this negative trait of his. I thought I had made my peace with it long ago. Now I was questioning whether it was a serious character flaw rather than an annoying little tic.

I was also questioning whether he was giving me the silent treatment because of our last conversation. I decided that was for him to deal with. I was going to live my life, and he could figure out how he wanted to fit into it. Yeah, right.

All of these comforting inspirational pep-talks came to a crashing halt when Karen emailed me Thursday afternoon, telling me she wanted to hold her first observation of my teaching Friday morning.

I'd be happy to have you come observe my class tomorrow morning, I wrote. *Which one?*

That entailed some confusion, but by supper time that night, it was agreed that she would come to my 9:00am class, and then meet with me promptly at 11:00 for a thorough review of everything she'd observed.

Sounds great! I wrote. *Looking forward to it!*

It was probably only my imagination that the words were smoking slightly from the pungency of that lie.

34

THE NEXT MORNING, FRIDAY, September 2nd, I hobbled into my first class on my crutches at 8:50am. I had decided to show up a little early just in case. That meant I had to sit and stew for an extra few minutes before class started.

Miranda, as usual, was the first one to arrive. "Hey, Professor Halley!" she said brightly. "What are we doing today?"

"Reviewing first-conjugation verbs," I told her. "And it looks like we'll have a guest today."

She brightened even more. "Like, that journalist friend you told me about? Or someone else cool?"

"Well..." I said. "Not exactly. I'm, ah, hosting a teaching observation this morning." When I said it like that, it didn't sound so awful. I wasn't sure how aware the students were of the various performance-enhancing protocols we were supposed to go through. Maybe they thought teaching observations were there to observe particularly stellar examples of teaching excellence.

"Oh." Miranda's face unbrightened. "Oh...wait. It's not going to be *her*, is it? Professor Dupont?"

"Yep," I said.

Miranda and Karen had a history. A history of mutual antagonism and contempt. Karen thought Miranda was an inveterate troublemaker who should be oppressed as much as possible, or possibly expelled. Miranda thought Karen was an asshole. Miranda, I felt, was the better judge of human nature.

"I guess we should be on our best behavior, then, huh?"

"Yep," I said.

Miranda set her mouth in a grim line, nodded once, like a woman about to perform an unpleasant but necessary task, and sidled around the too-big table to her usual seat by the board.

Jackson, slurping loudly on a large iced coffee, came in next, followed closely by Jessica and Isobel.

"Professor!" Jessica called from across the room. "I think there was a mistake in the quiz!"

Karen had always shown up late to observations before. Today she stepped into the classroom at 8:58am, just as Jessica's words filled the too-small space. Something like a sour smile crossed Karen's saggy mouth.

"Show me," I said to Jessica. I hoped I managed to suppress any kind of nervous glance in Karen's direction as I did so.

Jessica flourished our first quiz at me and started talking in an excited mixture of English, Mandarin, and Russian about how I had marked her prepositional case ending wrong for *aeroport.*

"Oh, well, if you remember, *aeroport* is part of that small class of masculine nouns that takes a stressed *-u* ending for the prepositional after *v* or *na*," I said.

Jessica made a face almost as sour as Karen's, and went on a diatribe about Russian case endings. Jessica was one of our Chinese foreign students, whom the university was recruiting more and more to help pay the bills. She was one of those straight-A students who argues over every tiny point off. Normally I appreciated her zeal. Today, though, she seemed determined to argue extra-hard, even though I was clearly right and could point to the exact chart in the textbook to prove it. I could see Karen watching the whole exchange with what looked like delighted *schadenfreude.*

By the time I got Jessica mollified and everyone in their seats and ready to work on first-conjugation verbs, it was 9:03. I saw Karen make an emphatic note on her notepad. Her pen made a spine-crinkling little *scritch scritch* with every stroke. Agh. I wanted to stop everything and point out that I had been in the classroom, talking to a student about a class topic, at 9:00am exactly. Would it do any good? It would not. I pressed on.

The students tried. They tried very hard. These were my second-year kids, who'd been through a trying couple of semesters with me, including hiding behind this very table from an active shooter. I had to assume most of them liked me, or at least we had trauma-bonded to an extremely high degree. But Karen's sour smile and the *scritch scritch* of her pen would have distracted a Zen monk.

Jackson, who was the poor unfortunate seated next to her, could hardly manage to look at the board. He alternated between sucking coffee loudly through his straw, rattling his ice, eyeing Karen nervously, and—it seemed to me—trying to read her notes when she wasn't looking. His face, I thought, was turning redder and redder with each sentence.

At 8:27 she caught him at it and tried to shift her body to shield her notes from his gaze. But she kept getting distracted and letting the notepad rest uncovered on the table, allowing Jackson another peek at it. Something he saw made a spasm of rage cross his face.

Oh God, I thought. *Is this going to go on my official performance review? Yes, yes, it is. That way, she can either take credit for improving my previously subpar performance, or justify terminating me.*

I set the students to working on a pair exercise. Jackson partnered up with Isobel, turning his back on Karen.

Good, I thought. *At least he'll get a few minutes of actual learning in today.*

Jackson and Isobel began working through the exercise together. Karen said something to them, too low for me to make out. Jackson gave a curt nod and turned away from her. Karen said something again, pointing to Jackson's large take-out cup of iced coffee. Something about the ring of condensation it was leaving on the table, I thought, and how that was interfering with Karen's ability to take notes.

Jackson stopped talking to Isobel, turned, and looked at Karen. His eyes flickered up towards me. Something in them alarmed me. They were too...resolute.

"Jackson!" I called. "Why don't you come over..."

"Sure," he said, apparently speaking to both me and Karen. "Just let me move my drink real quick."

He picked it up. The slippery plastic slid through his fingers, which caught the lid on its way down, tearing it off as the bottom of the cup hit the table. A wave of coffee, cream, syrup, and half-melted ice sloshed over the side and onto Karen's notepad.

She emitted an incoherent shriek of horror and grabbed at it. Her right hand connected with the cup, which was balancing precariously on the edge of the table, and swept it right off the table and into her lap, drenching her with a good pint of sticky, icy liquid.

Everyone gasped in shock. Karen shrieked again.

"Gosh, I'm *so sorry*," said Jackson. "Here, let me help you clean that up. I've got a pack of tissues on me somewhere."

He reached into his backpack. Instead of tissues, though, what he pulled out was a half-eaten pack of peanut butter crackers, which somehow flew out of their cellophane and straight onto the icy pool of coffee rapidly spreading across Karen's skirt and blouse.

Karen shrieked again, trying desperately to brush the melting ice and crumbs off her clothes, and rescue her notepad.

"Let me get that," said Jackson. He grabbed the notepad and ripped off the top several pages. "That should save the rest of it," he said, crumpling up the sodden pages into a ball and tossing it into the trash.

"Ah...ah...ah..." Karen was making strange little gasps. She looked around the room. Ten pairs of delighted eyes were fixed on her, and ten mouths struggled to contain their laughter.

"I'd...I'd...thank you...I'd better...I'd better go get cleaned up...Rowena, I'll see you later...yes, after I get cleaned up...I'd better..." She stood up, dumping ice and crackers all over the floor. She stood there for a moment staring at the mess in stunned perplexity. Then she threw back her shoulders and did her best to march out of the room with dignity.

It was badly spoiled by the trail of crumbs and coffee-colored water that dribbled behind her.

35

THE LAUGHTER THAT BROKE out after she left the room was long, raucous, and loud.

"Let's not laugh about it," I said, doing my best to give the students a disapproving look. "She can probably hear us." I remembered leaving the room after the impromptu campus interview at Carmel College last semester, and hearing the committee's laughter trailing me down the corridor. I'd never found out whether they'd been laughing at me or at something else. Either way, the memory still haunted me.

"She deserved it, Prof!" said Jackson. He was grinning broadly. So were all the others. Even Jessica was smiling in delight.

"That was real smooth," Miranda told him. "I've never seen such a good accidentally-on-purpose accident."

"My brother and I used to do that kind of stuff all the time," Jackson said. "We got real good at it. First time I've ever used it in a, like, real-world application, though. Whaddya think? Do I deserve an Oscar? Best actor in a revenge role? Best accidental special effects?"

"For sure," said Miranda.

"I think we're out of time," I said. "Jackson, would you mind cleaning up the mess?"

"No problem, Prof!"

During the break between classes he and Isobel cleaned up the spilled ice and coffee with a cheery efficiency that was only slightly marred by their frequent outbreaks of snorts and giggles. I said nothing. I didn't know what to say. I 100% agreed that Karen deserved it, and had done everything she could to bring it down upon herself. And Jackson had indeed been remarkably dexterous and clever, and I couldn't help but admire that. On the other hand, I couldn't condone that kind of thing. And I found myself feeling sorrier and sorrier for her.

The second class came in as Jackson and Isobel were dumping their sodden paper towels into the trash. Jackson told them he had "accidentally"—he waggled his eyebrows as he said it—knocked over his iced coffee, dumping it into Professor Dupont's lap. The second class appreciated this story almost as much as the first class. Karen, it seemed, was unpopular with students all over Crimson.

No spectacular accidents happened during the second class, but the aura of the coffee incident made it impossible for anyone to focus. It was a relief to dismiss the students. Or it would have been if it hadn't meant going and facing Karen.

She was sitting in her corner office with the door mostly closed. Her voice was subdued when she invited me to come in.

Her desk, which as usual was piled high with several geological strata of old tests and papers, scraps of notepaper, cough drop wrappers, and random bits of detritus, hid the lower half of her body, but I could see half-dried splash marks all over her blouse.

"Um..." I said. "Are you okay?"

"What?" She had been looking at a framed photograph. She placed it facedown on a precarious pile of what looked like old gradebooks, and focused on me. "Yes, I'm fine, of course, although, I have to say, Rowena, this incident only goes to show how unruly and disruptive your classes are."

"Mmmmm," I said.

"Although, to be fair, that student—Jackson; is that his name?—has a reputation for making trouble. I suppose you can't be held completely responsible for his behavior. Still, we *must* come up with a plan to bring him under control."

"Mmmmmm," I said again. As usual when dealing with Karen's "feedback," I felt like I was being targeted by a rape-y pickup artist in a sleazy bar, who was convinced that the way to my heart was by putting me down so that I would fall all over myself letting him help me back up—although not, of course, all the way up to his level.

"My notes were *ruined* during the, ah, *incident*, but fortunately I still remember many of the main points. Let me see...well, first of all, there's the fact that you were *late* starting class..."

Karen went through a litany of my supposed failings, beginning with starting class late, progressing to my teacher-centered mode of lecturing on grammatical points, dwelling on my use of English for explanations, touching upon my use of handwritten Russian on the board, which some of the students had had a hard time reading, and ending with my overly student-centered exercises in the latter half of the class.

"Uh-huh," I said. My sense of being targeted by a rape-y pickup artist increased. Everything I had done was bog-standard, super solid pedagogy for Russian. It wasn't that we didn't try new things, but a lot of the faddish approaches championed by Romance language instructors kept turning out to be failures when it came to Russian. Grammar had to be explained, and it had to be explained in English, and then the students had to be given a certain amount of time to mess around on their own and work through practice exercises. It was also helpful to expose them to handwritten cursive on a regular basis, and let them puzzle through it. Sometimes you could do fun things with authentic materials, but anything too complicated became an exercise in frustration rather than anything constructive.

But that left the overseers with little to do, so we had to pretend it wasn't true.

"And so I need a written response from *you*, Rowena, by next week—let's say Monday, shall we? No point in letting it sit around and go stale; better to work on it while this is all still *fresh*—so send me a written report by Monday on all these points and how you intend to implement an action plan for improvement. And then we'll hold a follow-up observation...let's see...in a month? Although this time I think I should observe your other class."

"Um," I said. I thought about asking how she would know if I'd followed up on my action plan if she observed a different class. Then I decided it was better for everyone if she stayed as far away from Miranda and Jackson as possible. "Sure, that sounds good," I said. "Just let me know when you want to come by."

"Yes...yes...let me look at my calendar for next month." Rather than turning to her computer, she began shuffling through the piles of paper on her desk. She moved the picture off the gradebooks in order to get at something under them, turning it over so that it was now face up. Without consciously meaning to, I looked.

The photo showed a vibrantly beautiful young woman, with a wild tangle of auburn curls caught in the wind and a look of exultant triumph on her face, standing with one fist raised and the other hand holding up a sign that said **TAKE BACK THE NIGHT: NEVER LET THE BASTARDS BREAK YOU**. Standing with one arm around her was an equally vibrant woman with an even wilder afro and a sign that read **BLACK FEMINIST POWER.** Other women were caught in mid-movement in the background, the camera preserving their purposeful, joyful strides long after the event and the women themselves had been forgotten.

I must have been staring at the photo too obviously. "You know, Rowena, you're not the only academic who can be pretty," Karen said. "I was quite the looker back in my day, too. I guess this is what time does to us all. It'll happen to you one day too, and sooner than you think." Her tone started off full of anticipatory *schadenfreude*, but by the time she got the end, it had changed, seemingly against her will, to regretful sadness.

I tried not to do too obvious a double take. It was astonishing, and more than that, it was horrifying, to think that this repulsive toad-woman in front of me had once been that gloriously happy and alive young woman, her face alight with purpose, her auburn curls streaming in the wind. The physical transformation was shocking enough, but even worse was the mental one. To think that Karen had once been so full of passion and purpose! To think that she had once wanted so openly and obviously to make the world a better place! To think that everything in that picture had been made into a lie, and the bastards *had* broken her, and remade her in their own image.

"Was that when you were in undergrad?" I said. It was the first thing I could think of that didn't involve howls of outrage and horror.

"First year of grad school," she said. Her expression and her voice were still bittersweet. "Delilah and I—such a beautiful name, Delilah, don't you think?—the woman standing next to me, we formed a chapter of Campus Feminists and started holding events. I don't know what we did right, but for that first year, people kept showing up, everyone kept telling us what a great thing we were doing. Then...then they started telling us we needed to focus on our scholarship instead of wasting our time on stuff like that. Delilah said that since she was planning to focus on black queer feminist studies, activism *was* part of her scholarship. They washed her out during her comps, told her she wasn't focused and committed enough. I lost track of her soon after that—once you leave academia, it's like you die for all your friends still in it. So...she went up for her comps ahead of me—she was always so smart, so over-prepared for everything—and so I saw what happened to her, and I said it wasn't going to happen to me. I said I wasn't going to give them any reason to wash me out. And I didn't. And...here I am."

"Oh," I said.

"Ah, there we are." Karen pulled a desk calendar, marked with numerous coffee-cup rings, out from under the gradebooks, releasing a large cloud of dust and cough drop wrappers. We both broke into a sneezing fit, which in Karen's case morphed into desperate coughing. She fished a half-empty bottle of water out from under another pile of papers, releasing another cloud of dust, and tried to drink from it, but that only made her choke so badly I started to wonder if I needed to attempt a Heimlich.

"Let's see..." she gasped, once she could talk again. "We're looking at October...I have that retreat...and then it's fall break...and then I'll be conducting oral midterms for my own class and I won't have time for anything else...and now we're in November...and I've got that conference...we're looking at November now, Rowena. The week of Thanksgiving. Let's make it that Tuesday. I *assume* you won't be leaving early?"

"No," I said. "Tuesday of Thanksgiving week sounds great."

36

AFTER THAT I WENT STRAIGHT home. I wanted to go for a run, but I couldn't. So I wrote up lesson plans for my classes on Monday, feeling doubt and confusion rise up higher and higher until they threatened to smother me. I was as sure as I could be that my teaching was about as good as it could be, or, at least, that Karen's suggestions would not improve it.

But as was often the case, receiving any kind of feedback, even feedback that was patently moronic and should be tossed off the steamship of pedagogy without a second thought, had left me confused and demoralized to the point of paralysis. If good teaching was measured by student satisfaction and high learning outcomes, then my best teaching was done when I was left strictly to my own devices. The more people tried to "mentor" and "guide" me, the worse my performance became.

And Karen's story had been so awful. Especially on top of her humiliation this morning. Once again, I couldn't help but agree that she had brought it upon herself, and thoroughly deserved it. If Jackson truly had done it on purpose, I could only sympathize with him, and feel that justice had been served.

But that didn't make Karen's unhappiness and embarrassment, no matter how richly deserved, any less. And her warning that "It will happen to you too, and sooner than you think it will" kept reverberating inside my head, like the ringing from a blocked eardrum that just won't go away. I wasn't so worried about my physical appearance. I knew that we all changed, and one day, providing I didn't get brutally gunned down or something in the meantime, my figure would change and my hair would turn gray and the lines on my face would be visible even in deep twilight. I accepted that, at least as much as anyone could accept that.

What I couldn't accept was that I might someday end up like Karen on the inside. She had once been happy. She had once been *good.* And now she was a force for misery in the world.

I figured you had to be ***bad*** *somewhere deep down.* Frank's parting words joined Karen's spiteful warning in the echoes inside my head. I had tried to shake it off then, just as I wanted to shake off Karen's words too. But I couldn't shake it off completely. There was a grain of truth in what they both had said, a truth that my friends would never admit to, but that my enemies, or at least my non-friends, had apparently seen straight to.

My phone *pinged.* I looked at it, glad for the distraction. It was a message from Madison.

Hey, Professor H! Hope you're doing okay. I wanted to send you something. This is what my cousins and my mom are up to. What do you think? Am I just being crazy? My mom says it's all the drugs I've taken that are messing with me. But I can't stop worrying about it. I saw her post about this yesterday, and it's been eating at me ever since, so I broke down and thought I'd ask you.

The message included a link to a website for Glorious Future. Feeling some trepidation, but deciding it would still be better than sitting with my morbid thoughts, I clicked on it.

37

THE WEBSITE HAD PICTURES of broadly smiling blond children playing soccer, doing handicrafts, and—there in the corner—dressed in camo and carrying guns. Two of them were holding what I thought were hunting rifles. One was holding what I was pretty sure was an AK-47. Just what everyone needed for a happy and wholesome childhood.

There was a link in the menu to a series of blog posts. The most recent post was in English, by a Brenda Melnichuk. Madison's mother, I guessed. Melnichuk, if I remembered correctly, was a Western Ukrainian name. It was the equivalent of "Miller" or "Millerson." There were about a bazillion of them all over the former USSR.

I started to read.

Raising Our Youth Right!

So many of us mothers know this heartbreak all too well: we give our children everything, lavish them with all our care, attention, and affection, try to set them up on the path to a good life, and what happens? They reject all our efforts!

When this happens it's easy to blame our children. Why won't they listen to us? Or we can blame ourselves. If only we could find the right way to reach them! We just haven't figured it out yet.

But in fact in most of these cases there are other forces at work that tear our children away from us and turn them against us. We've talked a lot here about the dangers of modern woke culture being force fed to our children in schools all over the world. Our children are being taught to love foreigners and hate their own countries and their own people, deny they were born a boy or a girl, and turn against their own families. Sometimes it seems like there's nowhere in America left where we can keep our children safe and raise them the right way.

That's why I was so glad to connect with my cousins during my trip to Ukraine last year. We had lots of long conversations about lots of interesting things. One of the main things we found out was that we share a lot of the same concerns. All of us see that our children are under constant threat of being taken away from us, by social services serving the Big State or by ideologies that want to turn our children into druggies and hate filled zombies.

I was very excited to find out that my family in Ukraine has already found a solution to this problem! By providing children and teenagers with a supportive atmosphere full of healthy activities that help grow their natural love for their families and their people, they've managed to stop the slide into self hatred, drug addiction and sexual impurity.

Through Glorious Future they've started a training camp for young people that helps steer them onto the right path. Young people work one on one or in small groups with adults who mentor them. At the Glorious Future camp, many of these mentors have already proved themselves under fire by bravely defending their homeland against the Eastern terrorists as part of the Anti-Terrorist Operation. This naturally makes a big impression on young people, especially teenage boys! Teenage girls also appreciate it too. The admiration they feel naturally translates into obedience and following in their mentor's footsteps.

That's why I'm very excited to announce a partnership between Glorious Future and the organization I founded with my good friend Carrie Ostermayer, Bright Dawn! At Bright Dawn we hold retreats for people wishing to get in touch with their roots and connect with other like minded individuals. I'm so excited to let everyone know that a group of mentors from Glorious Future will be joining us for a retreat this winter at the Bright Dawn retreat center. If you are interested in attending contact me directly!

Hmmm. I had to agree with Madison that it didn't look great. There wasn't a lot that was blatantly, flagrantly bad, but the whole thing could certainly be read as one giant dog whistle.

It also seemed so silly that I had a hard time believing anyone would take it seriously—but lots of people got sucked into things that I considered to be absolutely ludicrous. The attack on "woke" culture was sure to resonate with lots of people. I could even sympathize, on a certain level, although I doubted my critique of "woke" culture would align very well with theirs. My problem with woke culture was that it prioritized virtue signaling and vitriol over compassion and consensus-building. So even though I agreed with many of its basic positions, I disagreed very strongly with its tactics, in the same way that I disagreed with terrorism.

And Glorious Future, Bright Dawn, and their ilk, I was perfectly willing to believe, were either feeding into terrorist training camps, or were actual terrorist training camps themselves, under the guise of fighting terrorism. The Anti-Terrorist Operation, or ATO, was the Ukrainian name for Kiev's military campaign in the civil war/proxy war currently being fought in the Donbass. Declaring it an operation against terrorism rather than a war garnered lots of US support and, as I understood it, put it on a different legal footing than an actual war. And while some of the people doing the fighting were motivated by simple patriotism or self-defense, others were actively furthering a neo-Nazi agenda. This certainly looked like what Glorious Future and Bright Dawn were doing with their "retreats." Terrorist training camps for white supremacists. What could be more delightful?

I clicked on the link for the Bright Dawn retreat center. Pictures of a pleasant-looking center in the Catskills greeted me. Lots of rustic but still comfortable cabins, picnic pavilions, and glorious fall colors. I could easily imagine it being used as a gathering place for hikers, Girl Scouts, or the more peaceful sort of eco-knitting activists.

Several of the buildings had a round symbol of some kind on them. It was out of focus in all the pictures, but it looked similar to the logo of Bright Dawn. I zoomed in on the logo. It was a stylized sun symbol in a cheery yellow, with fat, almost childish-looking lines. The sun had your typical points all the way around the outside, like a sun emoji. Inside, in a faint pattern of yellow-on-yellow that was hard to distinguish, it had a central circle, with squiggly rays fanning out to a larger circle.

A *frisson* of revulsion went up the back of my neck. I opened up another browser and searched for "Nazi sun symbol." More than nine million results popped up.

I clicked on the Wikipedia page. Their examples were mainly black, with sharp, angular lines that were undeniably Fascist in their aesthetic. Bright Dawn's logo was much more reminiscent of Sesame Street than the SS in its initial appearance. But there was still no doubt in my mind that what I was looking at was a *Sonnenrad.*

38

I AGREE THAT IT'S POTENTIALLY concerning, I texted to Madison. *Have you reported it to your contact?*

What contact?

The person from the FBI who contacted you.

I guess he was from the FBI, she texted back. *Some alphabet agency, anyway.*

Well, whoever it was. Have you told him about it?

No.

After more than a minute, another text came through.

I'm scared to. What if he laughs at me and tells me it's nothing? Or what if it's something, and I get my mom in big trouble?

What if it's something, and you don't report it, and she gets herself in even bigger trouble? I wrote back.

I still think she'd never forgive me for it.

That was a fair point. This was a horrible situation for Madison to be in. I tried to think of something more morally fraught than snitching on your own mother. Off the top of my head, I couldn't come up with anything, other than maybe snitching on your own child. It was not something that was likely to be forgiven, no matter how justified.

Why don't I get in touch with my person, I wrote. *That way it'll be on me, not you.*

Thanks!

No problem, I texted. *Happy to help!* Then, ignoring the sinking feeling in my stomach, I pulled up Frank on my contacts.

He answered on the second ring. Squelching the sinking feeling in my stomach even more, I laid out the situation for him.

"I know you're probably not the person handling this, and you said you'd take it from here, but I wasn't sure what else to do," I concluded. "I didn't want to leave it unreported, in case it really is something."

"No, Ro, you did exactly right," he said. "I'll make sure it goes to the right people."

"Thanks," I said.

"Always glad to help." He sounded more sincere than I had felt when talking to Madison. He sounded more sincere than I felt 95% of the time when I said those words. The thought that Frank might be a more genuine and sincere person than me made my stomach sink even more.

"I really appreciate it." My mouth felt unpleasantly numb as I said the words. I *did* appreciate the trouble he was taking, both to help me with Madison's issue, and to be nice to me. I also sensed that I was, once again, being insincere. I didn't *want* to have to appreciate anything Frank did.

He laughed in my ear. It was the kind of low, intimate laugh that was so incredibly sexy in a man you were in love with. To my horror, I felt it breathe a little more life into the tiny, tiny spark of attraction I felt towards Frank.

"Well, maybe one of these days you'll get a chance to express your appreciation," he said. "I'm still hoping we can get you out here to the San Francisco office, Ro."

"Yeah," I said. "That would be great."

39

I TRIED TO FOCUS ON job applications. No dice. I tried to work some more on the article I'd started last week at Chloe's. Even fewer dice. I tried to do some of my PT exercises. My agitated state meant I hurt myself even more than usual.

Get a grip! I told myself. *Focus!*

But it was pointless. Between my meeting with Karen this morning, and my conversation with Frank this afternoon, I couldn't focus on anything. Anything other than my own self-doubt.

*What if the man you've been waiting for all this time is **Frank**?* That thought finally rose up from where it had been hiding, deep in the center of my subconscious, and showed itself to me.

My first impulse was a wild howl of denial. My second impulse, as was so often the case, was to examine the thought carefully, in case it had merit. I certainly had issues in the love department. My entire life, I'd been in exactly two serious relationships, both of which had ended with categorical rejection from the other person. Other than that, I'd never really had anything in that area. I'd never even been on a traditional 'date' as such. Men liked to look at me, but they rarely asked me out, and if I asked them out, they recoiled in terror. And I couldn't even complain about it without being accused of being manipulative and selfish.

Dima and Alex were both rebels, and I was pretty sure that's one of the things that had drawn us together. They'd been dead set on going against everything that society told them to do, and that included having ordinary relationships with traditional gender roles. But, it had turned out, they hadn't been able to handle any kind of meaningful relationship at all.

Frank, on the other hand, was a sexually harassing asshole. But he'd also—I hated even to think it, but it was true—believed in me in a way that neither Dima nor Alex ever had. When we'd been looking for Erin this summer, he'd called me a smartypants—but that had been his version of a compliment. He'd trusted me to go after her when all Alex had wanted to do was keep me away. I couldn't say that Frank was anyone's knight in shining armor, but he hadn't abandoned me in order to protect me when things got hard. Instead, he'd turned to me for help.

Plus, he seemed to subscribe to the idea that a man needed to be in a relationship to be living his best life. And he hadn't run from Erin, even when a person with better sense would have hightailed it in the opposite direction as fast as they could. Maybe he would have run in the end, but I also got the feeling that he wasn't the running kind.

Unlike Alex. Or Dima.

That thought seemed so terrible and disloyal that I felt dirty just thinking it. But it was *true*. Madison had had to face up to the fact that her mother was engaged in something she found morally abhorrent. I was having to face up to the fact that the men I loved hadn't lived up to my ideal of them. They hadn't been what I'd needed them to be. I'd wanted to be on a happy heroine's journey, where we all worked together to make things better for everyone. They'd seen themselves as on lonely hero's journeys, where love held them back and the only possible ending was bittersweet at best.

I'd bought into that for a long time too, but now I found myself rejecting it fiercely. Part of that was my own brand of idealism. Things *should* be good for everyone, dammit. Life didn't have to be a zero-sum game. We *should* be able to find a way to make mutually beneficial agreements.

Part of my current rejection was also my increasing understanding of just how much it would cost me to follow their path. My happiness...my self-respect...my chance at having the family I'd always wanted. I'd been bringing it up with Dima ever since we'd gotten engaged, more than ten years ago. When it had been just a distant fantasy, he'd been excited by the idea, but when I'd actually suggested taking concrete steps to realize it, he'd been against it. Like many other people in my life, he'd told me that having children, especially when I was so young, was selfish and irresponsible. It would ruin my career, be a burden on my colleagues, friends, and family, and make me a less socially engaged person, as well as dramatically increasing my environmental footprint. On some level, I was uncomfortably aware that many of these arguments might be coming from his own selfishness and irresponsibility, but that was too upsetting a thought, so I'd always squelched it. Instead, I'd gone along and believed him when he'd said we should wait, we still had plenty of time.

But now, as I slid into the latter half of my thirties, time was growing shorter and shorter. Every time I thought about being single and childless at forty, I felt like a bird of passage trapped in a cage. An unshakeable biological imperative was coming up against iron bars. Maybe having a bunch of children was selfish and irresponsible, but what about just one? Just one wouldn't be too bad, would it? Besides, who was going to take care of me in my old age?

Some days, I found myself wondering if my principled behavior, which had made me reject the age-old ruse of getting pregnant against my male partner's wishes, had backfired on me. Sure, I might have lost Dima if I'd done that. But I'd lost him anyway, and I didn't have a child, either. Being a broke and desperate single mother held little appeal, but my current state was so lonely and unfulfilling that I was starting to wonder if the single mom thing might be worth it.

To make matters worse, I couldn't even complain about it to anyone. When men say they desperately need sex, they get sympathy, but when women say they desperately need to have a family and children, they're figures of fun.

Stop, stop, stop! My throat was actually closing up with unshed tears of self-pity. This was no good. I needed to consider my options and come up with a plan.

I considered my options in the man department. Alex seemed like a non-starter. He was way too fucked up to be counted on right now, and maybe ever. He had the basic material to be a good husband and father, but he needed to get his head on straight before he could be counted on. I didn't want to waste any more time on hoping he would pull himself together.

Dima...Dima...Dima was going to do what Dima was going to do. He had lots of good basic material too, I was sure of that, but I should know by now not to build anything with him as its foundation. Everything I'd said about Alex was true for Dima as well, but squared, or possibly cubed.

As for Frank...I reluctantly admitted to myself that of the three of them, he might actually be my best bet. I suspected that his basic material was much less good than Alex or Dima's. But I also suspected that, if I played my cards right, I would have much better luck at actually getting him to marry me and even provide me with children. Sure, I figured there was at least a 50% chance that he'd cheat on me, and a 75% chance that we'd make each other unhappy, but the woman with the ring on her finger and the charming pets and 2.1 beautiful children in her pleasant family home would be *me*.

Hmmm. That didn't sound like healthy thinking at *all*. Although it did sound like a lot of the thinking that those of us on the marriage market were supposed to do. Weren't we supposed to reject unrealistically high standards and take what we could, realistically, get? That to me sounded like more of the "warm body" fallacy that our society was currently so immured in, where everyone was fungible and all you had to do was find anyone with a pulse in order to plug them into your impersonal system. At least until the long-promised AI developments allowed us to do away with actual people entirely, and just have digital avatars.

But I had never found that people were fungible and replaceable. For me, no matter how much I might wish it weren't true, each person was unique, and the people who really, really mattered for me personally were few and far between. Realistically, I was never going to be happy with just anyone just because we had a few similar life goals. Realistically, no matter how large a gaping hole their absence was leaving in my life, the ring on my finger and 2.1 beautiful children would never be enough to make up for the misery of being with the wrong person. I'd read enough literature from the arranged-marriage, pre-divorce era to know that those kinds of relationships often ended in tragedy for the whole family. And, while I might be engaging in wild fantasies of normalcy and domesticity right now, they were, in fact, unrealistic. Realistically, I had never been able to manage normalcy. Realistically, I had been born to be extreme, one way or another, and I wasn't going to be able to change that aspect of myself, no matter how much I might want to.

Besides, I told myself more optimistically, I had more than just three options. The rise of dating apps meant that I had literally countless options. In theory, there were thousands of others at least as extreme as I was, just waiting to meet me and declare me their soul mate. In theory. In practice I was more doubtful. But it seemed like, desperate as I was, maybe I should at least look at what was out there.

I took a few deep breaths to psych myself up. My knowledge of men was deep rather than wide. Well, that was about to change.

Internet dating was probably going to be some kind of *Brothers Karamazov* dive into the pettiness of the human spirit.

I flexed my fingers. I could handle it, right? I'd faced down loads of things much scarier and darker than a bunch of dating profiles. I could do this. I *could.* It could even lead to something new and wonderful in my life.

Maybe, I thought, if I kept telling myself that, it would be true.

40

SOME INTERNET RESEARCH told me that I could pay upwards of $50 a month for some of the dating apps.

"Welcome to capitalism," I said. Apparently money *could* buy you love. Although that had always been true. Maybe my problem was a lack of money. Maybe Mel was right and I should blame myself less and misogyny and late-stage capitalism more. In fact, I was sure she was right. But since I still had to exist in a society ruled by misogyny and late-stage capitalism, I had to figure out how to optimize my results given the constraints in which I was operating.

Given those constraints, paying $50-100 a month for the chance to have my profile shown to people who might be total psychopaths, or at least hopeless dead ends, was not an option. Feeling tearful and faintly queasy, I started a profile on a free app.

It took way longer than I had been expecting, and asked a number of what I considered rather impertinent questions. I supposed this was good information to have in these kinds of situations, but it also made me wonder how many of the people were here for cheap hookups. Lots, I concluded. I went to bed wondering how many messages from sexual predators I could expect to wake up to.

To my surprise, there was only one message from an obvious hookup artist waiting for me the next morning. What there was that

I had not been expecting were five other messages from obviously fake profiles.

Grimly, I sat down and went through some profiles myself, dutifully messaging those with a match rating of 90% or higher. Boy, did this feel like work. Also, the closest person lived in Atlanta, an hour and a half away.

It's still closer than California—or Russia! I told myself. *And you can't expect instant results. Everything takes work.*

That work was so dispiriting, though, that it was actually a relief to turn to working on my first job application. I updated my CV to reflect my teaching experience over the summer and swapped out the cut-and-paste sentences in my cover letter to say exactly what particular thing at that particular institution I would be happy (at the beginning of the letter) or even delighted (at the end of the letter) to do. Then I paid the necessary fees to have my confidential letters of recommendation forwarded to the institution, and, $18 lighter, sat back with the sense of a dirty deed done well.

The rest of the afternoon dragged. After spending the summer with Alex, and then Madison's impromptu sleepover, living by myself felt lonely and boring. I had Fevronia, of course, but she only tolerated about seven minutes of contact, max, before she turned on me with a whirlwind of fangs and claws. I could no longer go running or do yoga or hapkido, and my PT exercises took less than half an hour. In theory, I had an infinite amount of work I could do on my latest article, but I couldn't bring myself to do it. Somehow, Marina Tsvetaeva's 1913 poem "Passerby who looks like me..." felt distant and unimportant right now. I mean, I knew that on the grand scale of things, it was a work of timeless significance. But right now I was having a hard time focusing on it.

The result was that I spent the last part of Saturday afternoon reading about Bright Dawn, Brenda Melnichuk's organization. It was enlightening, to say the least.

Bright Dawn had been founded five years ago as a partnership between Brenda and a woman named Carrie Ostermayer. Carrie Ostermayer, I discovered after a little digging around, was part of a wealthy New York family with ties to the Republican Party. She did not, as far as I could tell, have a job as such, but after some kind of youthful indiscretion that was hinted at in the articles but never explained straight out, she had devoted herself to philanthropical work, with at-risk youth as her primary focus. She and Brenda, who had a background in hospitality, had joined forces in 2011 to create a retreat/outdoor center for at-risk youth and their families "to reconnect with each other against the healing background of the natural beauty of the Catskill Mountains."

That all sounded lovely. It sounded so sickeningly sweet and sincere that I started to experience doubts. Maybe I was totally misreading things. Maybe Glorious Future was itself innocent, or Bright Dawn's connection with it was, and what I thought was a *sonnenrad* in the logo was pure coincidence and me seeing things that weren't there.

Maybe it was intuition that made me keep reading. Maybe it was an intense dislike of being wrong. Either way, by suppertime I had read a short statement by Brenda saying they had chosen the name Bright Dawn to signify the new beginnings for these struggling families that they aimed to nurture, and also because of the similarities with the beautiful name Golden Dawn. A little more looking told me that Golden Dawn could refer to an early twentieth-century secret society dedicated to the occult—or it could refer to a current neo-Nazi Greek political organization. There was nothing from Brenda's statement that allowed me to guess which one she meant, or if she was referring to something else entirely.

Over the next several days, when I wasn't teaching, working on job applications, or grimly "liking" men on the dating app who never liked me back and blocking the scammers who kept messaging me,

I continued reading about Brenda, Carrie, Bright Dawn, Glorious Future, and the alt-right, white supremacist, and neo-Nazi movements in North America and Europe. By the end of the week, I was convinced that Madison was absolutely right to be concerned. My main fear was that she wasn't concerned enough.

As often happened when delving into fringe movements, I was disconcerted by how much I had in common with them. I had been brought up on the fringes myself, and although I had taken a few steps towards integrating myself into mainstream society, I still saw it largely from the perspective of an outsider looking in. This meant that I often had a lot in common with people who'd grown up in the mainstream and then become disillusioned with it. I'd noticed it before with evangelical Christians and anti-vaxxers. Although I didn't share many of the fundamentals of their movements, I did share some of their critiques of modern-day America. It was a society that had lost its moral compass, with a medical system that was more concerned with turning a profit than helping people. I just disagreed with the means that those particular groups took to rectify to situation.

I had always assumed, though, that I would have absolutely nothing in common with neo-Nazi extremists. That was completely beyond the pale. But no. We both, it seemed, felt like we were living a crumbling empire careening towards dystopia. Many alt-right or neo-Nazi extremists had been radicalized by their hatred of the Iraq war or their concerns about climate change. I shared both of those feelings. I just thought that using violence to create a white ethnonation would almost certainly cause us to plunge into dystopia even faster and deeper.

In the case of Brenda, she made frequent posts on social media about the need to protect our youth from dangerous outside influences and the harmful effects of modern drug culture. Given that she was Madison's mother, I could see why she would feel that way. Her hatred of drugs had then extended out to drug dealers, whom she apparently saw as being largely black or Mexican. She kept her public statements about them fairly veiled, but I gathered that she was edging ever closer to full-on white supremacy as her rage against drugs and drug culture grew.

As for Glorious Future, it held the same position as most of the rising right-wing groups from central and Eastern Europe: they were the last bulwark against the tide of degenerate liberalism coming from Western Europe, and the barbaric, Asiatic hordes of Russia. The fact that there was an actual war with pro-Russian separatists in the Donbass only strengthened their conviction that they were the last stand of European civilization.

Their message, it seemed, had resonated with Brenda, and she had brought it back to Carrie Ostermayer, who had also found it attractive. Now Bright Dawn was pivoting to a more hardline alt-right/neo-Nazi agenda, while still packaging itself as a cheery, family-friendly nature retreat for healthy outdoor activities.

I had to admire their strategy, although I wasn't sure how conscious it was. Neo-Nazism had always been very male-dominated, as far as I knew, and had a hard time recruiting women. But Brenda and Carrie, with their unaggressive, almost childish logos and statements, were making it seem like something that women, even women who abhorred violence and macho posturing and only cared about nurturing their families, might want to get involved in.

The only thing I didn't know was how dangerous their current plans were. Maybe they were just a couple of crackpots who weren't actually going to do anything that bad, and could be left alone, like a slow-growing tumor that it would be more dangerous to remove?

It was a comforting thought. I just hoped it wasn't wishful thinking.

41

I TEXTED BACK AND FORTH a few times that month with Madison, but she only said that her mother didn't seem to know that the FBI or whoever was after her, and had even tried to effect a rapprochement.

What do you think? Madison asked. *She still makes me want to puke, but maybe this would be a good way to get some inside intel?*

That seems like an awfully dangerous thing to do, I texted back. *If you want to make up with your mom, I say go for it, because being on the outs with your mother is awful, but don't do it so you can go snooping through her business. In fact, don't go snooping through her business no matter what.*

Do you really think she's that dangerous?

You know her better than I do, I wrote. *In fact, I don't know her at all, so I can't say. It sounds to me like she herself isn't particularly dangerous. But she's playing around with people who could be *very* dangerous. Do you know yet whom she's planning to bring over this winter?*

Not yet. Just that they're all glorious fighters who've proven themselves in the fight against the Russian terrorist aggressors. She thinks they'll make great role models, lol. Also, she told me several times that they're Russian speakers, so I can practice my Russian with them. It seems pretty messed up to me, double lol!

Such people are normally very dangerous, I repeated. *You do not want to get mixed up with them. They will not be good mentors or role models. At best, they'll radicalize you into a neo-Nazi jihadist. At worst, they'll get you killed—or kill you themselves.*

I felt bad as soon as I'd sent the text, certain I'd terrify Madison, or turn her against me with my overblown rhetoric, but she only texted back, *Yeah, no shit, Sherlock. These people scared the fuck out of me when we were over there, and they scare me even more now.*

I was pleased to see this rare sign of good sense in Madison. I just wished I had some good advice to follow it up with.

What does your dad think? I asked. *Have you talked it over with him?*

He knows why I left home. I think he believes me about the whole fucked up backstory with my mom's grandpa, he just thinks it's ancient history and I shouldn't worry about it now. He thinks I'm blowing things totally out of proportion with what my mom is doing now. He's convinced she's a saint.

Oh, I texted. *Well, okay.*

Actually, he doesn't think she's a saint, Madison texted back after a moment. *I just don't think he takes her seriously enough. I think he doesn't think she's smart enough to do something like this. He's always been so sure he's the smart one, and my mom and I are the ditzy girls who need to be watched over and guided. He can't believe she'd do something like this without him, or without him figuring it out. And Aunt Cybil is the same. Things are going really well with her, by the way! She's now saying maybe I can stay for the rest of the semester. She tells me all kinds of stuff, too. She doesn't like my mom at all, but she said something about her not having the gumption for something like this. I didn't know people still used the word gumption, lol.*

Some of us do. And you don't have to be a genius to get involved in something like this, I wrote. *In fact, I'd say most people who do this kind of thing *aren't* geniuses.*

LOL! Madison texted, and added a bunch of laughter emojis. *My dad just doesn't take us seriously. He'd never believe my mom could do something like this. So I can't talk to him about it.*

Okay, I said. *Well, be careful. Stay in touch with your alphabet agency contact, but don't go taking any risks. And do NOT go snooping through your mom's stuff.*

Sure thing, Prof! Madison answered. I told myself that I believed her. Well, I had no choice. I would just have to hope that Madison had enough self-preservation to not do something supremely stupid. She had never shown much sign of it so far, but people could grow and change.

I found myself praying to St. Fevronia or anyone else who was listening that Madison was growing and changing really fast.

42

THE SECOND WEEK OF October brought some pleasantly cool fall weather, meaning it was down in the 70s. It also brought fall break. The students were making plans to hit the beach and party. We faculty were making plans to catch up on our grading and, in the case of us visiting faculty, send out more job applications. For me, that meant buckling down and formally submitting my application for the Crimson tenure-track position, now that it had finally been posted on the JIL. The materials required were surprisingly reasonable—just a cover letter, CV, one-page teaching statement, two-page research statement, two sample syllabi, one or more representative articles or book chapters, and three letters of recommendation—but I had spent the past week crashing up against a severe emotional blockage. I finally battered my way through it Thursday evening and sent the damn thing out, and then collapsed on my bed, shivering, headache-y, and sure I was sick with the flu.

By Friday morning my stress-flu had passed. This meant I had no excuse to skip a family get-together. My parents were back from their stint with Doctors Without Borders and were eager to see everyone. John had been strong-armed into taking a day off and driving down from Camp Lejeune to spend a long weekend in Macon, Georgia, with my mother's parents. I, obviously, could not get out of this either. The only thing I could be grateful for was that I would not be spending the night there. Macon was close enough that I could sleep at home and drive back and forth for dinner.

I was ashamed, and somewhat puzzled, by my dread. I generally got along quite well with my family. Even with John, and *no one* got along well with John.

I consulted my feelings. Was it because I knew there would be fireworks between John and our father, like there always were? Nah, I was used to that. Was it because I thought it likely John would drink too much and be a pain in the ass? Nah, I was used to that too. Was it because I would have to face my whole family for the first time since Alex and I had called it quits? Bullseye. I was sure they would be disappointed and upset, which meant I would have to hide my own disappointment and upset, defend Alex to them, and pretend I was just fine with how things had turned out.

I came up with several strategies and talking points on the road to Macon. For the last ten minutes of the drive, I stopped strategizing and just focused on deep breathing exercises. Once I pulled up to the house, I sat for several minutes in the car, doing more breathing exercises and telling myself I could totally do this, it was hardly the worst thing I'd ever faced.

My subconscious, most unhelpfully, told me back that it might not be the greatest physical danger I'd ever faced, but it was certainly the worst example of personal failure I'd ever had to explain to my family. I'd never gotten arrested, or even detention or, for that matter, a grade lower than an A. I'd never done drugs. I'd never had an unintended pregnancy or even an STD. I'd never flunked out of anything, or gotten fired. I'd never even gotten so much as a parking ticket. And yet here I was, failing yet again at what was possibly the most important task in life: finding a life partner. And I couldn't even take comfort in a career to compensate for it. My career had been on a toilet trajectory ever since its inception, and most successful career women credited their husbands as being a major factor in their success.

Get a grip! My grandparents were coming out of the house, faintly puzzled expressions on their faces, like they didn't understand why I hadn't come in yet. Bursting into tears and blubbering all over their shirts that I was too scared to come in and face everyone was not going to make things any better.

"Weena! There you are! We were starting to worry you'd gotten into a wreck or something." My grandmother was a slender, fine-boned woman who was, somewhat intentionally, the epitome of steel magnolia Southern womanhood.

"Just got caught up in some work stuff," I said, extracting myself from the car and putting on an extra-bright smile. Maybe if I smiled big enough, I would start to feel some actual good cheer.

"Isn't it fall break for you, sugar?"

"It is," I confirmed. "But I've got a lot to catch up on. I'm glad to be here, though."

"You say that now, but Vannie and Bobby have been going at it hammer and tongs over politics ever since they stepped into the house. I don't know what to do about those two, I swear."

Vannie was my brother. Our parents had christened us Rowena Arwen and Ivanhoe Elladan. I continued to proudly bear my original name. John had added "John" as his legal first name when he turned eighteen, and had threatened death to anyone who called him anything else. Anyone except our grandparents, who still resolutely called us Vannie and Weena. Bobby, or Robert Halley, was our father. He and John routinely got into shouting matches over politics at every opportunity. As I stepped through the front door, I could tell that today was no exception.

"You cannot be SERIOUS!" our father was shouting. "I know you've been corrupted by the Marines, but...!!!!"

"Why not?" demanded John. "Bush and Obama kept sending me to shitholes like Iraq and Afghanistan. I hate 'em both. Trump's promising to pull us out of all these places."

"You're delusional if you think he's going to deliver on his promises!" our father shouted.

"Yeah, but maybe he'll have us invading fuckin' Toronto or something instead," said John. "I could do with a change."

I retreated to the kitchen. I had tried to convince my father many times that John loved winding him up about politics, and didn't actually hold most of the political convictions he professed to espouse. In fact, I knew that he was a card-carrying Democrat: he'd shown me his party membership card. But my father, who lacked the impish sense of humor and general desire to shock the world that John possessed in such abundance, fell right into his snare every time. Interfering would only be a headache with no gain.

My mother was sitting at the kitchen island, holding a glass of iced tea to her temple. She jumped up, gave me a quick hug, and poured me another glass. I promptly held it to my temple too.

"What do you think?" she asked. "Should we go in there and break it up?"

"Nah," I said. "This is how they engage in father-son bonding."

"True, darling, true, but I don't know how much more of this I can take."

"I'll go say hi," I said. "Maybe that will distract them."

I set down my glass and went over to the living room. John was slouching in a recliner, a tumbler of what I was pretty sure was neat Scotch in his hand. Our dad was pacing the middle of the room, gesticulating.

John and I both take after our mother and our mother's father: tall, rangy, dark hair, light eyes: typical "Black Irish" features all around. Our father, by contrast, was small, almost delicate in comparison, with light hazel eyes, sandy hair mostly gone to gray, wire-framed glasses, and an air of near-manic energy. After spending his twenties as a hippy advocating for a new society based loosely on Hare Krishna principles, he'd decided to take a more hands-on approach starting in his thirties and become a social worker in inner-city Atlanta.

It was easy to see where John and I both got our commitment to serving the greater good and having the courage of your convictions. The mere thought of spending several decades as a social worker in inner-city Atlanta sent chills down my spine. John had once confessed to me, after seven pints of Guinness, that it sent chills down his spine too. Neither of us were sure we'd have the iron stomach and steel backbone for it. But our father was still going strong twenty-five years later, helping the downtrodden and desperate of Atlanta, one person at a time. Druggies and drug dealers, abusers and abuse victims; he tried to save them all, with courage, compassion, and humility. No one, it was said, could get under his skin.

Except, of course, John. Now he was running his hands through his hair, which was already standing up in tufts, and saying, "I don't know what to say to you, I don't know *what* I can say to make you see sense..."

"Hi, Dad," I said. "Don't worry about John. He's just yanking your chain, you know that." I went over and kissed his cheek. Then I went over and gave John a high five. He grinned up at me and held up his Scotch tumbler with his other hand in a sloppy salute.

"I know he *revels* in getting my goat, but you don't...I mean, you don't *really* think he has a point?" my dad asked. He pulled at a tuft of hair sticking out over his temple for emphasis.

I recognized my own self-doubt. It was nice to know where I'd gotten it from. "I do," I said. "And we would be wise to pay heed to it. Otherwise we might get caught in a dangerous echo chamber." I thought about my recent deep dive into neo-Nazism. The canary in the coal mine? Should we be taking it a lot more seriously than we currently were, and asking what we could do about so many people getting radicalized? Probably.

I opened my mouth to ask my dad what he knew about neo-Nazism and what he thought about it—other than the obvious—when my phone buzzed against my thigh.

My dad and John were already back to arguing about Trump and the failings of the Bush and Obama administrations and how they had caused a deep disillusionment with the mainstream platforms of both parties. Behind me, I could hear my mom and my grandma talking quietly in the kitchen about dinner. My grandpa was nowhere to be seen. Probably in the back shed, hiding out from the chaos or plotting a new practical joke. He did like his practical jokes. I hoped he wouldn't do anything that would set John's PTSD off too much.

I turned so that I was slightly sideways to John and our dad, and pulled out my phone. Probably it would be something work-related, and I could ignore it until Monday.

It was a Signal message. *Darling Inna*, it read. *What do you know about your Security Solutions?*

43

NOT MUCH, I wrote back. *Why?*

Doing a little research for a story. Can't sleep. Homer. Taut sails...Instead of reading "The Iliad," I thought I'd check in with you))))

))))) I wrote back. It was a reference to the Mandelstam poem "Insomnia. Homer. Taut sails..."

I've got some questions that won't let me rest, and whom should I listen to? Homer is silent))))))

)))))) I wrote again, while I racked my brains trying to remember the rest of the poem so that I could come up with a witty rejoinder by quoting a line from it. That would be better than firing off an angry text demanding to know what he'd been up to, why he thought he could come waltzing back into my life asking for my help when it was convenient for him after ignoring me for more than a month, and the thing that was really eating at me: was he engaged to Polya yet?

I snuck a glance at John and our dad. Still arguing away about politics. They paid me no attention whatsoever as I tiptoed out of the living room and through the back door, onto the back porch.

By the time I got out there, another text was waiting for me.

I'm sorry I've been silent for so long, like Homer. It's been a difficult autumn. Mama really isn't doing well.

Oh no! I'm sorry to hear that. Give her my love.

Will do)))) That will cheer her up, at least. She isn't very happy with me—but when is she ever?))))) And the treatments aren't going *very well here, and there's still no word on when we'll get visas, or even *if* we'll get visas. I won't hide it, Inna: it's very scary, waiting like this, knowing your fate is in the hands of bureaucrats who don't care about you at all. They know about mama's health issues and they're still moving as slowly as honey in January. I'm feeling a lot of bad things about America right now. But I don't have much hope for other options. I asked about possible specialists in Canada, too, but it looks like the best specialists are in America.*

I tried to think of what to say. *Let me know if there's anything I can do to help*, I finally texted.

Will do)))) Meanwhile, I'm still working on something connected to your Security Solutions. They are mixed up in everything!

Something in Russia? I asked.

They are everywhere)))))

Is it dangerous? I asked.

Dangerous enough—but don't worry about me!)))))

The door creaked. I looked up. John was stepping out onto the porch, Scotch still in hand. It looked like he'd topped it up.

"Have you decided to stop tormenting Dad?" I asked.

He grinned. "It's good for him, Ro, you know that. He doesn't exercise enough. At least this way he gets his heart rate up. And it's another perspective and all. You said it: it's dangerous to get caught in an echo chamber."

"Uh-huh." I glanced back down at my phone.

"So who's the text from?" John grinned again. "A hot date, I hope."

I shook my head. "No hot dates for me, I'm afraid."

"Yeah." His face went sad for a moment. Then he forced out another grin. "You gotta get back out there, Ro. I know Miller was a loser in the end, but there're other guys. You just gotta give 'em a chance."

"Yes," I agreed. My fingers were itching to respond to Dima's text, even though I didn't know what I would say to it.

John eyed me suspiciously. "It's not Miller you're texting right now, is it? You're not trying to make things up with him, are you? 'Cause I don't think it's gonna work. And if you try, I'll have to do the big brother thing and step in and put a stop to it."

"No," I said. "It's not Alex. We, uh—" my voice caught embarrassingly—"we haven't been in contact much since I got back to Georgia. We're, um, still friends, but we're, uh, letting things calm down a little for now." I didn't tell John that Alex had sent me a couple more late-night texts recently, obviously looking for someone to pour out all his troubles to, and I'd sidestepped that conversation both times. As long as he was still mixed up with Erin, no good could come down that road, I was sure. The very thought of being the "other woman," even in a purely emotional way, made me feel ill. So I'd disengaged, as gently as possible, whenever he got into contact.

John, not knowing about my atypical hardheartedness on the Alex front, eyed me even more suspiciously. "So why the nervous face, then? Who *is* it? Someone even worse?"

"It depends on your perspective, I guess," I said.

John groaned. "It's not *him,* is it?"

"If by '*him*' you mean Dima, then yes."

"Fuck! Why the fuck are you even giving him the time of day, Ro?"

"I don't know," I said.

"He's not trying to get back together, is he?"

"I don't know about that either," I said. "Not as far as I can tell, at least for the moment. He just needed my help with something."

"And you were so fucking eager to give it that you ran out of the room to hide on the back porch and offer him whatever he needed!"

"Well..." I said. "It wasn't exactly as if that conversation between you and Dad had a lot in it for me."

"Fuck! Don't be like this, Ro. I've told you this before and I'm gonna tell it to you again, so maybe this time it'll sink it: You've gotta stop being an emotional support animal for fucked-up men who don't have a problem with wasting away the best years of your life."

"I know," I said. "But it was never my intention to be an emotional support animal for fucked-up men. It was always my intention to find true love and start a family. It just...didn't happen."

"Well, stop letting it happen. Stop letting men treat you like that. Put your foot down and make them toe the line."

"Does that work on you?" I asked. "Have your various emotional support animals ever managed to make *you* toe the line and stop wasting away the best years of *their* lives?"

"That's not what we're talking about here!"

"Yeah, it is," I said. "Do you think that other men are so much different than you? Do you think I'm so much different from all the women you've screwed around with and thrown away over the years?"

"I fucking well hope so!"

"Well, I'm not. As is abundantly clear by an objective assessment of my current situation."

John turned away to stare off across the yard, into the patch of kudzu and poison ivy affectionately known as "the back woods" by my grandparents. "Any woman who takes up with me isn't worth anything better," he said, not looking at me.

"Well, apparently that's exactly what all the men in my life have thought about *me*."

John turned back around. "So don't fucking fuck around with men like that, Ro! For Chrissake, pick better men!"

"I thought I was," I said. "Now I'm starting to wonder if there are even any better men to pick. These *are* the good guys, John. That's what's so sad about it. You *are* one of the good guys. And so were they. But they still fell down on the job when it really mattered."

John gestured angrily, sloshing half his Scotch over his hand. "That's not true!"

I looked at him, forcing him to hold my gaze. "It is true, John. That's the tragedy. I've spent all my life as one of the good guys, surrounded by other good guys. And they've still treated me like shit at every turn. My uber-idealistic, uber-progressive workplace keeps me broke and desperate and may be destroying my physical as well as my mental health. My uber-idealistic, uber-righteous boyfriends broke my heart and denied me the thing I wanted most from life—and the one thing I couldn't get on my own but needed their help with. My Land of the Free, Home of the Brave is a doublespeaking, dystopian nightmare..."

"That's not true!" John repeated, sloshing more of his Scotch out of his glass with an even angrier gesture.

"It's true to me," I said.

John made a face like he was trying to come up with a killer retort to that, one that would prove to me once and for all how incredibly wrong I was about everything, when our grandfather called from the back shed. "Weena? Vannie? Can you come give me a hand for a minute?"

"Sure, Grandpa," we yelled simultaneously. John gave me a wry grin and set down his now-empty tumbler of Scotch on the porch railing. We stepped off the porch and headed towards the shed.

When we tried to open the door, it was stuck. "Grandpa!" John yelled. "Grandpa, the door's latched on the inside! You gotta let us in."

"Hang on a minute," our grandfather yelled back. "It's been acting up lately..." There were some shuffling sounds on the other side of the door. "Try it now!" he yelled. "Let's make sure it's working right from both sides."

John and I exchanged glances. "Cover me, Ro, I'm going in," he whispered, and turned the door knob. This time it turned smoothly. Cautiously, so cautiously, he pulled on it. The knob flew off in his hand and a paper snake came lunging out through the hole, striking him square on the chest.

"FUCK!" yelled John, slamming us both against the shed wall.

"It's okay! It's okay!" I shouted. "It's just a paper snake."

John released his hold on me and gave me a shaky grin. "I fucking *knew* and he still got me."

From inside the shed we heard the sounds of uncontrollable laughter.

"Maybe I should be the one to actually go through the door," I said.

"I can't let a lady take the bullet meant for me," John said gallantly.

"He already got you. I'm going in." I brushed past him before he could catch me and stepped boldly through the door, my hands over my head in case of stray water bottles or buckets of paint.

Nothing. I took another step. A buzzing, rattling sound came from the floor at my feet. I looked down and screamed, simultaneously leaping into the air and throwing myself back through the door and into John's arms.

More uncontrollable laughter rang out from inside the shed.

"God *damn* it!" said John, although he was laughing, albeit rather hysterically, too. He sidled through the door, grabbed a rake on the wall next to it, and raked out the buzzing rattlesnake, which turned out to be made of rubber.

"Jesus Christ," I said. "I don't know how much more family togetherness I can take."

44

JOHN SAID HE WASN'T going to venture into the back shed again without full tactical gear, minesweeping robots, and air support. Eventually our grandfather came out to meet us. He was still shaking with laughter. We were just still shaking. Apparently my gentle hints to him that maybe he shouldn't leave booby traps for John, especially ones with explosives, hadn't sunk in yet. I wasn't too thrilled about the fake snake myself. I wasn't excessively scared of snakes, but I wasn't *not* scared of snakes, either. I was also starting to worry that this increasing obsession with wilder and wilder practical jokes was a sign of incipient dementia.

Fortunately for me, our grandmother came out then and scolded our grandfather roundly for scaring the bejeezus out of me and John, sparing me from having to do it and distracting me from my fears for his cognitive abilities. Then we all trooped inside for hors d'oeuvres before supper.

I managed to get in a quick text to Dima amongst all that, letting him know what was up and telling him I'd be happy to answer any questions I could. Of course he didn't respond.

I told myself not to fret over it, and braced myself for a grilling about my failed love life over cheese and crackers. But my grandmother, bless her, ignored me and turned to John, saying as she handed him a plate, "So, Vannie, how are things going between you and that girl you've been seeing?"

The rest of us all sat up and pointed like bird dogs. This was the first I'd heard of it. Judging by my parents' expressions, it was the first they'd heard of it, too, and they were so stunned they didn't know what to say.

"Fine," John mumbled into his Scotch, which he'd refilled first thing on coming back into the house.

"Better than fine, it sounds like to me, if you're still seeing her," said my grandmother. "It's been going on since this spring, hasn't it?"

John mumbled something that might have been an affirmative into his Scotch.

"Well, I sure hope we all get to meet her soon," said my grandmother. "What did you say her name was? It was something *so* pretty..."

"Camila," John mumbled. "Camila Rodriguez."

Our grandmother beamed. "*Such* a lovely name. What does she look like?"

John sighed. "Here. You're never gonna leave it till I show you a picture, so here you go." He pulled out his phone, pulled up a picture, and showed us the screen. We all leaned in, eyes bulging from curiosity.

The picture showed John with his arm around the shoulder of a woman dressed in running clothes, with a race bib on her shirt and a medal around her neck. She was a head shorter than him, with large dark eyes and dark hair pulled back in a sporty pony tail.

"She'd just won her age division of a local 5k," John said. "She's been a competitive runner since high school, and she's training for her first triathlon." He was smiling despite his best efforts not to. "You'd love her, Ro: you both love kicking my ass on the running course. I should get you two together sometime."

"Absolutely," I said, once I got my mouth unstuck from where it had been frozen in shock. "Although I'm afraid I'm not up for any running at the moment."

John grimaced. "Your knee still bothering you?"

I nodded. I was no longer on crutches at all times, although I still had to resort to them or a cane after a long day or after physical therapy. The first round of therapy I'd done had left me in significant pain and limping even worse than before. When I'd mentioned it and said I was thinking of stopping PT, I'd been convinced to switch to a different therapist who specialized in a different set of exercises. These had been slightly less damaging than the first ones, but still left me sore and incapacitated afterwards. I had used fall break as an excuse to get out of this week's session. I noted, with a mixture of scientific curiosity and gloom, that I was walking better after one missed session than I had in months.

"Well, as soon as you're back up to fighting fitness, I should get you together so you can run with her. Although...could be risky. She might get you hooked on triathlons, and that shit is expensive."

"Vannie!" Our grandmother swatted him, but she was smiling too much for it to have much force. I guessed she had seen the same thing I had, which was that this Camila was completely different than John's normal type. He generally went for cheap trashy blondes, preferably married. Camila looked neither cheap, trashy, nor blonde, and I saw no sign of either a ring or a suspicious tan line on her left ring finger.

"Well," said my mother. She was choosing her words very carefully. "I'm sure we'd all love to meet her whenever you think the timing is right. She looks like a lovely person. Now, Bobby and I have some exciting news of our own." She looked meaningfully around the room. "We've decided to sell our house."

"About dang time!" said my grandfather, while my grandmother said, "Praise the Lord!"

For the better part of twenty years my parents had lived in a very modest Cape Cod house on a very modest piece of property that they had done absolutely nothing to improve. The whole thing was about as boring and bland as you could possibly imagine. My parents had bought it in a fit of conformity, when they had decided that they really needed to give me and John a "normal" childhood and prepare us to enter the "real" world. John had already left for The Citadel by then, but I guess the thought counted for something.

To everyone's surprise, our parents had stayed in the house ever since. It was convenient to work, they explained, and the mortgage was affordable, even for them. My grandfather had opined on more than one occasion that it was a little *too* dang affordable, and he'd pay for them to move to somewhere nicer, or at least safer.

However, they had been untroubled by crime their entire time there. Probably everyone in the neighborhood knew there was nothing worth stealing in it. Or, my grandmother liked to say, they felt so sorry for the pitiful neglected place that they couldn't bring themselves to rob it. She'd tried more than once to get my mother to put in a few flowers or a couple of shrubs, or at least hang up some proper drapes, but my mother always claimed she simply couldn't be bothered. The bedsheets they'd hung over the windows the week they'd moved in had worked just fine ever since. My father mowed the lawn about once a month, and that was all the decorating and landscaping they could bring themselves to do.

"I know it's not from lack of knowledge, or get-up-and-go," my grandmother would say in frustration. "You built your own yurt and raised your own vegetables for years in that commune! You could at least put in a little garden bed out front!"

"I'm too busy with work now," my mother would say. "Besides, I got tired of it. Gardening isn't fun anymore when it's the only thing putting food on the table for your children."

"You can still go to the grocery store if you plant a few pansies!" my grandmother would say. "Or even some squash and beans!"

"I just can't be bothered," my mother would say. "I need a break from all that."

But now she was telling us that they had found a little plot of land out of town, and had just made an offer.

"That'll be a heck of a commute into the city," my grandfather said.

"Oh, well...you know...I haven't been talking about it because it's not quite settled yet, but it looks like I'll be setting up practice as a GP in the town nearby. You know, a proper small-town doctor. It'll be a nice change."

This announcement was greeted with more shock. Not that we thought my mother would be a bad small-town doctor. We just had never expected her to do something so eminently sensible.

"Well," said my grandfather, once he'd recovered a little. "That sounds great, hun. So are you planning to build your own place on this plot of land? That'll be nice. Do you have any plans drawn up yet?"

"Oh, yes!" My mother's face was glowing with enthusiasm now. "Bobby and I have been talking and talking about it, and we've decided it's time to get *serious* about reducing our environmental footprint, so we're going to hand-build a tiny home out of reclaimed materials."

My grandfather groaned. My grandmother shook her head and *tsked*. John gave a bark of laughter and went over to kiss our mother's head.

"You sure are a weirdo, Mom," he said. "But I wouldn't have it any other way. Probably in twenty years' time we'll all be doing the same thing. So if you need any help, let me know. I can pick up some tips for when the apocalypse comes and I need to get serious about survival."

Our mother patted his hand. "You really are a good boy," she said. "We'd love your help, I'm sure. And Camila's welcome to come see the place any time you care to bring her. We'll be building a guest house as well; you can tell us what you'd like to have in it."

I thought John would say something about how there was no way in Hell he'd be bringing Camila over, but he only grinned and said sure, whenever they were ready to show him the place.

I guess miracles ***can*** *happen*, I told myself. *Now even* ***John*** *is settling down. Can I be far behind?*

45

I ESCAPED AFTER SUPPER and went home to Fevronia, who seemed happy to see me after my absence. She was not a sweet and cuddly cat. In fact, she could best be described as blood-thirsty and vicious. But she had stood by me in thick and thin, which was more than I could say about most of the others in my life. I was aware that she had stood by me mainly because I kept her locked in the apartment, but that still had to count for something, right?

The next morning I headed back over to Macon for an entire day of family togetherness. John and I were supposed to do some work around the yard. Our grandparents were still pretty spry for people well into their 80s, but they preferred to leave the heavy lifting to us as much as possible. Actually, it would be more accurate to say that John had brow-beaten them into agreeing that they would leave the heavy lifting to us. If they'd had their druthers, they'd probably be out there doing their own roofing. But our grandfather had thrown his back out one too many times, and our grandmother had a tendency to get her "spells" when it got too hot, which was about nine months of the year in Georgia, so, in a rare moment of unity, John and I had stood strong together and insisted.

When I showed up that morning, John was already mowing the lawn and my mother was weeding the front garden bed. The sounds of vigorous sawing and hammering came from the back shed.

"It's Bobby and your grandfather," my grandmother told me when I got out of the car and nodded towards the noises. "They're building some kind of prototype for something in the tiny house Bobby thinks he want to build. Or rather, I should say, your grandfather is building it."

"No doubt." My father liked to dream up designs. He was less good when it came to the actual physical implementation of them. I had occasionally seen him with a hammer in his hand in my childhood, but 90% of the time that had been thirty seconds before some kind of catastrophic accident that at best involved losing a thumbnail, and at worst meant a trip to the ER. The rest of us had learned to keep him away from tools of all sorts for everyone's sake.

"He's planning to hire a builder for the actual house, right?" I asked. "He's not planning to build it himself?"

My mother, who'd gotten up from weeding and come over to us, sighed. "He *wants* to build it all with his own two hands," she said. "And I do too, for that matter. It would be very rewarding, don't you think? I don't know if you remember the yurt, Rowena..."

"I remember," I put in quickly. "That was awesome. But I thought *you* built it."

"I did. Bobby just helped a little. And it turned out pretty well, if I do say so myself. But it gave him an itch to build his own home that he's never been able to satisfy—until now." She sighed again. "I can do some of the build for the house, but I can't do everything. As it's currently planned, it will involve welding, plumbing, electricity...all kinds of skillsets I don't possess, and don't feel like learning. But your father is now talking about taking welding classes..."

She trailed off as my grandmother and I stared at her in horror. "I don't think he'll actually go through with it," she added hastily. "You know how he is about that sort of thing. But it's all he can think about right now. He wants to weld some kind of a bookshelf out of reclaimed steel, so he and your grandfather are putting together a wooden prototype right now."

I tried to envision a bookshelf hand-welded from reclaimed steel by my father. The mind boggled. "What kind of an aesthetic are you going for?" I asked cautiously.

My mother sighed again. "Not Rust Belt Chic. But you know how he is: you have to let him have his enthusiasms. Probably by next month he'll have given up on the welding and settled for something more sensible."

I nodded hopefully. It was true that my father, while prone to unwise enthusiasms, normally managed to see sense after a bit. He was, after all, extremely intelligent. He was also very competent in the areas where he was actually an expert. And he didn't like to hurt people. So altogether, it was normally not too difficult to persuade him to take the more practical course. But he was very easily swept away.

There was a shout of pain and surprise, followed by a sudden cessation of hammering and the sound of a pile of two-by-fours crashing down on the back shed's concrete floor. My mother, grandmother, and I shared a look of concern.

John stopped the lawnmower and went sprinting into the shed. A minute later, he came back out, ushering our father along beside him. Who had, I noted with alarm, a bloody rag held up to his face.

"Bobby!" My mother went jogging over to check on him. I palmed my car keys, ready to make a quick dash to the local ER.

After a thorough examination, though, my mother declared it unnecessary. It was just a simple nosebleed, which under her ministrations quickly stopped bleeding. Somehow, my father explained once he could speak, he'd lost control of his hammer and it had flown back and hit him in the face, cracking his glasses but, my mother declared, doing nothing worse than bruising the rest of him.

"Well," said my grandmother, once that had all been sorted out, "I do enjoy a little family excitement, I must say. Weena, darling, how do you feel about helping me put in some pansies?"

I spent the rest of the morning helping my grandmother put in her fall display of black and orange pansies. She liked to go all out for Halloween, including a themed flowerbed. As a child I'd thought it was hilarious. Now I wondered how she found the energy and enthusiasm. Then I wondered how I had gotten so much older and more jaded than my grandmother.

In the afternoon John and I attacked the kudzu that was constantly threatening to engulf the shed, the yard, and, if it had its way, the house. Our grandparents' property backed up to a creek bottom that was infested with kudzu (along with snakes, ticks, chiggers, and other unsavory things). Several times a year the kudzu had to be cut back with all the brutality we could muster. John had already mown everything he could reach with the mower. Now we went after the rest of it with clippers and machetes.

"God damn," said John, once we'd stripped all of it we could reach from the shed. He flapped the hem of his shirt, trying to get a little cool air onto his chest. "It gets worse every year. Maybe Grandma and Grandpa should try a flamethrower to burn the shit out of it."

"And set the entire property on fire?" I eyed the expanse of kudzu strangling the trees along the property line. "I've heard goats work," I said. "Goats and pigs. Maybe they should get a little herd of goats and pigs."

"Plus, then you'd get bacon! I'm sorry, I'm sorry. Someday you're going to think that's funny."

"I doubt it," I said.

"You need to live a little, Ro!"

"Mmmmm." I wiped some sweat off my forehead with my shirt and sized up the nearest kudzu-smothered tree. I was hot and tired and ready for a refreshing shower and a cool drink. On the other hand, I wasn't at work, so that was a major positive.

"What do you think?" I asked John. "Should I do a career change and go into landscaping?"

"Nah." He wiped sweat off his face too. "I've already looked into it. Thought about it as a possibility for once my twenty years are up and I leave the Marines. But the pay is shit. Plus you'd have to deal with rich assholes all the time."

"That's what I thought, too," I said. "But I've still been entertaining it as a happy fantasy."

John grinned. "We could do it as a family business. 'Halley and Halley.' You bring the charm and I'll bring the muscles. We could specialize in...I don't know...regenerative gardening or some shit like that. Is that a thing? It sounds like it should be a thing. It sounds like just the kind of shit that people putting in tiny houses made of reclaimed materials would eat up."

"I'm sure it is," I said. "And I'm sure other people have already thought of that and are moving rapidly into that niche."

"Yeah. And I don't think I'd actually be any good at it anyway. The only thing I know how to do in a garden is mow grass and whack back kudzu."

"Yeah," I said. "Not really a useful skillset, especially when goats can probably do it even better."

John was attacking the kudzu at the base of the next tree. "Seems like I should have a better set of skills," he said, his back to me. "Seems like I should be worth something after everything I've done."

"Yeah," I said. "You and me both."

"But so far the only places I've found that might be interested in me are law enforcement and private security."

"Uh-huh," I said. "And if it's something you are interested in, Brian Michaels has offered more than once to help out." Brian Michaels was the chief of campus police at Crimson. His son had served under John's command, and Brian had expressed his willingness to do whatever he could for the man who had straightened out his ne'er-do-well youngest child and, possibly, saved his life under fire.

"I should hit him up. I guess." John didn't sound very enthused. "And I've actually already had someone from Security Solutions reach out to me. Aren't they the folks who basically own Crimson?"

"More or less," I said. "That's proactive of them."

"I got the feeling they were real proactive people."

"Do you think you might take them up on it?" I asked cautiously. My heart sank at the thought of John taking up private soldiering in any form. But I also knew that he was right when he said he might not have a lot of other options. He was coming up very soon on his twenty years of service with the Marines, and was planning to leave then. Gung-ho as he'd always been, he was looking forward to getting out of the military. But he didn't know what he'd do next. Early forties was awfully young to retire, and he'd need some kind of an income to supplement his pension.

"Camila says she'll cut off my balls if I do."

"Well," I said. "That settles it, then." I tried to hide my surprise. Normally I'd expect John to respond to that kind of statement by breaking off the relationship with extreme prejudice.

"Yeah. She's had a few run-ins with them before, because of her law firm, and she pretty much spits with rage whenever their name comes up. She's trying to get me to go to law school instead."

I hoped that I was able to refrain from gaping like a fish. "Are you thinking about it?" I finally managed to ask.

"I'd never thought about it before. But once she suggested it, I started to think yeah, maybe I *could* be a lawyer. I mean, I'm no brain like you, Ro, but I'm not a complete idiot. I could probably get through law school. And there's a lot of work that needs doing out there."

"Uh-huh," I said, still trying to hide my shock. "You mean like...social-work kind of work?"

"It sounds stupid when you say it like that..."

"No, it doesn't," I put in quickly. "I think you'd do a great job of it, if that's what you want to do."

"I'm still thinking about it. Don't tell anyone, okay? Not until I've thought about it some more. But Camila thinks it would be great for both of us."

"In that case, she might have a point," I said. "And I'm sure you'd do great in law school. And I'd bet you'd make a great lawyer, too." The thought had never occurred to me, either, but now that I considered it, I could totally see John as a hard-charging lawyer.

My phone *pinged*. I stopped attacking the kudzu to pull it out of my pocket.

Darling Inna, said the text. *I really have a lot of questions about Security Solutions. Can we talk?*

46

"UH-OH," SAID JOHN. "I don't like that look on your face. Whoever sent that text, they're trouble."

"Probably." I wiped my hands off on my shirt and started typing a reply.

"Ro! What the fuck are you doing?!?"

"Living a little," I told him. "Isn't that what you want?"

"Not by messing around with whoever's sending you that text. Wait—is it *him*?"

"Yep."

"And you're gonna drop everything to text him back right now?"

"It's worse than that," I said. "I might even call him. Maybe even video chat."

"Jesus Christ, Ro! Are you trying to piss me off?"

I pointed a finger at him. "Got it in one. It's probably good for you. Just like it's probably good for Dad for you to yank his chain every now and then."

John groaned and threw up his hands. "What about that whole speech you gave me yesterday about how even the good guys let you down? Didn't you hear a word you fucking said? Why the fuck are you even giving this fuckwit loser the time of day? Why aren't you out finding some newer, hotter, richer guy who can take care of you properly?"

"So far my efforts in that direction have not been crowned with success," I said. "And besides, I've rethought everything I said about even the good guys letting me down. I mean, yes, so far for me it's been true. But seeing you saying you're seriously considering going to law school because Camila suggested it has made me believe in miracles. If she can be a good influence on you, what marvels might I accomplish?"

"God damn it, Ro!"

"Besides," I added, "he needs my help."

"Double God damn it, Ro! That's how they get you! I know because I've done it!"

"I know," I said. "But I'm going to help him out anyway. And I might ask you for help, too. Or at least Camila. He's looking into Security Solutions, and he wants more info."

John looked torn, like he wanted to cuss me out some more, but was also intrigued, and maybe wasn't against digging up some dirt on Security Solutions.

"You're just talking about Security Solutions?" he said finally. "Nothing...lovey-dovey?"

"Just Security Solutions," I said. I swallowed against the lump that had suddenly grown in my throat. "He's talking about getting engaged to someone else."

John looked even more torn, as relief and rage chased each other across his face.

"Well," he said eventually. "Guess I'm glad about that. You'll be better off when he's out of your life. But I want to kick his ass for being such a stupid motherfucker that he'd throw you over and take up with someone else."

"I think he spends a lot of time kicking his own ass," I said. "If you think you do a fine line in self-loathing and self-recrimination, you should see him in action. He's pretty much a world champion."

"Sounds like he should be," said John.

I resisted the urge to argue with John, and texted back, *What do you want to know about Security Solutions?*

After a moment, Dima texted, *Do you know anyone in the US who works with them? Works for them?*

As it happens, I wrote, *I might.*

Do you think you could get me an interview with them?

Let me ask. I looked up at John. He groaned. "What are you going to ask me?" he said.

"How soon would you feel comfortable introducing me to Camila?" I said. "And do you think she'd be comfortable talking to a journalist about Security Solutions?"

John groaned again. "See, this is why I didn't want to tell you guys about her. Now you can't fucking leave me alone about her."

"We don't have to tell anyone else that you're introducing us," I said. "It could be our secret. Mom and Dad, and Grandma and Grandpa, never have to know."

John groused and groaned some more, but his heart wasn't really in it. I was pretty sure that deep inside, he was eager to show off Camila to me. I even suspected he wouldn't be averse to her showing off her insider knowledge and helping me out when no one else could. He just had to put up a token resistance for form's sake. But by the end of the afternoon, not only had he agreed, he'd set up a video call between us for next week.

47

I HAD ALSO MET AN EMPLOYEE of Security Solutions myself on several occasions. His name was Carl and he had provided security for a couple of campus events. I was pretty sure he liked me, or at least found me vaguely amusing, and might be willing to give me some insider info. But I didn't know his last name, or what kind of details he usually worked, or how to get in touch with him.

I tried a few internet searches to see if I could track him down, but came up with nothing. I didn't dare reach out to the company itself. Not only did I not want to tip them off that Dima was interested in them, and that I was connected to Dima, but I was pretty sure I was right near the top of their shit list. Getting the company owner's son and heir arrested for drug dealing and sexual assault last spring had probably not ingratiated me with them at all. Better if I didn't bring myself to their attention.

But I still had Camila. She had agreed to a Skype call with me on Thursday afternoon. If that went well, she'd relayed through John, she'd consider talking to Dima.

At 2:00pm that Thursday, I was waiting by the computer, my stomach fluttering almost as much as if I were about to have—shudder!—an interview. I told myself there was no reason to be nervous. Camila was the one who should be nervous. In fact, she probably *was* nervous. But somehow, even so, I was nervous too.

When she appeared on my screen, though, she didn't appear nervous. From what I could see of her, she was on the short side, with a compact, athletic frame that her pantsuit couldn't quite disguise, long dark hair that today was pulled back in a low ponytail, and big dark eyes that had a no-nonsense look. She was in every way the opposite of every other woman I'd ever known John to go out with.

"Wow," she said as soon as the video and audio had synched up. "John said you looked like him, but I didn't realize how much." She had a faint North Carolina accent, with an even fainter underlay of Mexico. Born here, I guessed, but in a family that mainly spoke Spanish at home. So probably bilingual as well as a lawyer. I gave John even more kudos. I also wondered how on Earth he'd ended up with her. Asking Camila would probably be wrong, right? At least during our first chat. I'd interrogate her about it later.

"Two peas in a pod, that's us," I said.

"Though he said you don't act like him much."

"Well," I said. "It depends on how you define it."

Camila laughed, flashing straight white teeth. "I like it! A good lawyer answer. Although John says you're a professor."

"Yep."

"I guess it's kind of similar, though. You're always having to do lots of reading and research, and be clever with words."

"Pretty much," I agreed. Camila still didn't seem nervous at all. That only made me feel even more nervous.

"Anyway," she said. "John tells me you want to find out more about Security Solutions?"

I outlined the situation briefly, explaining that Dima was doing a story on them and wanted to talk to someone who might have some insider info, or at least had dealt with them.

"Well," she said. "I can't say I have insider info, exactly...although maybe...do you think he'd be interested in their ties with extremist groups?"

I sat up. "I'm sure he would be."

She nodded. "Okay. So...I guess I should give you a little background. Someone reached out to me a few months back. A friend asking for some advice. This friend had gotten out of the military and been hired by Security Solutions."

I nodded.

"He had some qualms about what they do, but he really needed the work, and they were the only game in town."

I nodded some more.

"And it first it didn't seem too bad, especially not for what it was. And he was mostly treated pretty well. It was a diverse group of employees—my friend is Hispanic—most of them ex-military, so he felt at home, surrounded by professionals. At least at first."

Camila paused. I nodded encouragingly.

"Then some new guys came in. And they weren't so welcoming and professional. A couple of them were ex-military, but several of them weren't, although they knew their way around guns well enough. And then my friend started noticing the numbers they had tattooed on their bodies. Numbers like 14, 18, 88, and 109/110."

"Neo-Nazi codes," I said.

Camila gave me an approving smile. "You know your neo-Nazi symbology, I see."

"Not very well, although more than I'd like to. I had to do a bit of a dive into it recently."

"Yeah. Me too. And for the amount of effort those people put into creating and deciphering codes and symbols, they could get a PhD in literature." She stopped. "Oops. I forgot. I didn't mean to offend you."

"No offense," I said. "And it might be true. Although I'd argue that those of us with actual PhDs in literature generally read better texts and provide more subtle and nuanced interpretations of them.

Hopefully more socially valuable interpretations, too. But it's the same basic impulse."

"Yeah. So, anyway, my friend asked me about it, and we both looked into it a bit, and it looks like Security Solutions has started hiring from a couple of paramilitary-type groups with extremist views and connections to white supremacy and neo-Nazism."

"Yowza," I said.

"Yowza indeed. Needless to say, my friend was not happy about it. He was even less happy about it when a couple of them started hassling him about it. They started telling him to go back home, and blaming him for global warming."

"Nice," I said.

"Real nice. First he complained to his supervisor, but that only got him more harassment. Eventually he found another job and left. His new job doesn't pay as well, but it involves fewer Nazis, so he was willing to make the trade."

"Makes sense," I said. "Although it sucks that he had to do it."

"Yeah. We talked about whether or not it was worth suing over, but he decided he didn't want to go through with it. But he might be willing to talk to your journalist friend about it."

"That would be great," I said.

"I've had some other run-ins with Security Solutions," Camila said. "They're based in Georgia, but they've been stretching their tentacles up here into North Carolina, hoping to get a piece of that private prison pie. We've been cutting back on them, but there are still a few, and SS—my nickname for them—would like to get some of that Raleigh money. So if you need more info, I might have it, but the neo-Nazi angle is the most lurid, so I led with it."

"Thanks," I said. "That was great. I mean, not what happened to your friend. That was terrible. But I think my friend might find the story very interesting, if you're willing to share it."

"I'll get in touch with my friend, and see what he says." She grinned. "And maybe one day soon, my people will talk with your people, and we'll set something up. Or something. And maybe some good will come of it."

"Yeah," I agreed. "Maybe some good will come of it after all."

48

I HAD BEEN FULL OF happy fantasies that Camila's friend would immediately agree, and we'd set up some kind of a meeting that weekend, and it would go really well, and this would in some way make my life go much better, but in fact she told me the next day that he was thinking about it, and would let us know at some point in the next few weeks if he would be willing to talk to Dima or not. So I had to put that project on the back burner, and focus on other things.

The other things I needed to focus on included applying for more jobs, polishing up the article I'd been slowly working on all semester, and keeping Chloe from going into a tailspin over the progress of her book, or lack thereof.

"I did the revisions over the summer, and sent them in three months ago!" she told me, as we sat over cappuccinos at Brew's Up on a Monday afternoon. I felt very conspicuous. It was Halloween, and most of the people in the shop were in costumes. Some of them were very sexy costumes. One of the benefits of living in Georgia was that Halloween was often still warm enough to make wearing nothing but a bra, miniskirt, and a pair of ripped stockings seem like a good idea. "But they haven't gotten back to me yet, and when I reached out to them about it, they just said it was a slow process, and not to worry about it!"

"Did they give you some kind of a timeline for when they *would* get back to you?" I asked.

"No! Just that it would be a while. What about you? Have you heard from your publisher yet?"

"Not yet." A publisher had requested a full copy of my manuscript at the end of the spring semester. They'd been sitting on it ever since. This meant I couldn't submit it elsewhere. Sometimes I thought about checking in with them, but I always chickened out. I was afraid they'd say no, or come back with a lot of really hurtful comments, and then I'd be back at square one as far as publication went, but more bruised and battered. So I'd elected to work on an article while I waited. I couldn't say that I enjoyed writing articles, but it felt productive, and during the drafting phase I didn't have to deal with the aggravation inherent in any interactions with editors and reviewers.

"Hi! I didn't expect to run into you girls." It was Diane, coming into the coffee shop with Julie. "Here to try the pumpkin cookies?"

"I saw them, but I was too scared," I said. Brew's Up was festooned with orange and black streamers, and there were trays of free cookies iced to look like pumpkins set out on the counter.

"Wise woman," said Diane. "They're crap, and all that food coloring can't be good for you. But they're free, so lots of people come and get them. Mostly students, but some faculty, too. You know how people are when there's free food. And I guess I can't blame them. I know one of our adjuncts recently had to apply for SNAP benefits to feed her kids. I was shocked, but that's how things are these days, I guess."

Chloe and I nodded.

"Is Melissa with you?" Diane asked, looking around.

Chloe and I shook our heads. "She's at the doctor's," I said. "She finally got in to see a specialist she's been trying to see for months, so she's off doing that."

"Hope it helps," said Diane. "But I was hoping to see her, since I think she'd be interested in hearing what I've got to say. Do you mind if I sit down?"

"Please." She and Julie took the other two chairs at our table.

"So," said Diane, once they were seated. She put her elbows on the table and rested her chin on her clasped hands. "Do you remember when we talked at the beginning of the semester? About the"—she looked around and lowered her voice—"mold?"

Chloe and I nodded some more.

"So, I ran some tests, like I said I was going to do. You know, taking samples, culturing them, that kind of thing. All in a day's work for me."

"Anything interesting?" I asked.

She swayed her shoulders from side to side in a maybe-yes, maybe-no motion. "There's a lot of mold in most of the buildings here on campus," she said. "But there's a lot of mold in most places here in Georgia. Some of what I found were species known to be toxic to humans, but again...people will tell you there's mold everywhere, and they're right. Most of it's benign, or in such low quantities that it doesn't matter to most people. Our buildings do appear to have a fair amount of some potentially dangerous varieties, but most health experts will tell you that it's only a concern for transplant or chemo patients, or people with late-stage AIDS."

"Of course, we probably have some of those people here on campus," Julie put in.

"I know for a fact that someone in our department is undergoing chemo right now, and someone in Chemistry just had a transplant," said Diane. "But that doesn't explain *our* problems. I did some reading, though, and it looks like lots of colleges are having this issue. Lots of students are complaining about getting sick from moldy dorms, and faculty and staff are complaining about getting sick from moldy offices and classrooms. *Something's* bothering them. I've read it could be some kind of an interaction between the mold and the building materials themselves. You know, most of our modern building materials are pretty toxic. The materials from a few decades back are full not just of lead and asbestos, but formaldehyde, and it turns out that's a lot worse for you than we used to think. Some of that's being phased out, but now we're just starting to find out how much of a problem these things called PFAS chemicals are, and they're in practically every part of our buildings. And our buildings aren't ventilated very well. They're designed to be efficient, not healthy. That's why when one person in your class comes down with a cold, everyone comes down with it."

Chloe stifled a sneeze. "Sorry," she said when she could talk again. "I'm actually just getting over a cold. Just like you said, someone came into my class with a cold after fall break, and a week later we were all sick."

Diane nodded. "That's how it works. And since I ran into you here, I thought I'd let you know what I've found so far. I'm going to keep reading, keep doing tests and cultures. I could get a major paper out of this. Or get terminated."

We sat there in a moment of silence out of respect for the risk to her career.

"Anyway, let Melissa know when you see her," Diane said. "If this turns into a major breakthrough for me, I'll owe her. I guess if I get fired, I'll owe her too, but in a different way. Although I decided to do this myself, so I'll have no one to blame but myself and the college's cowardice if they kick me out."

"Could they really do that?" Chloe asked. "Don't you have tenure?"

"They'd find a way," said Diane. "Even tenured faculty can be gotten rid of if the college wants to badly enough. And if I tell them all their buildings are death traps, they'll want to badly enough."

"Could you publish the results anonymously?" I asked. "Or anonymize the test sites somehow?"

"I'm thinking about how to do that," said Diane. "But then we'll have the issue of me knowing that we're working in an unsafe environment, and deliberately choosing not to do anything about it. Also not good, either for my conscience or my legal liability."

"Hmmmm," I said.

"But in the meantime, I'm going to keep on going. Just...don't tell anyone about it, will you? So far the only person who knows about it is Julie and you two. And Melissa, if you tell her. But other than that, let's just keep it our little secret for a little while longer, okay?"

"No problem," I said, while Chloe made heart-crossing and lip-zipping motions.

"And maybe don't spend too much time in any of our buildings," said Diane. "Just to be on the safe side."

We all looked around Brew's Up.

"This place seems pretty safe," Diane said. "Most of the samples I've taken here only show pretty low levels of stuff. And it smells okay, and you don't normally feel bad here, do you?"

Chloe and I shook our heads again.

"That's a good sign. We spend a lot of time teaching people not to jump to conclusions, which has somehow turned into teaching people not to trust their perceptions. But if you're going to deal with the real world, you have to trust your perceptions. A lot of the time, they're your best defense against danger. Believe in yourself, just like all the songs and motivational talks tell you to. Just don't stop using the scientific method while you're at it."

"Always good advice," I said.

49

IT WASN'T FOR ANOTHER three weeks, the Monday before Thanksgiving, that Raul, Camila's friend, was finally ready to talk. He had agreed to share his story with Dima, providing I was there to translate, and Camila was there to provide moral and legal support.

I was grateful he had agreed. I wished he had agreed at some other time. I had come back from the ASEEES convention in DC, where I had given a paper but not, alas, been invited for any interviews, late Sunday evening. I had class first thing Monday morning, our chat with Raul Monday evening, and Karen's long-dreaded second observation Tuesday morning, before spending the Thanksgiving holiday helping my parents with their new homesite. And I still had a couple more jobs I needed to apply to. So all in all, not a fun and relaxing week.

I tried to convince myself, as I anxiously checked my email for the thirtieth time Monday afternoon, that I had no reason to be nervous about talking to Raul. He was going to share his story, but it would have no real effect on me. I was just going to be there as an interpreter. An interpreter for Dima. I was going to spend a significant amount of time on the same video call as Dima.

You can do this! You've spent more time talking to him than you can count. My blatant attempts at psyching myself up rang hollow. Of *course* I was nervous about this. I'd spent a huge amount of time talking to Dima, I'd thought I was going to spend the rest of my life talking to Dima...and then he'd brought all those happy dreams to a crashing halt. I couldn't even begin to pretend I was indifferent about it.

Our video call was supposed to start at 6:00pm, Georgia time. That would be one in the morning in Moscow. I'd pointed that out and asked if we could move it to sometime earlier in the day, but Dima had said it was fine, he'd be happy to get up in the middle of the night to talk to a source.

Still suffering from that insomnia, he'd written to me. *Still suffering from those taut sails. Frankly, Inna, it will be a relief to not have to try to sleep through the night.*

That didn't sound very healthy to me at all, but this was his story, so I kept my mouth shut. Nagging Dima about taking care of himself was a counterproductive action in the extreme.

I ate an early supper, in order to stave off low blood sugar during the call, and then regretted it. My stomach was now gurgling unhappily as I waited by my laptop. I reminded myself that one of the benefits of a video call was that I could just mute myself and run to the bathroom whenever I needed to. I just didn't want to need to. I wanted everything to go perfectly smoothly, and...

Skype *blooped* on. I answered the call.

"Hello, Inna," said Dima. "You look great. I've missed you."

50

"I'VE MISSED YOU TOO," I said through numb lips. Then Camila *blooped* onto the screen, followed quickly by Raul. I made the introductions, and allowed Raul to start talking.

Raul was a slender man with large, intelligent eyes and dark hair that he still kept buzzed short on the sides. Like Camila, he also spoke with a North Carolina drawl with a tiny hint of Mexico underneath. I had already heard the basic outlines of his story from Camila. After he had gotten out of the military, he'd gone looking for work. The first work he'd found was with Security Solutions.

"First as a prison guard," he said. "But after a couple of months of that, they said they saw potential in me, and offered me a chance to move up in the world."

This initially meant private security. Then, after a couple more months of that, he'd been taken to their private training camp, where he'd been told about some of their more, well, private operations.

"They're looking to get into the mercenary business," he told us. "It's a profitable global market. Or it could be, except that US-trained soldiers cost a lot. Some companies cut costs by hiring guys from Venezuela, places like that. Security Solutions decided to try something different. Instead of hiring guys that'd already been trained, they'd hire people with less experience, and give them the training themselves. So they started recruiting from militia groups."

We all nodded.

"Of course, those guys think they're hot stuff, but most of them don't actually know shit—sorry, ma'am." Raul gave me an apologetic look.

"No worries," I said. "It's hardly the first time I've heard that word."

He smiled faintly. "So they need lots of training. And at first Security Solutions was using their own guys to do it. But then they came up with a better, ah, solution."

He paused. We all nodded encouragingly.

"So, I guess you all know..." Now he gave Dima an uncertain glance. "About the situation in, ah, Ukraine."

Dima and I nodded emphatically.

"So, it's, like, well, it's complicated. Originally I thought it was, you know, your archetypal good-versus-evil situation. Like, the evil Russian empire attacking poor little Ukraine." He gave Dima and me both another apologetic look.

"Believe me, there's normally a lot of truth in that story," said Dima.

"But then Security Solutions started bringing in their new trainers. From Ukraine. Battle-hardened soldiers from the ATO, the Anti-Terrorist Operation in Eastern Ukraine, they said."

We nodded some more.

"And I guess that was all true. But"—Raul's voice rose with indignation as he came to the crux of the story—"some of them were wearing the same Nazi shit that the militia guys were! And then Security Solutions started sending guys over there for training, and they'd come back even more indoctrinated in that shit than before! Like, I fucking kid you not, some of them were going around Sieg Heiling and shit! Like, right in front of the rest of us! Although, considering what just happened with the election just now and all, I guess I shouldn't have been too surprised. Anyway, when some of us complained about it, we were basically told to go fuck off. They said we were imagining things, or it wasn't that bad, or shit like that."

"Ah," I said. I translated it for Dima, although he'd been nodding along like he'd understood at least part of it already.

"Yes," he said when I was done. "It is hard to tell people here about it. It is a constant problem for us journalists. We're not supposed to talk about it much in our articles, and if we send in pictures of Ukrainian soldiers with Nazi symbols on their uniforms, the editors normally tell us that they can't print those pictures. We don't want to feed Russian propaganda, they say." Dima's mouth quirked. "Some people at a certain brick-red square in central Moscow would be very surprised to hear that I am guilty of feeding Russian propaganda. They are too busy accusing me of feeding Ukrainian and American propaganda."

Raul looked like he only partially understood what Dima was talking about, but didn't want to ask in case it plunged him into deeper waters than he felt comfortable swimming.

"So anyway," said Raul after a moment. "I realized I'd fallen in with a bunch of fucking white supremacists! Sometimes some of the trainers would talk about how they were defending European values from Russia. But by 'European values' they meant fucking fascism and white supremacy!"

Dima and I both nodded emphatically again. Camila looked faintly sick, even though she'd heard the story before.

"So anyway," Raul continued, "some of the trainees were sent off to Ukraine, like I said. As a special perk kind of thing, for special training. And when they got back, they were worse than ever. I mean, most of them didn't get in my face too much, although a few of them did. But I was seeing more and more that what was going on—it just wasn't right. Like, it seemed like Security Solutions was—I mean, it sounds crazy when I say it, but that's what it seemed like—it seemed like they were training these guys to become, like, jihadists or something. Whatever you call white supremacist jihadists. I mean, yeah, they were training them to be bodyguards and soldiers for hire, but I heard them drop some stuff when they thought I wasn't listening that suggested maybe they were doing something else, something more sinister, too."

"Tell me," said Dima, "did you ever hear anyone mention an organization called Kavboyets?"

Raul frowned when I translated that. Then his eyes lit up, and he nodded.

"Yeah! Only they didn't say it like that—actually, the trainers they'd brought over from Ukraine did, I guess. But the American guys didn't, so it took me a second. But yeah, I think that's what they were saying. I only heard them a couple of times. I couldn't figure out what they were talking about, not really. Just that Kavboyets had it all figured out, and we could be looking at a merger."

"Ah," said Dima. He looked extremely satisfied.

"What *is* Kavboyets, if you don't mind me asking?" said Raul.

"Another mercenary company," Dima explained. "But from the North Caucasus."

Raul looked like that didn't enlighten him too much, but he nodded anyway.

"They have global ambitions," Dima said. "Like your Security Solutions. A merger could make sense for both firms. Although politically...there could be some political problems. But with enough money, perhaps those political problems could be solved."

"Enough money can solve any problem," said Raul.

Dima shrugged. I guessed he was thinking that there were some problems that money couldn't solve. He'd told me so himself, several times. When you spent all your time seeing the kinds of crimes the very rich could commit, and how unhappy they were as they were committing them, you lost faith in the power of money. Or at least he'd always said so. This was normally as part of his explanation for why we were sharing a two-room apartment with his mother. I'd never complained about it, but he'd felt the need to justify himself at least once a year even so.

Dima asked a few more questions, but Raul had left Security Solutions shortly after that. His new company, he said, worked in the same general area, but they weren't actively recruiting and training neo-Nazi white supremacists, so that was a step up as far as he was concerned.

"I'm very grateful for your help," Dima told him at the end. "Can I talk to you again if I have more questions?"

Raul looked suddenly uncertain. "Uh...is my name going to appear anywhere?"

"Not if you don't want it to," Dima told him.

Raul didn't look like he put much faith in Dima's promise, but there wasn't much he could do about it now, so he agreed sure, Dima could contact him if he had more questions, and he'd think about answering them.

"Great," said Dima. "I'm very grateful. And to you, too, Camila, and to you, Inna. Inna, can we talk for a moment after this?"

"Sure," I said. "I'd be happy to."

51

RAUL AND CAMILA LEFT the call. Dima and I stayed on.

"Really, Inna, you do look great," he told me once we were alone again.

"How's Polya?" I asked.

He looked startled. It was a rare look for him. I savored it. "I don't know," he said after a moment.

"Oh?"

"Yeah." Now he was looking sheepish. It was an even rarer look for him. "She said...Inna, you warned me, and mama warned me, but I didn't listen...she said she didn't think I really cared about her at all, I was just using her, and she didn't want to be in a relationship with me if that was the case, so she was going to dump me. Then she said we'd never really been in a relationship anyway, so she couldn't actually dump me, but she'd break off contact with me, which was as close as she could get, so..."

"I'm sorry," I said automatically.

"Really?"

"Well...no. That always seemed like a terrible idea to me from the start."

"Yeah. Mama kept telling me the same thing. I just...I wanted to do right by everyone. But instead I screwed up big-time, didn't I?"

"Well..." I said.

"Inna," he said sternly, "even your angelic patience has to come to an end at some point. Let it be now."

"Well..." I said again. "Okay. But...I don't know...I've made a lot of mistakes too..."

"Not as many as me."

"I'm just full of doubts right now," I said. "So I don't want to condemn others."

"Full of doubts about what?" he asked.

"About me. About whether I'm a good person...is this what you wanted to discuss?"

"No, but this is ridiculous. You doubting that you're a good person! That's...that's...why on earth..."

"Sometimes it's good to doubt," I said. "And maybe neither of us know me as well as we thought. Anyway. What *did* you want to discuss?"

"Mostly I wanted to talk to you, Inna. Just...talk. But since you're asking, I wanted to tell you a little more about what I've found out. I thought it might help me to talk it over with you. And...I'm a little worried about you, to be honest."

A jolt went through me. "Worried? Why?"

"What this Raul told us only confirmed what I'd already suspected. Security Solutions are mixed up in some pretty dangerous stuff. And you're involved with them, aren't you?"

"Well," I said. "Only on paper, really. Yes, they donated a bunch of money to the university, but that's it."

"And they belong to the most powerful family in the university."

"Yes, that too," I agreed.

"Whose son you got into big trouble."

"Well...yes," I admitted.

"So they have reason to come after you. Personally."

"Well...I suppose so, but they haven't yet. I mean, that would be awfully obvious. I don't think they're going to do something like that."

"They might not try to get you fired, Inna. That might be too obvious for them, yes. Although they might be that obvious. But they might arrange something else for you. Some kind of accident or something."

I laughed. "Surely not!"

"Why not?"

"Well...most people don't do that kind of thing here. Especially not to people like me. I'm...nobody."

"A nobody who got the son of the owner of Security Solutions in big trouble, maybe ruined his life."

"I think he ruined his life himself," I countered.

"That's not how they think, Inna."

"True," I conceded. "But...I mean, I'm no fan of Security Solutions, but I have a hard time believing they'd break the *law* like that..."

"I don't." Dima's voice was forceful. "I'm sure they present a good front. But you heard what this Raul said. These are not good people. These are not nice people. And they're joining up with Kavboyets, who are about as not-nice as it's possible for people to be. All this Mister Anthony Wainwright II has to do is mention his little problem to his new friends at Kavboyets, and they'll take care of it, no muss, no fuss, no blood on his hands."

"Yeah, but...okay. Yes. I'm sure they're all terrible. How much danger do you think I'm really in? And what do you think I should do?"

Dima's face was somber. "I don't know, Inna. Other than be careful. Don't draw their attention to you. Don't go anywhere by yourself, or do anything where you might find yourself likely to have a convenient accident. Mama and I are hoping to get our visas soon.

We could be with you as soon as next month. Until then, be very, very careful."

"I will," I promised.

"And if you do happen to hear anything, let me know, will you?"

"I will," I promised again. "Hey, by the way, since we're talking about this kind of thing, what do you know about a group called Glorious Future?"

His face went still. "I only know a little about them. But what I know, I don't like. Why do you ask?"

"A former student has been asking about them. I just wondered if you happened to know anything interesting."

"Not much. But it's probably not a good sign that they've come up in my current investigation. So please, please, Inna, be careful."

"I will," I promised. "As careful as I can be."

52

I ENDED THE CALL WITH Dima feeling a mixture of elated, stressed, elated, terrified, and elated. Then I felt annoyed with myself. So Polya had broken up with him—although they'd apparently never been in a real relationship anyway, so she couldn't have actually broken up with him, which was wonderful, wonderful news...I tried to stop that train of thought. I was getting ahead of myself. I needed to have a good hard think about what I really wanted, and what was actually good for me, before I decided that getting back together with Dima was a good idea. And then I needed to have a little self-counseling session to figure out if it was even feasible, and how I would cope if it didn't work out.

The warning he'd given me I immediately dismissed. Then I told myself that maybe I should be taking it more seriously. He wasn't wrong. I *had* pissed off the head of Security Solutions—I assumed—and bad things could happen as a result. I'd been blithely assuming that US legal processes would protect me from retaliation, and so far I'd seen no sign of it anyway.

Anthony Wainwright, III, the son and heir of the owner of Security Solutions, was currently being prosecuted for multiple counts of sexual assault, and maybe some drug-related charges as well. And yes, I was the one, or at least one of the ones, who'd gotten him caught. But there'd been surprisingly little blowback for me so far. The university was too busy distancing themselves from the whole affair and loudly proclaiming their innocence to come after me. But that didn't mean someone *wouldn't* come after me. And if Security Solutions was in fact working with Kavboyets, well, Kavboyets had people who did that kind of thing.

A jolt of fear went through me as I thought that. I wasn't afraid of Security Solutions, but I was afraid, viscerally afraid, of Kavboyets. I found myself thinking of how to convince them not to come after me, that I wasn't going to do anything to bother them. But the problem was that I'd already done what I'd done. For all I knew, the Wainwright family had sworn blood vengeance against me, and was just waiting for the right time to send Kavboyets after me.

Don't be ridiculous! And don't panic. It all sounded so remote and over-the-top. And yet it *could* happen. There just wasn't a lot I could do about it, other than take those basic safety precautions Dima had recommended.

And in the meantime, I told myself, *you have that observation and performance evaluation to look forward to.*

53

NO ONE LEAPT OUT AT me as I got into my car the next morning, or rammed into me as I drove onto campus, or met me with a hail of gunfire as I got out of the car and started my slow way towards Bedford Hall. More's the pity.

I didn't really mean that, but I would have welcomed almost any non-lethal way to get out of the observation and evaluation. Since Mel was leaving straight from campus to go to her family's place in South Carolina, we were driving separately. This meant I had to park my car in the faculty lot and hobble all the way past the stadium and the dorms to the central quad. I could do it, and without crutches, which was a vast improvement over the start of the semester, but it still wasn't easy or pleasant. On the other hand, since I had stopped going to PT, my pain levels had decreased dramatically, so that was something.

Karen had, with surprising good sense, elected to observe my first-year class, where the students didn't know her, rather than return to face Jackson and the rest of the gang in second year. So I had all of my 9:00am class to stew and sweat before she showed up for the 10:00am class.

Miranda provided some welcome distraction during the first class. "Oh, Professor," she said when I came in. "I wanted to thank you. That friend of yours, you know, the journalist? He finally got in touch with me. I had an email from him waiting for me when I got up this morning. Finally something good! You know I've been in such a funk ever since the election...but now it feels like maybe there's something right in the world again."

My first, supremely irrational, emotion was jealousy. *I* hadn't had an email from Dima waiting for me when I'd gotten up this morning. Then I told myself how ridiculous that was. Dima and I had actually video-talked last night. And I doubted he would be interested in Miranda in that way. And...

"Can you take a look at the email, Professor?" she continued. "I *think* I understand it, but I'm not sure. And I'm kinda nervous, to be honest. Can you help me write the response? And, like, if he asks to talk to me, can you help translate?"

I gave my jealousy a small, triumphant smile. "Sure," I said. I glanced at the clock. 8:59. "I've got class right after this, and then a meeting, but maybe we can meet after that?"

"Can you do it at the end of class? It should only take a minute. It's not a long email, and I think I got most of it already."

"Um," I said. "Sure. I'd be happy to."

Miranda settled into her seat, looking happy. Everyone else squeezed in where they could, and we started reviewing the instrumental case. Or learning it for the first time, since half the students reacted to it as if they'd never seen it before in their lives.

Everyone but Miranda scrambled for the exit as soon as I called an end to the lesson at 8:48, glad to leave two minutes early. Miranda came over to me and showed me the email from Dima. Sure enough, it was very short.

Esteemed Miranda!

Your professor, Rowena Halley, has said you are interested in journalism and would like to speak with me about it. I would be happy to answer any of your questions I am able to. Let's set up a time to talk. Perhaps Professor Halley will be so kind as to interpret for us if necessary.

With respect,

Dima Kuznetsov

Miranda had managed to get about 80% of it. It was, she told me, a great personal triumph. But she also felt totally out of her depth actually responding, or communicating with him in any way. Could I help?

"Sure," I said. "Why don't we work on an answer together. But later. I've got class now."

"Oh. But I've got to head out soon to join the fam for Thanksgiving. Maybe you could just give me a few hints right now? It should only take a minute."

"Um." I looked up to see Karen coming in through the classroom door. Five minutes early, which was unlike her. But maybe she'd learned to arrive early in order to get the best spot. "Looks like I've got a guest. Can we email about it later?"

"Okay, sounds good! Talk to you then..." Miranda turned and saw Karen. Her face twisted up in an inadvertent expression of extreme dislike. Karen's own face mirrored the expression with almost comic accuracy.

"Bye!" said Miranda, and rushed out of the room.

"That girl," said Karen once Miranda was gone. She shook her head. "You know, Rowena, you certainly got some of the hardest students in the college. I have to hand it to you for sticking with them for so long. This is, what, your third semester with that Arenson girl?"

"Um," I said. "Yeah."

"And she actually seems to *like* you." Karen sounded more wondering than accusatory. "Were you helping her with some extra work there as I was coming in?"

"Um," I said. "Yeah. I, uh, put her in touch with a journalist I know. Because, um, she's interested in journalism."

Karen nodded. "That's *just* the kind of thing we like to see Crimson faculty doing."

"Oh," I said. "Um. That's great." I resisted the urge to go over and see if there was some sign that Karen had been abducted by aliens, or replaced with a robot simulacrum. I found myself examining her out the corner of my eye as I erased the board and wrote up bullet points for the next class. No sign of a charging port that I could see. I wasn't sure what kind of visible marks alien abduction was supposed to leave.

The students for my 10:00am class filed in and took their seats. I started class. Karen sat there quietly, her face as close to pleasantly neutral as a face like hers could be, occasionally making brief notes to herself. Sometimes she gave a faint smile as she made the notes. Not a smirk of delight at catching someone out in an error, but a smile of appreciation for a job well done. It was so unnerving I had a hard time concentrating on teaching.

When class was over and all the students had filed back out, Karen stood up, gave me another vague smile, said, "Come by and see me when you're ready, Rowena," and left.

I started erasing the board. What on earth, I asked myself, had gotten into her? And what diabolical action did it presage?

54

KAREN LOOKED UP FROM her computer as I stepped into her office a few minutes later. She gave me another smile. It was a bland, slightly weird smile, but it was a smile nonetheless.

Even more unnerved than before, I looked around her office, searching for clues. The same disheveled piles of books, gradebooks, papers, notes, and trash still covered every available surface. Including the chair. I removed a stack of stained quizzes from its seat, and sat down. I felt the back of my trousers catch on whatever the sticky thing was that had never been cleaned off that chair. Oh goody.

"Well, Rowena," Karen said. "I'm *very* pleased to say that you have obviously implemented my suggestions from my previous observations. I saw *real* improvement in your teaching today. I was particularly pleased since I know this is a very *trying* time for everyone. Things are very divisive right now because of the election. But your students all got along great. As I said, you've improved by leaps and bounds since you've started here."

"Um," I said. "That's, uh, great." I thought about asking what, exactly, she had seen. I'd taught exactly the same as I always did. My hackles were also starting to rise, just as they always did around her. It was good to know she probably hadn't been body-snatched, at least.

"Yes." Now she did smirk. Just a little, and then she caught it before it spread all over her face. "I have to say, at first I wasn't sure if you were going to be able to raise yourself up to the Crimson standard, but I'm *extremely* pleased to say that I think you have the makings of an *excellent* Crimson faculty member, given the right kind of mentoring."

"Oh," I said. "I'm, ah, glad to hear it."

"Yes. And speaking of such things, while I have you here, I wanted to talk to you about your candidacy for our tenure-track position."

"Uh-huh?" Cold sweat started trickling down my sides. I shifted in my seat, and then regretted it as my trousers ripped free of the sticky thing with a faintly rude noise.

"Yes, I'm *very* pleased to inform you that the committee was favorably impressed by your application, and we would like to invite you to a first-round interview this winter."

"Oh," I said. "That's great!" It should have been the most sincere thing I'd said in a while. Instead, a wave of dread washed over me. An interview! Ugh! And if it went absolutely perfectly, then I would probably have another, extremely grueling, round of interviews to follow. And if all that went great, then I would end up working here at Crimson for the rest of my life, or at least the next several years. And, it sounded like, being "mentored" by Karen. The prospect was stark.

"Yes. I can really see you joining our happy Crimson family for the long term, Rowena!"

"I'd be *delighted* to," I said.

55

I LIMPED OUT OF KAREN'S office and made my slow way out the building and towards the parking lot. I tried to tell myself I should be pleased. I should actually, for once, be delighted, just like I kept saying I was. But I wasn't.

Partly, I was annoyed—no, I was *enraged*—with what I now saw to be Karen's manipulation. She'd played bad cop all along, and now she had switched to good cop in order to show me and everyone else what a great mentor she was. We'd just moved onto the next phase of the hazing process, where she laid off the active attacks and started bringing me into the group, now that I'd been sufficiently broken down and was willing to accept the group's hierarchy and dynamics.

But I really needed this job, so I'd have to go along with it. Maybe for a few more months, maybe for the rest of my working life. Maybe ten or fifteen years from now I'd be the one hazing new faculty and acting like an asshole in the corner office. Because maybe I was *bad*.

I thought about that picture of Karen I'd seen at my previous visit. For a while, she'd been a lot like me. She'd said so, and for once, I was sure she was being sincere. No, that wasn't right. I was pretty sure she was almost always sincere. It was just that her sincerity generally came from a place of meanness and brokenness. We'd all be a lot better off if she learned to be a little less sincere.

I assumed that another major driver behind her sudden niceness was that they'd seen the candidate pool for the tenure-track job, and realized that it would be hard to replace me. While there were probably ten qualified Russian professors for every decent position, most people didn't consider a job in small-town Georgia to be a decent position. The competition would be much less than for a job in the Mid-Atlantic. As I'd guessed all along, there was probably hardly anyone actually available who could do the job I was doing.

On one level, that made me feel better. Unless something absolutely terrible happened, there was an excellent chance that I had a job, providing I could make myself jump through all the hoops ahead of me.

On another level, it was forcing me to realize just how little I wanted to stay here for much longer. Even nice Karen made my hairs bristle, and all the other decent colleagues I had didn't make up for that. And while I didn't hate Greenfields, I had a hard time imagining myself living here for another ten, twenty, or thirty years. I supposed it might be all right for people who already had families. Property prices were low and the area was generally safe, so a family could, for example, get a nice little farm on the edge of town and raise goats or alpacas or something as their hobby. But for an unwillingly single person, Greenfields was a dead zone. My reluctant forays into dating apps had only underscored how few potential partners there were within a two-hour drive of here. Taking this job would probably mean saying goodbye to any hopes I might still entertain of ever finding love or having a family.

Maybe the FBI will come through! They hadn't yet, though. I knew it was a slow process, but I had to assume the fact that I hadn't heard a peep from them for months was a bad sign. They'd probably gotten bogged down in my background check, and were now seriously second-guessing their decision to consider me at all. Weirdly, ridiculously, crazily, horribly, it looked like my best bet for a steady paycheck was going to be my abusive old flame, academia.

56

THE NEXT MORNING WAS the beginning of Thanksgiving break. But since scholarship never stops, I got the official email of invitation to the interview for the tenure-track position at Crimson. I officially wrote back saying I would officially be delighted to be interviewed. The interview, I was told, would take place after New Year's, via Skype. This would make it more fair for all the other candidates.

We want to make sure we are ***scrupulously*** *fair in the job search process,* Karen wrote. *It is very important for our institutional reputation, and our very accreditation by SACS, that there be not even a hint of favoritism towards an inside candidate.*

Of course, I wrote back. *I understand.* I tried to tell myself I did. In fact, my strongest feeling was one of resentment. Of course the process wasn't fair. I'd already been working there for a year and a half. Shouldn't that count for something? Or was this more hazing? I suspected that it was.

Well, nothing I could do about it right now. Or maybe ever. It was looking more and more like I was stuck in this hazing hell. Although if I got a job in some other field, would it be any better? I'd gotten quite attached to the idea of working for the FBI, but my common sense told me that the reality would probably be full of petty annoyances and, most likely, hazing. Probably I was better off with the devil I knew. And it looked like I might be stuck with him, in any case.

In the meantime, I was going to go see my parents' new plot of land and the beginnings of their tiny house project. Part of me was genuinely interested, even excited. It brought back all kinds of happy childhood memories of alternative lifestyles that were starting to seem more and more attractive.

I'd turned my back on that kind of thing as a teenager and had gone through a fairly normal college and grad school process, with the intention of living a fairly mainstream life. Well, if you could call being a Russian professor married to a Russian opposition journalist "mainstream." But my plans hadn't involved living in a hand-built yurt or tiny house. A charming hand-built dacha outside of Moscow, maybe, but that was totally mainstream for Russia.

The mainstream hadn't been nearly so welcoming as I'd imagined, though. Or at least, it hadn't been nearly so simple to navigate. It was tempting to think, when you were on the outside looking in, that those on the inside had it easy. They were following a well-defined path, with all the advantages that entailed.

But, I thought sourly, *that path is actually the Highway to Hell.* Then I lectured myself about not being such a grumpy-pants. At this rate I was *definitely* going to turn into Karen. Either that, or join Brenda Melnichuk and her cronies as an extremist masquerading behind a bland, well-intentioned exterior.

Fortunately, I had my family to save me from that. I scratched Fevronia behind her ears, neatly dodging a nasty swipe from her claws, and headed off to see my parents' new, non-mainstream, life project.

57

MY PARENTS' NEW PIECE of land was a little north of Macon, near the Piedmont National Wildlife Refuge. It was a couple of wooded acres overlooking a creek, nestled in amongst farmland and a respectable number of churches. It had a long gravel drive, almost a road, through the woods, ending at a cleared spot with a ramshackle old barn in the middle.

"This used to be a homestead," my mother was telling my grandparents as I got out of the car and came over to join them. "But the only thing left is this barn. At first we thought about restoring it—Bobby thought it would be a charming cottage—but then we decided against it."

My grandfather had closed his eyes in horror when my mother had mentioned restoring the barn. Now he reopened them and nodded with vigorous approval. "Good, good," he said. "Restoring something like this would be a nightmare. Don't look like there's anything worth saving left, anyway. Whole thing'd crumble to dust as soon as you so much as pointed a hammer its way."

"That's what Bev said," my father agreed. Bev was my mother. Bev O'Malley had married Bobby Halley. They found it almost as funny as I did. I could also sympathize with why they'd given me and John such outlandish names. "I thought it had potential," my father was saying. "But Bev said no, and the structure would be too big for what we were looking for anyway, so we agreed we'd pull the whole thing down, reclaim what we could of the materials, and design the new house to honor this old structure. Include similar motifs, things like that."

My grandfather nodded slowly, looking like he wanted to agree, but was afraid that behind this façade of common sense, madness lurked. That was often how he felt about my father. Deep down, they actually had pretty similar morals. Both of them believed in hard work and helping others over self-aggrandizement and greed. And they often said things that seemed to agree on the surface. But their ideas of how to implement their ideals were normally somewhere between 90 and 180 degrees off. It made for an interesting relationship.

"You got any blueprints drawn up?" my grandfather asked, speaking with the caution of a man who has often been disappointed in the past, but in whom hope springs eternal.

"We've been drawing up sketches," my father said. He pulled off his glasses, which were still cracked from the hammer incident over fall break, and cleaned them on his shirt, a sign that he was particularly excited. "Bev has them. We can show you. And we thought, since we have you here today, we could start marking out the foundations. You know, actually mark it out on the ground and see how it looks, how we feel about it, start to visualize it as a material reality rather than an abstract idea."

My grandfather nodded again, still with cautious hope and approval. "That sounds like a fine idea. I take it y'all aren't planning to put it exactly over where the old barn is now?"

"We're not sure," my mother put in. "We thought about having it tucked in under the trees over there." She pointed to the edge of the clearing. "But that's why we wanted to start marking out the foundations."

"We brought string!" my father said enthusiastically. "And tent pegs! And even marking chalk!"

"Great," said my grandfather. "Great. Y'all have thought about this real thoroughly, I can tell. That's good. Why don't we get to marking, then? Y'all have your plans with you?"

My mother pulled out a notebook of sketches while my father trotted over to the car to get the string and pegs. My grandmother came over to me while we stood there.

"Weena, darling, have you heard? John is actually spending Thanksgiving with Camila and her family. Isn't that just...darling, has he *ever* spent Thanksgiving with a woman before?"

"Not that I can remember," I said. "Gosh. He *is* a changed man."

"It sure seems like it, doesn't it? And to be honest, I'm actually glad he won't be with us this Thanksgiving. I mean, I'll miss him something terrible, but I just don't think I can handle the arguments he and your father would get into over politics after this *terrible* election. So I'm glad he'll be spending it with Camila instead. And I think she's *so* good for him, don't you? I mean, she sounds like a little...well, I was going to say *ballbreaker*, but maybe martinet is more polite, isn't it? But you know what I mean. And normally I wouldn't want that, but with John, well...it's probably what he needs, isn't it? And it's what he's used to, isn't it? After all those years in the military? He probably feels happiest when someone's telling him what to do. Most women just didn't have the backbone to give him what he really needs, but maybe this Camila does."

"Yeah," I said. "I think she just might."

"That's right, you actually talked to her, didn't you? Well, tell me all about it!"

My parents had assembled all the necessary equipment for marking out the foundations. We moved forward to take our places, my grandmother sticking by my side.

"Well," I said. "She's, uh, well, she seems like a good person to me. A bit of a ballbreaker, I'm sure, but basically a good person. I think I liked her."

"Of *course* you did, darling. She sounds a lot like you, actually."

"Um," I said. "Maybe. I guess..."

My phone *pinged.*

"Hang on," I said. "I'd better check this. You guys go ahead."

I stepped away from the potential construction site and pulled out my phone. A big part of me was hoping it was a message from Dima. Had he remembered that it was a holiday in the US, and was writing to congratulate me? Or to update me on the visa situation for him and Galina Ivanovna?

Hey Prof H! the text said. *Can you talk for a minute? I think I've got a big problem.*

58

THE TEXT WAS FROM MADISON. Of course she had a big problem. I repressed a sigh. Then I felt bad. She probably did have a big problem. It could even be a real problem. It could even be a problem that she had not created directly herself.

Sure, I texted back. *Do you want to talk or text?*

Can we talk? I feel weird talking about it in writing somehow. I guess I'm super paranoid or something but I don't want it recorded anywhere so Verizon or whatever can get into my records.

No problem. Should I call you now?

Please do.

That "please do" worried me. I tried to remember Madison ever using a phrase so appropriate and polite. I couldn't think of a single instance. She must really be in trouble.

I looked over at the others. My father was reading from the sketches and fiddling with a measuring tape while my mother was discussing something with my grandparents. It looked like they were trying to decide the best location to put in the first corner peg. My dad looked up and said something to them. He gestured towards a particular spot in the ground, forgetting about the measuring tape he'd pulled about a foot out of its case. The metal tape zipped back into the case when he let go of it, catching on his thumb and drawing blood with its sharp edge. Yelling and swearing and general consternation on all sides erupted.

I turned away. It wasn't a mortal wound. My mother was already fishing an alcohol wipe and bandaid from the large supply she always kept in her purse. Just another fun afternoon doing manual labor with my dad. I hit "Call" on my phone screen.

"Hey, Prof!" Madison answered on the first ring. She was trying to sound breezy, but her voice caught, and she ended in a strangled gulp.

"Hey, Madison," I said. "What's up?"

"Oh, you know...school's going well, Aunt Cybil's actually, like, really cool. And I guess she thinks I'm pretty cool too, since she's saying not only can I stay till the end of the semester, maybe I should stay for next semester too. That'd be awesome, 'cause I'm having a great time in NYC. And my dad's being less of a dick than usual. Oh shit. Didn't mean to...anyway. Things are going great. Only...you know the election last week and all the like, craziness and shit?"

"Yes," I said. "I do know."

"First time I ever voted," Madison said. "Huh! Big fucking whoop-de-whoop. Don't know why I bothered."

"Well," I said. "Sometimes you just have to do the right thing no matter what."

"Yeah, I guess. It just seemed like a total fucking waste of time...but anyway. That's not why I called. It's, like, my mom."

"Uh-huh?" I said, when she didn't say anything for a moment.

"Yeah. We're kinda, like, talking again."

"That's great," I said.

"I don't know about that, Professor H. I think I might be, like, what's the word? Aiding the enemy or some shit like that?"

"Um," I said. "How so?"

"Well, so, it's like this. I agreed to go spend Thanksgiving with my mom. Big fucking mistake."

"Uh-huh?" I said again, after another long pause.

"Yeah, so, we'd been, like, talking and shit for a few weeks now. And she'd been talking about the election, politics, all that...I didn't want to argue, so I just kinda like nodded along and went 'Yeah, yeah, sure, Mom, sure,' the whole time. So I guess she thought I, like, agreed with her a lot more than I do."

There was another pause. "Uh-huh?" I said, to jolly the conversation along.

"So, I, like, showed up at her place like, last night. And we had, like, a guest for dinner. Carrie Ostermayer."

"Mmmm?" I said.

"You know about her, right? She was, like, in the stuff I told you about earlier, right?"

"Uh-huh," I said. "I read about her and your mom working together."

"Yeah. So I'd, like, never actually met her before. But there she was, large as life, sitting across the dinner table from me."

"Mmmm," I said.

"So she and my mom started talking. About politics and stuff. And from what I gathered...it sounded like...it sounds crazy, but I swear it's true, cross my heart and hope to die...it sounded like they were saying that if the election had gone the other way like we all thought it would, then they'd been, like, planning...I can't believe I'm saying this shit about my own mom...they'd been planning to carry out some kind of terrorist operation."

59

"HAVE YOU TOLD ANYONE?" I asked. "Have you told your alphabet agency contact?"

"No. I...I, like, I *can't*. I can't snitch on my own mom that way. 'Sides, he'll probably laugh in my face."

"Madison," I said. "We've been through this before. He's not going to laugh in your face. This is why they contacted you. They're very, very interested in this kind of thing. They *need* you to tell them."

"You think so?"

"I know so. This is what they exist for."

"Yeah, but...it's just all so vague...it's not like I heard them say 'Tomorrow at dawn in front of the Capitol.' I just kinda...guessed from what they were talking about that they'd had some kind of plans..."

"Even so," I said. "Maybe they're hearing other, similar rumors. This could help them confirm their hunch, triangulate in on the truth. Maybe something that was meaningless to you will be meaningful to them. I really think you should tell them, Madison."

"Okay." She still sounded skeptical. "And I guess I should remind them about the guys from Glorious Future coming over too for this retreat, huh? I, like, know who they are now, so maybe they'd, like, want to know? And I, like, looked them up, and it was, like...they're pretty scary guys. At least I think so."

"Yes," I said. "You should *definitely* tell them about that too."

"They're not going to do anything," she said. "No one does anything. This whole country is going to crap. Maybe they're in on it too."

"That seems unlikely," I said.

"Yeah. I guess. It just all feels so useless right now. I kinda...I mean, I think my mom's, like, crazy, and her whole family's crazy and maybe kinda evil, but, like...I get why they do what they do. I just, kinda, like, feel like joining them now. I mean, not, like, joining *them*. But, like, doing what they're doing. Starting my own movement instead of trying to do stuff that's never going to work."

"I know the feeling," I said. "But really, in this case, I think you should tell your contact. I mean, I don't know what you could do that would work better."

She was silent for a moment. "Yeah," she finally said. "I guess so. Well, I guess I'll call him. Maybe he'll answer. Oh, and if you want a laugh, you should look up Vadim Zhuraev. I can't believe he's my cousin. I can't believe he's real. Maybe he isn't. Maybe he's, like, I don't know, a plant or a fake or something. You should look him up and let me know."

"Um," I said. "Sure. I'll do that."

"Great." She was starting to sound like the breezy Madison of old. "Meantime, I'll call my alphabet agency guy and see if he laughs in my face or what. Tell you what, Prof: this has been a pretty cool semester all around. I mean, it's not what most people probably want, right? But it's actually been pretty cool. And even if alphabet guy laughs at me, that'll be kind of cool too. I mean, it'll be, like, an experience."

"Yeah," I said. "For sure."

"Cool. Well, talk to you later, Prof. And seriously, go look up Vadim Zhuraev right now. You'll be glad you did."

60

I HAD TO WAIT UNTIL the evening before I could go look up Vadim Zhuraev. First I had to spend the afternoon helping my parents measure out the potential foundations for their proposed tiny house. This involved a lot of discussion, debate, and two more minor injuries for my father. By 4:30pm, they still weren't 100% certain about where they wanted the foundations to be, but my grandmother was clearly drooping, so my grandfather said we had to call it a day and go get cleaned up and get dinner.

"We'll come back on Friday," he declared. "It'll be clearer with fresh heads."

My parents agreed, reluctantly, that he spoke sense. We all piled into our cars and drove back to the house in Macon, where we took turns washing off and then sat down to a light supper. We were hungry enough that we would have liked a hearty supper, but my grandmother said it would be good for us to build our appetites for the feast tomorrow.

By 8:00 I was able to escape and drive back home. When I got back to the apartment at 8:30, Fevronia was waiting for me, mewling impatiently. I gave her some attention and some cat crunchies. By then it was 8:45. I told myself I was just going to take a shower and go straight to bed. I could have fun on the internet tomorrow.

But when I got out of the shower, it was only 9:00pm and curiosity was eating away at me. I told myself I would do just a quick search for Vadim Zhuraev. At least I'd have an idea of why Madison thought he was so important.

My first few searches turned up a dentist in Moscow, a college student in Novorossiysk, and a car mechanic with a side hustle as a DJ in Tomsk. None of them seemed like likely prospects. Surely Madison had had someone more extremist in mind.

I added "neo-Nazi" to my search term string and got an immediate hit.

This Vadim Zhuraev, I read, had been born in 1980. Just like me. Only he'd been born in Donetsk, in the Donbass region of Ukraine. His family had moved from there to Moscow, and then Minsk, where they'd been living when the Soviet Union collapsed. This meant that they had become citizens of Belarus, despite being a Russian family from eastern Ukraine.

Vadim and his family, I gathered, had been dismayed by this circumstance, as had the many millions of people who had suddenly ended up citizens of a foreign country after the dissolution of the USSR. The problem had been dramatically compounded in recent years by the increasingly strained relations between Russia and Ukraine. The original idea, I knew, had been for Russia, Belarus, and Ukraine to remain very closely tied, with a mutual military-defense agreement. This is why the Crimea, and in particular the naval port at Sevastopol, had been left with Ukraine, even though technically as an item of all-Union significance it should have been returned to Russia. Now the fraternal squabbling over the family estate had escalated into occupation and war. For the actual families caught on both sides of the divide, the tragedy only continued to grow.

In Vadim's case, he had started working for the Belarusian security forces after getting out of school. This had somehow been parlayed into a job with the Russian FSB. But then he'd left them and ended up leading the White Wolves, a group with strong ties to fascism and neo-Nazi ideology, as well as a kind of neo-Soviet nostalgia. This was all part of the "red-brown" movement that had been growing in the former USSR following its collapse.

While involved in the White Wolves, Vadim had been implicated in various murders of rivals within the organization, as well as attacks on Caucasian and Central Asian minorities living in Moscow. He had eventually been forced out of the group, only to resurface in Kiev as a vlogger about Ukrainian nationalism. Almost preternaturally handsome, with a high forehead that suggested an intellectual bent and pretty-boy features that were gradually morphing into ruggedly sexy good looks, along with a quick tongue and a voice that somehow sounded like melted chocolate, he had quickly gained a following.

In 2013-2014 he had led a group of protestors on the Maidan, the square in central Kiev where the main protests and clashes had taken place. His group was also one of the right-wing groups implicated in the killings of both protestors and police. Rumor had it that Vadim had bragged afterwards about taking out two policemen himself.

Afterwards, while still maintaining an active vlogging presence, he had led a paramilitary group against the Donbass separatists, before being folded into the main Ukrainian military. His social media feeds had been full of videos of heroic deeds in the Anti-Terrorist Operation by him and his group, and he had become a sex symbol amongst women the world over who sympathized with Ukraine and the Maidan movement.

Less heroically, rumors of rape, torture, and extrajudicial executions of separatists, as well as firing on civilians and the brutal hazing of his own fighters, surrounded his unit, although nothing had been proven definitively. Journalists who had tried to publish pictures of fighters in his unit wearing swastikas, *sonnenräder*, and other Nazi symbols had had their stories canceled, and in some cases had been threatened and even beaten. There was no room, they were told, for negative depictions of the brave fighters against Russian aggression. People needed heroes, especially during such divisive times, and Vadim was the hero of the moment. If that meant looking the other way when certain unpleasant facts came to light, so be it. If someone wouldn't listen to reason, then Vadim and his men were extremely capable of silencing people more permanently.

The author of the final report I read on him, from a small human rights group dedicated to researching and exposing neo-Nazi and white supremacist ideology, speculated that he was actually a Russian plant sent to undermine Ukrainian independence from within. Why else would a Russian/Belarusian neo-Nazi be fighting against the pro-Russian separatists in the Donbass?

Other authors suggested that he was a committed white supremacist who had found a particularly congenial environment. Neo-Nazism and white supremacy had become global movements that were separating themselves from nationalism per se, although they still often existed side-by-side with it.

With the collapse of the Soviet Union, some people had clung to communism and Soviet nostalgia, but lots of others had gone searching for other ideologies to replace it. Neo-Nazism had become popular in Russia in the early 2000s, but now, as far as I could tell, was being subsumed by a Russian nationalism that was more interested in Russia as a great, and therefore multi-ethnic, empire than as a white ethnostate. Meanwhile, the ideals of white supremacy aligned closely with the ideals of Ukrainian independence and Ukraine as a wholly European nation, upholding European values. This was particularly the case since previous iterations of the Ukrainian independence movement had been closely tied to fascism and Nazism.

That meant that now true believers in white supremacy were gravitating towards Ukraine and Kiev's so-called Anti-Terrorist Operation in the Donbass. So Vadim could be a Russian plant, sent to destroy Ukraine from the inside, or he could be a fervent white supremacist, fighting to defend Europe from the ravening Asiatic hordes. Or he could be both. In my experience, one should never underestimate the presence of agents of chaos.

I checked the time. 10:00pm. Which meant it was five in the morning for Dima. I shouldn't bother him. Either he was sleeping, or he was trying to sleep. He didn't need a text from me. And I was about to go to bed. I should let both of us sleep. And maybe by tomorrow my questions wouldn't seem so pressing anyway.

Those were all sensible thoughts. None of them stopped me from taking out my phone and writing, *What do you know about Vadim Zhuraev?*

61

AFTER I SENT THAT TEXT, I made myself set my phone down and get into bed. Fevronia came out from where she'd been skulking under the bed and climbed onto the spare pillow, the one that was supposed to be for lovers but actually just collected cat hair, and gave me a meaningful stare.

"You have food," I told her.

She gave me another, even more meaningful, stare.

I cautiously reached out a hand and tried to scratch behind her ears. She ducked her head and jerked away. I put my hand under the covers and tried to look as unthreatening as possible.

Fevronia gave me another meaningful stare. When I responded by staying completely still and ignoring her, she crept closer. I looked straight ahead, pretending she wasn't there. She crept a little closer and nosed at my hair. There was a faint rumble by my ear. Was she purring? I tried to breathe as shallowly as possible. The rumble grew louder. Then there was a tug at my hair.

*Is she **chewing** on my hair?* I resisted the urge to turn my head and look. The tugging on my hair grew stronger, as did the purring. She was definitely chewing on my hair.

*I **guess** this is a good thing?* I wondered how much damage she was doing to my hair. Then I wondered how much it would actually matter. My hair care routine consisted of trying to keep it reasonably clean and tangle-free, and occasionally snipping it back to just above my shoulders when it starting catching on the strap of my purse. Probably a little cat chewing wouldn't make any difference at all.

My phone *pinged.* I reached out for it. Fevronia scuttled away under the bed again.

Hello, Innochka! I know more about Vadim Zhuraev than I'd like, the text read. *Why do you ask?*

It looks like he might be coming to the US, I wrote back. *And you're up awfully early.*

Insomnia, taut sails again)))))) Partly from worrying about guys like Zhuraev. Why is he coming to the US? You're not going to have anything to do with him, are you?

No, I assured him. *He should be in a completely different state, far away from me. Someone just told me about him recently, and I was wondering.*

He's a bad guy, Inna. Stay away from him.

I intend to, I promised.

Do you know why he's coming to the US? Dima asked. *Seems like he should be busy with the ATO.*

I think he's coming over to meet with other like-minded people here. Probably to give inspirational speeches.

I can't believe the US government would let him come over, Dima wrote. *He's a really dangerous guy. Aren't they supposed to keep terrorists out?*

To them, he's probably not a terrorist, I wrote back. *He's a brave defender of his homeland, democracy, and European values.*

And the Taliban, al-Qaeda, and ISIS are brave defenders of their homelands and eternal religious values, Dima wrote. *That doesn't mean you should invite them over as guests.*

I know. But it's not my decision.

True. Anyway, it's funny you should ask about Vadim. I've been looking into him myself.

How come? I asked.

Some threads that might be between him and Kavboyets.

I see. That was only sort of true. Kavboyets was a Chechen-based mercenary company full of radical Muslim fighters that probably answered to the Kremlin. It seemed like it should be on the opposite side of anything Zhuraev supported. *Do you think Moscow planted Zhuraev in order to undermine the current Kiev regime?* I asked.

That was my first thought, Dima wrote back. *But the more I look into him, the less likely it seems. It seems to me that he sincerely believes in his fascist ideology. It also seems to me that he serves no master. No one can keep him under control.*

Then what's the connection with Kavboyets from? I asked.

I wish I knew)))) I've just heard reports of him doing something with Kavboyets, maybe drug smuggling or drug development. They may be trying out new drugs on the field in the Donbass. But how or why he and Kavboyets would be working together on this when they're supposed to be on opposite sides, I don't know.

I tried to think of some kind of clever and insightful response to that, something that would illuminate what Zhuraev and Kavboyets were doing. Instead I wrote *There are a lot of bad people in the world.*

There are, Dima agreed. *But there's good people in the world, too. Like you, Inna.*

And you, I wrote back.

I try))))) But mostly I fail)))))

You succeed, I wrote.

Not enough. I've been thinking, Innochka.

I waited. Nothing. *Yes?* I prompted.

I've been a total shit to you, haven't I? I mean, I meant well, but I've been a complete asshole to you. I have ever since we first got together, and it's only gotten worse over the years.

What brought this on? I wrote, rather than responding directly. Because of course it was true, but I wasn't going to tell him that.

*I've been thinking. A *lot*. Because of work stuff, and especially because of mama's situation. It's made me do a lot of soul-searching. And, you know, I've always been an idealist.*

There was another pause. I waited some more. *I know*, I wrote.

*I was an idealist when I joined OMON—yes, I did it because I needed the money, but I also *believed* in it—and an idealist when I quit and became a journalist and joined the opposition, and an idealist when I proposed to you, and an idealist when I broke up with you. All of those actions were prompted by idealism. I truly thought I was doing the right thing, and I was trying as hard as I could to act for the best.*

I know, I wrote again, when no more was forthcoming.

And all of those things were bad. They made me do bad things, betray the very ideals I'd meant to serve.

Thanks, I wrote.

I guess that sounded bad when it came out like that, huh? But what I meant was that...well, let's talk about you. About you and me.

Okay, I wrote.

*Inna, I really loved you. I really did. I'm as sure of that as I am of anything. But I also started going out with you, and proposed to you, because of idealism. Not because I loved you. Because I thought doing it would serve some higher ideal. You and I were going to change the world together. And marrying a liberal American was another way of thumbing my nose at the Powers That Be, whom I'd sworn to overthrow. I didn't do it because of you. I didn't do it because of me. I did it because of *them*.*

Okay, I wrote again.

Only after a while I started to think that maybe I was doing the wrong thing. After all, being with you wasn't helping my cause. It was hurting it. A connection with an American just showed that I was a degenerate foreign agent who'd sold out to America, not a principled patriot of Russia.

Is that how you actually felt? I asked. We'd never discussed this aspect of our relationship. I'd worried about it too much to have the courage to bring it up with him, in case he said exactly what he'd just said.

*No. I didn't feel compromised at all. You never asked me to compromise anything. But I worried that I was and didn't know it, and I *knew* that that's what others thought. What do they say? "Bad optics"? The optics of our relationship were very bad.*

I know, I wrote. I was NOT going to cry. Absolutely not. The part about bad optics was true, and all the crying in the world wouldn't make it any less true. I just hated the thought of Dima weighing our relationship on the balance of PR, and finding it wanting. It made me think less of him. While no one—other than maybe his mother—was as aware of his faults as I was, I still thought of him as fundamentally brave and true, someone who acted according to his beliefs, not what the public thought of him. Losing that faith in his essential heroism would be almost as painful as losing him.

*And then when that incident happened, when they threatened you, I realized how I truly felt about you, and it was so scary. Because I cared about *you* more than I cared about any ideal, or about *Them*. And I also realized that I was hurting you. I was hurting you by putting you in danger, but I was also hurting you by acting according to my ideals instead of according to what was best for you. And I couldn't figure out how to reconcile those two things. So I broke up with you, and I told us both it was for the best. It was best for *you*. But you didn't think so, did you? You tried to tell me—you *did* tell me—that it wasn't best for you, but I wouldn't listen. I *couldn't* listen. I couldn't even listen to myself, let alone someone else, even you.*

But now you can? I asked. The tears threatening to choke me started to recede. Maybe Dima really was the hero, or at least the decent man, I'd always believed him to be.

*I don't know. Maybe. Maybe not, but at least I know I *need* to listen. I *need*—I *have*—to find a way to reconcile my ideals with my life. I just don't know how to do that yet. But by following my ideals at the expense of everything else, I've broken the very ideals that I was trying so hard to follow. And now I don't know what to do. I *need* ideals, Inna. I can't live without them. They're my daily bread. But they're tearing me apart. They're making me betray them. I've come to a dead end and I can't figure out how to get out.*

Sometimes, I wrote, *I find that the best way out of a dead end is to do something totally unexpected.*

Totally unexpected? That's wise, I suppose. So...totally unexpected...I totally unexpectedly))))) humble myself))))))) before you, Inna, and ask you for help and advice. What would you advise me to do, Inna? How can I stop betraying my ideals by attempting to follow them?

I wish I knew, I wrote. *I keep asking myself the same thing. The only thing I know for sure is that if you want to act well, you can't treat people badly. How you treat one person is how you treat the world.*

Hard wisdom, Innochka, but true. I'll have to think on it. I know you're right, but I don't know yet how I can live by that. And Homer is silent)))) Whom should I listen to?

Mandelstam, maybe, I wrote. *When he said that everything is moved by love.*

Everything is moved by love))))) As always, Mandelstam knows all. I'll think on it, Innochka. I don't know what conclusions I'll come to, but I'll think on it. I've sworn to myself that I'll let you go, and I've sworn to myself that I'll take you back, and neither of those things have come to pass. Maybe I should stop swearing to myself and start listening to you instead.

Yes, I said. *Maybe you should.*

I'll try, Innochka. It will be an unaccustomed exercise, but I'll try. And now it must be late for you. No reason for you to have insomnia along with me. I'll let you sleep. Although maybe I'll come up to the head of your bed, like the wine-dark sea, in your dreams))))

Maybe, I wrote. *Good night. Or good morning, rather, for you.*

Good morning, Innochka. Sleep well))))

62

MY TALK WITH DIMA HADN'T kept me up that late, but I lay awake for a long time afterwards, feeling the wine-dark sea of confusion and uncertainty sloshing around my bed. Occasionally I smiled up into the darkness like an idiot.

When I woke up the next morning, Fevronia was purring and chewing on my hair again. I felt remarkably cheerful and energetic, despite only getting half a night's sleep. The three messages from dating site scammers that greeted me when I checked my phone failed to ruin my mood. So far, this experiment hadn't broadened my knowledge of men so much as made me realize how few non-scammer, non-predator males were out there. And the few non-sociopaths I'd encountered had been totally incompatible. Pretty depressing results for a pool of thousands of potential matches. But I didn't need lots of men. I only needed one. After a moment of indecision, in case I was jinxing myself, I set the app to "snooze" for 30 days. A great feeling of freedom washed over me, lifting my mood even further.

I continued to feel remarkably cheerful and energetic as I drove over to Macon, and as I helped with the prep for Thanksgiving dinner, and as I fielded prying questions about my work and personal life. My good mood continued the next day, when we eschewed Black Friday and went back to the new house site, where we spent most of the day measuring things and discussing, sometimes in heated tones, what we were measuring. My dad suddenly got it into his head that they should build a treehouse, and to everyone else's outrage I accidentally backed him up on it.

"A treehouse would be *awesome*," I said.

"But not at all practical," said my mother. Behind her, my grandparents had both gone round-eyed with horror.

"Well, no...maybe you could have a treehouse as the guest house you were talking about?"

My dad said that was the best idea he'd ever heard, so by the end of the day, it was agreed that they would have a treehouse as well as the regular tiny house. I could tell that my mom and grandpa, who would be doing most of the actual construction work, were less thrilled with the idea than my dad and I were, but what could I say? A treehouse *would* be awesome. I might even be willing to help build it.

Despite the treehouse disagreement, it was one of the most harmonious and productive weekends I'd spent with my family in my entire adult life. By the end of it, though, I was starting to get antsy. The pressures of work were staring me in the face again, and I hadn't heard from Dima since that talk we'd had on Wednesday. Should I text him? He didn't tend to respond well to me reaching out to him. That was probably a very bad sign. Borderline abusive, in fact. Why had I been so happy at the thought of maybe, possibly, someday getting back together with him? Why was I such an idiot? Why had I ruined my life so badly?

I was contemplating these thoughts Sunday night when a text from Madison popped up on my screen.

OMG, check the news right now!

What am I checking for? I asked.

In response she sent a link to an article.

POPULAR EVENT ORGANIZER CARRIE OSTERMAYER ARRESTED FOR INAUGURATION DAY CONSPIRACY.

63

I SKIMMED THROUGH THE article. The headline said it all. Carrie Ostermayer, a well-known local event organizer and co-owner of the resort Bright Dawn, had been arrested Sunday morning after an anonymous tip had led to an early-morning raid.

According to the article, despite her current wholesome outward appearance, in her younger days Carrie had been a "known associate" of a member of the Aryan Brotherhood, a white supremacist prison gang that ran a wide variety of criminal activities. She was suspected of having smuggled messages from her then-boyfriend in prison, thus helping organize drug deals and possibly at least one murder.

Now the FBI were saying they had "credible evidence" that she had been involved in a conspiracy to lead some kind of disruptive, possibly terrorist, action on election night if Clinton had won. Clinton hadn't won, so the action had been called off, but they had discovered evidence of a potential plot to carry out a similar action on Inauguration Day.

It was unclear what that action would be and why she and her group would want to do something to disrupt the inauguration of a president they presumably supported. She was maintaining that it was simply a march in support of the new president and new administration. But law enforcement agencies had evidence that this march might involve extremist groups. Public safety was crashing up against free speech, and it wasn't certain yet how it would shake out.

Yikes! I texted Madison.

What am I going to DO???? Madison texted back. *My mom is super pissed! Can we talk? On the phone?*

Sure, give me a call.

Thirty second later, my phone rang. "What am I going to DO!?!" Madison repeated as soon as I picked up. Her voice was shaking and had risen up to near bat-sonar levels. "I didn't want to text about it...what if my mom reads my texts and finds out about...what I did? Or what if my text records get, like, what's the word, subpoenaed? Is that the word?"

"Something like that," I said. "I'm sure she'll be pissed, but..."

"It's not just her I'm scared of." Madison cut me off before I could finish. "It's those crazies she runs around with. Did you read about Vadim Zhuraev?"

"I sure did," I said.

"He's, like, my fourth cousin or some shit like that. Crazy, huh? I met him when we were there last summer. Scared the absolute shit out of me. Like, for real. Like, after I talked to him I had to go running to the fucking *outhouse*, 'cause they didn't have real bathrooms there, and, like, take a massive dump...sorry, Prof. Probably not what you want to hear. But you get what I'm saying."

"I do," I said. "Realistically, how much danger do you think you're in right now?"

I heard her take a deep breath on the other end of the line. "Realistically? Probably not a huge amount right now. My mom's, like, batshit crazy, but I can't imagine her actually bursting into Aunt Cybil's apartment and actually *shooting* me or some shit like that. But as soon as Vadim and his posse get here, I don't know...and my mom knows where I am...oh shit! Oh fuck! She could tell them to go after Aunt Cybil! She's always fucking hated her. She might not want to shoot *me*, but I bet she'll be totally okay with taking out Aunt Cybil.

She might even do it herself. And it'll be my fault! I tipped off the feds, and I put Aunt Cybil in danger, and..."

"What about your dad?" I interrupted. "Can you go to him? Will that be safer?"

"Nuh-uh. My mom knows where he is too, of course. And, like, he's a total dick, but I'm not gonna lead a bunch of killers straight to his door. I just...I just *can't*."

"Have you told your contact about this?" I asked.

"What? Of course. I was the one who snitched. I mean, gave the anonymous tip. However you wanna say it."

"But have you expressed your concerns that your life and the lives of your family might be in danger?" I asked.

"I kinda said something about it, but he said he didn't think I had any real reason to be worried, but if I was, I could, like, get out of town or something and it'd probably be fine. I don't think he thinks much of me. And I don't think he takes my mom and Carrie and their gang all that seriously. He thinks they're a couple of soccer moms playing at being Nazis. He doesn't understand about my cousins. I don't think there's gonna be much help from him."

"Okay," I said. "Well, maybe you should just leave. You know, just to be on the safe side. How much more class do you have? Just one week?"

"Two weeks," said Madison. "Plus finals. But fuck finals. They're not worth dying for, right?"

"Right," I said. "And if you tell your professors that you have an emergency, you might be able to take an Incomplete and finish up the semester later."

"Cool," said Madison. "I'll do that, then. So, like...can I come stay with you?"

"Um," I said. "Do you think it will be safe? I mean," I added hastily, "you're always welcome here. But will coming to me actually accomplish what you want to accomplish?"

"It'll slow 'em down," Madison said. "My mom probably wouldn't think to tell 'em about you. My dad might guess, but he wouldn't tell them...unless they tortured him. Oh fuck. Do you think they might torture him?"

"From what I can gather, Zhuraev has a history," I said.

"Fuck, fuck, *fuck!*"

"But I really don't think you're in immediate danger from him," I said. "He's not in the US yet, right?"

"No. Right. He won't get here for a few more days."

"Okay. So you probably have a little time to figure something out."

"Okay. Great. So can I come stay with you while I'm doing that? I just...I can't stay here. And I'm...I'm scared. I can't stand the idea of being alone in some skanky hostel or something. And you...you saved me once before. You know how to deal with stuff like this. So can I come stay with you? Please? I promise I'll leave soon. I won't be with you by the time he gets here. I just need...I need..."

"Sure," I said. "Why don't you come stay with me for a couple of days while we figure something out. I'm sure nothing will happen."

64

MADISON AND I AGREED that she would get tickets to come down to Georgia within the next couple of days. I offered to meet her at the airport, but she said she was afraid to fly.

"To much of a trail," she said. "Anyone could follow me. I'll take the bus. More flexibility."

I didn't think the bus would necessarily be any safer, but it made her feel better, so I didn't argue. She would call me when she got to the bus station at Macon, and I'd pick her up then.

"It might take me a couple of days," she warned me. "I'm going to lay a false trail."

"Okay," I said. I didn't know how necessary that actually was, or how effective it would be, but again, I didn't argue. If Zhuraev really was after us, I figured he'd make a beeline for Madison, and it wouldn't take him much work to figure out that she might run to me. By coming to me, she was only endangering me further. But if she disappeared into the American hinterland, which I thought was her best bet, Zhuraev would still probably come to me once he'd shaken down her family and come up with nothing. So either way, it probably didn't matter. We'd just have to hope he didn't come after her.

I debated about texting Dima about the situation. Maybe he would have good advice. Maybe he just needed to know. Or maybe his texts would get read by the wrong person, and we'd both end up in danger. And besides, our recent rapprochement was still very fragile. No point in stressing it if I could avoid it. Some part of me thought that if I turned to him for help, he'd freak out and run the other way. I decided to hold off for the moment.

Then I started wondering if I should tell Alex. Maybe he would have good advice. Maybe—I was ashamed of the thought as I thought it, but I thought it anyway—he would drop everything and come running all the way across the country to help me out, and I wouldn't have to go through this alone.

Part of that was fear talking, and part of it, I knew, was jealousy. Some small, weak, pathetic part of me was still mad that Alex had dropped everything, including me, to go running to save Erin when she'd needed him. I wanted someone to do the same for me. But it was unfair and just plain wrong to ask Alex to do that because I was feeling insecure, especially after I'd been dodging all his attempts to reconnect all semester. Plus, I had a strong feeling it wouldn't end well. Alex seemed able to function only as a knight in slightly battered armor. Once I stopped needing a savior and started needing a man, he'd probably fall apart all over again. So maybe I should just hold off until things started looking really desperate. Or maybe...no, maybe...but maybe...

When I got into Mel's Jeep Monday morning, I still hadn't decided any of these things. Looking at my reflection mirrored in her sunglasses, I wondered if maybe I should tell her. She might have good advice. She might even be able to protect me and Madison somehow. At least she'd be a good backup.

"Guess what!" Mel said, as soon as I had scrambled up into the passenger seat. "I have fucking Lyme disease! I finally got the results back from that specialist clinic." She grinned. "Most people don't get all happy about a nasty diagnosis, but in this case...from what I've heard, I'm not alone in being thrilled. At least I've got some kind of an answer now."

"Um," I said. "That's great. Uh...what can you do about it?"

"Antibiotics," Mel said. "Fuck tons of antibiotics, apparently. Plus a lot of herbs and weird alternative shit. It's supposed to make you sick as a dog." She grinned some more. "But then you feel better. You hope." Her grin faded a little. "Apparently it can be a pretty rough road. Some people never get better at all, or only after years. But still!" Her grin returned. "At least I've got an explanation for all the weird shit that's been happening to me for the past year and a half. And some treatments to try. I'm going to start as soon as finals are over, get the really bad shit over with over break, and hope I'm feeling better by January."

"That's great," I said. *I guess I shouldn't be asking her for anything right now*, I thought. *She's got enough going on as it is.*

"Anyway," Mel was saying, "I was thinking: we should try to get together for one last research meeting before the end of the semester. You know: actually hammer something out we can submit over break. I know we all like to tell ourselves we'll get our writing done during break, but I can't fucking delude myself like that this time. Apparently I've gotta be prepared for seizures and projectile vomiting and not being able to get out of bed for days."

"My God," I said. "Are you sure that's how it's supposed to go? That doesn't sound right at all. Treatment shouldn't make you worse."

Mel shrugged. "Didn't your PT make your knee worse at first?"

"Yeah," I said. "And I only got better once I quit." I flexed my left leg experimentally. "For a given value of 'better,' that is. But I was getting worse and worse while I was in treatment. Once I stopped going, I started improving."

Mel shrugged again. "Sounds about right. But what else am I going to do? I can't stand the idea of keeping on like I've been going, feeling like shit half the time and with weird freaky stuff happening to my body out of nowhere. Weird freaky shit that's been getting worse and worse. I was so tired after I got home from the clinic that I couldn't walk. My mom had to come out and help me stagger in from the car. Then I was better the next day, but...I can't face it, Ro. I *can't*. If taking vomit pills and causing the nasty little monsters inside of me to explode and spew endotoxins all over my insides is what I have to do to have a chance of getting better, then I'll do it. Because it sounds better than going on like I've been."

"Okay," I said. "I can't blame you. I'm sure I'd do the same thing if I were in your shoes. Just let me know if you need any help while you're going through this, okay? And in the meantime, when do you want to do this last research meeting?"

"Let's talk to Chloe about it," Mel said. "She's the one who's always kicking our butts into doing what we need to do. Let's let her do her thing."

65

WE RAN INTO CHLOE AS soon as we approached Bedford. She was sitting on a bench outside the door, fanning herself.

"Whoa," said Mel. "What's the matter? It's not that hot." Now that we were in the last week of November, the morning temperatures were a cool and pleasant 50 degrees.

"Panic attack," said Chloe. She sounded more resigned than actually panicked. "Or whatever it is. My dad keeps talking about hypoglycemia and diabetes and pre-diabetes. He wants me to see a friend of his." Chloe's father was a surgeon with a lot of connections in the Atlanta medical world.

"Maybe that's a good idea," I said.

"Yeah...I've been too scared to actually start measuring my blood sugar regularly. What if it *is* diabetes?"

"Then you'd want to start getting it under control ASAP," I said.

"Yeah...I think I'd rather not know. But..." She looked around. Students and faculty were streaming past us, hurrying to their morning classes, but no one appeared to be paying any attention to us at all. "I hate these whatever-they-are episodes! I feel like I'm letting everyone down. Not just myself, after all the work I put into getting this far, but my family, and my professors, and my advisor, and—I know it sounds hokey, but, like, my people. I knew it was going to be tough, being the only black tenure-track faculty member here, singlehandedly integrating a college that used to be a plantation, but I was proud to be the one to do it. Only I'm failing at that too. Failing everyone."

"You're not failing them," I said. Okay, I wasn't going to be able to ask Chloe for help either. She already had enough on her plate.

"Fuck no," said Mel. "Especially if the reason you feel so bad is because of all that fucking poisonous ex-plantation air, or all the toxic mold or whatever shit is in all these buildings. If anything, *they're* failing *you.*"

Chloe sighed. "That doesn't help me very much. If I'm the failure, then at least there's something I can do about it."

"Yeah," said Mel. "Hey, speaking of doing something...how do you feel about a final research meeting? Maybe on Thursday? We need you to kick our butts into finishing our articles."

Chloe smiled. Faintly, but she seemed to be recovering from her attack of whatever. "I've never been called a butt kicker before. I like it. And I'd love to kick your butts, but it can't be on Thursday. I'm actually supposed to go see my family. One of my aunties is doing poorly. Can we do it Tuesday afternoon instead?"

Mel and I looked back and forth and nodded. "Tuesday afternoon sounds great," Mel said. "Be there or be square."

66

MADISON AND I TALKED again Monday night. She was still in New York, she said, but was planning to catch a midnight bus out of the Port Authority Bus Terminal.

"And then I'll like, disappear," she said. "Only to, like, resurface at your place a couple days later. Is that okay?"

"Sure," I said. "Have you heard anything from your mom?" I asked. "Or anything about the whole situation?"

"Nuh-uh. She hasn't talked to me, and I've been too scared to reach out to her. But Aunt Cybil said some stuff that made me think my dad's talked to her and he thinks she might be, like, in danger of going to *jail* over this."

"Wow," I said. "Uh, well...honestly, I don't know what to say. It would be rough for all of you if she went to prison, especially over something like this. But I can't really condone what she's been doing."

"Yeah...I don't know how I feel about it either, to be honest, Professor H. Except I *know* I, like, really don't want Vadim to catch me, especially if I think he had anything to do with all this."

"When's he supposed to arrive in the US—if he still comes?" I asked.

"Dunno. The retreat/gathering thingy is next week. Mom said something about having me come meet him beforehand, you know, for some fun cousinly togetherness. That was supposed to be this upcoming weekend. So I'm guessing he and his buds are supposed to get here on, like, Friday or something. Unless they're already here. I think there's, like, five of them all together, though only Vadim's actually related to me. And I'd think Mom'd tell me when he gets here, 'cause she really wants me to spend more time with him. She thinks he'll, like, straighten me out or something. She thinks he's, like, a good role model for me."

"Oh," I said. "Well, hopefully you've got some time, then."

"Hopefully. Anyway, I'm off to Port Authority. Wish me luck, Professor H, and I'll call you in a couple of days to let you know where I am."

"Good luck," I said. "*Ni pukha, ni pera.*"

"Yeah...aren't I supposed to say, like, 'Go to hell' in response?"

"Indeed," I said.

"Okay, then, go to hell, Professor H, and I guess I'll see you there, or something." She laughed. "Sounds awfully dramatic, doesn't it? Bet this whole thing'll, like, turn out to be a big nothing. But I still can't shake the feeling that I need to get the fuck out of town, so I'm doing it. I already managed to get most of my professors to agree to give me Incompletes for the semester. I'll figure out what to do about that next semester. If I *live* that long." She laughed some more, reveling in the drama of the situation, but with an undertone of real fear.

"You know where to find me if you need me," I said. I wasn't quite sure how I felt about Madison's dash for supposed safety. On the one hand, I thought it might be good for her. She needed the opportunity to get out and do stuff on her own, and here she was, getting out and doing stuff on her own. On the other hand, I was genuinely worried for her, and it was adding to all my other worries and my general sense of anxiety and dread. I didn't think that Vadim Zhuraev and his cronies were a danger—yet. Once they came over to the US, they could be very, very dangerous, in a way that even

Madison didn't quite seem to understand. Just thinking about what they might do if they actually did decide to come after us made me feel sick, and want to go run and hide, hide, *hide,* throwing myself down some deep, dark hole where no one could ever, ever find me.

In the meantime, though, I was more worried that Madison would do something stupid or run into the normal dangers that attended travel, especially sudden travel, especially sudden travel by bus by a naive young woman on her own. And my worry, I assumed, was just a faint echo of what Madison's mother felt for her every day. When I thought about it that way, I could sympathize with why Brenda might do something crazy if she thought it would protect her daughter. It was just unfortunate that she was probably putting her in the worst danger she'd ever been in and hopefully ever would be in, in her entire life.

I counseled myself not to do something stupid like Brenda, and let Madison take off on her bus trip. The most likely outcome was that she would have a little adventure, probably with some minor unpleasantnesses but nothing actually dangerous, and then she'd have to deal with the fallout of running off at the end of the semester, and it would be a funny story that she could tell later in life. The best thing I could do for her was to be on standby if she needed help.

And while I was on standby, I should go work on my article. It was one of those important-but-not-urgent things that always got pushed to the back of the queue of tasks, until one day you realized you hadn't done it and were going to end up unemployed and unemployable as a result. Or something equally dire. It was easy to get caught up in the drama of extremists maybe coming after you with evil intent, but what you *really* needed to worry about was your own inability to motivate yourself to do tedious but essential tasks that no one else was going to make you do.

Telling myself this, I set off Tuesday afternoon for Chloe's.

67

WE HAD AGREED TO MEET at 2:00pm at Chloe's. Mel had some errands she needed to run, so we'd decided to take separate vehicles over there. I pulled up to the curb just behind her.

"Hey, Ro," Mel said, jumping out of the Jeep and coming over to me before I could extricate myself from my car. "Need a hand with anything? Want me to carry your laptop in for you?"

"Well...aren't you the one who's supposed to be really sick?"

She shrugged. "Yeah, but today's a good day. I woke up in the middle of the night, sweating and shaking and thinking I was going to throw up, but after an hour or so it passed and now I feel fine. Well, except for my knees hurting. And my elbows. And my fucking thumbs. I swear to God, you don't appreciate your thumbs until you have to try to go without them. Anyway, want me to carry anything for you?"

"I can get it," I said. "I'm feeling remarkably healed. My knee feels almost back to normal, knock on wood." We both looked around for some wood to knock on, and settled for knocking on our heads. "I just probably shouldn't run on it," I said.

"Yeah. And hey, at least we got out of the Pre-Turkey Trot this year. I'm hoping we get out of the Lamb Chop Trot in the spring, too."

"Every cloud has a silver lining," I said. Crimson had a 5k race for faculty each semester, one right before Thanksgiving and one right before Easter. Once it had been discovered that both Mel and I were good runners, our voluntary participation had been mandatory. While in general we had nothing against running a 5k, being forced to run in a race that involved parading in goofy costumes in front of the entire college had been decidedly non-awesome. Plus we'd both gotten injured. Having a legitimate reason to sit this year's races out was a welcome side effect of our otherwise miserable health problems.

Chloe met us at the door. Her normal expression of shy reserve was replaced with a smile that was almost glowing.

"Well, look at you," said Mel as she stepped inside. "What's up? Have you fallen in love? Found some replacement for that loser you showed us earlier?"

"What? What loser...oh, him. Yeah, whatever. I don't care about him anymore. I just got word. The book! They're going to publish the book! I mean, they've accepted this round of edits and sent it on to copyediting! They're expecting it to come out soon, maybe as early as next summer! I'm going to have a book!"

"Congratulations," Mel and I both said at once.

"Yeah, I know...It's just *such* a long, difficult process...although it's been quick and easy compared to what I've heard about from other people, but it *felt* long to me...almost a whole year...and it won't come out for another six months at least...and I'm just...it's like having a *child* or something, isn't it? Like, it's practically that exciting, isn't it?"

"Something like that," Mel said. "You've created something! You're putting it out there in the world. That's awesome."

"Thanks! I'm just...I'm just so excited..."

Chloe chattered away as we got set up at her dining room table, telling us what a relief it was, what a vindication, what a feeling of accomplishment to finally have a book.

"I guess I should stop going on about it," she said eventually. "It's just...I've been working towards this for more than half a decade. And it's finally here! Well, almost here. It will be here in six months. Oh God. What if something goes wrong! I don't know if I can stand it if something goes wrong..."

"Nothing's going to go wrong," Mel and I said together.

"But it *could*."

"Anything *could* happen," Mel said. "But dollars to doughnuts, that book's going to come out, and right on time."

"Yeah...so anyway...what's new with you?"

"Nothing much," said Mel. "What about you, Ro? By the way, how's that internet dating thing you said you were going to do? Any luck?"

"No luck whatsoever," I said. "In fact, I quit without getting a single date. But that's okay. I've got enough to deal with right now." For a moment I thought once again about telling them about Madison, but then nixed the idea. If anyone did come after her, we needed as few people as possible to know where she was. Instead I told them about my parents' house-building adventures, and how I might have gotten volunteered to help out with it.

"That could be cool," said Chloe. She sighed. "I've never gotten to build anything before. My life has always been about school. School, school, nothing but school. And that's okay, especially now with the whole book thing, but...sometimes I want something more. Do you ever feel that way?"

I nodded. "Fuck yeah," said Mel. "I was in the fucking military, remember? I wanted to devote myself to a higher purpose, serve the greater good, all that shit. And I thought I would do a great job at it. Only, the whole time I was there, I was always being measured by my ability to be a man, so I was always coming up short. Fucked me up big-time. Now I gotta figure out how to live my life as a woman. A butch woman, sure, but a woman. And I don't know exactly what that means, but I don't think it's just about school. Even if females *are* on average better at it."

"Yeah." Chloe sighed again. I could see the high from the book news draining out of her, like watching a balloon deflating. "I always figured I'd do the whole being-a-woman thing by getting married and having a kid. I mean, not as a substitute for the school thing, but as a complement. And I figured it would just happen, like it did for my mom and most other women I knew." She snorted. "I don't know *why* I thought that, since socialization was always my weak point. But I just thought...hey, life finds a way, right? Only it hasn't for me yet. So far it's only found a way for other women. Women whom I want to call basic bitches."

She put her hand over her mouth. "I'm sorry! I shouldn't have said that. But it's how I *feel*. And I'll be thirty in a couple of years. Being almost thirty and single and childless was the thing I feared most for myself. I mean, other than washing out of school. And now that it's here, I just don't know if I can stand it. And I feel so anxious and messed up most of the time that even if I could find a man, which I can't, my body is probably now a toxic waste dump. If I had a baby, it'd probably be a Ninja Turtle or something, and not in a good way."

"Hah," said Mel. "Wait until you're almost forty and a single and childless toxic waste dump. Then you'll know the true meaning of loneliness and despair. I don't even want to think about what it's going to be like when I'm fifty."

"You're a lesbian," said Chloe. "What do you want marriage and kids for?"

We both looked at her. "Oh, shoot," she said. "That was one of those things you're not supposed to say, right? I mean, you know I put my foot in my mouth every time I open it. My mouth, not my foot...you know what I mean. I just...I didn't mean to hurt your feelings..."

"I know," said Mel. "And a lot of lesbians don't want marriage or kids. But the ones that do, really, really want it. And it's starting to eat at me."

"I'm sorry," said Chloe. "It's eating at me too, and I don't even want it as a life goal! It's just...Argh! Why does it have to be so hard! I guess this is why I'm good at school stuff, though. Sublimation, or whatever it's called."

"Yeah," said Mel. "So we can devote ourselves to our students, like Ro does." They both turned to look at me.

"I don't think my devotion to my students is my way of sublimating my maternal instinct," I said. "Oh, wait: maybe it is." Another example of how my job was taking everything that was best and most precious to me, and using it to make money for other people.

"Well, look at it this way," Mel said. "Given the state of the environment and all that, maybe the most loving maternal act we can make is *not* to have children."

"That's too depressing to think about," said Chloe.

I wanted to agree. But I also suspected that Mel might be right.

"Books," I said out loud. "We should concentrate on our books. We don't have anything else right now, and we may never have anything else. So let's make them good."

68

OUR SUPER-DEPRESSING conversation at Chloe's stayed with me the rest of the day, and the next day, and the next. My main takeaway from it was that once again, I was being used. No, I was letting myself be used. I should stand up for myself! I should...what? Not help other people who needed my help?

Madison texted Wednesday night to tell me she was safe. Then, as I was staring out at the dreary, rainy Thursday morning that was the first day of December, the first day of Advent, she knocked on my door.

"Surprise!" she said when I opened it. "I'm here!"

"Wow," I said. "Uh, come in. I thought you were going to call me first."

"I was, but then I thought it would be better to surprise you. Make it more of a secret. Did it work? Are you surprised?"

"A bit," I said. "Glad you made it safely. No one's been asking after you here. Have you noticed anyone following you?"

She shook her head. "Nuh-uh. Although Vadim and the rest of the cousins are only coming in today. I think."

"Well, good, I guess," I said. "Have you heard anything more from your mom?"

She shook her head again. "I talked to her a couple of times, actually, to try to throw her off the scent. She's upset about what happened to Carrie, but so far she's stayed out of jail herself. She was just hauled in for questioning a couple of times, which she's super pissed about. But she's planning to go ahead with the retreat thingy."

Madison took a deep breath. "It occurred to me after I left that maybe me running off like this would look suspicious, so I told her I was having problems and was checking into rehab again. She was super pissed about that, too. Or, like, well, she was pleased that I was doing it voluntarily. But she was super upset about me needing to do it. She started to cry and everything. And she really started to put on the pressure to get me to come to the retreat. I almost said yes, just to scope it out."

"Don't do it," I said. "If you thought it was dangerous, then going to it deliberately with the specific intent of scoping it out would be even more dangerous. Stay far away."

Madison gave me a double take. "Jeez, Professor H, you *are* spooked about this thing. I thought you didn't really take it seriously and were just, like, humoring me about it. But you think it's dangerous too, don't you?"

"I think it could be," I said. "I think if you have a gut feeling that it's dangerous, you should stay away. Besides, you wouldn't enjoy it, would you?"

"Nah. Sounds like a real drag at the best of times. Glad I have a reason to get out of it. But"—she swallowed hard—"I'm feeling kinda bad for my mom. Like, she was *really* upset when she heard I was going back into rehab. She was so upset, I felt bad even telling her about it, even though it's not true. She's gonna be hurting real bad over it for a while, and it's a lie. That's not a good feeling, especially when it's your mom, you know what I mean?"

"Yeah," I said. "But she's also put you in a really bad position. It's not like you're doing this just to be mean to her. And maybe if she's separated from this Carrie person, she'll straighten out and you can be friends again and you won't have to deceive her for her own good anymore."

"Maybe," said Madison, sounding skeptical. "So what's up for the rest of the day?"

What was up for the rest of the day was me writing my final exams and review exercises, while Madison mooched around the apartment, watching videos on her phone and heroically trying not to complain about being bored. We discussed the possibility of her going out and doing something, or of introducing her to my friends so that she'd have someone else to talk to, but we agreed it was too dangerous. If we were operating under the assumption that someone with the ability and the will to cause grievous bodily harm might have a grudge against Madison, and might carry that grudge so far as to track her down, then she needed to be in hiding. It was just that being in hiding was boring. Very boring.

Madison's boredom was alleviated when Fevronia came slinking out from under the bed to check her out.

"Oh, hey, kitty," Madison said. "Good to see you again. You and me are friends, aren't we?" And she proceeded to dangle the drawstring from her hoodie in front of Fevronia's face, encouraging her to play. To my extreme astonishment, Fevronia batted at the string. First with one paw, then with the other, and then she was leaping and pouncing and rolling like a kitten.

"I've never seen her do that before," I said. "I got her some toys and tried to get her to play with them when I first brought her home, but she never seemed interested in them at all. Mostly she just seems to like being ignored."

"You gotta do it right," Madison said authoritatively. "Cats know if you want to make them play, and they won't. You gotta want to play, but not try too hard. You gotta..." Her phone *pinged*. A second later, my phone *pinged* too.

We looked at each other, our eyes wide and staring with sudden alarm. *Probably a complete coincidence*, I told myself. But it felt ominous.

"Go on," Madison said. "I'll check mine if you'll check yours. It's probably nothing, right?"

"Right," I said. I looked at my phone. The message was from Frank.

Ro! Call me as soon as you get this. We need to talk ASAP. IMPORTANT!!!!

69

"IT'S A MESSAGE," MADISON said. Her eyes were wide again. "From my alphabet agency contact. He wants me to call him right away."

"Then you probably should," I said. "And I've got someone who wants me to call too. Let's do it."

We instinctively turned away from each other and went into opposite ends of the apartment, Madison into the kitchen and me to the far end of the dining room table. Before I could call back on the message, my phone started to ring. Frank.

"Ro," he said as soon as I picked up. "You're here. Good. I wasn't sure whether to call you or text you. Decided to try both. Listen. Something's come up. Something big. Where are you? Are you safe?"

"I hope so," I said. "I'm in my apartment. Why?"

"You know that organization you told me about? Those guys that are supposed to come over?"

"Uh-huh," I said.

"Well, they're here. I was hoping to stop them from coming over, but I couldn't. They arrived late last night."

"Uh-huh," I said again.

"And we monitored some disturbing conversations from them."

"Uh-huh," I said for a third time. I wanted to ask how Frank had gotten assigned to the task force or whatever it was that was following this group, and how he had gotten permission to monitor their communications, and in general what was going on. I decided to hold off on that until I had a clearer picture of how life-threatening the danger I was in, was.

"It sounds like they want to come after you. Specifically, the leader, Vadim Zhuraev." Frank did a surprisingly passable job of pronouncing his name.

"Oh, dear," I said.

"No fucking kidding. What did you do to piss this guy off, Ro?"

"I'm not sure," I said. "There are several possibilities."

"Jesus Christ, Ro. You need to be more careful."

"I know," I said. "So what should I do about it?"

"For the moment, sit tight. Don't go out, don't let anyone in. I'm on my way now."

"You're coming here?" I felt slow and stupid.

"Yeah. On my way to the airport right now. Should be there by first thing tomorrow morning. Meanwhile, don't open the door to anyone but me."

"Um," I said. "Okay. But why? I mean, why are you on your way here?"

"Because," he said, speaking slowly and clearly, as if to a confused toddler, "you might be in danger, Ro."

"Yeah, but..."

"And this is my case. Partly. I got myself put on it because of my connection to you, even though I'm on the wrong side of the country. So sit tight, wait for me, and don't so much as stick your nose outside your door until you hear my voice. Got it?"

"Um," I said. "Sure."

"Tell me you've got it, Ro. I'm fucking serious here."

"I've got it," I said. "I'll be very careful, I promise. I take these guys seriously, I really do. I won't do anything to endanger myself."

"Good. I'm gonna hold you to that, Ro. Okay. I'm at the airport now. I'll let you know when I've boarded, and again when I arrive.

And I mean it: if the Virgin Mary asks you to open your door, don't do it. Don't so much as peek out of it until you hear my voice."

"Got it," I said. "I won't."

"Good. You alone?"

"Um...no...?"

"Oh." There was a short pause. "Who's with you? A friend? Boyfriend?"

"Um," I said. "Not exactly. Madison. The, uh, person who, ah, has the original connection with these guys."

"Oh. Great. *Great.* We've been looking for her too. Only anything that makes it easier for us to find you, makes it easier for them to find you. So be doubly careful, okay? Promise me you'll be careful, Ro. Careful for both of you."

"I promise," I said. "Um...should we, like, keep all the lights off and pretend not to be here?"

"Might not be a bad idea," he said. "I was going to tell you to get out and check into a hotel, but I'm afraid they'll already be watching the place. They were supposed to fly into Newark, but instead they flew into Atlanta. They could be there already. Assume they *are* there already. Keep your blinds drawn and your lights off. You got any rooms there that don't have exterior windows?"

"Just the bathroom," I said.

"Maybe hang out in the bathroom until I get there."

"That could be, what, twelve hours?" I said. "That's a long time to hide in the bathroom, especially with someone else."

"Fair enough. But don't hesitate to shelter in there if you think something suspicious is happening. If they knock on your door or something, don't answer, just go straight into the bathroom and lock yourself in. It has a lock, doesn't it?"

"It does."

"Great. Do you have a gun? Any kind of weapon for self defense?"

"Just a couple of kitchen knives."

"Kitchen knives won't do much against firearms. But it's better than nothing, I guess. Keep them close at hand."

"Okay," I said. "Will do."

"Great. Great. I'm approaching security. I'll keep in touch. Answer me right away, okay?"

"Okay," I agreed. "And, uh, thanks. I appreciate it."

"Sure thing. Stay safe. 'Bye."

The call clicked off. I got up and looked over at Madison, who was standing by the sink, her eyes deer-in-the-headlights wide.

"They think..." She choked, swallowed, and tried again. "They think they're after me! Vadim and the other cousins. They said they're in Atlanta. Somehow they found me already."

"I think they might have found me," I said. "You just happen to be here."

"They said to stay put and hide! They said someone's coming from the Atlanta office, and to stay put until then. But it might not be for another couple of hours. What do we do!?!"

"We stay put and hide," I said. "Preferably with the blinds drawn and the lights out."

We both looked at the big window looking out onto the parking lot from the living/dining room area. It faced west. The sun, red and fat, was just sinking below a crimson horizon, filling the parking lot and the room with an eerie, bloody glow.

"I'm scared," Madison said in a small voice. "I'm scared to go over to the window and draw the blinds."

"I'll do it. I'm closer." I stepped over to the window, trying to stand to the side of it, but aware how I was limned by the setting sun and the ceiling light, no doubt starkly visible through the glass. My fingers felt stiff and slick as I pulled on the cords of the blinds. I pulled on the cords unevenly, letting down only one side of the slats, and had to raise them all the way up again and try a second time before I got them fully lowered.

"Turn out the light," I said, stepping back. My heart was racing and sweat was trickling down my sides.

Madison switched off the light, plunging us into a crimson, shadowy twilight. "There's another window in the kitchen," I said. "Can you go lower those blinds?"

"I'm scared." Madison's voice was shaking.

"I know. But you're closest. Do it quick."

Madison took the one step to the window over the kitchen sink. It took her three tries to lower the blinds. As soon as they were down, she ran around the kitchen island to come stand beside me, hugging herself and visibly trembling.

"I'll go close the blinds in the bedroom," I said. "And then we can share notes, make a plan."

"My face feels funny," Madison said. "Like I've taken too much coke. But I haven't touched any in months, I swear."

"It's just fear," I told her.

"It's stupid! We're probably not actually in any real danger anyway! But..."

"But we *could* be," I agreed. "So we think we are. And it's scary. But help is coming. I'm going to go shut the bedroom blinds, and then we'll...cook dinner in the dark, or something. It'll be like camping."

"I fucking hate camping," said Madison. Her voice sounded stronger.

"Good. It'll help keep your mind off things. I'll be right back."

I walked through the twilight into the bedroom. I was already feeling much calmer. Sure, it was scary, but seriously, how much danger could we really be in? Vadim and his cronies weren't going to snipe through the windows at us, were they? They were probably waiting to grab us in the parking lot. *If* they were here at all. Maybe they hadn't gotten here yet. Maybe they had no intention of coming here at all. Madison and I were just minor annoyances to them, right?

My bed was right under the bedroom window. I climbed up onto it to reach the cords for the blinds.

Something flashed in the parking lot. I froze, outlined against the bare glass. Something flashed again.

A phone screen, I thought. *It's just a phone screen. Someone's sitting in their car, looking at their phone.*

I looked down. A car was parked in the spot directly opposite my bedroom and living room windows. Two people were sitting in the front seats. Two bulky men. Both of them were looking up at me.

One of them held up his phone in front of him.

He's taking a picture, I thought. Then: *He's taking a picture of* ***me!***

70

I JERKED BACK FROM the window, fumbling with the cords for the blinds and almost pulling the whole thing down and falling off the bed in my haste. Then I stumbled out of the bedroom, closing the door behind me, as if that would make things safer.

"I think they're watching us from the parking lot," I told Madison. "What did your contact say? That they're sending someone from Atlanta?"

"Uh-huh. Should get here in about two hours."

I wavered for a moment. Then I called Frank.

"Ro. What's up?"

"I think they're here. In the parking lot. I was closing the blinds, and I'm pretty sure someone took a picture of me from inside his car."

"Shit."

"Yeah. Listen. Madison's contact is telling her that they're sending someone over from Atlanta. Do you know anything about this?"

A pause. Then Frank said, "Let me get back to you about that."

He hung up. Madison and I turned off the kitchen light and sat at the dining room table in the reddish twilight filtering in through the blinds. It felt horribly exposed. I was terrifyingly, dreadfully aware that there was nothing but a piece of glass and some slender metal slats between me and men who might want to kill me. My whole body hurt with the knowledge, as if their presence were a special kind of radiation that was stripping away my skin, exposing the raw nerve endings underneath.

I found myself thinking of what I could do to get them to go away. They didn't want me for me, right? They were after me because of Madison and Dima. Could I talk my way out of this? I'd had luck with that before. I was a persuasive talker, especially under pressure, and people liked me. For all I knew, Vadim and his cronies would be easily turned in my favor. I'd tell them how much we had in common, how we could find a common ground, how Madison was really their close kin and they shouldn't hurt either of us, they should let us go...

My phone rang. I jumped in my seat, suppressing a shriek. Across the table, Madison yelped in fright.

"It's okay," I told her, with what I hoped was a reassuring smile. "It's Frank. My friend in the FBI who's on his way here. Help is coming."

"Not fucking fast enough," said Madison. She was hugging herself and shivering slightly. I gave her what I hoped was another reassuring smile, and answered the phone.

"Ro," said Frank. "What's up? Are they still outside?"

"I don't know," I said. "I closed all the blinds and turned off the lights. Now I'm sitting in a darkened room waiting for help to arrive."

"Good. I mean, that's the right thing to do. Listen. I checked in with Atlanta. They are sending someone. You know how it is: coordinating even a small operation like this is a total bitch. Anyway. They're sending a guy named Xavier Thornton over. I don't know him, but I just talked to him, and he seemed solid enough. He's trying to coordinate with local law enforcement right now. It might delay him a little, but it'll mean someone could be coming over to you a lot sooner than he or I can get there."

"Okay," I said. "That's good."

"Yeah. Just...be really, really sure that if someone comes up to the door and says they're law enforcement, that they're actually law enforcement. Make them show you their badge through the peephole before you open the door to them. And even then be careful. I don't like this, Ro. I don't like the idea of a bunch of guys I don't know walking in there. But I like the idea of you by yourself with some bad guys out in the parking lot taking pictures of you even less."

"Yeah," I said. "Me too. We'll be super careful. Xavier Thornton, you said? Do you know what he looks like?"

"Black guy, older, heavy Southern accent."

"So we're unlikely to confuse him with a thirty-something Ukrainian white supremacist."

Frank let out a harsh laugh. "Yeah. That makes me a feel a little better. And he really does seem on the ball. I just won't feel okay until I'm over there. Oh shit. They're calling my flight. I've gotta board now or I'll miss it. It's a nonstop to Atlanta. Four and a half hours. I'll call you as soon as I get in."

"Okay," I said. "And, um, thanks. And, uh, have a nice flight."

"Take care of yourself," he said, and hung up.

71

"WHAT'S THE NAME OF the guy from Atlanta who's supposed to be coming?" I asked Madison.

She frowned. "Something weird. Shit! I can't remember. They told me, and I'm totally fucking blanking on it."

"It's okay," I said. "It's from nerves. It happens a lot. It wasn't Thornton, was it?"

"Yeah! Something Thornton. Xander...no, Xavier. With an X. They spelled it out for me."

"Okay. Good." I felt marginally more relaxed having a double confirmation that someone named Xavier Thornton was on the way from Atlanta. I would feel even better if I knew that the local police were on their way too. Couldn't they just arrest the guys in the car? I was hazy on the legality of that. The FBI had gotten permission to monitor these guys' phones, which implied a warrant of some sort. But did that mean that the Greenfields police could arrest them for sitting in their car and maybe taking some pictures?

Even if they couldn't, I told myself, they could show up, which might be deterrence enough. Although it might make Vadim run off, and maybe they wanted to catch him. Maybe they were using me and Madison as bait...

My panicked musings were interrupted by blue and red lights filling up the apartment like strobe lights at a disco.

"Thank God!" Madison cried.

"We're not safe yet," I warned, but I felt my whole body unclench. Madison got up and went over to the window.

"Be careful!" I cried as she made to look through the blinds. "You don't know..."

"There's a car parked right across from us with a couple of guys in the front," she said. "And...looks like they're starting up their car...they're leaving...looks like the police are following them."

I got up and peeked through the blinds too. Sure enough, the car with the guys who had been watching me earlier was pulling out of the parking lot. The police car, still with its lights on, was following it.

"We're safe!" Madison said.

"For now," I said.

72

THE TWO CARS WENT OUT the front gate of the apartment complex, but then stopped on the side of the street leading to the gate. Madison and I watched as one of the police officers got out of his car and went over to the window of the other car. We stood there watching for so long that my left knee started to ache as the police officer talked to the driver, and then talked into his radio, and conferred with his partner, and talked into his radio some more, and then went back and talked to the driver again. A second squad car arrived, and there was some more talking and conferring with partners and radios. Then all three cars set off in a caravan, with the men who'd been photographing me still in their vehicle, which was in the middle of the three-car parade.

"Huh," Madison and I said together.

A few minutes later Madison got a call. It was Xavier Thornton, on his way down from Atlanta. The men in the car had agreed to voluntarily report to the local police station for questioning, he told us. He was on his way straight to the station. He'd probably be by to talk to us later this evening. Meanwhile, we should sit tight and not go anywhere.

"You're probably safe enough now," I heard him tell Madison. He did indeed have a heavy Southern accent. It went well with the deep, gravelly voice of a heavy-set older man and long-time smoker. "But just in case, stay indoors until we give you the all-clear. Got it?"

"Got it," said Madison. She sounded remarkably subdued. "We won't go anywhere until we see you, I promise."

"Good. Talk to you in a bit."

Madison ended the call and looked up. "Can we turn on the lights now?" she asked plaintively. "And have some supper? All of a sudden I'm *starving*."

"Sure," I said. I went around flicking on all the lights in the apartment. I even found myself checking out the bathroom, but the only thing I found there was Fevronia, who had been napping on a spare bath towel in the cabinet under the vanity. She gave me a one-eyed glare and went back to sleep. I backed quietly out of the bathroom, but I left the bedroom light on and the blinds drawn. I was creeped out by the idea of darkness, but I was also creeped out by the idea of someone being able to look in through my windows.

With the apartment firmly closed up to the outside world, Madison and I made a meal of pasta and tomato sauce. For the first half of it, Madison was silent, still uncharacteristically subdued. Once she'd downed a plate of pasta, she started talking, growing more and more hyper. If I hadn't been as sure as I could be that she'd had no access to drugs for hours, I'd have assumed she was high on speed or coke.

When we were done with supper, there was still no news, so we settled for watching a movie. Madison said any kind of crime thriller or horror was too scary right now, so we settled for some kind of teen romance about an ordinary American girl who wins the love of a European prince. Madison kept making retching noises throughout it, but watched it until the end, eyes rapt.

"Maybe that's what I need," she said when it was over. "To, like, run off with some prince or something."

"Easier said than done," I said. "It's a fantasy for a reason."

"Yeah, but it's a fun fantasy. Right?"

"I guess," I said.

"Jeez, Professor H. You should lighten up a little. Learn to have some fun."

"U-huh," I said. "I guess...is that your phone?"

Madison's phone was buzzing. It was Xavier Thornton again, calling to tell us that they were still questioning the two men who'd been in our parking lot. They were indeed from Glorious Future, and said they'd been sent here by Vadim Zhuraev to keep an eye out for his cousin Madison, who had run away from home. They swore they had no ill intent, either towards Madison or America. They appeared to be cooperating to the fullest extent possible.

"So you may have nothing to worry about now," I heard Xavier tell Madison. "But just in case, keep your doors locked and don't go out alone. I'll be in touch if I find out anything more, or once you're safe to go about your business again."

"Thank you," said Madison, once again sounding uncharacteristically subdued, not to mention polite. "I really appreciate it."

"Just be careful, young lady, and stand by for updates. It probably won't be until tomorrow morning unless it's something really big, though, so you might as well get some sleep while you can."

"Okay," said Madison. "Thanks. We'll try." She hung up. "He thinks we're pretty safe now," she told me. "He said we should try to go to bed and he'll get back to us in the morning."

"Sounds good," I said. "And by morning Frank will be here too. We'll just sit tight tonight, and hopefully by morning it will be all sorted out."

73

BY THEN IT WAS ALMOST 10:00pm. Bedtime. If we could sleep. Madison was yawning cavernously, the reaction to the adrenaline of earlier finally setting in. She set up her bed on the floor with no complaints, leading me to conclude she was almost comatose.

I was also feeling the post-adrenaline crash setting in, but when I got into bed and turned out the light, I could feel my body buzzing faintly against the sheets. Ugh. And I had class tomorrow morning. The last day of class. Kind of an important class to hold. It would be good to be rested and refreshed for it.

My left knee buzzed extra hard, and cramped. I turned onto my side to try to relax it. The motion made it cramp harder, and then release into an even fiercer buzzing. Argh. And I hadn't even done anything to strain it. It did this buzzing thing sometimes, but only after I'd overused it. But all I'd done all afternoon and evening was sit inside my apartment.

My phone lit up the darkness with a soft glow and a faint *ping*. Normally I put it on silent for the night, but tonight I was leaving it on just in case. Good for safety. Not so good for sleep.

I picked up the phone. Just in case. But it wasn't Frank, who was probably somewhere over the Mississippi right now, or Xavier Thornton, or anyone like that. It was Dima.

Insomnia again and taut sails))))) I hope I'm not bothering you, Innochka.

I've got insomnia too, I wrote. *What's up?*

I don't know. I just wanted to talk to you. What time is it there? It's bedtime, isn't it? Probably too late for a video call, isn't it?

Yes, I wrote. *And I have a guest here. A former student who's having problems. And we've had a bit of a situation.*

What kind of situation?

You remember Vadim Zhuraev and Glorious Future?

Of course.

Well, they're here, I texted. *And a couple of Vadim's guys came looking for us this evening.*

What happened?

The police came and took them away. They told us it's probably all been taken care of.

But not certainly? Dima wrote. *Where's Vadim?*

That I don't know, I wrote.

But he's in America?

I think so, I wrote.

I don't like this at all, Innochka.

Neither do I, I admitted.

Are the police looking for him?

I think so.

But they might not find him. He's pretty cunning, Inna. He's a dangerous guy.

I know, I wrote. *We won't go outside. We'll stay inside the locked apartment.*

Good. Do you have a weapon of some kind?

Just kitchen knives.

Kitchen knives are better than nothing. Go get the biggest one and keep it by you. You remember what I showed you about knife fighting?

Yes. I didn't say that I hadn't really absorbed that lesson at the time, and I doubted I would be any better at it now. Dima had always been mad for self defense. It was logical enough for a former OMON officer with a lot of enemies. It was annoying when he had been constantly forcing me to practice this or that self-defense technique, as well as keep up with my physical fitness. But it had saved me more than once. Maybe it would save me again.

I'll go get the knife right now, I wrote, and tiptoed into the dark kitchen. Madison lay on her improvised bed, apparently deeply asleep. I pulled my largest knife, an eight-inch stainless steel chef's knife that I occasionally sharpened in a desultory fashion, out of the knife drawer and tiptoed back into the bedroom.

Got it, I wrote. I laid it down on the floor next to my bed. Then I imagined stepping onto it in the middle of the night when I got up to go to the bathroom, and driving it right through my foot. I shoved it under the bed. Less handy, but also less likely to require emergency surgery from a moment of inattention. I was reminded why I disliked weapons so much. Anything you could use to hurt an enemy, you could also use to hurt yourself, often by accident. Maybe I needed a lifestyle that required less need for weapons. Of course, that's what I'd been aiming for when I'd decided to go to grad school. Funny how that had worked out.

Good, Dima wrote. *Okay, Inna, I'm about to do something crazy.*

What?

I'm going to call Vadim Zhuraev.

You have his number? That was not the only thing about that statement that surprised me, but it jumped out at me.

I have one of his numbers. I've actually talked to him a few times. Weirdly, I don't think he completely hates me)))) I said that he was a lunatic, but a lunatic who believes in his lunacy and has the courage of his convictions, and he took that as a compliment. That's not how I meant it, but it's not my fault that he's not good at literary analysis)))))

I'm going to try to contact him. Maybe he'll tell me what he's up to. If it's something about you, maybe I can convince him to leave you alone.

Thanks, I wrote. *I'm really grateful for your help.*

Of course, Innochka. Now sleep well.

74

I THOUGHT I'D NEVER sleep, but I must have dozed off at some point, because I jerked awake, my heart racing.

Something's wrong. Why was I thinking that? What had woken me? Was it...Fevronia was no longer on the other pillow. She must have jumped off. Maybe that was what had woken me up. Oh. And my phone screen was glowing.

I reached down and grabbed it, my fingers brushing against the handle of the knife I'd shoved half under the bed. Why did I have a knife...oh, right.

I held up the phone, squinting at the too-bright screen. 3:47am. I'd gotten a respectable amount of sleep. There was a message. From Dima. I opened it.

Inna, I read. *I talked to Vadim. He's in America. I think he's in Georgia, where you are. He's obsessed with some girl named "Madison." Do you know who she is?*

Yes, I wrote back. *She's here with me now.*

Okay. I think Vadim is coming after her. I couldn't convince him not to. I think he's on his way there right now. You need to get ready.

How? I wrote.

Do you trust the police?

Yes.

Call them. And don't let anyone in until they get there. And keep your knife handy. I'm going to try to call Vadim again, talk some sense into him.

Okay. I'll call them now.

I dialed 911, then hesitated for a moment. What if this was all an embarrassing misunderstanding? But no. It probably wasn't. And even if it was, better to be embarrassed than shot or knifed or otherwise horribly killed.

When I explained to the woman at the other end of the call what was happening, she promised to send a squad car around to check on it. She didn't sound super urgent. Maybe that was how she always talked. The police would be here soon, I told myself. Hopefully, soon enough.

I got up. I'd wake Madison up just in case, I decided. Better to miss a little sleep than to be surprised by a dangerous home invader.

When I padded over to her makeshift bed, though, she was already awake.

"Something doesn't feel right," she whispered. "Can you sense it?"

"No...but Vadim might be on his way."

"Shit!" The words came out in a strangled hiss. She crawled out of her bedroll. We were both in t-shirts and running shorts, the nightgowns of champions. At least our movements wouldn't be hindered if we had to fight or flee.

"I need a weapon," she whispered. "Do you have a gun? I wish I had a gun."

"No gun," I whispered back. "You could go get a knife. Or a frying pan."

She weighed the options. "Knife," she decided. "But I'll set the frying pan out within easy reach...do you hear something? Something isn't right, I swear it."

"Don't move. Let me listen." We both froze, trying not even to breathe. At first all I could hear was the blood rushing through my veins. I let myself take a breath. Now all I could hear was my own breathing, and Madison's. And...

"Is that a third person breathing?" I whispered.

We held our breath again. Nothing. Nothing. Nothing...

There was just the faintest hint of a sigh. It could have been a stray gust of wind. It could have been my imagination. Or it could have been someone trying to breathe very softly despite being out of breath.

Madison and I stared at each other in the dark. By the blue light coming in from the parking lot through the blinds, I could see the whites staring all the way around her eyes. I probably looked the same.

"Is he...*inside* here?" she whispered.

We went absolutely still again, straining to listen some more. There was another soft sound, like someone shifting position. From the door.

Madison and I looked at each other again. "I think he's on the other side of the door," I whispered into her ear.

She nodded, the movement almost imperceptible. Then we looked at each other some more. I could see the question in her eyes as clearly as if she'd spoken it out loud. What did we do? Confront him? Scream bloody murder? Take shelter in the bathroom?

I had just decided that the last option, taking shelter in the bathroom, was the best choice, when another soft sound came from the direction of the door. The sound of someone ever-so-gently trying the doorknob.

Madison gulped hard, like she was swallowing back a desperate shriek.

There were some more soft sounds coming from the doorknob. Very gentle scraping and clinking sounds. Like someone fumbling with a key. Or, I thought with a thrill of horror that made every nerve ending on my body scream in pain, like someone picking a lock.

The security chain is in place. But I'd heard so many times that security chains were basically useless for stopping a determined intruder. A clever door-breaker could unhook them from the outside, and a strong one could burst through them.

I have to confront him. The thought was very unwelcome. I'd been about to drag Madison back into the bathroom and lock us inside, but then it had occurred to me that it probably wouldn't do much good. If the person out there was willing and able to pick my front door, a little bathroom lock wasn't going to stop him. And if he was really ruthless, he could shoot us through the door. It was just hollow wood, and we'd be trapped in there. We needed to stop him from ever coming into the apartment at all.

Maybe we can scare him off. If I called out to him, would that drive him away? He'd been trying to be quiet so far. Maybe the threat of a little noise would send him packing. It was worth trying. I *had* to try it.

I opened my mouth. The only thing that came out was a sad, strangled croak. I cleared my throat and tried again. "Vadim?" I hissed. "Vadim, is that you?" Then I said it in Russian for good measure.

No response. Although I could no longer hear the tiny clinking and scraping noises coming from the doorknob. I listened hard. No sound of retreating footsteps, either. After a moment, the clinking noises started again.

"Vadim!" I said more loudly. I used Russian to make sure that he understood. "I know you're there. I've called the police."

The lock-picking noises went silent again.

"I called the police," I repeated. "They'll be here soon."

There was a loud *thud* and the door jumped on its hinges. He'd changed from picking the lock to kicking the door down. I tried to convince myself that it was a new door and it could withstand even a determined assault. There was another loud *thud* and it jumped on its hinges again. My confidence in its ability to protect me faltered.

I have to go over there! I needed to brace the door. And maybe I could talk to him, talk some sense into him. I *needed* to go over to the door. But my feet were frozen. I couldn't make them move me towards the door, towards danger. All they wanted to do was run, run, *run* as far and as fast as they could. But there was nowhere to run to. The only way out was through the door that Vadim was currently trying to kick down.

"Hey!" Madison's voice cracked. She gulped and tried again. "Hey, Vadim! I know it's you. It's me. Madison. Your cousin. The cousin you've been looking for. That's why you're here, isn't it? To come get me?"

The door stopped jumping on its hinges. Surely we'd woken up my neighbors. Surely someone would have called the police by now. Maybe a second call would get them to come out here at top speed.

"Madison." The voice on the other side of the door was youngish, male, Slavic. He was speaking English, but with a heavy accent that only strengthened that chocolatey timbre that people loved so much. "Madison, why you do this thing? Madison, you..." He trailed off, then switched to Russian and said, "Madison, you betrayed your mother, your family, and your people. How could you do this?"

Madison looked over at me questioningly. Her Russian probably wasn't good enough to understand everything he'd said. I tried to force myself to speak, to translate his words for her. But my mouth wouldn't open. I couldn't seem to get air out of my lungs and through my larynx.

Suddenly, I felt so tired. I was tired of all of this. I was tired of struggling and fighting to get by, and I was tired of being surrounded by fuckups and gangsters and extremists, and I was tired, so mortally tired, of people wanting to hurt me for something someone else had done. More than anything in the world, all I wanted to do was turn around, throw myself facedown on my bed, and never move again. Let Vadim come get Madison. Who was she to me, anyway? A student I'd had for one semester who'd almost gotten me killed once, and might be about to get me killed again. That didn't make sense. Whatever. What did any of it matter? None of it mattered at all.

If I exhibited superhuman strength, speed, cunning, and courage, and saved Madison by defeating Vadim in single combat, in the grand scheme of things it wouldn't matter. Madison would probably still go on to be a drug-addicted screwup who wasted her life on stupid pleasure-seeking. Vadim would still carry on being a neo-Nazi white supremacist, hurting others in the name of truth, freedom, the American way, democracy, European values, or whatever jingle they were using now.

Even if I got him arrested, he'd probably just get released again. Even if I killed him, the movement would carry on, stronger than before, with him as a martyr and me as a murderer. I'd complete my descent into the dark side of what I'd always wanted to be, and all our lives would be ruined. I should just give up now, leave it to other people, and not care about the outcome.

My phone, which I'd stuffed into the pocket of my running shorts, *buzzed* against my hip and lit up, causing me to emit an eerie green glow in the darkened room. Mechanically, wearily, hopelessly, I pulled it out, my fingers barely able to hold onto it.

It was a call. A video call. From Dima.

75

ANSWER? OR DON'T ANSWER? Answer? Or don't answer?

I answered. If he was calling at four in the morning, he must have a really, really good reason.

"Inna? Where are you?"

"In my apartment," I told him. "With Madison. And Vadim is at the door."

"I thought so, fuck his mother. I tried to talk to him earlier, but he wouldn't take my call. Can he hear us?"

"Probably," I said.

"Hold the phone up to the door. I want to talk to him."

I held the phone up towards the door, although I was still too afraid to get any closer to it. Or too apathetic. Dima's attempts to talk to Vadim were doomed to failure, I was sure of it already. I really should have gone and locked myself in the bathroom and curled up in the bathtub. At least that way I would already be lying down when the bullets from the gun I was sure Vadim was carrying pierced my flesh. Cleanup would be expedited, too.

Of course, I probably wouldn't have to worry about that, but my mom or my grandma might. I was able to summon up a flicker of feeling for them. If I was horribly slaughtered in my own apartment, would they have to go through my things and clean up the bloodstains in order to get my deposit back? Probably. Maybe I should try to stay alive in order to spare them that.

"Vadim," Dima said. "Vadim, do you hear me?"

Silence from the other side of the door.

"Vadim!" Dima shouted. "Answer, you lousy fascist motherfucker!"

"Or what?" came Vadim's voice from the other side of the door. Even in the middle of the night, through a door he was trying to break down so he could attack me, I could hear the charisma that had made him an internet icon the world over. Right now, it made him even scarier. "You'll scold me like a naughty schoolboy, right?" he was calling to Dima. "Oooo, I'm so scared! I'm shitting my pants right now! I fought your kind in Kiev, in the Donbass, I faced them down and I killed them, the fucking imperialist murderers. But now I'm going to do whatever you say because you're shouting at me? Of course, of course. You Moscow men are all the same, you think the world belongs to you..."

"If I'm not mistaken," Dima said, "you lived for a long time in Moscow yourself. In fact, I believe you still technically have Moscow residency. So as one Muscovite to another..."

"I am *not* a Muscovite!" Vadim's voice was growing increasingly agitated, losing its polish of confidence and cleverness that gave it such a sheen. Surely this was waking up the neighbors. Surely the police were going to show up at any moment. Surely this whole ridiculous farce would end soon, and I could go back to bed without actually having to do anything.

"Suuuuure," said Dima. "You know, the Westerners and the L'viv liberals like to talk about how the Nazis doing all the fighting and killing and dying for them are actually Russians. Because—subtext—that's all Russians are good for: the dirty work that these *European* intellectuals don't want to spoil their soft, white hands with. I used to think they were talking a bunch of shit.

"But then I met you, and I realized they weren't completely lying. All these Westerners and holier-than-thou liberal intellectuals are panting to lionize you, throw their panties at you like you're John Lennon—as long as you mouth the words they want to hear and take out their shit.

"Face it, Vadyusha. You're being used. I know you are, because I've been used to do other people's dirty work myself. I've even thought of going down your path and making my living by trash-talking Russia to the Western press that's just drooling for the kind of stories I could tell. We both might hate to admit it, but we're the same. Right down to our blood and bones. After all, you're practically as Russian as I am. And I bet you've got some Jewish blood, even some Tatar blood, just like I do. You're a steppe mongrel just like me. You just despise yourself too much to admit it."

"Fuck you." Vadim's voice was distinctly poisonous now. "You know, I think I'm going to fuck your girlfriend. I bet she'll enjoy it, too. It'll be a nice change from your limp Moscow Jew-boy pencil-dick."

Probably I should speak up now, defend Dima's figurative and literal manhood. I should at least intervene before Dima got us all killed even faster than we were going to get killed already. He had always been better at confrontation than common ground and de-escalation. But I couldn't summon the courage, or the caring, or anything. Even the thought of being raped by a crazed neo-Nazi couldn't summon up more than a faint feeling of *ick*. And seriously, where were the police? Why was I still having to stand here and listen to this?

"Vadim." Dima's voice was hard and serious now. "Listen to me very, very carefully. I was speaking honestly when I offered you a chance to tell your story. As God is my witness, I will interview you, and write what you say, and make you sound at least semi-sane. You say you're not a Nazi, you're a true patriot and son of Ukraine? Fine. Tell me about it. Tell me about it, and let me publish the story in some big-time Western publication, and let the public decide."

"You're lying," said Vadim.

"I'm not lying. And I'm lying even less when I tell you that if you harm even one hair on my fiancée's head, I will hunt you down, and I will rip your head from your spine and your skin from your body, and I will wear it as a trophy."

"You don't scare me! You don't do that kind of thing anymore. I'll bet you *never* did that kind of thing. And you don't have any backup, any protection. You'll never be able to get to me, let alone hurt me."

"I have friends in surprisingly high places," said Dima. "How do you think I'm still alive? Not everyone at a certain brick-red square in downtown Moscow hates me. And a lot of my former comrades in arms are still...comrades in arms. We may not see eye to eye about everything, but I'll bet my life they'd still love to come help me out with something like this."

"You're lying." Vadim spoke loudly, but he was sounding less and less certain. Good. Or was it bad? Was Dima just goading him into doing something even stupider and more violent? Where *were* the police?

"I'm not lying." Dima's voice was calm and flat. "Come on, Vadyusha. Talk to me. Give me that exclusive interview I've been hounding you about for months. It'll help you out a lot more than attacking a couple of Americans. You don't want to fuck with the American police."

"I'm not afraid of the American police!" Vadim insisted hotly. "Compared to you guys, they're just a bunch of pussies."

"Maybe," said Dima. "But what do you think will happen to you if you attack a couple of unarmed American women? In America they have freedom of the press. It's a strange concept for both Moscow and Kiev, I know, so let me explain it to you. A journalist could decide to write a story about how you, the leader of an organization with murky Nazi ties and ill intent towards the

American government, broke into an American woman's apartment and violently assaulted her. And no one would stop him! Then this journalist might start to say things like, 'Should we really be sending all this money and guns to these people? Should we really be supporting this cause? Maybe these aren't the glorious heroes we thought they were.' And *babakh*! Instead of throwing him in jail, people in high places might start to listen to him. All those tasty American dollars, not to mention all that breathless Western adulation and those eager volunteers from all over the world, could dry up. You could go from being the toast of the free world to being just another group of grubby terrorists, like the mujahideen. And all from you having a rush of blood to the head. So don't do it, Vadim. Just walk away. Walk away from the women, and talk to me instead."

Silence from the other side of the door. Then retreating footsteps.

He's leaving! The relief was so great my knees actually went weak. My left knee twinged as I caught myself before I went down, and then started buzzing.

The retreating footsteps stopped. Then they picked up speed. And loudness. Why were they getting louder? Why...

There was a loud *thud*, and the door jumped on its hinges, harder than before, like from the impact from a large, strong man throwing himself as hard as he could against it. Madison screamed.

"It's okay," I started to say. "He can't actually kick the door down..."

She screamed again and grabbed at my arm, pointing with her other hand. I followed her pointing finger with my eyes.

The doorknob was visibly looser and was rattling in its hole. He must be trying to pick it again. It looked like he was messing with the latch itself, not the keyhole. It was a spring lock. Spring locks, I thought hazily, could be opened with a credit card if they were facing the right way. Was my lock facing the right way? I had no idea. I couldn't bring up an image of it in my mind.

"We should brace the door," I said. Or tried to say. Madison didn't seem to hear me. I wasn't sure if the words had actually left my mouth.

"We should try to brace the door," I said again. This time I was sure I had managed to make myself heard. Madison took a half-step towards the door. I took a half-step behind her.

There was an ominous *click*. The door swung open.

76

MADISON SHRIEKED. THEN she threw herself at the door, as if trying to close it. She made it just in time to get smacked in the face. She reeled back, clutching at her nose.

"Hah!" said Vadim. He stepped inside. Good God, he was handsome. The sexiness that pulled people in on his YouTube videos was almost overpowering in person, even under such inauspicious circumstances.

The sexiness was slightly spoiled by the gun he was holding out in front of him. An elegant little handgun, but deadly enough. All thoughts of tackling him fled.

He swung the gun first towards Madison, then towards me. "Hands up," he told me.

I put my hands up. In my right palm, my phone was warm, the tiny fan whirring. Dima must still be on the call. In my left palm, the handle of the knife I'd grabbed from the kitchen was slick with sweat.

Vadim's eyes went wide when he saw it. Then he smiled. "Drop the knife," he ordered. He backed up the command with a sharp motion with the gun.

I dropped the knife.

"Good girl," Vadim said. He turned away from me, to Madison, who had retreated into the corner and was huddled there, hands over her bleeding nose, a feral look in her eyes.

"Madison," said Vadim reproachfully. "Why did you betray your family like that? Your *mother*? You should know better. When I spoke with Brenda, she couldn't say who had tipped off the police, but when she told me how you were on the outs with her, I knew. I remembered what you are like, Madison. You were a difficult girl, an obstreperous girl, a disobedient girl, a girl who cares nothing for family, for homeland, for honor, when you were with us last summer. We tried to help you, but some people can't be helped. Maybe it is the corrupting effect of America. That is why I am going to take you back to Ukraine with me. Once you are with your people again, once you spend enough time with them, you will come to your senses."

Madison stared at him blankly. He had been speaking Russian. She had probably only gotten one word in five, if that.

"Go...Ukraine?" she finally managed to say in Russian, her American accent even more apparent than usual, her voice thick and clogged with tears and blood. "No! *NO!* I no go! NO!"

She was shouting as loudly as she could through her bleeding nose. Where *were* the damn neighbors? Couldn't they hear us?

Almost idly, I realized that Vadim had his back to me. He was so focused on Madison he seemed to have forgotten me entirely. The door was still open. If I were quick and quiet, I could run out onto the landing before he stopped me. He might come after me, or he might not. It seemed like he cared more about Madison than me. I could escape from this completely unscathed, and take shelter elsewhere to wait for the police to come deal with him. I didn't have to face this myself. I didn't have to face it at all.

You can't abandon Madison! The thought was slow, sluggish and distant, like it was putting up a token resistance and nothing more. And I wouldn't be abandoning her, another part of me argued. From outside, from safety, I could summon help more easily. It would be the smart thing to do.

You've already summoned help. It's not going to come any more quickly than it's coming.

Vadim was stepping over to Madison, holding out his hand, almost as if he wanted to make peace with her. She eyed him balefully. He laughed. Then, as easily as if he were swatting at a fly, he slapped her open-handed across the face, hard enough that her head snapped to the side, spraying blood all over him and my off-white carpet.

There goes my deposit. Unless I can get hydrogen peroxide into it real fast.

"Come on," Vadim told her. He was speaking genially, as if he hadn't just hit her in the face. "Let's go. Let's go to your mom. I know she wants to talk to you. And then we'll go back home to your family. To your motherland. It will do you good."

Madison shook her head, although I could tell she hadn't understood half of what he was saying. "No!" she said loudly, first in English, then in Russian. "No! I no!"

Vadim laughed again and took her arm, gesturing at her with the gun in his other hand. He was holding it loosely, comfortably. It might be easy to knock out of his hand. Or not. He certainly looked like he knew how to use it. I'd probably do more harm than good if I tried anything.

Vadim started to back up, dragging Madison with him. She struggled, crying out and clawing at his hand with her fingernails. He only laughed more and jerked at her, making her stumble towards him.

"Inna."

I jumped. What? Where...my phone. Dima was still on the call with me. And now he was whispering to me, trying to get my attention.

Slowly, smoothly, surreptitiously, I lowered my hand, bringing the phone to my face. Vadim, occupied with Madison, didn't seem to notice.

"*Inna,*" Dima whispered. "*You can stop him. Kick him in the balls.*"

I eyed Vadim. He had his back to me, his legs braced apart as he tried to drag Madison towards him. I could indeed kick him in the balls. In theory. And if I missed? Or my knee gave out on me? Then he'd be pissed at me.

"*Kick him in the balls,*" Dima whispered. "*Then hit him in the back of the neck. Then grab his gun if he drops it. Grab your knife. You can DO it! Do it! Now! Before he turns around!*"

Vadim had succeeded in pulling Madison over to him and was turning towards the door, ready to drag her out of the apartment. In a second he'd be out of range. I had to do it now.

The light from the phone was giving everything a strange, flickering, discoball, horror-movie glow. As smoothly as if I were doing forms, I pivoted on the bare ball of my left foot so that I was perfectly aligned with Vadim.

Flicker.

My right leg chambered for the kick.

Flicker.

Vadim paused, as if sensing danger.

Flicker.

My right leg unchambered and struck out.

Flicker.

My right instep flew between Vadim's spread legs and connected solidly with his groin.

Flicker.

He yelled in shock and pain.

Flicker.

He dropped Madison's arm and spun around to face me, even as his body crumpled up in a reflexive crouch.

Flicker.

His gun came up to point at me.

Flicker.

My right hand swung out, smooth and confident from all the hundreds of times I'd practiced this move, and knocked the gun out of his hand, sending it spinning through the air and into the kitchen.

Flicker.

Vadim launched himself at me, his handsome face distorted in a rabid snarl.

Flicker.

He slammed into me, making my left knee buckle and taking us both to the ground.

Flicker.

He had his hands around my throat. I scrabbled at them, my nails making no impression on his skin.

Flicker.

Light glinted off the blade of the knife I'd dropped.

Flicker.

I drove the nails of my right hand into his skin while my left hand let go of him and reached for the knife.

Flicker.

My left hand came up, operating as if on its own, and drove the tip of my knife into his right forearm.

Flicker.

Vadim screamed and stared at the knife in enraged horror.

Flicker.

He drew back his left hand and struck at my face.

Flicker.

I got my right arm up just in time to block his strike. The impact sent my phone sailing out of my hand and off into the darkness.

Flicker.

Vadim drew back his left hand again. Both my arms felt numb and slow. I wasn't going to be able to block him in time.

Flicker.

Madison screamed and grabbed at Vadim's back, stopping him from hitting me.

Flicker.

He shrugged her off and grabbed for my throat again with both his hands.

Flicker.

I tried to drive my nails into the backs of his hands. He didn't seem to feel it.

Flicker.

The flickering was growing worse. Was I blacking out? I couldn't get air...there was so much shouting...Dima was shouting...Madison was shouting...someone else was shouting...Vadim's weight was dragged off me.

I gasped for breath, choking and wheezing. Madison threw herself down beside me.

"Are you okay? Are you okay?" she was crying frantically.

I nodded, still not able to speak. Where was Vadim? There was so much shouting and struggling...What was going on...

Light suddenly flooded the entrance. Someone had switched on the lights. Vadim was facedown on the floor, his hands cuffed behind his back.

Standing over him was Frank.

77

FOR A MOMENT I COULD only stare at him blankly, gasping in breath through my tortured throat. What? How...?

"You made it," I said. Or tried to say. My memory, which had been totally subsumed by the moment-to-moment struggle to stay alive, returned, and I knew how and why Frank was here. My throat, though, still didn't want to talk.

"You okay?" Frank asked. He looked over at Madison, apparently seeing her for the first time. "Both of you okay?"

Madison and I nodded tentatively.

"Good. Where the fuck are the local boys? They should be here by now."

Right on cue, the green and white glow from my cell phone was cut by the harsher blue and red of police lights.

Vadim started to struggle harder, bucking and writhing so that his whole body was bouncing off the ground with the agility of a breakdancer.

"Stop it," said Frank. When Vadim didn't obey, he placed his foot firmly on Vadim's back, between his shoulder blades, forcing him down onto the floor.

"You're bleeding," Frank observed, looking over at me. "Your face is all bloody."

I felt at my face. "It must be his blood." This time the words came out. They came out as a tortured rasp, but they were audible. "I stabbed him with a knife," I explained.

Frank gave a low whistle. "Damn," he said. "I'm impressed. That why his right arm's all covered in blood?"

I nodded. That set my throat and neck to spasming in protest again.

Frank bent down and gave Vadim's arm a cursory examination. "I don't think you're gonna bleed out," he told him. "I don't even think you're gonna have much of a scar. That knife wound's the least of your worries, believe you me."

Heavy footsteps were coming up the stairs. In a moment my apartment entrance was filled with what felt like the entire Greenfields police department, plus Xavier Thornton and at least one other FBI agent, plus Brian Michaels from campus police, plus, as they were carting Vadim away, Mel.

"Ro!" she shouted, pushing her way through the officers milling by the door. "Ro! You okay? What happened?"

"I'm fine," I croaked. "She's a friend," I told the officers trying to stop her from coming in. "She's here to help me."

It was agreed that she could come in to be with me. I had scooted over to sit with my back to the cabinets separating the kitchen from the rest of the apartment. Madison was huddled next to me, her arms around her knees, rocking slightly back and forth. Mel sat down on the other side of me, looking me over.

"You look like shit," she said. "And you've got blood on your face."

"It's not mine," I told her. "It's Vadim's."

"He the one?" she asked, nodding towards the door that Vadim had just been hauled out of.

"Uh-huh."

"Looks like you won in the end, though," she said.

"I had some help," I told her.

Mel looked over at Madison.

I nodded. Then I nodded at Frank, who was talking animatedly with Brian Michaels and someone senior-looking in a Greenfields police uniform. Xavier Thornton had already left with Vadim.

Mel gave Frank a look through narrowed eyes. "Is he the asshole from California?" she whispered.

"Uh-huh," I whispered back. "But he came through when I needed him. And he's not the only one."

I glanced down at my hands. I was still clutching my phone, which was becoming uncomfortably hot. Dima was still on the call. He hadn't left me. It must have been terrible for him, to watch helplessly while others fought, but he hadn't left me. And he was still here.

78

BY SIX IN THE MORNING the bustle around my apartment had mostly cleared away. I'd had to end the call with Dima around five, when the battery was down to 10% and the phone itself was desperately blowing out a steady stream of overheated air. He'd made me promise to call him again later today, whenever I was ready.

Mel sat with me until all the police had gone. Then she helped me to my feet. When I tried to stand, my left knee buckled beneath me.

"Damn," I said. "There goes four months of healing down the drain."

"It doesn't look as bad as before," Mel said.

"Really?"

"I don't know. I was just saying it to sound comforting. Did it work?"

I flexed the knee experimentally. "Maybe. It doesn't hurt as much as before, at least. But it feels messed up. I don't think I can put much weight on it."

I hobbled into the bathroom with Mel's support. When I stepped out of the shower, I found Fevronia peering out from under the sink. She must have spent the entire fracas hidden away there. Good. The best place for her. I gave her a scratch behind her ears. Instead of swiping at me, she purred.

When I hobbled back into the front room, Madison was on the phone with her dad.

"*No,* Dad, I'm *fine*," she was saying. "I'm, like, totally *fine*. There's no need for you to come get me." She paused. "Although I might need some therapy later."

Agitated words came over the phone. She let them go on for a few sentences, before cutting in with, "Fine, *fine*. Fly down to Atlanta and come get me, if it matters so much to you. If you can find the time. Next week's the last week of the semester. Don't you have a lot of big, important meetings and stuff you've got to attend?"

More agitated words on the other end of the call. Madison grimaced and held the phone away from her ear, looking over at me with almost comic despair.

"I'm going to hand you over to Professor Halley, Dad," she finally said, interrupting the flow. "That way she can tell you directly how she feels about me being here."

She held out the phone to me. I took it.

"Rowena?" It was Erik Johnson. "Rowena, my God, are you all right? Madison is saying you were *attacked*...I've been trying to get the story from her, but I can't get a straight answer..."

"I'm fine," I said. "We're both fine. More or less."

"More or less?" Erik repeated.

"I may have reinjured my torn ACL," I said. "But in the grand scheme of things, we're both fine."

"That sounds serious...you'll have to let me know if you need help with that...what *happened*?"

I gave him a short abstract of the action, downplaying the physical danger and completely leaving out my own internal debate over whether or not to run from the scene and let Vadim take Madison. I reassured him again that Madison was not, as far as I could tell, physically harmed other than a bloody nose. The paramedics had checked her out on the scene and assured her it wasn't broken. It was unlikely, I said, that we were in any more danger, with Vadim and two of his cronies taken away, although I supposed the other two of the five who had come over to the US could still be on the loose.

"Actually," Madison piped up from where she was sitting across the table, "Xavier Thornton texted me while you were in the shower and told me they'd been picked up in New York, at Bright Dawn. They showed up there as originally planned. And I think they picked up my mom as well."

"*What?!?*" Erik shouted over the phone. "Brenda's been *arrested?!?*"

"She deserved it, Dad," Madison said coolly.

"Mother of God...!!!"

It was my turn to wince and hold the phone away from my ear. When Erik calmed down, I said, "So it sounds like we're all safe now. Madison and I are fine. She's welcome to stay here as long as she likes. Whatever you guys decide."

"I'm coming down," Erik said firmly. "On the first flight I can get out of Newark. I'll let you know as soon as it's booked. Hopefully, I'll be there by this evening. And when I get there, Rowena, we should talk."

79

MEL CAME BACK AROUND 8:00 to see if I wanted a ride over to campus for class, or if I was planning to cancel and stay home. She was in favor of the latter.

"When have you ever canceled class?" she asked. "Live a little. See what it's like on the Dark Side. Besides, you were up half the night fighting off crazed extremists, and now you can hardly walk again. You're not really in prime teaching shape, if you'll excuse my saying so."

"I know," I said. "But I don't feel that bad, I really don't. If I cancel class, I'll just sit around here feeling anxious and miserable and fielding panicked emails from students. Easier just to go in and teach."

Mel conceded that point, and agreed to drive me over to campus and drop me off as close to Bedford as she could get. My knee, while not wrenchingly painful as long as I didn't twist it, was visibly swollen again, and buckled every time I tried to put weight on it. I had to dig out my crutches, and when I stood at the top of the two long flights of stairs leading from my apartment to the parking lot, I almost rethought my decision and canceled class anyway.

When I hobbled into the classroom, squinting against the migraine scotoma that had appeared as soon as I stepped into the building, all the students exclaimed over the crutches, demanding to know what had happened.

"I turned suddenly," I told them, with total, if not totally complete, truthfulness. "Must have strained something. Hopefully it'll go away soon. Now, let's talk about what's going to be on the exam..."

When I hobbled out of Bedford three hours later, it was with the surreal sensation that you get after too much stress and not enough sleep. I was waiting near the door for Mel to bring the Jeep around when I saw Chloe on one of the benches nearby. Instead of being by herself, though, she was talking to Diane and Julie. All three of them were speaking animatedly, but with smiles on their faces, like they were enjoying each other's company.

Well, look at that. Chloe has finally found friends amongst the tenured faculty. I debated hobbling over to say hi. I didn't want to end the semester without talking to all of them. But I didn't want to interrupt what looked like a great bonding moment between the three of them, either.

Chloe looked up and caught sight of me. She lifted up her hand as if about to wave me over, then saw the crutches, froze, and said something to Diane and Julie. They all turned, surveyed the crutch situation, and came over to me.

"What *happened*?" asked Julie.

"Long story," I said, again with total, although not totally complete, truthfulness. "Hopefully I won't be back on them for too long."

Julie nodded, her nose wrinkled. "Yeah. As I'm sure you know, campus is a nightmare to get around if you have any kind of mobility issues. I was on one of those scooter thingies for a month a couple of years ago after I cracked a bone in my foot. I found out really quickly just how many stairs there are in this place, not to mention doors you need two hands to get through. I brought it up with the college faculty and the administration at the time, and they basically said someone would have to bring a lawsuit to them over it for it to be worth doing something about. We don't have people here who have difficulty getting around campus, so what's the problem?" She took a deep breath. "I said...well, never mind. You get the picture. Anyway. We've got something now that the college is going to hate even more than their lack of ramps and accessible doors."

Diane nodded. "Some really gnarly samples from most of the buildings on campus," she said. "Various varieties of mold that are known to be toxic, plus some really alarming levels of formaldehyde and PFAS—nasty chemicals. Oh, and a lot of the rooms have worrisome carbon dioxide levels in them during full occupancy, and I think I discovered at least one carbon monoxide leak."

Now I was the one wrinkling my nose. "Can't carbon monoxide kill you?"

"It sure can," said Diane. "Like I said, the college isn't going to like this one bit. We're looking at massive and very costly renovations if they decide to do anything about it."

"So we're forming a committee," Chloe put in. "An ad hoc, unofficial committee on campus safety. Maybe, if we work at it, we can push some change through before anyone gets seriously sickened."

"It's a problem all over the country that's starting to get some exposure," said Diane. "So we figured now might be the time to convince the college that they don't want any bad publicity over this. Start renovations now, so they don't have to do them all at once, under the threat of legal action."

"I know it's a risky thing to do," said Chloe. "I know it could get us in trouble, and I know I have the most to lose here. But it feels important. It's sad, but for the first time since I came to Crimson, I feel like I'm doing something important. And I've found other people who want to do something important too. It's nice, you know? I feel much more like a part of this campus now than I ever have before."

"That's great," I said.

"And if you'd like to join us, Rowena, you'd be welcome to," Diane said. "I know it'd be particularly risky for you, but if you'd like to be an unofficial member, as it were, we'd be glad to have you join us."

"Yeah," I said. "That sounds good."

80

"YOU LOOK SURPRISINGLY good for a woman who almost got killed last night," Mel said when I climbed into the Jeep.

"I'm feeling hopeful," I said. "Maybe it's the beautiful Advent season."

Mel looked expressively out the window, where a December rain had just started. December wasn't the prettiest month in this part of the South. No snow, but plenty of cold rain and sleet, along with inadequate heating.

"Or the end of the semester," I said. "We made it through another semester. That's a triumph, right? And you're about to start treatment, which is hopeful, right? And it looks like Chloe is starting to feel comfortable here, and my brother's life is looking up. And maybe mine is too."

"Is that so," said Mel, giving me another expressive look. "How so?"

I shrugged. "It just feels...hopeful."

"Well, I guess I'll take that. Lord knows we could all use some hope right about now. And you're right: I *am* excited about starting treatment, horrible as it's supposed to be. At least I'll be doing something. And hopefully once I'm through the bad bit, I'll start feeling better and better. And Karen, to my immeasurable surprise, hinted that they might want to keep me here for another year, *and*

I've got an interview coming up next week." She cleared her throat. "For another job in LA."

"Do you still want to move back to LA?" I asked. Mel's ex-girlfriend lived in LA.

Now she shrugged. "I dunno. But I like the idea of having options. I kinda feel like I've got a lot of options opening up in front of me right now. Not all of them are gonna be pleasant, but I've got them, and that's the main thing. You know, after the election, I was pretty much in despair. I'm sure on Inauguration Day I'll be in despair again. But right now, I feel like there's stuff I can do. Life isn't over. It's still possible for good things to happen."

"Yeah," I said. "It is."

At the complex, Mel helped me up the two tall flights of stairs to my apartment, and Madison opened the door for me. Mel gave Madison a critical once-over and said, "Nice shiner, kid. Makes you look tough."

Madison almost bridled for a moment, but then burst into a big grin. "Ouch, shit, that hurts! But it does, like, make me look really tough, doesn't it! You know, I've never had any kind of a real injury before. My mom tried to get me to go skiing, but I never really liked it enough to hurt myself, and I wasn't allowed to do other stuff. But now I've got a black eye from an actual *fight*. Pretty cool, huh?"

"Damn straight," said Mel, and held up her fist for a fist bump. Madison enthusiastically complied, staggering back slightly when her fairly anemic swing connected with Mel's rock-solid stance. Mel laughed and told her they'd have to practice if Madison stuck around.

Then Madison filled us in on a call she'd just had from Xavier Thornton, who, she said, was feeling bad about leaving us to be attacked by Vadim, and was trying to make up for it by feeding Madison as much information as he felt he could legitimately release. Madison's mother had been arrested, along with the other two men from Glorious Future and the entire Bright Dawn staff. A large stockpile of weapons had been discovered, suggesting that they had indeed been planning something nefarious. It was currently believed that they'd been planning to attack the Obamas, the Clintons, or the Carters during the inauguration events. Or maybe they'd just hoped to spread some mayhem and terror.

"So it's good I pissed Vadim off so much he came after us," Madison concluded. "Right? Because that way it was all discovered." She felt at her bruised nose. "I kinda wish we coulda done it without me getting, like, punched in the face, but whatever. A small price to pay for glory, right?"

"Right," I said. "And you did what you said you wanted to do, too: you saved my ass."

"Only after almost getting you killed—*again*. And I did a shit job of it."

"Vadim might have come after me anyway," I told her. "And you jumped him at just the right moment. You came through when it mattered."

Madison grinned, and then clutched at her nose. "Oh, and my dad's gonna get here tonight," she said through her fingers. "He's booked rooms at a hotel and he wants me to get ready to check in with him when he gets here. I *told* him I wanted to stay here, but he said"—her voice took on a faux-stuffy male tone—"'You've trespassed on Professor Halley's kindness too long,' or some shit like that, and I'm supposed to sit tight until he gets there and then go straight over to the hotel with him."

"Whatever you want to do," I said.

"I *want* to stay here," she said, rolling her eyes. "But maybe I need to be with my dad. I think he's pretty upset about the whole thing. He's all broken up about my mom getting arrested. Besides, this way I can flash my shiner at him and make him feel guilty." She grinned some more at that.

"Great plan," I said.

"Yeah...is someone coming up the stairs?" For all her bravado a moment ago, Madison was shrinking in on herself at the thought of someone coming to the door.

"Hang on." I went over to the peephole and looked out it. "It's just Frank," I said. I opened the door before he could knock.

"Good to see you up on your feet, Ro." He tried to give me a raking "elevator eyes" up-and-down, but it fell rather flat. He looked like someone who'd been on a red-eye flight from California, gotten into a fight upon arrival, and then spent all morning at the police station. His normal air of a vigorous clan chieftain was much more muted than usual.

"Thanks. Want to come in?"

He looked through the door at Mel and Madison, and visibly hesitated.

"Or we could go for a walk," I said.

He looked down at my knee, and up at my face, and quirked a brow.

"Let's go for a drive," he said. "You can show me this campus I've heard so much about. And I can fill you in on how everyone's doing back in California."

"I've gotta go shopping," Mel said. "I bet Madison has some stuff she needs to get too. Why don't we go do that now."

"I don't need..." Madison began.

"I'll bet Rowena needs groceries," Mel said, cutting her off. "What with the two of you here, and her having a busted knee and all. Let's go grab some stuff for her right now, before the store gets hit by the after-school crowd."

Madison looked like she was going to protest again, but when Mel jerked her head at her, she followed her out the door, giving Frank a curious glance as she passed him. He nodded courteously at her in response, which seemed to only stoke her curiosity further.

"This place looks a lot different during the day," said Frank, looking around the entrance as he stepped through the door. "Funny, isn't it? It seemed like some scary cave or something...supernatural last night. But it's just a cheap apartment. Uh, sorry. Didn't mean to..."

"No worries," I said. "It is a cheap apartment. That's its main glory."

"Did you get the blood off the carpet okay?"

I looked down. "I left Madison with a bottle of hydrogen peroxide, a roll of paper towels, and instructions on how to use them. Judging by the pink wet spots, she took a stab at it but didn't get very far."

"Yeah. Kids, huh? You don't have any of your own, right?"

"Nope," I said.

"Me neither. Funny. A lot of my buddies ended up with kids they didn't want, from relationships they shouldn't have had. But I never did. At first it seemed like I was the smart one. Now I wonder."

"Yeah," I said.

"Anyway...you need to sit down? You look like you're about to fall over."

"Sure," I said. We both took seats at the table.

"So," said Frank. "Lots to talk about." He gave me one of those surprisingly shrewd looks he could deploy upon occasion. "Alex's doing well, by the way. I told him I was going to see you. I made it clear it was to help out with FBI stuff." He smiled thinly. "I don't think he was too happy about it even so."

"Oh," I said.

"Yeah. Anyways. Lots to talk about, like I said. I don't even really know where to begin. So maybe let's start with the big stuff." He gave me another one of those shrewd looks. "Let's talk about your boyfriend."

81

"WHICH BOYFRIEND?" I said. Then I really wished I hadn't said it. Especially not like that.

Frank's eyes were crinkled up in suppressed laughter. "Good for you, Ro. I didn't think you had it in you."

"I don't," I said. "I just don't actually have a boyfriend right now that I'm aware of. So you must be referring to an ex. And I have more than one of those, I suppose."

He sobered up. "Yeah, I guess so. And you're probably thinking I want to talk about Alex. I still see the guy, you know." He smirked. "Guess that came out wrong too. You know what I mean. I still keep in touch with him, see him around sometimes. It seems only right. And he's...he's doing okay, I guess, but he could be doing better. You were a good influence on him, you know that? 'Course, I'm sure you're a good influence on anybody.

"Anyway, he's still working, still holding it together as far as I can tell, but he's not looking too happy. Still trying to help Erin get her shit together. Only she doesn't want to get her shit together, so now both of 'em are in the shit together."

"Uh-huh." I wished I hadn't sounded so cynical when I'd said that. As Frank had remarked before, I didn't like Erin. From my perspective, she'd jerked around Alex for years, even after they were no longer together, even after he was with me and she was with Frank *and,* it had turned out, another man as well. It was extremely hard for me not to say some very harsh things about her that would go against my policy of sisterly feminist solidarity.

Frank's eyes were crinkled up in a smile again. "That may be the most unkind thing I've ever heard you say, Ro. And you didn't even say anything."

"Uh-huh," I said.

His smile widened. "I told you that you were *bad*. Glad to have some visual proof of it. Or whatever that was."

"Sure," I said. "I'd argue that I should get a pass on Erin, but how you treat your enemies really is the ultimate test of morality. Or one of them, anyway. I'm sorry Alex isn't doing as well as he could be. I take it Erin isn't either?"

He was shaking his head, still grinning. "Nope. I wouldn't be surprised if she finds herself seeking other employment soon. And Noel"—the other man in Erin's life—"is still stringing her along, messing her up and leaving it for Alex to pick up the pieces. He's doing it, but one of these days he's going to get tired of it. Like I already did. She's already come crying back to me a couple of times, but I sent her packing."

"Oh," I said.

"It's the best thing for her," he said. "I know it seems cruel, but as long as people keep cleaning up her messes, she's never going to learn how to take care of herself."

"If she ever can," I said. "Tough love sounds attractive, especially when aimed at her, but it only works some of the time."

"Fair enough," he said.

That was an awfully agreeable statement for him to make. I thought about asking him if he'd been hit on the head during his altercation with Vadim. Instead I said, "So if it's not about Alex, which boyfriend do you want to talk to me about?"

"Your Russian one. Our boy Vadim's pal."

"He's not my boyfriend," I said reflexively. "And he's not friends with Vadim. I'm sure of that if I'm sure of anything."

"Maybe 'friends' is the wrong word," said Frank. "'Associates' might be better. But they know each other."

"I know," I said.

"He knows a lot of bad guys," said Frank.

"True," I said.

"Which is good for us, but maybe bad for you."

"Oh?" I said.

"Yeah. You still haven't gotten your security clearance, have you?"

I shook my head. "The hiring process seemed to be going pretty well at first," I said. "But the last time I heard from them was a couple of months ago, and they said they were bogged down in the security clearance, and I shouldn't expect to hear from them for a while."

He nodded. "Yeah. Figured as much. Dammit. I'll keep my fingers crossed for you...but with these connections you have to this Kuznetsov fellow, it'll be tough for you to get cleared. And you'll probably have to cut off ties with him, or with a lot of your other Russian friends, or both."

"Oh." I'd known that was a possibility. That was one of the reasons I'd resisted applying for any kind of a job that required a security clearance. I'd just been desperate, and had thought that my future lay in America, with Americans, and I'd decided to give it a go.

"By the look on your face," Frank said, "you're not ready for that."

"I thought I was," I said. "But things might have changed."

"Yeah. I get that. You were all set to hook up with an American and, hopefully, move out to California. Then that all went to hell. For what it's worth"—he quirked one side of his mouth—"if you're still interested in hooking up with an American and maybe moving to California, I might be able to help you out with that."

"Thanks," I said. "But I wonder how serious you'd be about it if I actually showed up at your doorstep, saying I was ready to take you up on that offer. In my experience, lots of people say they'd like to get together and start a life together, blah blah blah. But when push comes to shove, they run."

Frank gave me an appraising look. That unexpected shrewdness filled his eyes. "Yeah. And I might have done the same thing a time or two myself. I'd like to say I've grown out of it, but no one's ever put me to the test." He shrugged, a little half-smile on his face that suddenly made him look much younger. "I guess if you wanted to put me the test, I'd let you. But maybe you're right to be wary. I don't really have the best track record."

"That's okay," I said. "Neither do I. So I'm not sure either of us should put each other to the test just yet."

"Fair enough," said Frank. "We can just keep it as Plan B."

"Um," I said. "Sure."

He grinned, still looking unexpectedly shrewd. "I'm not gonna take that as a 'Yes.' Or even a 'maybe.' But keep it in mind, okay? It might go better than you think."

"Sure," I said.

He grinned wider. "I'm hurt! That was damn near sarcastic."

"I didn't mean it that way," I said.

He wagged a finger at me. "I know. But deep down, you're *bad*, Ro, and it has to come out somehow. If sarcasm with me is what gets you off, well, so be it. You can even tell yourself you're not being bad, since I'm so bad myself it's okay to treat me like that."

"That's not how I roll," I said. I paused for reflection. "I hope not," I added. "That's not how I *intentionally* roll, anyway."

"That," said Frank, "is maybe the most sickeningly goody-goody thing I've ever had anyone say to me with a straight face. And I think you meant it, too, which is the worst part. I don't know how you put up with this Kuznetsov fellow, I really don't."

"We're both kind of goody-goody," I said.

Now the look he was giving me was narrow, sideways. "He's not a goody-goody kind of person, Ro."

"Well," I said. "Maybe in some aspects, no. But..."

"But nothing, Ro. He walks on the fucking dark side, and this is *me* saying that."

"Well..." I said. "Maybe in the past..."

"I'm not talking about his fucking past, Ro. I've been reading up on him. He's become a person of interest, you might say. To the US government, since he's applied for a visa to come over here, and to me personally, since you're mixed up with him. And he's...yeah, he's a hero, I get that. The kind of Russian opposition figure you liberals like to go gaga about."

"Um..." I said. "That's not...I mean, yeah, I suppose so, but that's not why I..."

"Listen." Frank cut me off, his voice hard and intense. "He's mixed up with some bad people. I don't just mean his old comrades, or the people back in Moscow who'd love to take him out. I mean people like Vadim. People with one foot in the Taliban or al-Qaeda or C14 or the Aryan Brotherhood or some shit like that, and the other foot high up in Kremlin politics. *Bad* people. Bad people who could kill you as soon as look at you."

"I know," I said. "I know that very well."

"And you don't fuck around with people like that. You don't fuck around with people like that because they'll kill you soon as look at you, and you don't fuck around with people like that because before you know it, you're one of them. Believe me, I know."

"Yeah," I said. "I believe you. And I know. I've been careful, and I'll go on being careful."

"It might not be enough." Frank's face was set in grim lines. "You were careful here, weren't you? And this fuckface Vadim still broke into your apartment and damn near killed you."

"Maybe I wasn't careful enough," I said. "I didn't take it seriously until it was actually happening."

"You took it seriously enough to call me, didn't you? You took it seriously enough to lock yourself in your apartment and set out weapons. That's about as seriously as an amateur like you can take it, Ro. I don't mean that in a bad way. But you *are* an amateur. You're in over your head here, and *he's* the one pushing you under, whether he means to or not."

"I guess," I said.

"You don't guess," Frank told me. "You know. You know I'm right, don't you? You know he's mixed up in bad stuff, and you know he's bringing it down on you. You just don't want to run away."

"No," I said. "I don't. I've done a lot of running away. Sometimes it's saved me. And I thought about doing it again this time. I really did. Sometimes you have to run for your life. But sometimes you have to stand and fight. And I think I've come to the standing and fighting part of my journey."

Frank stood up. "I can respect that," he said. "Sometimes that's what you gotta do. I get that. And if you need help standing and fighting, you call me, okay? It's one of the few things I'm pretty good at."

"I'm sure you're good at other things," I said, standing up too. "But I know you're good at standing and fighting. And whenever I've seen you run, you've always been running towards me in order to save me. Maybe someday I'll be able to come running in order to save you."

Frank grinned. "I sure hope so. That'd be something to see. And thanks, Ro. Hearing I'm a hero from someone like you means a lot." He leaned over and put his arms around me. He felt solid and strong and incredibly attractive, just as I'd known he would. He almost groped my ass, just as I'd suspected he would. I resisted the urge to roll my eyes.

"I've gotta go," he said, stepping back from the embrace. "Duty calls, and all that. I've got a flight out of Atlanta tonight. Better hit the road if I want to make it. But if you call, I'll come running."

"Thanks," I said. "I appreciate it. You're a good man, Frank McAvoy, even if you hide it well."

He laughed all the way out the door.

82

I HAD OFFERED, WITHOUT a huge amount of enthusiasm, to pick Erik up at the airport, but he had declined. He texted us once to tell us he was at Newark, and again a couple of hours later to tell us he'd landed at Atlanta. He texted a little after six to tell us he'd made it to his hotel in Greenfields, and wanted to take us to dinner.

"Do I *have* to?" Madison asked.

"Well," I said. "Technically, no. Since you're now an adult, you have no legal obligation to go see him at all. If you're desperate not to, I'll make your excuses. But I'd strongly advise you to at least have dinner with him."

"*Why?*" she moaned.

"Because he's your dad?" I said. "The only dad you've got? So you might as well try to maintain a decent relationship with him? And right now he's probably pretty stressed out, so you would be making the world a better place by being nice to him?"

Madison gave me a skeptical look.

"Think of it this way," I told her. "By going out to dinner with him this evening and being reasonably polite to him, you will reduce the amount of suffering in the world. And you will probably benefit from it materially yourself, in the form of plane tickets, tuition, room and board...you get the picture."

"That sounds so *cynical*," she said. "Like I'm just being nice to him so he'll buy me stuff. I don't want to be nice to him so he'll buy me stuff. I want him to be nice to me instead of trying to buy me off with stuff."

"Maybe you should tell him that," I said.

She gave me an even more skeptical look. However, she allowed me to drive her over to the hotel, which was an upscale affair on the far side of campus. Greenfields, thanks to the college, had a small but very nice downtown that included a five-star hotel with a fancy fusion cuisine restaurant, as well as a smattering of elegant boutiques and faux-English tea shops. I hardly ever went there, because there was nothing there I could afford, but it added an air of elegance to what otherwise would have been a cheap Southern town in the middle of nowhere.

Erik was pacing the hotel lobby when we arrived. As usual, he was dressed in a suit that probably cost more than my whole wardrobe, but today it was rumpled and tired-looking, like he'd thrown something on at six in the morning and slept on the plane in it. His haircut probably cost more than...I rarely spent money on my hair, so I didn't know what to compare it with, but it was also expensive. And right now, even more rumpled than his suit. I guessed he'd been running his hands through it in his distraction.

"Thank God!" he said when we stepped inside. He came over and grabbed Madison by the shoulders as if he wanted to hug her. She stiffened. He stopped himself from going for the full hug, and looked her over.

"Your face!" he said. "It looks so bad...I thought you said you weren't hurt!"

"Chill, Dad," she said. "It's nothing. Just a bruise. No biggie. The paramedics said I'm gonna be fine."

"Your nose is swollen, and you have two black eyes. That doesn't look like nothing. We'll get you checked out first thing tomorrow, as soon as we're back in New Jersey."

"I want to go back to New York," Madison said. A distinctly sullen edge was creeping into her voice. "I want to go back to Aunt Cybil."

"Cybil may not want *you* back, Madison. And in any case, it's best for us to be together right now. We need to support each other and present a united front as a family, what with your mother's...situation."

Madison opened her mouth, clearly about to argue further. Then she caught my eye, and to my astonishment, said, "That's a good point, Dad. How *is* Mom? Have you talked to her yet?"

He shook his head. "They haven't let me speak to her yet. I think the only person allowed access to her right now is her lawyer. Or maybe she doesn't want to talk to me. She must be feeling..." He trailed off, unable to come up with the words for how she must be feeling. I repressed any thoughts of however bad she was feeling, it probably wasn't bad enough. Was she rethinking her involvement with Carrie, Vadim, and their ilk? Somehow I doubted it. Probably she was just doubling down on her convictions now.

"Anyway," Erik said. He cleared his throat and looked over at me. "It's good to see you, Rowena, although I wish it had been under more auspicious circumstances. Are we all ready to go into the dining room...what happened to your leg? Was that from the...altercation?"

"It's an old injury," I said. I had, with more pride than sense, disdained the crutches for the evening, but I had my knee in a brace and was using a cane. "It just...got a little re-aggravated during the fight."

Erik winced at the word "fight," and again when he saw my hobble as we started towards the dining room. "You'll have to tell me if you need...help with this, Rowena," he said as we made our slow way across the lobby. "I know how expensive some of these specialists can be...does the college provide benefits for contingent faculty? I imagine it's not great."

"They do," I said. "And it's not great, but there's not a lot you can get done around here anyway, so it doesn't really matter that much most of the time."

"Still," he said. "Let me know if you need any help with that. It's only fair."

I gave him a polite smile. He was perfectly right in assuming that I wouldn't be able to afford any kind of extensive treatment on my own. And it was probably right of him to offer to help pay for it, since I had sustained my injury while protecting his daughter. But the thought of owing him anything, even just a favor, didn't sit right with me.

I'd owed him before and it had been fine, and in the grand scheme of things it could be argued that he would be forever in my debt, but still, the thought of getting drawn deeper into his orbit didn't appeal. I had always been chary of taking him up on the various things he had offered me, but had been willing to consider it. Now, though, it felt like my life was heading in a different direction, one that hopefully wouldn't mean having to rely on him. I certainly didn't want to make him my enemy, but I didn't want to make him my patron (with benefits?) either.

A strained semi-silence hung over the table as we ordered drinks, and perused the menu, and ordered our food. Erik kept looking back and forth between me and Madison, his face changing from joy to relief to horror to outrage and back again.

"How much more of the semester do you have left, Rowena?" he said abruptly, as we were finishing our main course.

"Today was the last day of class," I said.

He winced. "Tough day to miss."

"Actually, I went in and taught," I said. "I didn't have anything better to do, so I decided to go ahead and do it."

His face tried to take on several different expressions at once. "Rowena, I..." He glanced over at Madison. "I know we've taken advantage of your...of everything...of, of you in a way we can't ever truly repay you for, but...I..." He shrugged helplessly. Then he said, speaking directly for the first time that evening, "What do you need? How can I help you?"

I tried to come up with something that he could give me. He obviously needed to do it, and it might be useful to me, too. But I couldn't think of anything off the top of my head. He couldn't singlehandedly get me a job, and certainly not one that would be any better than the one I already had. He couldn't fix my relationships. He could pay for treatment for my knee, but that might not actually fix anything. He could give me money, but I didn't want to take money from him. Certainly not for this.

"I didn't do any of this for gain," I said.

"I know you didn't." He made an angry gesture with his hand. "But I still want to help you out. I *need* to."

I nodded. "I understand. I would feel the same way. But I just can't think of anything right now. Maybe...maybe the thing I want most is for you and Madison to get along."

He nodded. Tiredly. "That would certainly make your life easier."

"Not for that reason. Because it would make me feel like the world had become a tiny bit better if you could be kind to each other. Like I'd done some real good in the world. Like everything I'd done hadn't been in vain."

Erik smiled lopsidedly. "That's a pretty big ask. But I guess I asked for it, didn't I? I just...I wish I knew how..."

"Maybe you should ask her," I said, nodding towards Madison.

"Yeah. Jeez. I'm, like, *right* here," she said. She was trying to play the part of the sulky adolescent, but she wasn't quite pulling it off. Her voice trembled like she was about to cry.

Erik smiled lopsidedly again. "So, Madison, what do *you* want? What can I get *you?*"

Madison looked over at me. Then she looked back at him and said, "I want you to spend time on me, rather than money."

Erik went still. "That *is* a big ask," he said. "But a good one." His voice was starting to shake too.

"Excuse me," I said. "I'll be right back." I slipped—well, staggered—away from the table and over towards the ladies' room. I didn't actually have to go, but I figured I'd be more likely to get what I'd asked for if I weren't there.

83

MADISON AGREED TO SPEND the night in the hotel room Erik had gotten for her. We met again the next morning for breakfast before they set off for the airport. Madison's swollen nose and black eyes were at their impressive peak.

"Everyone's going to think I can't take care of you," Erik said. *And they're right*, his face added silently.

"Jeez, Dad," she said. She tried to roll her eyes, and winced. "I'm, like, 21 years old. A *grownup*. It's not your job to take care of me anymore."

Erik opened his mouth, obviously to argue, then took a deep breath and shut it. Progress. I *had* done something good here, I told myself. Maybe all I was good for was picking up other people's pieces, but that was a good thing, and I had done it.

"I wonder what I should tell people," Madison said, prodding speculatively at her nose and wincing again. "I mean, it sounds all badass and all until I say I got smacked in the face by a door. That's, like, so *gay*. Shit. We're not supposed to say that, right? What should I say instead? Lame? That's so *old*, though."

"And maybe problematic in itself, too," I said. "You could just go for an oldie but goodie like 'embarrassing.'"

"Yeah. Whatevs. I think I'll go with the truth, but without the most embarrassing parts. I'll just say I got it in a fight. That's true, right? So I wouldn't be lying. I just don't have to say that I got smacked in the face by a door."

"Sounds good to me," I agreed.

After I saw them off to their rental car, I hobbled back to my own car and spent the weekend off my feet as much as possible, in hopes of avoiding another medical visit.

By Monday afternoon, when I had my first final, the swelling in my knee had noticeably gone down, to my profound relief. By then the news about Vadim and his gang had gotten out, albeit in simplified form, and the students knew I'd been involved in it somehow. There was a fair amount of curiosity and admiration evinced, along with concern for my knee. I assured them, with a lot more certainty than I felt, that my knee would be recovered by the next semester, and shouldn't interfere with my teaching in any way.

And by Friday afternoon, when I had my second final, I was walking with hardly any sign of a hobble at all. I counted that as a major win. I wasn't quite ready to take up running again, but it was starting to seem like a possibility six months in the future.

When I got home from the exam Friday evening, there was an email waiting for me from the publisher who'd requested the full manuscript of my book last semester.

Don't get your hopes up! I prepared myself to read a rejection, probably couched in humiliating terms, with a multi-page explanation of why the readers considered my book unworthy of publication. From what I'd heard, that was the normal hazing procedure, done under the guise of giving useful feedback.

Dear Rowena (if I may), I read.

I am delighted to inform you that the reader feedback on your manuscript was largely positive overall, and we are very interested in publishing it. If you would like to go further with this, please look over the attached contract.

At first I couldn't understand what I was reading. Then I realized this was not a rejection. This was an offer of a book contract.

A scream started to well up from somewhere deep within my chest. I swallowed it back, but a small *yip* of joy still emerged. Fevronia peered out from where she'd been sitting under the table, and then dashed for the safety of the bedroom.

I opened the contract, but couldn't make any sense of the small type and legal language. I closed it. I'd read through it later, when I was calmer. I opened the reader comments, hoping to see something encouraging. My eyes immediately fell on the words *...the author doesn't appear to understand the meaning of the terms they use...insufficient justification for the chosen theoretical basis...potentially problematic...amateurish writing style that sometimes borders on the hysterical...*I shut that document as well, shuddering to think what kind of comments a book that was actually rejected got. I'd deal with all that later. No doubt it would be exploitative and horrible, but if I could get through that gauntlet, *I'd have a published book.* I'd have something that I'd actually *done*, a concrete accomplishment that I could point to for years to come.

I responded with a short email saying I'd gotten the letter, I was very interested, and I'd peruse the contract over the weekend and get back to them if I had any questions. Then I turned to the problem of supper.

The kitchen felt very empty and quiet without Madison there. I put my laptop on the counter and set YouTube to playing some music videos before starting to make pasta for the third time that week.

In the middle of Lindsey Buckingham doing an acoustic version of "Trouble," my phone *pinged*. I picked it up, keeping it carefully away from the steaming water.

Darling Innochka, the message read. *I've been thinking of you. Would you like to have a video chat?*

84

I STARTED TO TEXT A response. Then I pressed the "Call" button instead.

Dima answered on the first ring. He was lying back on what I recognized as the fold-out couch that had been our bed when we'd lived together in his and his mother's apartment in Moscow. The lights were off, and his face was grainy and lit by a greeny-orange glow from the screen.

"It must be late," I said. "Aren't you afraid of waking up Galina Ivanovna?"

"It's after midnight," he said. "Mama's spending the night in the hospital for some tests. I can't sleep. The apartment doesn't feel right without her or you here."

"Oh." I swallowed, trying to force down the lump that had suddenly grown in my throat.

"I've always had a problem with insomnia," he continued. "Ever since I was a little boy. Except when you were with me. Then I slept like a baby."

"Oh," I said again. My memory was that he hadn't slept very well when I'd been with him either, but maybe it had been better than at other times.

"I've been thinking," he said. "A lot. I've been thinking and thinking. About what happened last week."

"Oh?" I said. We'd texted a few times since then, mostly me reassuring him that I was fine, and that Vadim was safely locked up and was no longer a danger to me. There was a fair amount of disagreement, I understood, about what to do with Vadim. Some people wanted to hold him in the US and charge him under US law. The Ukrainian government, it seemed, was agitating quietly for him to be shipped back home. He was a war hero and essential for their Anti-Terrorist Operation, after all. What would actually happen to him was still far from clear.

I, cynically, assumed he would be sent home with a slap on the wrist. Unless his case got a lot of publicity and someone did, as Dima had suggested, make a stink about someone with known neo-Nazi ties attacking a couple of unarmed—not counting our kitchen implements—women in their own apartment. Then the Ukrainian government might wash their hands of him, as a sign of the hard line they took against extremists. The likelihood of that seemed vanishingly small to me, though.

"Yes," he said. "You know, it was pretty much my worst nightmare. Watching you be in danger, but not being able to do anything about it. Having to sit there completely helplessly while you faced a danger that I'd caused."

"It wasn't just you," I said. "In fact, it mostly wasn't you."

"I still had a hand in it. I pissed off Vadim, and people who are a lot scarier, too. I'm a chaos-bomb, Inna. I don't mean to be, but I am." He inhaled deeply through his nose, and blew out a breath. "I used to worry a lot about being evil. I still do. But I've come to realize that I'm worse than that."

"Worse than evil?" I asked. "How?"

"Evil is rational. It's predictable. I know what those corrupt oligarchs I go after want. I know what the people who run organizations like Kavboyets want. I even know what guys like Vadim want. It's all simple and straightforward. They act in accordance with their desires, and their actions have consequences, and other people suffer from those consequences. It's not good, but it's easy to comprehend.

"While I...I have desires, but I don't act in accordance with them. I act in accordance with what I *think* is right, and my actions have consequences, but those consequences are just as likely to have bad outcomes as good ones. And not even I can predict what will happen. I mean to be a hero, but I'm an agent of chaos."

"Chaos isn't always bad," I said. "Isn't chaos the start of everything else? I think you have to have chaos in order to have life."

"Maybe, but you need something other than chaos in order to continue life. You can't *just* have chaos. But that's all I have."

"That's not all you have," I said.

Dima shook his head. "I might as well, for all the good I've done. And this time, once again, I set something terrible into motion. I sent Vadim to come after you, even though that was the exact opposite of everything I would have wanted. And then I had to watch while someone else rescued you."

"It was good that Frank came," I said.

"Is that his name? Frank? He's not...he's not your American man, is he? The one in California?"

"No," I said. "He's a friend of his." That was stretching the truth pretty thin, but I didn't want to get involved in lengthy explanations of trivialities.

"So he's probably a good man too."

"Sort of," I said. "At least, he's a less bad man than I originally thought."

Dima smiled at that. "Is he an agent of chaos too?"

I thought about it. "Maybe. Not as much as you, though."

Dima smiled a little more, but it was a sad smile. "It's good to be special and unique, I guess. Although I would have liked to be special and unique in a good way."

"You are," I said. "And Frank helped, but you helped too. Before Frank ever arrived, you were the one who helped me fight Vadim. I had given up. I didn't tell you before, but I had given up. I just wanted to run away."

"Running away might have been a good thing to do in that situation, Inna," Dima said.

"And leave Madison? Leave her to face Vadim on her own?"

"Or save her by calling for help," said Dima. "But you didn't run. You stayed, and you fought, and you saved both of you."

"Yes," I said. "And that was all because of you. *You* didn't run, Dima. You stayed by my side—metaphorically, at least—and you helped me. Just when I thought I was going to betray everything I believed in, when I thought I was going to run away and abandon someone who depended on me, *you* gave me the courage to stay and save her. You weren't an agent of chaos that night, Dima. You were an agent of courage. And I think it might have been the bravest thing I've ever seen you do. I know how hard it was for you to watch that..."

"You don't know," he interrupted.

"I think I do," I told him. "How many times have I had to see you in danger? More than I can count. I know *exactly* how hard it is. But you don't. You've always hidden your face or run away from it. Until that night. That night you didn't turn away, or run away, or abandon me. You stood by me and gave me the courage I needed to live up to my convictions."

"Well..." Dima swallowed. He rubbed at the bridge of his nose. Rubbing away tears, I realized. Or the faintest sheen of moisture that might hint at tears. I'd never seen him cry. I'd never seen him come *close* to crying. But now he was choking up.

"You're not evil," I told him. "And you're not an agent of chaos." I smiled, to overcome the lump in my throat that was threatening to choke me, too. "Well, not just of chaos. You can be a force for good, too. And you *are*."

"I don't know how," he said. He sounded weaker and more bewildered than I had ever heard him. "I thought I did, but I didn't. And now I don't know what to do." He scratched at the bridge of his nose again, and swallowed hard. "Maybe Mandelstam will tell me, eh?"

"Maybe," I said.

"Everything is moved by love," he said softly.

"It is," I agreed.

"I don't know what that means, Innochka. And if I did, I don't know that I could live by that rule. But I can try."

"That's all any of us are doing," I said. "Trying."

He took another deep breath. He seemed to be having trouble drawing in air. "I don't know much, Innochka. I've read the story only to the middle, and now I'm cast adrift in these wine-dark seas. And I'm afraid I'll drown in them, and drag you down as well."

"Or maybe," I said, "if you stretch out your hand, you'll pull me to safety."

"But I don't know that! *You* don't know that! No one does!"

"No," I said. "But it's worth trying."

"And maybe if I try, I'll be able to bring my actions and my desires together, so that they don't work at cross purposes," he said. "Or maybe I'll cause even more chaos."

"Or maybe you won't," I said.

"Or maybe...maybe we'll find out. This isn't what I'd meant to tell you. What I'd meant to tell you is that we got our visas, Innochka. Mama and I are coming to America. We'll be arriving in Atlanta on New Year's Day."

"That's...that's only three weeks away," I said.

"It is."

"Three weeks seems like a very long time right now," I said.

He smiled at that. Then he turned serious again. "I can't promise anything, Inna. I don't even know...all I know that is we're flying into Atlanta on New Year's Day."

"I'll come get you at the airport," I said.

"You don't have to."

"I do have to," I said.

He smiled some more at that. "Then...maybe this New Year will be a new start, Inna. For all of us. Maybe this time we can get it right."

"I have faith," I said. "Everything is moved by love, after all. I'll meet you at the airport on New Year's Day."

THE END

Dear Reader! Want to find out more of what Dima (and Vadim) were up to over the fall? Scan the QR code below to get your FREE novella and sign up for my mailing list (but only if you want to).

From the Author

LIKE THE OTHER BOOKS in the *Doctor Rowena Halley* series, *Under Review* is fiction, but fiction that is heavily inspired by real-world events and my own personal experiences. The basic plot line, of US and Ukrainian white supremacists/neo-Nazis engaging in joint training and recruitment activities, is closely based on reality, as reported for example in Newsweek (https://www.newsweek.com/ukraine-war-draws-us-far-right-fight-russia-violence-home-1665027) and TIME Magazine (https://time.com/5926750/azov-far-right-movement-facebook/). The plot to disrupt the 2017 US inauguration is loosely based on the January 6, 2021 attack on the US Capitol Building, which included a few Ukraine-trained participants. Rowena's explanation to her students that you have to be white to join a white supremacist organization is pretty much a verbatim description of my own conversations with some of my students who were seduced by the Azov Battalion's snazzy training videos aimed at recruiting adolescents for their youth training camps. Meanwhile, certain aspects of the biography of Vadim Zhuraev are very loosely based on those of various current military and political leaders in Ukraine.

This book was written against the backdrop of the phase of the war in Ukraine that began with Russia's full-scale invasion of the country in February 2022. However, that is in many ways merely an expansion of a civil war that had been taking place within Ukraine since 2014, which became externalized into a great power conflict/proxy war. This has caused investigations into the Ukraine-based white supremacist movement, always anemic, to come to a grinding halt. Meanwhile Facebook, for example, removed its ban on posts about the Azov Battalion, allowing further dissemination of pro-Azov content.

As of the time of writing (2023) it's unclear how this will all shake out, but a quick look at, say, Afghanistan does not fill me with confidence. Is the US arming and training the next Taliban/al-Qaeda/ISIS, but this time in Europe and North America? Already several mass shooters, most notably the perpetrator of the 2019 Christchurch shooting (https://www.nytimes.com/2019/03/15/world/asia/christchurch-mass-shooting-extremism.html), have explicitly listed Ukraine and the Ukrainian-based white supremacist movement as a key inspiration for their actions. Meanwhile, Russian neo-Nazis operating out of Ukraine are becoming increasingly emboldened, and appear to have considerable support from the Ukrainian, and therefore US, government (https://www.nytimes.com/live/2023/05/26/world/russia-ukraine-news, https://www.nbcnews.com/news/world/belgorod-raid-russian-volunteer-corps-freedom-russia-legion-rcna86168). The post-Maidan Ukrainian government, which evidence increasingly suggests was founded on an act of deliberate betrayal and violence against its own supporters (https://brill.com/view/journals/rupo/8/2/article-p181_5.xml?language=en) is also continuing its alarming slide into authoritarianism with a distinctly fascist edge (https://jacobin.com/2023/02/ukraine-censorship-authoritarianism-illiberalism-crackdown-police-zelensky). Only time will tell whether there is more to come.

About the Author

SID STARK LIVES A LIFE very similar to her characters', only with more grading and fewer exciting chase scenes. She did once get held up in Heathrow on suspicion of being a Russian criminal traveling on an American passport, though, which was fun. She loves to hear from her readers, and can be reached by email at sidstark@sidstarkauthor.com, at her website at https://sidstarkauthor.com/, on Facebook at https://www.facebook.com/SidStarkAuthor/, and Twitter at @SidStarkAuthor.

Don't miss out!

Visit the website below and you can sign up to receive emails whenever Sid Stark publishes a new book. There's no charge and no obligation.

https://books2read.com/r/B-A-NVEK-FPSJC

BOOKS 2 READ

Connecting independent readers to independent writers.

Also by Sid Stark

Doctor Rowena Halley
Campus Confidential: An Academic Thriller
Permanent Position: An Academic Thriller
Summer Session: An Academic Thriller
Trigger Warning: An Academic Thriller
Honor Court: An Academic Thriller
Total Immersion: An Academic Thriller
Under Review: An Academic Thriller

Doctor Rowena Halley Boxed Sets
The Doctor Rowena Halley Series Books 1-4: Four Dark Comedy Mysteries

www.ingramcontent.com/pod-product-compliance
Lightning Source LLC
LaVergne TN
LVHW041106080826
845145LV00007B/1698

* 9 7 8 1 9 5 2 7 2 3 4 1 4 *